Praise for Renee Ryan

Journey's End
"Utterly charming and not to be forgotten, *Journey's End* is Gilded Age delight."

—Victoria Alexander, #1 *New York Times* bestselling author

"Powerful and inspiring. *Journey's End* is a wonderfully rich and rewarding book."

—Gerri Russell, bestselling author of *Flirting with Felicity*

"Renee Ryan's heart-tugging story set in New York's Gilded Age kept me turning the pages well past my bedtime!"

—Winnie Griggs, award-winning author of inspirational historical romance

"Ryan's written a touching story of family, forgiveness, and a forever sort of love."

—Holly Jacobs, award-winning author of *These Three Words*

The Marriage Agreement, an RT Top Pick
"Fanny cares for Jonathon deeply, but she won't marry him without his love. At a crossroads, Jonathon will have to choose whether to walk away or be the man that Fanny believes him to be. The elements of Christian faith are superbly woven into the story, and fans of this delightful series will surely enjoy this sweet tale of forgiveness, hope and redeeming love."

—Susannah Balch, RT Book Reviews

A Touch of Scarlet

ALSO BY RENEE RYAN

Gilded Promises historical series

Charity House historical series

World War II historical series

Village Green contemporary series

Stand-alone works

Heartland Wedding

Homecoming Hero

Mistaken Bride

"New Year's Date" in *A Recipe for Romance*

Wagon Train Proposal

"Yuletide Lawman" in *A Western Christmas*

Stand-In Rancher Daddy

Published as Renee Halverson

Extreme Measures

RENEE RYAN

A Touch of Scarlet

A GILDED PROMISES NOVEL

Waterfall
PRESS

Published by Waterfall Press, Grand Haven, MI

www.brilliancepublishing.com

Amazon, the Amazon logo, and Waterfall Press are trademarks of Amazon.com, Inc., or its affiliates.

ISBN-13: 9781503938663
ISBN-10: 1503938662

Cover design by Kirk DouPonce, DogEared Design

Printed in the United States of America

To my beautiful daughter, Hillary Anne Nolan.
Not only because you cried when I told you the plot
of this story, but also because you inspire me daily.
You are good and kind and courageous. All my heroines
have a little part of you in them.

For the Lord seeth not as man seeth; for man looketh on the outward appearance, but the Lord looketh on the heart.

1 Samuel 16:7

American girls are pretty and charming—little oases of pretty unreasonableness in a vast desert of practical common-sense.

Oscar Wilde

Chapter One

New York City, 1901

Her chance for a happy future lay on the other side of the door. Elizabeth St. James simply had to enter her grandfather's private study, say the words she'd practiced with her maid, and her course would be set.

She reached for the handle, paused as her composure slipped. Fear of the unknown scorched through her. She nearly turned back. The safety of her comfortable life beckoned. It would be so simple to continue on as before, to pretend she *could* go on as before. But the need to start anew was too strong to let cowardice win.

This was her opportunity to take control of her life.

Elizabeth placed a palm on the door, fingers splayed over the carved wood grain. She knew she was stalling, knew she was losing her resolve with every second she faltered.

How could she not be nervous? Once she pushed through the door everything would change.

Shoulders squared, she shoved into the room without knocking. The smell of lemon oil, handcrafted leather, and freshly polished wood greeted her.

The man seated behind the large mahogany desk did not.

She'd made a mistake. No one entered this room without permission. For Elizabeth to do so now proved just how anxious she was to settle her future.

The pounding of her pulse grew loud in her ears, a heavy, echoing thump, thump, thump. She looked up at the dark-paneled ceiling. The loops and swirls blurred before her eyes. She firmed her chin.

Uncertainty had no place here. Though she'd celebrated her twentieth birthday two full months ago, for the first time in her life Elizabeth held the power. Well, a portion of it, anyway. And . . .

She was stalling again.

Lowering her gaze, she moved deeper into the room, one foot in front of the other. A few more steps brought her to within inches of the desk. She studied the head bent over a stack of papers.

That she'd come to her grandfather, rather than seeking out her father, spoke of the role Richard St. James played in their family. Even at seventy years old, he was in peak physical condition with a full shock of silver hair, handsome features that had weathered over time, and a tall, lithe frame.

Elizabeth admired him greatly. He'd grown a meager railroad venture into a vast empire that included everything from shipping and oil to a garment factory and a ladies' magazine.

Not many dared question Richard St. James's mandates. Even fewer rebelled. His only daughter had been one of the few, to disastrous results.

Something to keep in mind, Elizabeth.

Her heartbeat picked up speed, hammering wildly against her ribs. Not from fear but from nerves. She was intensely aware of the door behind her, of the growing desire to turn and run. Then what? Disappearance into the demi-existence of her life?

Unacceptable.

"Grandfather?" Even to her own ears, her voice sounded hollow. Empty. If Elizabeth were to convince the St. James patriarch she wanted to take this step, she must be bold. "May I have a moment of your time? If you're not too busy, of course."

At last, he looked up, pen in hand, a smile on his face. "I'm never too busy for you."

The startling green eyes that connected with Elizabeth's were filled with affection and mild curiosity. He started to stand, but she waved him back in his chair.

"To what do I owe this impromptu visit?"

Clearly, he had yet to guess the reason for her intrusion.

Her stomach dipped, feeling as if it were filled with a lump of cold steel. Despite the urge to flee, Elizabeth held herself perfectly still. She would see this through.

"I have made my decision."

"What decision is that, my dear?" Her grandfather's voice came out calm and steady, completely at odds with the importance of this moment.

Elizabeth took a quick, steadying breath, prayed for some semblance of control. "I will go to London as you and father have requested."

There. She'd said the words.

She could breathe again. The hard part was over. The rest of the conversation would go easier now. Except . . .

After the first rush of relief, her shoulders tensed and her mind filled with worry. Her grandfather had not yet responded. Why wasn't he speaking?

She angled her head, more than a little confused. It was as if this were just another ordinary conversation, on another ordinary day.

If only that were true.

Surely, he recognized the magnitude of her announcement. "Grandfather, did you hear me?"

He set down the pen and then leaned back in his chair. A succession of creaks and groans accompanied the movement. "I heard you."

He fell silent again.

Elizabeth's nerves frayed even further, nearly tattering at the edges. A part of her wanted to prolong this conversation, to wield the power she held, if only another moment more.

Regardless of her grandfather's lackluster reception, her decision to travel to London affected him as much as it did her. Richard St. James had riches. He had prestige and privilege. But he lacked the one thing only Elizabeth could give him.

This was what he wanted. What he'd requested of her. And yet, he seemed so . . . unmoved.

She had just agreed to journey to England and join other American heiresses who sought a husband from the British peerage. With her sizable dowry, she would purchase a husband for herself and a title for the family. "You are not pleased?"

"I am very pleased. I only wonder if—"

The rest of his words were cut off when the door swung open and Elizabeth's father entered the room.

"I have the Leighton contracts you requested. There are a few points that still need discussing. With Jackson on his honeymoon, it falls to us to decide the—" Marcus St. James stopped abruptly. "Oh, Elizabeth. Hello, darling."

"Good afternoon, Father."

He smiled broadly, the gesture a bit too cheerful, the look not quite authentic. "I thought you were having tea with your friends today."

Elizabeth resisted the urge to sigh. Her father's assumption that she had nothing better to do than take afternoon tea was a reminder of how useless and empty her life had become. Or rather, how useless and empty her life had always been.

"I came to speak with grandfather." She captured her father's gaze, held it one beat, two, and on the third she broke eye contact. "But now that you are here, I will tell you as well."

He nodded.

She opened her mouth to continue, but he wasn't looking at her any longer. He continued through the room, only stopping once he was behind the large desk where her grandfather sat.

Still not looking at her, her father set down the stack of papers he carried and said something to the other man, something Elizabeth couldn't quite decipher. Something to do with the contract he'd just set down.

Both distracted by the pressing matter before them, the two men fell into a hushed conversation. This wasn't the first time business had taken precedence over Elizabeth. As she'd been trained to do, she waited for them to finish their discussion. She tried not to let resentment take hold. It helped watching the two interact.

I won't see them like this much longer.

The younger was an exact copy of the older in height, in stance, and, as of late, in personality. Her once mild-mannered father was gone. In his place was a man she hardly recognized. He no longer laughed, and he never suggested frivolous outings for just the two of them.

There were other changes, as well.

He'd aged considerably in the past three months. He was still handsome, with salt-and-pepper hair, sculpted patrician features, and broad shoulders. But he was no longer the carefree father Elizabeth had always known.

Sorrow rippled through her. Then morphed into something darker when she thought of her mother and what she'd done to her father, to their family.

All the antagonism Elizabeth had been holding back threatened to spill over, filling her until she thought she might explode. Her mother had ruined two innocent lives for nothing more than money and social standing. Even worse, the two women hadn't been strangers. They'd been treasured family members, one lost forever, one recently found.

Elizabeth knew the Lord called His children to forgive. She couldn't find it in her heart to do so, not where her mother was concerned.

Resentment flared again. This time, Elizabeth let it come, let it burn through her calm.

"You look terribly serious, darling." The words, as much as the worry in her father's voice, jolted Elizabeth's attention back to him. "Has something happened to upset you?"

The gentleness was from another time, when they'd been close, when her life had been full of parties and her mind challenged with nothing more complicated than deciding what dress to wear. "No, Father, nothing is wrong."

Nothing she was willing to admit aloud. Not to him, at any rate. There'd been a time when she'd told him everything. Those days were gone forever. "I have agreed to travel to London and do my duty for the family."

It was somewhat of a shock that the words spilled from her lips with such ease, such conviction. For weeks, she'd struggled with what to do, unsure if she had the courage to leave the comfort and security of the only home she'd ever known.

What choice did she have, really?

Her world, which had once seemed so large and safe, had been built on deception. The family had secrets now. Lies had to be told to protect the St. James name, and Elizabeth's reputation.

As though there weren't whispers about her already. The man everyone thought would become her husband had married her cousin, a woman Elizabeth hadn't known existed four months ago. No one cared that Elizabeth had been happy about the match. They saw her only as the injured party and lauded her for putting up a brave front in the face of such scandalous behavior.

"Very good, darling. As always, you've made the right decision." Her father gave her one firm nod and then leaned back over the papers.

Her grandfather followed suit.

Elizabeth blinked. She'd been dismissed.

Where was their gratitude? The acknowledgment of her sacrifice? She'd just agreed to travel across an entire ocean for the benefit of the family. If she found success, she would never return.

They didn't seem concerned about that part. They seemed to care only that she'd bent to their wishes. Obviously, it had never occurred to them she might say no.

"You knew I would choose to go to London." She could not keep the hurt from sounding in her voice.

"Of course." The response came from her grandfather.

"But how could you have known?" She hadn't made her final decision until a few hours ago.

"My dear child." The older man regarded her with pointed patience. "You may always be counted on to do what we ask."

You may always be counted on to do what we ask.

In that moment, Elizabeth wished she were more like Libby St. James, the aunt she'd been named after but had never met. She wanted to be bold and brave, to rebel against society's rules. She wanted the courage to run away from duty, all for the sake of love, for romance and passion.

Apparently, she didn't have it in her, as evidenced by her grandfather's matter-of-fact statement. *You may always be counted on to do what we ask.*

This was to be her life, then. She was forever to be the dutiful daughter and granddaughter, the good girl who could be counted on to obey without question.

Elizabeth pushed back a devastating pang of remorse. She'd fooled herself into thinking she'd had a choice. There'd been no choice, only duty. No real option but obedience.

Suddenly, she couldn't get out of this house, this country, *this family* fast enough.

She was mildly aware her grandfather continued speaking. His voice, usually so strong and firm, seemed to come at her through a wall of water. She fought for her next breath. And then the next. Each one came faster, harder, dragging her toward a dark pit in her mind. She thought she might be sick.

Breathe, Elizabeth. In and out. Yes, that's it.

She tried to focus but caught only snippets of the plans already underway for her impending departure. The final string of words had her stiffening: "You set sail in two months."

Two months?

Too soon.

Not soon enough.

She pulled in a slow, bracing breath.

For months, she'd felt like an exotic bird trapped in a gilded cage. A delicate creature adored from afar, lauded for her beauty and very little else.

The truth hit Elizabeth like a punch to the heart. This wasn't her moment of triumph. She wasn't breaking free of her mundane life. She was merely trading one cage for another.

She'd hoped that once she was away from New York she would finally have a life she chose for herself, not the one her mother had created for her.

"You may begin purchasing your wardrobe immediately." Her grandfather's calm voice only agitated her further. "My cousin Matilda will help you. Having recently returned from London, she will know the styles you should choose to gain the appropriate attention from English gentlemen."

Elizabeth nodded, not really caring what English gentlemen thought of her. Her grandfather's money would secure her a husband, not her clothing, looks, or accomplishments.

"Do you have any questions?"

She shook her head.

"You may go." He gestured toward the door.

The conversation was officially over.

She turned.

At the door, she looked back over her shoulder. A sigh leaked past her lips. The two men she loved most in the world were happily sending her to another country to find a husband with a title. Once she boarded the ship, she might never see her family again.

Her stomach roiled at the thought.

As she stood there, staring at her father and grandfather, she realized just how little she wanted to go to London. It wasn't merely because she would miss her family. Of course she would miss them. It wasn't that she didn't want to marry. She did, one day. The problem was that Elizabeth wanted more. More.

The word whispered through her mind, again and again.

More.

She wanted more than duty. More than blind obedience. More than marriage to a stranger for the sake of the family.

A thread of rebellion slipped through Elizabeth, a weak but steady throb thrumming through her veins and strengthening her conviction. She had two months before she left for London.

She had time. Not much. But some.

All was not yet lost.

* * *

After shutting the door behind her with a firm click, Elizabeth found herself alone in the hallway once more. Tears threatened. She blinked them back, determined not to cry.

Disappointment gnawed at her like little rat teeth, urging her to give in to her distress. When a woman made a life-altering decision, she expected a bit of enthusiasm in return. Her father and grandfather's lackluster reaction stung.

You may always be counted on to do what we ask.

Words of praise she'd once coveted now seemed the ultimate insult.

She opened and closed her fists, then set out for the refuge of her room, navigating the labyrinth of hallways with restless, choppy strides. At the end of the corridor, she turned left and continued moving at a clipped pace.

St. James House was massive, claiming nearly an entire block near Madison Square. The building itself was a twelve-bedroom structure made of imported marble, limestone, and brick. The interior was over-furnished due to four generations of input yet still tastefully decorated. Every inch of the walls was filled with paintings and portraits done by the masters. Rembrandts shared space with pictures painted by Monet and Degas. There were even a few of the American Impressionists' works, Elizabeth's favorite done by Theodore Robinson.

She was fortunate to live among so much luxury, for no other reason than she'd been born a St. James. It wasn't that Elizabeth didn't appreciate her blessings. She lived a charmed life. The Lord had been good to her, when she'd done nothing to deserve His favor. The Bible called that grace.

How could she enjoy such plenty and still feel trapped?

The emptiness that had plagued Elizabeth for months seemed to grow stronger by the day. She feared the sensation would swallow her whole if she didn't do . . . something.

Exasperation propelled her around the next corner. What would her grandfather and father do if she rebelled? Not in a grand manner, but in some small, unassuming way?

At the moment, even that seemed beyond her.

Elizabeth came to the end of yet another hallway and, finally, escaped into her room. Guided by a ray of sunshine spilling through the enormous window overlooking the streets of New York, she collapsed into her favorite overstuffed chair. As she threw her legs over one of the arms, a sigh leaked out of her. "What now?"

When no answer immediately came to mind, she allowed herself another, longer sigh.

"The conversation with your grandfather went that poorly?"

"Oh." Elizabeth gave a little start. "Sally, I . . . you . . ." She swiveled her head in the direction of the adjoining room that led to her maid's private quarters. "You startled me."

"Forgive me." The young woman flashed an apologetic grimace. "That wasn't my intention."

"Of course it wasn't." Swinging her legs to the floor, Elizabeth smiled at her lady's maid silhouetted in the doorway.

Sally wore a nondescript black dress under a long white apron tied in a neat bow at her back. The bonnet on the young woman's head hid most of her hair, but not all. The maid was a blue-eyed blonde like Elizabeth. They were close to the same age, identical in height and build. They could pass for sisters, at least in looks.

In personality, they were complete opposites. Elizabeth was more reserved and always tempered her speech. Sally was often frank with her opinions and carried an aura of mystery that hinted at secrets and silent pain. So much so that Elizabeth doubted whether her last name was even Smith, as she claimed. But Sally never spoke of her past, and Elizabeth never pressed.

At the maid's lifted eyebrows, Elizabeth realized she hadn't answered her question.

"The conversation went . . . Oh, Sally." She sighed heavily. "It was a complete disaster from start to finish."

"I'm sorry."

The simple, sympathetic response had Elizabeth swallowing back a sob. Until that moment, she hadn't realized how much she'd come to rely on her new maid, not merely in her official capacity but as a friend.

Sally had originally served Elizabeth's cousin. Instead of continuing on with Caroline after her wedding, the young woman had surprised everyone and just over a month ago requested a position with Elizabeth. At the time, Elizabeth had been grateful. Her mother's treachery had been revealed days prior, and she'd been more than a little lost.

As it turned out, Sally had been a godsend. The maid understood Elizabeth in ways no one ever had before, except perhaps her former governess.

"Well?" The maid moved to the bed, idly picked up a blanket, and began folding it into a neat square. "Are you going to tell me what happened?"

Not wanting to relive the conversation but needing to unburden herself, Elizabeth shut her eyes and gave Sally an abbreviated version. "My grandfather and father weren't a bit surprised by my announcement."

"Oh, dear."

"Arrangements for my passage are complete. All that's left is for me to choose my wardrobe."

Sally paused mid-fold and tilted her head. "Why do I get the sense you are leaving a portion of the tale untold?"

Not quite meeting the maid's eyes, Elizabeth lifted a shoulder. "Those are the important highlights. Their lack of surprise was disheartening."

"I imagine it was." Sally enunciated each word in her flat midwestern accent, which didn't quite match her delicate features and fine bone structure.

"I only have myself to blame." Elizabeth blew the hair off her forehead with an impatient huff. "I've never given them cause to expect anything but my absolute obedience."

"You are too compliant."

Elizabeth didn't disagree.

Twenty years of perfect behavior was entirely too long. The spurt of rebellion she'd felt in her grandfather's office came to life once again. "Something has to change."

With great care, Sally set the blanket back on the bed and turned to face Elizabeth. Her eyes were filled with wisdom far beyond her years. "I have often found that taking one small step can result in surprising benefits."

"One small step. You make it sound so simple." *So achievable.*

"The first step makes the next one easier."

The seed of rebellion dug deeper, growing tender roots. If Elizabeth had the courage to disregard convention, if only a little, what would she do?

The clock on the mantelpiece struck the top of the hour, startling her to her feet. She glanced at the time. The afternoon had gotten away from her.

"It's getting late. Long past time you dressed for tonight's ball." Sally moved toward the closet, threw open the doors, and disappeared inside.

Elizabeth didn't want to go to another ball. She'd already been to four this season. She didn't want to smile and pretend all was well. But she could not avoid this evening's celebration honoring her best friend's engagement. Penelope Griffin hadn't always had an easy life. Elizabeth was happy she'd found love and wanted to congratulate her with the rest of New York society.

"What dress shall you wear?" Sally returned holding two exquisite gowns, one in each hand. "This one?" She lifted the pretty blue dress designed specifically for Elizabeth. "Or this one?" With a hitch of her chin, the maid indicated the pale-green silk with corded gold trim.

Elizabeth considered her choices. The blue gown had arrived from her mother's favorite Parisian couture house just two days ago. Elizabeth had worn the green dress last week, at a soiree given by one of her grandfather's business associates. The gown had hung in her closet for nearly a year prior to that event.

Her mother's voice consumed all other thought: *No woman of fine breeding should be caught in last season's design. And she must never be seen in the same gown twice.*

Sighing, Elizabeth reached for the blue dress, hesitated, frowned. Even now, with Katherine St. James banished to their family estate in Florida, Elizabeth had nearly submitted to her mother's wishes.

One small step.

One tiny rebellion.

What could possibly go wrong?

"I'll wear the green silk." Her mother would be appalled.

Sally gave an approving nod. "Excellent choice."

Heart infinitely lighter, Elizabeth allowed herself a small, secretive smile. The party she'd been dreading moments before suddenly held endless possibilities.

And tonight, she would face each of them in last season's gown.

Chapter Two

Barely an hour after arriving at the party, Elizabeth thought she might suffocate under the enormous weight of her disappointment.

Her first act of defiance was a complete and utter failure. The greater portion of party guests had treated her with their usual smiles and kind remarks. Several had even complimented her dress, including a few who'd attended last week's soiree.

One small step had turned into one large letdown.

Frowning, she retreated into the shadows of a sizable potted plant. She wasn't hiding, precisely. She simply needed a moment to recover her composure.

Dancers twirled past in a silken spool of colors and textures, stirring the dark-green leaves beside her. A young woman giggled from somewhere nearby, the shrill sound at odds with the soft romantic notes of the waltz.

Desperately wishing the evening were over, but knowing she couldn't leave for hours yet, Elizabeth melted deeper into the shadows. She'd never felt more out of place, or more like a fraud. She certainly couldn't drum up the enthusiasm to join in the celebration of her friend's impending wedding.

How could she? Everything Elizabeth thought she knew about marriage was based on lies and half-truths.

She thought her parents had married for love. Her father had. Her mother had not. The St. James name and overflowing coffers had wooed Katherine into the match. God's design for marriage had never entered the equation.

Is going to London seeking a husband with a title any different?

Elizabeth dismissed the disturbing thought with a swat at a wayward branch swaying in front of her face. Unlike Katherine St. James, Elizabeth wasn't marrying for personal gain. Her match was solely for the benefit of the family.

What of love? What of passion?

There'd been a time when Elizabeth had dreamed of both. Now, she wanted out of New York and away from a life that was tarnished beyond all repair.

Lips pressed in a flat line, she slipped her gaze over the glittering crush of silks and satins. Everyone seemed so happy, so full of joy. Everyone but Elizabeth. She wasn't happy. She was . . .

Feeling sorry for herself.

She *hated* feeling sorry for herself. It spoke of a selfish nature far too similar to her mother's.

Sick of her own company, Elizabeth set out for the refreshment table. Perhaps a glass of lemonade would settle her nerves. She'd hardly taken a step when two female voices fell over her. They spoke in hushed whispers.

Elizabeth froze. She'd stayed in the shadows too long. Now she was trapped, with no easy escape in sight. If she moved, the women would see her and probably suspect she'd been listening to their conversation.

Hoping to block out their voices, she focused on the music. She nearly succeeded. But then she heard her name.

"Elizabeth St. James is such a lovely girl."

The other quickly agreed. "She is perfectly well mannered. She would have made him a proper wife."

Elizabeth stifled a gasp. They were speaking about her and Jackson.

"Thrown over for her own cousin; it's simply too dreadful to contemplate."

And yet, of course, they proceeded to *contemplate* the matter in excruciating detail. They had no shame, saying mean, hurtful things about Jackson and his new bride, Caroline. Two people Elizabeth adored, who'd done nothing wrong other than fall in love.

Elizabeth desperately wanted to step out of the shadows and call the women out for their atrocious behavior. Didn't they know gossip was a sin?

She shifted slightly, now hoping to draw attention to herself. Unfortunately, the women were too deep in their conversation to notice her. She made another attempt, then paused as she remembered the promise she'd made to Caroline and Jackson. She was not to defend them in public, under any circumstances. Caroline had made Elizabeth vow not to jeopardize her reputation for the sake of theirs.

How she regretted agreeing to their request. Even if she hadn't made that promise, she couldn't confront the women. This was Penelope's engagement party. *Nothing* must spoil her friend's evening.

"That boy proved to be just like his father."

Elizabeth gritted her teeth at the flagrant inaccuracy. Jackson was nothing like his father. Edward Montgomery had run off with his wife's sister without a single concern for how his behavior would affect others.

Jackson had come to Elizabeth directly. He'd explained why he wasn't going to ask for her hand in marriage.

Elizabeth hadn't been surprised. She certainly hadn't been hurt. She'd been relieved and so very happy for Jackson, for her cousin Caroline, and most of all, for herself.

"That poor, tragic girl. She's so brave."

Tragic? Brave? Elizabeth was neither.

"His rejection must have been beyond humiliating."

Jackson hadn't rejected her. He'd given Elizabeth her freedom. *Are you really free?*

She would be. In two months.

"I hear her mother was so distraught she took to her bed for weeks."

Fury rushed through Elizabeth, heating her cheeks and increasing her heartbeat. Her mother had not taken to her bed. She'd been banished to the family's estate in Florida for what she'd done to Caroline's mother.

Oh, how Elizabeth wanted to tell the gossiping old biddies the true story. But it wasn't hers to tell. Stepping into the middle of the conversation would only complicate matters for two people she loved.

Just as Elizabeth thought she couldn't bear another moment of hearing the gossips discuss her family, they turned to another topic, something about an unfortunate young woman whose parentage had recently been thrown into question.

Honestly. That was really quite enough.

Elizabeth slipped out of the shadows.

Almost immediately, a hand clasped her arm. "There you are. I've been looking for you everywhere."

Forcing a smile, Elizabeth swiveled around to face her oldest and dearest friend in the world. "And now you've found me."

"So I have." Penelope laughed. The sound was full of unbridled joy.

A rush of relief flooded Elizabeth. "You look terribly happy, Penny."

"Of course I'm happy, divinely so." Penelope's responding smile brightened the entire room. "Simon is my perfect match in every way. He's simply, why, he's simply *wonderful.*"

She laughed again, a sweet, tinkling, infectious sound.

This time, Elizabeth joined in her friend's merriment.

As a child, Penelope had struggled with a pronounced stammer. Her inability to speak clearly had earned her ridicule from other girls their age.

Elizabeth had stood up for her friend, but the cruelty had taken a toll. Penelope had become painfully shy. Though she'd grown into an attractive woman, with a lovely oval face, light-brown hair, and eyes a rich amber color, Penelope was still cautious and overly timid.

Tonight, she didn't look cautious or timid. In a gold silk dress that matched her gorgeous eyes, she looked radiant. All because of Simon Burrows.

"Speaking of your fiancé, where is he?"

"Here I am." A tall figure appeared at Penelope's elbow. The couple stared at one another, both caught up in the moment. Simon's wide shoulders and considerable height nearly overwhelmed Penelope's petite frame.

They shouldn't look good together, but they did.

At last, Simon turned his attention to Elizabeth. "Good evening, Miss St. James."

"Good evening, Mr. Burrows."

For the next few moments, they spoke of nothing more significant than the weather. Elizabeth was struck by Simon's relaxed manner. The man came from an old New York Knickerbocker family. He was known for his rigidity and strict adherence to a moral code of behavior based on biblical precepts.

Elizabeth was suddenly very—*very*—glad she hadn't confronted the gossips.

"I hope you don't mind, Miss St. James, but I'm afraid we'll have to continue this conversation another time. I was sent to fetch my fiancée." The smile he gave Penelope was full of warmth. "Mother wishes to speak with you, something about scheduling a trip to the shore after our honeymoon."

"Oh, yes, of course." Penelope turned to Elizabeth, a question in her eyes. "You don't mind if I desert you?"

"Not even a little."

"We'll talk later?"

Elizabeth would like nothing better. "You may count on it."

The happy couple said their farewells.

The moment they were swallowed up in the crowd, Elizabeth decided to make her own escape from the maddening crush. She needed a temporary respite and knew exactly where to find it.

Decision made, she set out at a fast pace.

* * *

Five minutes later, Elizabeth slipped out of the house through one of the French doors thrown open to let in the crisp night air. A light breeze stirred a tendril of hair that had fallen loose from its pins. Gaze lowered, she moved quickly across the large tiered terrace, down the marble steps, and into the sunken gardens below.

Shrouded in the safety of the inky night, she looked up. At the same moment a clump of swift-moving clouds covered the moon. Elizabeth let the resulting blackness embrace her. She didn't need to see to know where she was going. She'd played in these gardens as a child. With the house still in view, she leaned against an ivy-covered wall and released a deep sigh. She hated that she'd become the sighing sort.

Arms wrapped tightly around herself against the chill evening air, she whispered, "What if I didn't return to the house? Would anyone notice I was gone?"

A deep, masculine chuckle sounded from the shadows. "Make no mistake, my dear. Your lovely presence would most definitely be missed."

The husky baritone sent a spattering of nerves tripping down Elizabeth's spine. She knew that voice, knew the owner. Lucian Griffin. Penelope's older brother. He'd recently returned to America after living in London for three years.

A ripple of longing flowed through her before she ruthlessly shut down the sensation. Of all the people to come upon her, of course it would be *him*.

She shot away from the wall, the pounding of her heart loud in her ears. "Luke . . . I, I didn't realize you were there."

"Evidently." Humor still sounded in his voice. And something else. Something she was too nervous to define.

Not sure whether this chance encounter was a good thing or a very, very bad turn of events, she attempted to slow the pounding of her heart, to no avail.

This is Luke, she told herself, *Penelope's older brother and one of your good friends.*

"It wasn't wise to come out here alone, Little Bit."

Little Bit.

Only Luke called her by that name, and not for many, many years. She couldn't imagine why he did so tonight.

Squinting past the dark, she could barely make out his form. He was maybe four feet to her left, possibly five. Not that it was necessary to see him. She knew his face by heart, knew every handsome plane and sharp angle.

She sighed again.

Penelope's brother had been the cause of several girlish dreams in Elizabeth's youth. Now, she stood alone with him in the black night.

"Any number of people could have come upon you," he added. "Some with wicked intent."

The brotherly concern was the final humiliation in a long, trying day. Elizabeth did something she'd never expect of herself. She took her frustration out on him.

"Yes, well, you really shouldn't sneak up on people in the dark. It's not very gentlemanly."

"My apologies." He didn't sound sorry. Not in the least.

The dark outline of his tall, lean body sent a tremble through Elizabeth. She pressed back into the shadows, not from unease or fear but from irritation.

What was he doing skulking in the dark, anyway? He should be inside the house.

So should you.

With chilled, trembling fingers, she reached for the stone wall behind her, found a reassuring anchor when her palm pressed to the cool ivy branches.

"I believe I've had enough fresh air." She cleared her throat and attempted to put confidence in her words. "I should return to the party."

"Yes, you should."

Her feet refused to cooperate.

How much worse could this evening get?

After a moment, Luke spoke again. "Has someone upset you?"

"No."

She felt rather than saw him take a step closer. "Tell me what sent you running from the ballroom, Little Bit."

"I didn't run."

"No?"

She lifted her chin at a haughty angle, desperately wishing she could read his expression yet overwhelmingly relieved he couldn't read hers. "I walked quickly."

His responding chuckle warmed her to her toes.

"My mistake. You weren't running. You aren't upset. You are merely taking some fresh air."

He was laughing at her. She heard the amusement in his voice. Something inside her broke a little. There'd been too many secrets in the past three months and far too many times she'd pretended nothing was awry when matters were far from ideal. She couldn't bring herself to continue evading the truth with Luke. He was her friend.

A friend who made her heart trip and wish for things that could never be.

"Perhaps I am upset," she admitted in a small voice. "But only a very little."

"Tell me what's happened." He spoke quietly now, his words pitched at a soothing octave.

On the surface, his concern was kindness itself, even heroic. But all Elizabeth could think was that Luke sounded far too much like an older brother.

She had wished for many things concerning Luke. She had never wished for him to be her brother.

"I"—she swallowed—"it's just . . . Oh, Luke, it's the gossip about Jackson and Caroline. They don't deserve the censure."

"No, they don't." As Jackson's closest friend and staunchest ally, Luke knew the story, all of it, including the role Elizabeth's mother had played.

It was a relief to speak with someone who knew the truth.

"The gossips don't even have the facts straight."

"Darling girl." His voice flowed over her, soft and rich as velvet. "Gossips rarely care about the facts."

"It's not right."

Luke reached out and took her hand. "No, it's not."

He pulled her a fraction closer.

Her breath caught, rendering her momentarily speechless. She marveled at the way she responded to a simple touch. She wore gloves, and so did he, yet she could feel Luke's warmth seeping through her chilled fingers. He towered over her with six additional inches of height, yet she wasn't the least intimidated.

This was Luke. Her friend's brother. Perfectly harmless.

But then the clouds parted slightly. A thin stream of moonlight cast a surreal glow over the garden, giving the moment a romantic, dreamlike feel. *Not so harmless anymore.*

She pulled her hand free and, legs a bit wobbly, moved to a small wrought-iron bench next to a birdbath. She sat, taking great care settling her skirts around her legs.

Luke came to stand beside her. "While I'll admit I hate hearing my friend's character thrown into question, and that of his new bride, at least the gossip is not unkind about you. That's worth a lot."

Was it? Her good name had escaped any lasting damage, but at what cost?

Elizabeth balled her fists in her lap, then forced her fingers to relax. Hands shaking slightly, she smoothed her palms across her skirt once again. "It's been nearly a month since their wedding. I don't understand why they are still a favorite topic of discussion."

Luke joined her on the bench and gave her one long look. Something almost tender moved in his eyes before it was gone.

Unable to resist, she leaned closer to him, just a fraction more, until their shoulders nearly, almost touched. "I can't help feeling partly responsible that Jackson and Caroline are shunned from proper society."

"You aren't to blame."

She wasn't as confident as he. "If I'd had the courage to speak candidly with Jackson sooner, he and Caroline would not be the source of gossip."

"That's not entirely true."

She opened her mouth to argue but shut it again as she remembered that Luke knew what had brought her cousin Caroline to New York.

She'd traveled from London seeking revenge on their mutual grandfather, believing he'd turned his back on her mother during her time of need because she'd fallen in love with someone beneath her station. The truth was so much uglier. Richard had been as much a victim as his daughter.

Elizabeth still couldn't understand why her own mother had gone to such lengths to prevent Aunt Libby from coming home. "I never thought my mother capable of such treachery."

"How could you have known? None of us did."

"I can't find it in my heart to forgive her."

There was a long stretch of silence before Luke's hand touched hers. "The wound is fresh. Give it time."

Time wouldn't change what her mother had done.

Elizabeth turned her head to say as much, but her breath caught in her throat. Every feature of Luke's handsome face was thrown into stark relief. The pale moonlight defined the sharp lines of his jaw and cheekbones, the sweep of his upturned lips. Even his golden hair had taken on a silvery glow.

His concern for her was also clearly illuminated.

No. No, no. She would not be the object of this man's sympathy. "Please don't look at me that way."

"How am I looking at you?"

"As if you feel sorry for me."

"I don't feel sorry for you." His eyes met hers, unguarded and earnest. "Never think that."

His sincerity seemed real.

Her stomach dipped in a very unsisterly manner. A ferocious blush burned across her face at the direction of her thoughts. The longer she stayed secluded in the darkened gardens with Luke, the more chance there was of exposure.

As if his thoughts had taken a similar journey, Luke gave her chin a light tap. "You, Miss St. James, must return to the house before your absence is noticed."

He rose before she could respond, reached out his hand.

She placed her palm against his, the move as natural as breathing, and allowed him to pull her to her feet. He was so tall, so masculine.

She wanted to rest in his strength a moment longer. Just one more moment.

"Have faith, Elizabeth." Luke released her hand. "All will turn out as it should."

His eyes were sincere as he spoke, unguarded, with not a hint of irony in his voice. Elizabeth wanted . . . She wanted . . .

What did it matter what she wanted?

In two months she would board a steamship heading to London. She would miss her family, her friends, and this man. Especially this man.

Luke attacked the world head-on, without reservation or timidity. He'd rebelled for a short time in his younger days. Elizabeth had heard the rumors. He'd fallen in with a wild crowd, but the names of his cohorts remained a mystery. Despite his scandalous past, Luke was considered quite a catch.

One small step.

Elizabeth pressed a light, trembling touch to Luke's shoulder. The muscles beneath her hand bunched. "Thank you, Luke."

"For . . . what?"

"For listening."

He held her gaze, saying nothing.

Her pulse pounded in her ears, nearly deafening her with its roar. She took a miniscule step forward. In all her twenty years, she'd never been a party to something so . . . scandalous.

He didn't seem to mind, proving he hadn't reformed completely. The discovery made her blood charge through her veins. She took another step.

As if compelled by some invisible force, he moved forward as well. The gap between them all but disappeared. He leaned down and pressed his lips to her . . .

Forehead. Her forehead!

It was quite the brotherly show of affection. One more insult to add to all the others she'd endured this day.

She caught her sigh before it embarrassed her. The entire situation was utterly hopeless. Elizabeth didn't doubt Luke liked her. They'd known one another for years, since she'd been a child and he a bold, brassy youth testing the boundaries of propriety as only a male child in their world could. He wasn't a young boy anymore.

She wasn't a young girl, either. But to him she was still his Little Bit.

Even if she could get him to see her as a grown woman, Luke deserved someone who knew her own mind, who didn't allow others to dictate her future.

Elizabeth was not that woman. Not yet.

Chapter Three

Luke was well aware he stood entirely too close to Elizabeth. He couldn't find the incentive to create a polite distance between them. Cloaked in shadows dusted with silvery moonlight, she had an ethereal, vulnerable quality that called to his protective nature.

Elizabeth was one of the few people who'd accepted Penelope without judgment. Her kindness during his sister's most trying years had earned her a permanent place in his heart.

Lately, however, his affection had morphed into something charged with tension and awkward pauses.

The shift had started almost immediately upon his return from a three-year residency in London. The moment he'd laid eyes on her, at another party thrown in this house, Elizabeth had thrown him off balance.

He was still trying to catch his breath.

She'd always been a pretty girl. But she'd become a beautiful woman with pale-blonde hair and blue, blue eyes framed by long, spiky black lashes. Her eyebrows were two shades darker than her hair. The startling contrast was eye-catching, mesmerizing.

For a moment, he wanted to bask in her goodness. A precarious prospect, loaded with hazards. Luke could harm Elizabeth simply by being caught with her in the dark.

There, at last, was the motivation he needed to step away from her. "I bid you a good night, Elizabeth."

He turned to go, paused when she whispered his name.

"Please don't leave." A rustle of silk and a faint touch to his arm accompanied the request. "Not yet."

"It isn't wise for me to stay."

"Please."

Elizabeth's fresh scent of lilacs and soap overwhelmed the other aromas of the garden, luring Luke to abandon his good sense. But it was the soft plea that had him spinning back around.

At the sight of her delicate frown, everything in him softened. The gossip about her cousin had put her in a vulnerable state, making her easy pickings. If some other man came upon her . . .

The possibility made him grind his teeth.

Luke closed the short distance between them, knowing he was as much a threat as any other man and simply not caring. But then, as his wits returned, he cared very much. Elizabeth's sterling reputation would take a hit if they were seen together, alone in the dark. All it would take was one person watching.

Someone was always watching.

"Go back inside, Little Bit."

She winced. He'd insulted her with the use of the childhood nickname. It couldn't be helped.

Luke made yet another attempt to get rid of her. "Since you refuse to think of your reputation, I will have to do so myself. Good evening." He gave her a curt nod of dismissal and once again turned to leave.

Once again, her voice stopped him.

"Luke." She reached for his sleeve with the barest whisper of a touch. "May I make a confession before you go?"

An innocent woman should not sound so sultry. She should not look so attractive. The way she'd secured her hair in a tumble of curls around her face displayed her arresting features in startling detail.

Leave her, Luke.

"If you must confess to someone, it might as well be me." He'd keep whatever secret she wished to share.

"I am wearing last season's gown." She sounded very pleased with herself, as if she'd just declared she'd mastered a complicated piano concerto.

Which meant, very likely, she was trying to tell him something significant. "I'm not sure I understand."

Elizabeth nibbled her lower lip, looking very adorable and utterly tempting. He secured his gaze at a spot above her head.

"My mother always said a young woman of quality should never be seen in last season's gown."

Ah. "I see."

"Do you? Do you, really?"

"I do." Perhaps a bit too much. Luke knew what it felt like to miss the mark in a parent's eyes, to always fall short no matter how hard he tried to win approval, then to do the opposite because a grievous slipup was treated the same as missing the mark by a hair. "You wore the dress to challenge your mother's ridiculous guidelines for proper behavior."

She beamed at him. "Precisely."

Wearing last year's gown was relatively tame, as disobedience went. Still, Luke knew better than most that Elizabeth was entering perilous ground. A small act of defiance led to another. And then another, until one's good character was thrown into question and innocence was gone forever.

He wanted to warn her to be careful. But then he remembered this was Elizabeth. She respected authority, always did the right thing. There was no cause for concern.

Unless, of course, someone came upon them.

His patience evaporated. He took her shoulders and gently turned her toward the open terrace doors before dropping his hands.

She smiled at him over her shoulder. "Good night, Luke."

"Good night, Little Bit."

She floated up the marble steps like a snowflake, slowly, smoothly, as graceful as a well-trained dancer. Once she'd completed her ascent, she swung back to face him.

Luke's heart kicked an extra-hard beat.

What a picture she made in the soft glow of the moon. No longer a child, no longer his *Little Bit*. But a fascinating woman. She looked untouchable. Not a hair out of place. Not a wrinkle in her gown.

Luke feared that elegant façade hid a penchant for rebellion that matched his own.

He wanted to go to her.

He resisted—barely—then, out of self-preservation, made an exaggerated shooing motion with his hand.

She let out a soft laugh, the musical lilt turning his guts to mush. Still smiling, she gave him a small wave, nothing more than a wiggle of her fingers.

It did not occur to him to return the gesture.

He was too enthralled watching her spin around and slowly place one foot in front of the other. She was being so very, very deliberate and working so very, very hard to force herself to enter the house.

Luke had his own decision to make. He could follow Elizabeth inside and claim the next dance. He could hold her in his arms and spin her around the parquet floor, letting her sweet, endearing laugh wash away the gloom building steadily in his heart.

Or . . .

He could enter the house from the back and forget their accidental meeting had ever happened.

There was only one choice.

Luke turned his back on Elizabeth and took off in the opposite direction.

Disaster averted. Temptation squashed. Problem solved.

* * *

Luke took the most circuitous path around the house, wanting to put distance between himself and the highly attractive Elizabeth St. James.

He shoved the woman out of his mind. He'd made mistakes in his past that could not be repeated. Though he'd escaped scandal—barely—there had been whispers, most of them true, none of them favorable. For his sister's sake, Luke needed to maintain the respect he'd cultivated since returning to America four months ago. Until Penelope was happily settled, he must be on his best behavior.

Objective clear, he strode around the back of the mansion his father had built for his mother over two decades ago. Griffin Manor was one of the largest of New York's private palaces, second in size only to the one built by Elizabeth's grandfather, Richard St. James.

Luke's mother had decorated the home in grand fashion, her reward for marrying a man solely for social status. His chosen route took him past the smaller building attached to the larger house. The private theater lay in darkness this evening. In less than a month, a production of *Carmen* would be presented for his father's closest friends and business colleagues.

Warren Griffin had a fondness for opera. And a passion for opera singers. Dishonoring his wedding vows didn't seem to bother the business titan. His infidelity certainly bothered Luke's mother.

Luke was also repelled, more now that his father was pressuring him to marry and produce a son to carry on the Griffin name. There weren't enough words in the English language to convince Luke to enter into a marriage like that of his parents.

His breath burned white-hot in his lungs. This was Penelope's engagement party, not the time for moralizing. Or, perhaps, this was the precise time for moralizing. By all accounts, Simon Burrows was a righteous man who followed a strict moral code. He'd chosen Penelope because of her impeccable reputation. Any hint of scandal could jeopardize the engagement.

Simon must not find out about Warren's well-kept secret, far more scandalous than his affairs.

Luke felt the burden of protecting Penelope, not only because of his father's transgressions but also because of his own. The cost of his youthful indiscretions had been high.

An image of Elizabeth St. James flared in his mind.

Her desire to defy her mother's rules struck an unpleasant cord. The recklessness of youth, the need to push against the constraints of a controlling parent, was too familiar.

Luke battled against old memories. They came stronger tonight, bringing back the guilt for hurting a woman who'd misunderstood his intentions.

Furious at the direction of his thoughts, he shoved into the house through a back door and made his way to the library on the second floor. He went directly to the bookshelves lining an entire wall, floor to ceiling, and randomly ran his finger along the spine of a book.

The din of conversation and high-pitched laughter from the party grated on him. He reached to close the door, but his hand fell away when he spotted the man standing on the threshold.

"Lucian, there you are." His father entered the library, the requisite scowl on his face. "Your mother and I were concerned you'd already left."

The reproach was unmistakable in his low tone. It exasperated Luke that his parents questioned his word, yet he kept his reaction hidden behind rigid control. "I said I would remain the entire evening, and so I will."

"Your absence has been noted by several of our guests."

"Then I will return to the party at once." He stepped toward the door.

His father barred his exit, feet spread, hands clasped behind his back. "Before you go, I'd like a quick word."

Luke adopted a similar pose and waited for the older man to stop scowling and state his business. In his mid-fifties, Warren Griffin was still handsome, still as fit as a man half his age. He'd come from a wealthy banking family and had been given all the advantages of a privileged birthright, including an education from the finest schools in the country.

The same privileges Luke had received as Warren's only son.

Always the outward picture of propriety, Warren wore one of his hand-tailored suits. The tall, leanly muscled build and classically handsome features fooled many. He was considered a man of impeccable taste, with a mind for business and a heart for philanthropy. Even Luke's closest friend, Jackson, considered Warren an upright example to be imitated.

Ah, but Warren Griffin was not what he seemed.

Like recognizes like, Luke thought, a harsh reminder of the things he'd done to prove he wasn't his father's son. Only to make choices that made him, in fact, *exactly* like the man he'd tried so hard not to be.

Though Luke's choices had been in reaction to his father's hypocrisy and impossibly high standards, there was no excuse for most of the things he'd done. He would have much to answer for when he faced the Lord.

Sobering thought.

His father continued eyeing him with a disapproving look and, finally, broke his silence. "I understand you are contemplating a new investment."

Luke covered his surprise with a bland stare. How his father knew about his recent discussion with Ryan Pitney was more disturbing than the accusatory tone. "I am."

"It's unwise to go into business with a friend."

Luke thought he'd given up winning his father's approval. Yet he still felt the need to defend himself. "I'm not going into business with Ryan. I am planning to purchase his company outright."

Once he secured another investor.

"Even worse."

Luke forced calm into his voice. "Motorcars are the future."

With slow, deliberate movements, his father unclasped his hands and balanced evenly on both feet. "I have attempted to teach you sound business practices, yet you refuse to learn."

Luke struggled to contain his bitterness, telling himself he was no longer an impressionable boy facing a disapproving parent. "Let me remind you, Father, that in my three years working out of the London offices, I turned Griffin Shipping into an international success."

Warren's mouth went flat. "That may be. But you take too many risks with your personal finances. Continue on this path, and you will lose everything."

Or gain a fortune.

Luke had already made several successful investments. He'd also had a few setbacks.

His father only pointed out the failures.

"You should be using tonight to reacquaint yourself with the young ladies of New York society."

And they were back to Warren Griffin's second-favorite topic. "You mean the unmarried ones."

"There are many suitable matches."

Luke couldn't argue the point. Elizabeth St. James came to mind. The image of her smile chased every other thought away. The way her beautiful eyes had softened when he'd leaned over and . . .

He beat the memory back.

"We've been through this before. I want Penelope settled first. I also want—" He darted his gaze around the room. This was yet another conversation he didn't want to have with his father. "I'm not ready to marry."

"No man is ever truly prepared for marriage."

Luke's friend Jackson had been, almost as soon as he'd laid eyes on Caroline St. James.

Warren's features turned distant, his mind clearly lost in thought. "While I have you here, there's something else you should know."

Luke waited.

"Esmeralda Cappelletti is returning to America next month."

Every muscle in Luke's back coiled and tightened.

"She has agreed to give a private performance in my opera house immediately upon her return."

Esmeralda was the previous century's most celebrated diva. Warren had launched her career in his private opera house a decade ago. "Will Sophie be with her?"

"Yes."

Luke closed his eyes, fought off a frown as he did a quick mental calculation. Sophie had to be twenty-one years old by now, possibly twenty-two. He remembered her as a young girl. She'd been Penelope's friend, along with Elizabeth St. James. For a time, the three had been inseparable.

"Does Mother know about Esmeralda's return?"

"I will tell her in good time."

Throat tight, Luke tried to empty his mind of all thought, but a distant memory shimmered to life. His mother working in her garden, day after day, her hands covered in dirt as she waited for her husband to tire of his latest opera singer and return to her.

Warren always returned.

As a boy, Luke had been too young to understand the strange dynamics between his parents. He wasn't sure he understood any better as a grown man. God's design for marriage did not include paramours who sang opera.

"I expect you to welcome Esmeralda and her daughter with the cordiality that is their due."

A spurt of outrage ignited in Luke's chest. He had the presence of mind to sit in a nearby chair. As if in a dream, he was transported back in time, to the night he'd discovered the truth about his father and Esmeralda, about the true parentage of Esmeralda's child.

Luke barely heard his father explaining the need for discretion. "For Penelope's sake, we must be circumspect."

A part of Luke listened, taking it all in. The other part was unable to forget that he and this man shared the same blood. They came from the same world, where a man could have a mistress and a wife, so long as he was *circumspect*.

Luke surfaced back into the conversation at the word *mistake*. "What did you say?"

"Simon Burrows must never know about my mistake."

Warren was referring to Sophie Cappelletti—his own daughter—as a mistake?

Disappointed in the man who'd fathered him, Luke remained outwardly calm. Inside, he burned. He thought of the days after he'd uncovered the truth about Sophie, his half sister. Warren's duplicity had been too much to bear. As a result, Luke had made choices he would have to live with for the rest of his days.

And he walked in all the sins of his father, which he had done before him . . .

Luke shuddered, thinking of his carelessness and the pain he'd caused.

"I trust I can count on your cooperation in this matter."

Luke cleared his face of all expression. "I will do everything in my power to protect Penelope's future."

"That's all I ask."

Luke rose. "If you'll excuse me, I've neglected our guests long enough."

"As have I." Warren wrenched open the door, exiting first.

In silence, Luke strode down the hallway beside his father. Out of the corner of his eye, he caught a glimpse of them in a gilded mirror on the wall. There was no denying he was Warren Griffin's son. They had the same build, an identical breadth of shoulders, and a similar stubborn angle to their chins.

While Luke may resemble his father on the outside, he would not become the same man on the inside. "I bid you good night."

Warren started to speak.

Luke continued on without looking back. He entered the ballroom, his gut roiling. With the din of at least a dozen different conversations buzzing around him, he made a silent promise to himself. No other woman would suffer because of him.

As if to test his certitude, he caught sight of Elizabeth St. James on the opposite side of the room, surrounded by several young men her age. She looked troubled and entirely too unhappy for a woman of twenty.

Luke took an involuntary step toward her. His wits returned almost immediately. Elizabeth was a grown woman, not a child. She didn't need rescuing. He turned in the opposite direction, then went in search of his sister and her fiancé.

Smartest move he'd made all night.

Chapter Four

The morning after Penelope's engagement party, Elizabeth woke with gritty eyes and a conflicted heart. She was pleased her friend had found love. In truth, she'd never seen Penny happier. But the evening had been distressing for Elizabeth. Overhearing the gossip about her family had been bad enough, but those precious few moments in the garden with Luke had been positively dreadful.

Under the intimacy of the moon and stars, when everything was possible and anything could happen, he'd kissed her—on the *forehead*.

Some things never change.

Something has to change.

She couldn't go on like this. She couldn't travel to London and begin a new life with so much uncertainty plaguing her.

Looking for guidance, she retrieved her Bible from the nightstand and opened it to a random page. She attempted to read, but the events of the previous evening kept intruding. Hand flat on the open book, she looked to the ceiling. There was no inspiration to be found there, either.

Her world had tilted off-kilter, and Elizabeth couldn't seem to find her balance. She'd tossed and turned most of the night. When she finally did fall asleep, she'd dreamed of Luke in the garden, smiling at her with a look that was far from brotherly.

Luke.

He was so handsome, so familiar, so much a part of her fondest childhood memories. If she was honest with herself, Elizabeth would admit she hardly knew the man anymore. He was different since his return to America. He certainly didn't know her. Like every other male in her immediate acquaintance, Luke treated her as if she were a parian doll.

Surely there was more to her than a blank-eyed, pretty plaything.

What if there isn't?

What if she was nothing more than the finished product of her mother's grooming, a woman bred to marry, to drink tea with friends, and to raise her daughters to do the same?

Teeth clenched, Elizabeth set her Bible back on the table.

The direction of her thoughts was only adding to her distress.

She threw off the covers and climbed to her feet. She was Elizabeth St. James, a grown woman who could take care of herself. To prove it, she didn't ring for her maid. She dressed quickly in a cream-and-coral-striped dress with matching accessories and low-heeled ankle boots.

At the mirror, she gathered her mass of unruly curls in a simple twist atop her head, smoothing and tugging until only a few wisps were left curling around her face.

She'd barely secured the final pin when Sally entered the room, carrying a tray laden with toast points, pastries, a pot of tea, and a soft-boiled egg nestled in an enameled cup.

"You're up." The maid's feet ground to a halt. "And ready for the day."

Annoyance flared. Elizabeth tapped the emotion down with a hard swallow. "I'm perfectly capable of dressing myself."

"Of course you are." Sally continued through the room. "I didn't mean to imply otherwise."

Giving Elizabeth a sidelong glance, the maid set the tray on a table near the large picture window currently hidden behind heavy green drapes. Hints of sunshine streamed through the center slit, then burst into the room when Sally tossed back the curtains.

Momentarily blinded, Elizabeth covered her eyes. By the time she lowered her hand, Sally was already bustling through the room, tidying as she went.

Elizabeth took her place at the table and silently watched the young woman go about her chores. What was it like, she wondered, to work for another person, as Sally worked for her?

She found herself asking, "Do you enjoy your position here at St. James House?"

Hands pausing over the bedcovers, Sally answered without turning around. "There is dignity in a life of service," she said in a carefully restrained tone. "The Lord himself came to serve His flock."

The maid's response didn't really answer the question, and yet Elizabeth suddenly felt small and insignificant. Sally had a purpose. She did not.

Something has to change.

How many times had she said that to herself in the past two days? Too many. Lips pressed tightly together, Elizabeth drummed her fingers on the table. Her first act of rebellion had been a futile attempt at best, hardly worth noting.

She needed to take a bolder step.

If only she knew how, what? With whom?

If only her mother were here to consult. If only . . .

Elizabeth stopped herself, appalled at where her thoughts had led. The mother she'd relied on in the past didn't exist. In truth, she'd never existed.

Even when she was young, it hadn't been Katherine St. James she'd sought out for counsel; it had been Hester. Elizabeth's former governess always gave good advice. Why had she not thought of that sooner? She would visit Hester this very morning. The decision made her feel marginally better.

"You're not eating." Sally came up beside her, arms overflowing with Elizabeth's clothing from the night before. "Are you feeling ill?"

"I'm perfectly well, thank you."

A worried frown marred the maid's delicate features. "You are certain? You're looking quite pale."

"I'm fine, Sally. Truly." Elizabeth made a grand show of placing a napkin on her lap.

For the maid's benefit, she forced a smile, picked up a spoon, and tapped the top of the egg. A series of cracks webbed across the shell. As she picked away the tiny fragments, she added, "I'm going out this morning."

"What time will we be leaving?"

"This is something I'd prefer to do alone." Hester would be more open and forthright if it was just the two of them.

Sally continued eyeing her, looking as though she had something more to say. "What about the menu for Thursday's dinner party? I thought you wished to reconsider the selections for several of the courses."

"I do, and I will review those with Mrs. Crawford once I return from my errand."

The party was in celebration of Caroline and Jackson's return from their month-long honeymoon. Wishing everything to be perfect, Elizabeth had made detailed lists. She'd checked and rechecked each of them a dozen times. She would probably do so a dozen more before Thursday evening. Nothing could be left to chance. The evening was too important.

"Do you wish to discuss the flower arrangements?" Sally persisted. "You said you wanted my ideas."

"I most definitely do." Sally had an eye for color like no one Elizabeth had ever met. "We will discuss them when—"

"You return from your errand."

"Precisely."

42

At last, Sally relented. "Very well. If there's nothing else, I'll leave you to your breakfast."

"Thank you, Sally."

The maid exited the room, looking back several times before finally shutting the door behind her with a soft click.

Less than twenty minutes later, Elizabeth dashed through St. James House. The trip to Riverside Drive would take at least a half hour, and only if she could coax her grandfather's chauffeur to drive her there in the motorcar.

She passed the formal dining room, then stopped and retraced her steps. She'd completed the seating chart a week ago and had reviewed the layout several times since. Nevertheless, she couldn't help worrying she'd missed something that would cause a problem the night of the dinner party.

Another look couldn't hurt.

Standing on the threshold, Elizabeth surveyed the room. The table was already set for the thirty-two invited guests. Her grandmother's silver looked spectacular next to the imported Irish crystal and bone china decorated with a swirling blue-and-gold pattern. All that was missing were the flower arrangements Sally would help Elizabeth design later that afternoon.

Something still felt . . . off.

Eyes narrowed, she wound her way around the table, checking the place cards one by one. Halfway through her inspection, she caught her mistake. She'd placed Jackson's mother directly across from Caroline.

"How did I miss that?" She whispered the words aloud, though she was the only one in the room.

Lucille Montgomery was still furious with her son for choosing Caroline over Elizabeth—as if there'd actually been a choice. Caroline wasn't especially fond of her new mother-in-law, either. On a good day, Mrs. Montgomery was a trying woman. On a bad one, she was impossible.

But she was Jackson's mother, and so, regardless of her challenging temperament, she must be included in the celebration. Of course, the evening would go better for everyone, especially the guests of honor, if the difficult woman wasn't forced to look at Caroline all evening.

Elizabeth thought a moment, searching the table carefully. At last she found her solution. She picked up the place card and moved Jackson's mother next to Mrs. VanDercreek, an older woman of fine breeding and upstanding morals—one of the few people who tolerated Lucille Montgomery's unpredictable moods.

As Elizabeth changed the woman's seat, she realized she'd originally sat Luke beside Mrs. VanDercreek. By swapping his position with Jackson's mother, Luke was now seated next to Elizabeth.

She was flooded with emotion—anticipation, excitement, and something else she couldn't quite define. She lost herself momentarily in the sensations. Her eyes fluttered shut, then snapped back open. She was doing it again, thinking of Luke in ways that would only lead to disappointment.

Sighing, Elizabeth reached for the place card, paused.

What harm would come from having Luke as her dinner companion for one night? It was actually quite practical. Elizabeth could use the occasion to quiz him about British society.

Satisfied with her reasoning, she exited the room and slammed headlong into a wall of hard muscle encased in thin black wool.

"Oh." She stumbled backward, arms flailing. "Oh, my."

A hand reached out to steady her. "Easy now."

Her breath burned hot in her lungs, only to turn ice cold half a second later. "Luke." His name came out on a whoosh of air. "I didn't see you there."

"I gathered."

His deep, gravelly voice washed over her, causing her heart to pound madly in her chest, the only part of her that seemed capable of moving. She couldn't even manage a fidget.

"Finding one another in unexpected places is becoming a habit." He leaned in close, humor in his eyes. "I like it."

Elizabeth felt her lips curve. The man was beyond charming. He left her quite tongue-tied.

As if she were prey caught in the hunter's snare, all she could do was look into his penetrating eyes. The unusual golden color reminded her of a tiger.

Say something, Elizabeth. Do something.

She couldn't move, could hardly breathe.

Luke didn't seem to notice her humiliating reaction to his nearness. Amusement continued dancing in his gaze. "Tell me, where are you headed off to in such a hurry?"

He punctuated the question with a smile. *That smile.*

"I have a . . . an"—she shifted her stance—"I have an appointment on the Upper West Side."

"It must be very important."

"I . . . well, yes. It is."

Outrageously nervous, she desperately wanted to smooth a hand across her hair and tuck away any loose strands. If only Luke weren't standing so close, she might be able to think properly. She could smell his familiar scent, a pleasant mix of shaving soap and some woodsy spice all his own.

The man should not smell so good.

The humor in his eyes moved into his voice. "I, too, have an important appointment this morning."

"Here?" She couldn't imagine what would have brought him to St. James House at this early hour.

"It's with your grandfather."

That was odd. Why hadn't he approached Grandfather at his office? Elizabeth waited for Luke to explain.

He said nothing.

He simply continued staring at her with that half-amused, overly patient expression she was growing to dislike intensely. She'd seen him give Penelope that very same look. When her friend was ten years old.

Frustration coursed through Elizabeth. After their encounter in the gardens last evening, she'd hoped matters had changed between them. Nothing but wishful thinking on her part.

"Well, then. I won't keep you." She attempted to step around him.

He barred her escape, his piercing gaze boring into her as if he could see straight into her soul.

"Elizabeth." He touched her sleeve, casually drew his hand back. "I can't help thinking I've somehow upset you just now."

He had, though she'd never admit such a thing out loud.

"Not in the least. I was . . ." *Think, Elizabeth. Think of something smart and clever to say.* She blurted out the first thing that came to mind. "It's just that my head is full of plans. I have much to do in the next two months."

"What happens in two months?"

Why had she said anything at all? Now she had to explain herself. "I set sail for England."

His eyebrows slammed together. "I didn't realize you were going on a tour of the British Isles."

"I'm not."

"Then why are you sailing to England in two months?"

"I am going there to"—she forced herself to hold his gaze—"find a husband."

* * *

Throat burning, heart pounding, Luke stared at Elizabeth in muted shock. For a moment, he thought he must have misheard her. She couldn't possibly be planning to travel all the way to England to find a husband.

"You wish to marry . . . a Brit?"

"Is that so hard to believe?"

"Actually, yes."

"Well, it's true." Elizabeth's stiff spine and lifted chin spoke of female mutiny, as if she expected him to laugh.

Luke had no desire to laugh.

He tried to swallow the lump in his throat but couldn't. Elizabeth wouldn't be the first American girl to travel to England in search of a husband with a title. There'd been a steady stream of wealthy young heiresses for twenty years, ever since King Edward VII, while still the Prince of Wales, had developed a fondness for them.

Luke couldn't tolerate the idea of Elizabeth joining their ranks. "Why go to England when there are plenty of eligible men in New York?"

"I should think it obvious."

"Not really." He couldn't keep the incredulity out of his voice. The woman belonged in America with her family and friends. "Help me understand."

She tilted her head, her thoughts whirling in her gaze, her hands clasped at her waist. "My family has prestige, money, and social status. They lack only one thing."

"The St. James family lacks for nothing."

"We don't have a title."

Luke considered himself unflappable. It was one of the traits that made him successful in negotiating difficult business deals. Yet, with a single, unexpected phrase, Elizabeth had managed to throw him completely off balance. "You wish to marry a stranger to acquire a title for your family?"

"Precisely."

Some of his puzzlement edged into irritation. "That's absurd."

A small defeated sigh whispered out of her. "It's the one thing only I can do for the family."

Remorse hit him hard and intense. His words had been full of disapproval, making him sound far too much like his father. He needed to apologize, immediately. "Elizabeth, don't misunderstand me. I didn't mean—"

"I know what you meant." She blew out a fast puff of air. "You don't believe I can entice a man with a title."

Clearly, he'd insulted her. Luke reined in his frustration and spoke from the heart. "I believe you will take England by storm."

For the span of a heartbeat, she blinked up at him with a sweet, grateful smile that reached inside his chest, gripped his heart, and tugged. Hard.

Warning bells went off in his head, loud and insistent.

Standing in the dim light of the hallway, he could not look away from those sculpted cheekbones, the perfectly bowed lips, and the pretty blue eyes the color of summer skies.

When had Elizabeth become so enticing? When had she grown into this stunning blend of delicate and exotic, innocence and boldness? And she wanted to marry a man for his title? The thought annoyed him.

"Do you have any advice for me?"

"Concerning . . . ?"

A half smile played across her lips. "How I can make myself more agreeable to the eligible English gentlemen."

She wanted to be *more* agreeable?

The emotion that swept through him was like a summer thunderstorm, violent, unexpected, blowing in out of nowhere.

Needing a moment to calm his chaotic thoughts, he gave her a frank appraisal. A mistake. She looked young and fresh this morning. The cut of her dress showed off her curves, reminding Luke she was no longer a child but a woman. The moment she entered her first English ballroom, she'd be the talk of the entire British Isles.

Every man in England would clamor for her attention. Some would be genuinely interested in her. Others would have their eyes solely on her grandfather's money.

Elizabeth was worth more than a hefty dowry.

And . . . she'd asked him a question.

"You will be a grand success, no matter what you do."

It was the simple truth, and he hated it. An odd response, to be sure, one he'd have to explore later. When he wasn't listing to port thanks to this strange, unnerving conversation.

"There must be something I can do to make myself more engaging."

The muscles at the back of his neck knotted. Elizabeth St. James was already too engaging for her own good. The British didn't deserve her. They wouldn't appreciate her.

"Your family has agreed to this ridicu—" He took a deep, steadying breath. "Your father and grandfather approve of this scheme?"

"It was their idea."

"I find that hard to believe."

She performed a delicate shrug.

"Why did you agree to their request?" He couldn't believe she wanted a title for herself. The Elizabeth he knew was not that superficial.

"I need a change, Luke. And I want to start over in a place where people don't know my mother."

Hearing those halting words, spoken in that low, vulnerable tone, Luke could find no fault in Elizabeth wishing to flee New York. He wondered why she hadn't done so sooner. "The business with your mother has truly upset you."

She nodded, looking as miserable as he'd ever seen her.

A burst of sympathy filled his chest. He knew the pain that came with discovering beloved parents weren't who—or what—they seemed.

"You lived in London for three years," she said. "You must know the British people well enough to suggest a few things I can do to set myself apart."

"You're perfect just the way you are."

"That's kind of you to say."

Kindness had nothing to do with it. "It's the truth."

"You don't have one piece of advice to share?"

Don't go.

The plea swept through his mind. "Be yourself."

"But, Luke, don't you see? That's the problem." Her fathomless blue eyes held a large dose of anxiety. "I don't know who I am beyond the most obvious character traits I present to the world. What if there is nothing more to me than meets the eye? What if I lack . . . substance?"

"Elizabeth, where is this coming from? I've never known you to question yourself like this."

Eyes not quite meeting his, she rolled her shoulders as if ridding herself of a heavy weight. "I haven't felt myself for some time now."

Of course she hadn't. She'd experienced a great shock several months ago. He wanted to shield her from further discomfort. Unfortunately, facts were facts. Elizabeth had a family secret that must be hidden from the world.

Luke knew all about keeping family secrets.

Compelled, he lifted his hand in her direction. He wasn't sure what he meant to do. Perhaps he simply planned to offer a comforting touch to her arm. Perhaps he meant to cup her cheek and tell her she was more than a pretty face.

He would never know, because she stepped out of his reach before he could make contact.

"The hour grows late." This time, her gaze didn't quite meet his. "Good-bye, Luke."

His hand dropped to his side and his voice went hoarse. "Good-bye, Elizabeth."

A heartbeat later, she was on the move once again.

Luke stood immobile, watching her until she turned the corner and the sound of her footsteps faded.

He'd felt a connection with Elizabeth this morning, stronger than what he'd experienced the night before, deeper than attraction, a sort of solidarity. Her concern that she was nothing more than the product of her upbringing hit close to home. Luke had been groomed to take over his father's business.

He wanted nothing to do with maintaining Warren Griffin's legacy, however, hence his meeting with Richard St. James. No matter how the conversation went, he would continue building his fortune in his own way, on his own terms.

His only obligation was to Penelope.

Her future must be secure before he made the final break from his father. Now that Penny's engagement to Simon Burrows was official, Luke was nearly satisfied his sister was in good hands. He had some digging left to do.

So far, her fiancé was exactly what he seemed. That didn't mean the man was free of secrets. If he was hiding something dark, deceitful, or dishonest, Luke would ferret out the truth.

But first . . .

He took off down the corridor with purposeful strides, his heels striking the hardwood floor like hammers to nails. He caught the sounds of piano music coming from deep within the house. Someone was playing the first strains of a concerto from the opera *Carmen*. It was the dimmest of sounds, but enough to send a jolt of shock quivering through him. Luke's steps abruptly halted.

Carmen was his father's favorite opera. All of Warren's paramours eventually sang the lead role in his private theater. Esmeralda had begun the tradition a decade ago.

Luke remembered the last time he'd seen the celebrated diva. He'd come home a day early from boarding school. His grades had been good enough to earn him the honor of salutatorian. He'd wanted to tell his father personally. He'd found Warren in the opera house, in an intimate embrace with Esmeralda—

Luke shoved aside the image. If he continued clinging to unpleasant memories, he would forever be tied to the past.

The creak of an opening door jerked his attention to his right. A shadow flickered across the floor, elongated, and then formed into a man as Marcus St. James stepped into the corridor.

His gaze locked with Luke's.

"My father and I were just speaking about you and your promising new venture." Marcus joined him in the long, empty hallway. "He is waiting for you in his study."

"Thank you, sir. I know the way."

"Yes, yes, of course you do."

They had a brief discussion about the future of motorcars—clearly, the St. James men had done their homework—and then Luke continued on to his destination. He stopped before the gleaming ebony door Marcus St. James had left ajar.

A rush of—*something*—skittered though him. This was the next step in breaking from his father once and for all.

After a cursory knock on the doorjamb, Luke entered Richard St. James's private sanctuary, fully prepared to leap over another hurdle standing between him and total freedom.

Chapter Five

Elizabeth instructed her grandfather's chauffeur to drop her off two blocks from Hester's building. She wanted to walk the remainder of the way, not only to clear her head after her recent interchange with Luke but to enjoy the cool spring air.

The picturesque Riverside Drive always captured her imagination, as did the eclectic town houses. The beauty of the brownstones ranged from elegant to ornate. Elizabeth was grateful her grandfather had made sure Hester had the money to live in comfort now that she was retired from service.

Eager to visit her old friend, Elizabeth rushed up the front steps leading into Hester's building. One of the original brownstones in the area, the town house was separated into two units per each of the three floors. The interior of the structure was as impressive as the exterior.

Sunlight spilling through the beveled windows provided enough illumination for her to see that the wallpaper was a pretty floral pattern. The wood banister gleamed from a new coat of lemon wax. This house suited Hester. Every time Elizabeth asked her beloved friend if she was happy here, Hester would speak of her friends, her church, and the life she'd built for herself.

Elizabeth climbed to the second-floor landing and knocked on Hester's door.

A series of locks releasing and a knob turning filled the air moments before the door swung open. "My dear Elizabeth, what a treat it is to see you."

Hester's cheery British accent matched the welcoming smile. The happy expression enhanced the older woman's pleasing features. A beauty in her youth, Hester had golden-brown hair that was now streaked with threads of gray. Her face also held the signs of time passing in the spiderweb of wrinkles around her eyes and mouth.

The woman was clearly pleased to see her, but on closer inspection she also appeared paler than usual. She was gaunt in the cheeks, and her shoulders were hunched. Even worse, her too-thin frame seemed almost emaciated this morning.

Elizabeth felt a stab of panic.

Was Hester ill?

"I hope I've come at a good time."

Hester's smile never faltered. "The very best."

Fighting off her apprehension, Elizabeth lifted the basket she'd filled with several of Hester's favorite items before leaving St. James House. "For you."

"Look at those lovely flowers." She lifted faded blue eyes that lacked their usual sparkle. "Yellow roses are my favorite."

"I remember."

"Where are my manners?" Hester opened the door wider. "Do come in."

Elizabeth stepped inside the tiny entryway.

Hester's movements were unnaturally stiff as she turned and led the way deeper into the apartment.

The main living area was small but elegant. Everywhere Elizabeth looked, she saw Hester. In the brocade furniture, in the rose-patterned wallpaper, in the basket of unfinished knitting and the books perched on every available tabletop.

The clutter added a lived-in feel. The smell of mint, jasmine, and lemon oil took Elizabeth back to her childhood, when she'd been as close to her governess as her own mother, perhaps even closer.

It had been Hester who held her when she cried, Hester who taught her to love unconditionally while requiring nothing in return. Hester who told her she was smart and beautiful no matter what dress she wore or circle of friends she chose.

"We'll sit in here." Hester directed her to a tiny parlor where two identical chairs were positioned on either side of a small round table.

Taking the basket, the older woman tilted her head at a curious angle. "To what do I owe this unexpected visit?"

"Would you believe me if I said I was in the neighborhood?"

"I would not."

"It's the truth. I was not more than two blocks away." She smiled innocently. "Once Grandfather's chauffeur let me out of the motorcar."

"Oh, well then, I stand corrected." Hester's soft laughter served to relieve Elizabeth's mind.

But then the older woman broke off abruptly and gave in to a fit of coughing that threw her off balance. Elizabeth was immediately by her side, holding her steady until she was breathing easy once again.

When their eyes met, Elizabeth's throat closed up tight. She had to swallow several times before she could speak. "Hester, are you unwell?"

"Of course not." The answer came quickly, too quickly.

"If you were sick, you would tell me?"

"Absolutely, I would."

Elizabeth almost believed her. But Hester's weakened physical state was impossible to ignore. Something was wrong with her.

"Stop fretting over me." Hester brushed her away and buried her nose in the basket, rummaging around with concentrated focus. "I merely slept poorly last evening."

"You are sure that's the whole of it?" Elizabeth reached out and touched the very edge of Hester's shoulder. "I don't mind sending Dr. Miller over to examine you."

"Please don't do that." The woman made a soft sound of protest, barely audible. "All I need is a good night's sleep, and then I'll be right as rain."

Short of calling the woman a liar, Elizabeth was forced to take Hester at her word. Though it scared her to think her former governess was ill, there wasn't much she could do but pray for her health and happiness.

She smiled fondly at Hester's bent head. "I'm glad I stopped by this morning."

At last, the woman looked up from the basket. "You never did reveal the reason for your visit."

No, she'd been too distracted by the obvious signs of Hester's physical decline. "I came to tell you I have decided to go to England as my father and grandfather have requested."

"Ah." Understanding filled the older woman's eyes. "I'll make tea, and we'll have a good, long talk."

"I can help with the tea."

"No need, you'll only be in the way."

Elizabeth wanted to protest, but Hester had already disappeared around the corner. While her friend puttered in the kitchen, Elizabeth took the opportunity to shed her coat and gloves. When the older woman returned, she'd just picked up the open book on a nearby footstool.

"You are reading *Pride and Prejudice* again." She returned the book to its original spot. "This must be the . . . what? Tenth time you've read the story?"

"Closer to twenty." Laughing softly, Hester set down the tray and poured the tea. "I do love a happy ending."

So did Elizabeth.

Would her own story end happily?

Her mother had taught her how to dress in the latest fashions, how to run a large household, and how to plan a dinner party. These were important skills in her privileged world. So why did her life feel shallow and frivolous, perhaps even a little empty?

Hester settled back in her chair and picked up a teacup.

Elizabeth followed suit.

"Now tell me, dear. Does your decision to leave the country have anything to do with the return of your cousin and her husband from their honeymoon?"

"No. *No.*" She answered with more emotion than she'd meant, but it was important Hester understood her decision had nothing to do with Caroline and Jackson.

"You are not a bit . . . jealous?"

"Not even a little." Well, maybe a little, but not because she wanted Jackson for herself. What she wanted was a love like Jackson had with Caroline. "I'm happy they found each other."

"Even though he was to be your husband?"

"We weren't engaged." The agreement between their mothers didn't signify. "And we certainly didn't suit one another."

Hester studied her over the rim of her teacup. "Everyone thought you did."

Elizabeth couldn't argue the point. Like her, Jackson had been a favored member of New York society, welcome in every home because of his sterling reputation.

That had changed when his relationship with Caroline became known. Because of her notorious beginnings, she'd been shunned from society. No proper New York hostess wanted a "filthy street urchin" in her home. Jackson had stood by the woman he loved, and had been shunned as well.

Oh, to be loved like that.

Though he'd forfeited his place among the New York elite, the man Jackson had become was far better than the one he'd been before meeting Caroline.

Pondering the change, Elizabeth wondered about her own future. Would her choices make her a better woman? That was the real question she'd been grappling with since her mother's departure.

"If I am to be completely honest"—she took a sip of tea out of reflex rather than desire, then set down the cup—"I have decided to go to London primarily because I wish for a fresh start."

"This is what you truly want?"

Elizabeth thought of Luke and their recent encounter. He'd claimed she would be a success in England, and that the British would find her pleasing. She hoped she would discover what she was missing in her life there.

"I cannot go on as before," she admitted.

"Is running away the answer?"

Words of denial were there in her mind, struggling up her throat and onto her tongue. She wanted—needed—to defend her decision. But the argument wouldn't form. She'd come for advice.

Why couldn't she ask for it?

Sweeping an unsteady hand over her dress, Elizabeth smoothed out a nonexistent wrinkle. The dress she wore was like all the others in her closet, made especially for her by expert hands in Parisian couture houses.

"And I would hate for you to make a similar mistake."

Elizabeth blinked. While she'd been mounting a defense for her decision, Hester had continued speaking. Elizabeth filed through the woman's words, trying to capture what she'd missed.

"There comes a time when we have to accept things cannot go back to the way they once were."

Elizabeth cocked her head in confusion. Was Hester speaking about herself or Elizabeth? The woman had a faraway look in her eyes, as if caught in a distant memory.

"Regret is a terrible bedfellow."

"You have regrets?"

"Far too many, I'm afraid." Hester's hands reached for each other, twisted in her lap.

"You've always been so steady."

She didn't look steady now. She looked sad. So very, very sad. Maybe even a bit broken.

"Life is all about choices, Elizabeth. A series of bad decisions, no matter how small at the time, can add up and eventually lead to a lifetime of regret."

Elizabeth took two, three shallow breaths. What terrible act had Hester committed that caused such remorse? She took the older woman's hand and squeezed gently. "Whatever you've done, you may tell me. I won't hold it against you."

"Oh, dear, dear girl, I do not regret what I've done."

"No?"

Hester shook her head. "I grieve for all that I didn't do, the chances I never took, the roads I never traveled. Missed opportunities, those are what haunt me and keep me awake at night."

For several heartbeats, Elizabeth could do nothing but blink at the woman she thought she'd known so well. Hester had always been so sure of herself, so ready to guide Elizabeth when she faltered. Her words of wisdom had spoken of a life well lived.

To discover that hadn't been the case was a shock.

"I have something to show you." Hester stood.

Elizabeth attempted to stand as well, but the woman motioned her back into the chair. "Wait here. I won't be a moment."

Watching her steady, practical governess leave the room, Elizabeth felt a crack of uncertainty split through her heart. Hester claimed she agonized over the roads not taken and chances not seized. Was Elizabeth headed down a similar path?

Hester soon returned with a small rectangular box. The wood looked old and worn. The wildflowers and ivy swirls painted on the lid were all but faded away.

After smoothing a hand across the top of the box, Hester carefully removed the lid. Elizabeth leaned in close and peered at the contents inside.

There wasn't much to see, just a nest of tissue. Anything could be hidden beneath the paper—a pair of shoes, a journal, something else entirely. "What is it?"

"Patience, dear."

Carefully peeling away the paper, Hester revealed a scarlet-colored shawl. The rich, vibrant color was too red, too scandalous, and yet the shawl was the most beautiful creation Elizabeth had ever seen. Such a garment could never be worn in polite society, at least not by a young, innocent woman seeking a proper husband. An unmarried woman should wear only subdued colors, mostly pastels. Nothing too bold, nothing too bright, and, most definitely, nothing that would draw unnecessary attention. Other than in the subtlest of embellishments, red was out of the question.

Which was utterly ridiculous. This was 1901. A new, modern era had begun. One red shawl couldn't harm a reputation. It could, however, throw it into question. Compelled by the beautiful color, Elizabeth reached out to touch the fabric. The smooth silk was cool beneath her fingers.

"It's lovely," she whispered, the word so inadequate. She looked up and found Hester staring at the shawl with something that could be described only as longing. "Where did it come from?"

"It doesn't matter." Hester sounded even more tired than before. Each word she spoke seemed to drain her energy. "I purchased the shawl years ago with the idea of wearing it on my first real adventure."

The idea of her staid, perfectly upright governess embarking on an adventure made Elizabeth smile.

"I have never worn it, not once."

Elizabeth's smile vanished. She placed a hand to her forehead and shoved aside a stray lock of hair.

Hester sighed heavily. "Now you know my biggest regret."

Lowering her gaze to the box, Elizabeth didn't have to feign confusion. "You regret having never worn this gorgeous shawl?"

"Yes and no." Hester sighed again. "I regret not living a life that would have afforded me the opportunity to wear this shawl. At my age, it should be in tatters from constant use."

With great care, Hester folded the tissue paper over the garment, then closed the lid and set the box on the table. "You are still young, Elizabeth, with a full life ahead of you. I urge you not to make the same mistake I did."

"You're telling me to go to England."

"I'm saying no such thing." Hester closed her eyes a moment. "I merely want you to think carefully about your decision. Go for the right reasons or not at all."

Good advice. But what were the right reasons?

Duty and obligation were noble pursuits. Or so Elizabeth had convinced herself. After presenting her decision to her father and grandfather, she'd attempted to tuck away her doubts in a quiet corner of her heart, along with her desire to marry for love and her wish to experience passion.

Her misgivings had refused to stay put. That's why she'd come here, seeking advice from the most trusted person in her life. Instead of finding certainty, Elizabeth was more confused than ever.

Going to London was supposed to be an adventure, wasn't it? Or was it simply relinquishing her hopes and dreams for the sake of duty?

As if reading her mind, Hester took her hands, her grip surprisingly strong. "I tell you this because I love you. Think hard about your decision. Make sure it's what you want."

Elizabeth nodded, her head spinning with too many thoughts to sort through at once. One thing was certain. From the drawn look on Hester's face, this visit had caused her governess pain.

"I've stayed too long." Elizabeth pulled her hands free. "I should let you rest."

The older woman didn't argue, which only confirmed Elizabeth's suspicions. Standing, she quickly donned her coat and gloves.

"I'll see you out." At the door, Hester paused. "Whether you go to London or choose to stay home, do not be afraid to take chances."

This was the advice Elizabeth had come for, though not in the form she'd expected. She started to respond, but Hester wasn't through.

"Be bold, Elizabeth, and never settle for a life half lived."

There was a note of finality in Hester's voice that cut a swath of fear straight through the remaining shreds of Elizabeth's composure.

"I love you, Hester." She leaned over and kissed her weathered cheek. Trying her best to keep the panic out of her voice, she added, "Please take care of yourself."

"I always do." She patted Elizabeth's arm, then opened the door.

Elizabeth left the town house full of worry. Outside, she lifted up a fervent prayer.

Lord, I fear Hester is in dire need of You. Take care of her. Give her healing and the comfort of Your presence. May Your peace be with her now and always.

Elizabeth owed so much to her former governess, more than she could ever repay. And today Hester had done more than given Elizabeth advice. She'd planted a seed.

Would Elizabeth water it? Or would she let it die in the ground, swallowed up by choices borne from duty and obligation?

She had much to think about in the weeks ahead. And possibly, if she was bold enough, a few chances to take.

* * *

Luke arrived at the Harvard Club twenty minutes past noon. His meeting with Richard St. James had gone better than planned. There were details yet to be worked out, and further research to be done, but he was confident he had his first significant investor, possibly the only one he needed. Soon, he would be ready to launch his automobile company.

Flush with success, he hesitated outside the club. The building was constructed in the neo-Georgian style, made exclusively from Harvard brick—of course—and Indiana limestone. Not that Luke was an expert on such things. He was aware of this obscure architectural fact because all members were required to know the club's history before joining.

The building's façade was reminiscent of the ones on Harvard's campus. It was as if he'd been dropped into a slice of Cambridge in the middle of New York City. There were plans to add a second library, another billiard room, and two additional floors of guest rooms. There was even talk of adding a swimming pool one day.

The amenities were top notch, but Luke was a member solely for the contacts. Some of the most powerful and influential businessmen in New York belonged to the Harvard Club, men who were building America one railroad, one oil line, one electric power plant at a time. Luke planned to join their ranks once he launched his latest venture.

But today wasn't about his financial independence. He wasn't here to make business contacts but to ensure Penelope's future was secure. Luke would discover any secrets Simon Burrows hid beneath his virtuous, haughty veneer.

As he stepped beneath the awning of the most exclusive club in the city, resolve spread through him. Luke would not rest until he was convinced his sister was marrying a good man who would treat her with the love and respect she deserved.

The doorman greeted him by name. "Good afternoon, Mr. Griffin."

Luke nodded. "Winslow."

The short, barrel-chested man had thinning hair and a smiling mouth full of crooked teeth. He was dressed in crimson-and-gold livery.

Harvard colors. After twenty years on the job, Winslow was as much a part of the club as the scarlet drapery. He knew every member, their various routines and individual connections to one another. He was a plethora of information.

"Is my father inside?"

"He left ten minutes ago, after taking an early lunch with your future brother-in-law."

Wasn't that interesting?

"And Mr. Burrows?"

"He left as well." The doorman pulled open the gold-plated door and stepped aside.

"Thank you."

Luke climbed the long flight of stairs that led to the main gathering area, touted as an oasis of calm in the midst of hectic New York. The smell of expensive tobacco and freshly polished wood mingled with the scent of leather, books, and old New York money.

The décor was similar to all the great mansions in the city— ridiculously high ceilings, chandeliers made from imported crystal, and dark wood-paneled walls.

Making his way through the cavernous hall, Luke nodded to familiar faces, including a few from his days at the prestigious university. Not surprising, since election for membership, with only a few exceptions, was limited to Harvard graduates and tenured faculty.

Luke sauntered into the dining room and took a quick inventory of the men gathered for lunch. Any number of them could give him the information he sought about Simon. The trick was choosing the right fellow and asking the proper questions, nothing too obvious.

"Luke, my good man." A hand clasped his shoulder. "I had a feeling I'd find you here."

Smiling, Luke twisted around to face his oldest and most trusted friend. Dressed impeccably in a black business suit and crisp linen shirt,

Jackson Montgomery was the quintessential picture of a successful man of means. His face was clean shaven, his black-as-midnight hair perfectly cropped.

"I wasn't expecting to see you until Thursday evening at your welcome-home party."

"That was the plan. However, we arrived back in New York a day early. Normally I would be enjoying time spent with my new wife, but she kicked me out of the house." The deadpan delivery didn't fool Luke.

He laughed. "Comes as no surprise. I'm only amazed it took her this long to see the error of her ways."

"Shows how much you know. I was sent away while Caroline unpacks our trunks. Apparently"—he gave a self-satisfied grin—"I'm a distraction."

Luke heard the affection in his friend's casually spoken words, and the happiness. The change in Jackson was astounding. Where once his posture had been stiff and unbending, he now held himself with easy assurance. His stance was more relaxed, and his guarded gaze was less, well, guarded.

Marriage obviously suited him.

"So you're a free man."

"For a few hours, at any rate."

They were interrupted by the club's venerable maître d'hôtel. "A table for two?"

As they were led to their table, Luke noticed several heads turning in their direction, making eye contact without actually making eye contact. There was never a stare more blatant than the one that didn't quite meet its target. Jackson had been a favorite among their peers, but clearly no more. It wouldn't make a difference in his business dealings with these men, but socially he'd become an outcast. He would no longer be invited into their homes or to their parties.

Much had changed in a mere handful of months. Jackson had once been consumed with restoring respectability to his family name. Part of his plan had been to marry a woman with an impeccable standing in society. He and Elizabeth St. James, the most sought-after debutante in the city, had been pledged to marry by their families.

Luke had been against the match from the start. Elizabeth deserved more than marriage to a man who wanted her good name and little else. He thought of her going to London to find a husband.

Blood roared in his ears. What was she thinking?

Jackson chuckled softly as he sat and glanced around the room. "It would appear our roles have been reversed."

Luke didn't pretend to misunderstand what his friend meant. By marrying Caroline, Jackson had given up all hope of restoring his family's good name. Luke was now the more respectable of the two.

Ironic, when his transgressions were far worse than his friend's. "For my sister's sake, I have made it my mission to garner society's good opinion."

"I don't give a fig what they think of me. Marrying Caroline was the wisest decision I've ever made."

The man had been laid low by love. Luke couldn't help but envy the poor sap. "How did you enjoy Europe?"

"I expected to hate touring half a continent. However—"

Jackson broke off when their waiter appeared. They gave their orders, and the man slipped away again.

"*However*," Jackson repeated, smiling broadly. "I found touring museums and cathedrals, while in the company of a beautiful woman, gratifying in ways I never imagined."

The pleasure in Jackson's face told its own story.

The man was smitten with his wife. Not for the first time, Luke was glad Jackson had married Caroline instead of her cousin.

A vision flashed of Elizabeth in the sunny parlor, pretty and fresh, smiling up at him. The image had him clearing his throat. "You are a changed man, Jackson Montgomery."

"I am, indeed." He leaned forward. "I highly recommend taking the marital plunge."

Luke remembered the last time the two of them met at this club. They'd spoken of marriage back then as well, but the conversation had been vastly different. At the time, Jackson had been close to offering for Elizabeth's hand.

Jackson was better off for making the break.

Was Elizabeth?

Luke stretched out his legs, needing the movement to sort through his thoughts. Until recently, Elizabeth had belonged to the man sitting across from him. Part of Luke still considered her off limits, a friend of the family, nothing more. And yet, somehow, *friendship* didn't accurately describe their connection. The term was entirely too tepid. He couldn't imagine standing by and watching her marry a British lord for the sake of acquiring a title for her family. She deserved better. The thought was becoming something of a mantra.

"You're frowning, my friend."

No doubt he was. Elizabeth's wish to abandon everything and *everyone* she knew concerned him. Jackson was her family now. Where Luke had failed, perhaps his friend would succeed. In a precise, emotionless cadence, Luke told Jackson about Elizabeth's plan to journey to England and why.

"That's absurd."

Luke's sentiments exactly. "She claims it's her way of contributing to the family."

Jackson's eyes narrowed. "You have spoken with her about this matter?"

"Just this morning."

"What counsel did you offer?"

"It's not my place to tell her what to do." Except, somehow, Luke felt that it *was* his place. "Elizabeth's future is hers to do with as she wishes."

"That hasn't stopped you in the past."

Luke winced at the reminder. By insisting Jackson be completely honest about his intentions, or rather his change of heart, he'd already interfered in Elizabeth's life. Jackson had railed against the unsolicited advice in the beginning. But in the end, he'd admitted Luke was right.

Luke was right about Elizabeth's current situation as well.

She didn't need to travel to England to find a husband. Her family didn't need a title. Someone should tell her those things.

That someone would not be Luke. It wasn't his place.

He hoped if he told himself that often enough, he'd refrain from interfering in her life again.

Chapter Six

Late Thursday afternoon, Elizabeth studied her closet with a critical eye. The custom-made gowns that had once held such appeal were now a physical reminder she'd allowed her mother to control her decisions for entirely too long. Though beautiful and exquisitely made, the respectable pale colors and conservative cuts were also unremarkable and lacked glamour.

Yet, even now, Elizabeth fought the reflex to choose the unworn blue silk for tonight's dinner party.

The woman wears the dress. The dress does not wear the woman. More advice from her mother Elizabeth wished to disregard. Why could she not get Katherine's voice out of her head?

Because not all her advice was wrong, nor were all her intentions evil.

Frowning, Elizabeth glided her fingertips along the pleated skirt. Indecision kept her from handing the gown over to Sally, who stood beside her in the closet.

"Which one is it to be?"

Elizabeth took a breath. "I don't know."

Sally turned her head to look at her directly. There was enough light in the tiny space to illuminate the maid's patient expression. Elizabeth appreciated the other woman not pushing her to make a decision, especially since Elizabeth didn't have an endless supply of time. There were at least half a dozen details to review before the guests were due to arrive.

A dress caught her eye.

Elizabeth took a step forward for a better look. The gold taffeta was of the finest quality, but what stood out about the dress was the barest trace of scarlet ribbon lining the bodice, neckline, and sleeves. The color was similar to that of Hester's shawl. The one the former governess had never worn and that now represented a lifetime of regret.

Tears gathered in Elizabeth's eyes. Hester had seemed so defeated. She'd gazed at the shawl with such longing . . .

Elizabeth reached for the dress, paused a beat, then ran her finger along the scarlet trim.

Was there more to Hester's story? Surely there had to be a reason for the choices she'd made and the ones she hadn't. Elizabeth would ask her when next they met.

For now, tonight, she would pay homage to her friend in the only way she knew how. "This one."

She plucked the gold taffeta dress free from its place among the others and passed it over to Sally. The maid gave a murmur of approval.

Forty minutes later, Elizabeth stood before the mirror in the dress, her hair arranged in a complicated twist atop her head. Sally tugged and pulled at the glittering material, ensuring it fell evenly to the floor from every angle, while Elizabeth stared at her reflection.

A thrill slipped along her spine. The modern cut of the gown set off her trim figure. The gold taffeta worked well with her skin tone. But it was the scarlet trim that drew her eye.

Never settle for a life half lived.

Elizabeth had a long way to go if she wished to follow Hester's advice.

"There." Sally stepped back and studied the result of her efforts. She circled Elizabeth one more time, stopping at a spot directly behind Elizabeth's right shoulder.

Their gazes met in the mirror. "You are ready."

"I believe I am."

"What's next?" Sally moved to the writing desk, where Elizabeth had laid out her lists—all five of them—for tonight's party.

She joined the maid and silently reviewed each piece of paper, top to bottom, left to right. "I can't help thinking I've forgotten something."

The statement earned her a soft laugh. "You never miss a detail."

Then why this nagging sense of worry nipping at her?

Nerves, she told herself, certainly understandable. In the months since her mother had moved to Florida, Elizabeth had taken over running her grandfather's household. She'd turned an already efficient staff into a well-honed machine. But tonight's party was the first party she'd planned without her mother's input.

Elizabeth glanced at the clock on the mantelpiece. She had a little more than an hour before the guests began arriving. Plenty of time for her to look in on the kitchen staff and check the dining room, if she didn't dawdle.

She dismissed Sally with a smile. "I'll take care of the rest." At the young woman's protest, she added, "You still have to dress for the party."

A horrified look crossed the maid's face. "You know I cannot attend."

"Of course you can."

Sally looked positively stricken with . . . fear? No, that couldn't be right. Why would she fear going to a private dinner party with only family and close friends in attendance?

"It is not appropriate," Sally argued.

Probably not, Elizabeth silently agreed, if her mother were still living in St. James House. But she wasn't, and Elizabeth was in charge of the evening's festivities. She had full say over the guest list. One small step.

One tiny rebellion.

"We've been through this already. You're Caroline's closest friend. She'll be hurt if you don't attend a party in her honor."

"She will understand."

"I won't hear another word of protest." Elizabeth took the young woman's hand and pulled her toward the adjoining room. "I expect to see you in the drawing room no later than seven o'clock."

"You're very persistent once you get an idea in your head."

"I am." Elizabeth gave the maid a toothy grin. "Now go."

She gave Sally a little push past the threshold, then shut the door behind her.

Pleased she'd won the argument, Elizabeth decided to go forth with confidence from that point forward. For Hester's sake, she would enjoy every bit of the evening. She would even look for opportunities to be bolder.

Flush with anticipation, she gathered up her lists, rushed out of the room, and then sped down the back stairwell.

The noise level increased with each step she conquered. Under Mrs. Crawford's efficient leadership, the kitchen was a hive of activity. A sea of staff dressed in formal black moved with purpose and efficiency.

Leaving them to their work, Elizabeth entered the dining room next. She pressed the switch on a raised panel. The recently installed Maria Theresa chandelier came alive with light. Airy and delicate, the handblown glass and crystal ornaments twisted around the gilded frame, giving the illusion of a floating waterfall.

Elizabeth's decision to go with a blue-and-gold palette to match the St. James china pattern had been a good one. The flower arrangement in the middle of the table, with its array of blue dahlias, was the final touch that pulled everything together.

Pleased by the overall effect, Elizabeth practically floated through the room. She checked each place card and then, satisfied, moved on to the drawing room, where the guests would gather before being called in to dinner.

The stillness in the air was disconcerting. This was her favorite room, but only when it was filled with voices and laughter. She fluffed a pillow, then another, then took note of the placement of the flower arrangements throughout the room.

Each was a smaller, identical version of the ones she and Sally had put on the dining table.

"Perfect," she whispered.

"Yes, you are indeed a vision of perfection."

* * *

Pulse racing, Elizabeth took a moment to gather herself before facing Luke directly. With slow, careful movements, she pivoted on her toes.

Their gazes met, held, held. *Held.*

Her heart took a fast, hard dip.

To the average observer, Luke would appear every inch the easygoing, wealthy gentleman with nothing but unlimited time on his hands. One shoulder propped against the wall, arms crossed over his chest, he watched Elizabeth with eyes lowered to half-mast.

A sense of déjà vu shook her to the core. He'd looked at her like this once before, only a few days ago, under the moon and stars in the sunken gardens of Griffin Manor. There was nothing casual about his deceptively relaxed manner then or now.

Elizabeth scanned his face, seeing something quite wonderful in his eyes, something soft and approachable and solely for her. She was staring, she knew, but couldn't seem to stop herself. Luke was spectacular dressed in black formal attire. He'd never looked more handsome, or more accessible.

He blessed her with that lazy smile he'd given her in the moonlit garden.

Her heart took another tumble.

The way he looked at her. A sensation akin to floating poured over her. She felt weak and strong at once, fearful and daring.

But then, he spoke. "Good evening, Little Bit."

Little Bit.

A thick, hot wall of disappointment crashed into her.

"Luke, I . . ." Taking a breath, she pulled the remaining shreds of her composure about her like a shield of armor. "You are early."

The lazy smile turned into a rakish grin. "For the party, yes. But my meeting with your grandfather, for that I'm right on time."

"You have another meeting with Grandfather?" She cocked an inquiring eyebrow. "So soon after the last?"

He nodded, his expression giving nothing away. "When I want something, I go after it quickly and decisively."

Oh, my.

How very intriguing.

The soft glow of the wall sconces defined the angles of his face. His hair had darkened during the years he'd been out of the country, and smile lines now appeared around his eyes, both of which only added to his appeal.

Luke was not a man who needed added appeal.

He pushed away from the wall.

Elizabeth searched her mind for something to say; anything would do, anything at all. But she couldn't seem to make her mind cooperate. He filled the room. His scent, his voice, his smile. He always exuded refined elegance, but tonight—*tonight*, he was even more compelling.

"I assume you are meeting with my grandfather about a business matter?"

"That's correct." His molten amber eyes roved across her face. "Had I known I would come across you looking so lovely, I would have arrived sooner for the sheer pleasure of admiring you."

Coiling warmth spread through her, weakening her knees. She had no idea what to do with these strange new feelings Luke inspired.

"Next time," she said in a trembling vibrato.

"Next time, Elizabeth, I will definitely plan accordingly."

Elizabeth. He'd called her Elizabeth.

Her heart raced so fast and hard, she worried if one of her ribs would crack from the added pressure.

Though he'd intimated he was running late, Luke didn't take his leave. Instead, he glanced at her gown, then raised a single eyebrow. "New?"

"No." He remembered their conversation in the garden. Elizabeth couldn't hide her pleasure. "It's from two seasons ago."

Appreciation filled his gaze.

He took a step toward her. And another.

Elizabeth held steady, unmoving, eager to see how near he would come.

He stopped his approach at a polite distance but close enough for her to see the flecks of gold in his eyes.

For the span of three rib-cracking heartbeats, Elizabeth simply stared up at him. A sigh slipped past her lips. The sound was far too tremulous. "My mother will never know of my impertinence, but I will know. And now, you do, too."

"Elizabeth." A look of strain tightened around his eyes and mouth. "A little rebellion isn't necessarily a bad thing."

His tone said otherwise. He definitely had more to say on the subject; she could see it in his eyes.

Bracing herself, she urged him to continue. "However . . . ?"

"I feel the need to warn you."

Said the big brother to the little sister.

She made a face, which he promptly ignored. The man was on a mission now.

"What starts out as a small defiance can take a devastating turn very quickly."

"It's a dress, Luke."

"It's more, and we both know it." His tone turned grave. "Cross the wrong line, and you will end up hurt, or worse, you will hurt another."

She heard something besides gravity in his voice: sadness, secrets, hidden pain. She'd heard the same emotions in Hester's voice two days ago. But where Elizabeth's former governess clearly mourned the things she hadn't done, Luke seemed to mourn the things he had.

Doubt left Elizabeth feeling unsettled. She didn't want to go through life without experiencing at least one real adventure. Perhaps even two. All right, three. Three was the absolute limit.

But what if she went too far?

What if she, as Luke suggested, crossed the wrong line?

"I would not wish to do something I could not take back," she murmured.

"I would not wish that for you, either." Luke spoke equally softly.

Although he stood no closer than before, Elizabeth was aware of his presence with sharp-edged clarity. His scent overwhelmed her, a pleasant blend of bergamot, masculine spice, and . . . him.

Something unspoken hovered in the air between them, communicated in a language Elizabeth should know but couldn't quite comprehend.

"Be careful, Little Bit."

Little Bit. He was feeling protective again. His concern was sweet but misguided.

Did he not know she already had regrets, for not having the courage to question the direction of her life sooner? Her greatest fear was that she'd waited too long. Freedom felt a long way off, close enough to wish for but too far away to grasp.

"Elizabeth, did you hear what I said?"

"I heard you." Her voice sounded as discouraged as she felt. "You want me to stay locked in my safe, sheltered world."

"That is not at all what I said. I am simply warning you to think before you act. Consider your reputation. One misstep is all it would take to smear your good name."

She couldn't prevent a feeling of disappointment. Luke was like all the other men in her life. *Be a good girl, Elizabeth. Do what you're told.*

Her desire to push against the boundaries returned with renewed vigor. "I do not think a little harmless rule-breaking will permanently stain my good name."

He scowled. "There is no such thing as *harmless* rule-breaking. Every rebellion has a cost."

Who was this man? And what had he done to the adventurous Lucian Griffin that Elizabeth knew? "You're certainly full of advice. Yet you rebelled once, and your reputation survived."

A shadow passed across his face. "I'm a man. The rules are different."

"That's terribly unfair."

"Perhaps, but don't think that simply because I have been forgiven for my mistakes that I don't still suffer the consequences. If I could erase my transgressions and the harm I inflicted, I would."

Elizabeth heard the guilt in his voice and wondered what he'd done to cause such remorse. Luke was a good man, an honorable one. Whatever he'd done couldn't have been too terribly awful. He was being too hard on himself.

He was also being too hard on her.

"I wish I were a man," she blurted out.

"You . . . *what?*"

"You heard me."

"You cannot mean that."

"Oh, but I do. Then I could do whatever I wanted whenever I wished." *I could ask you questions about your past, and you would answer me honestly.*

He made a sound of impatience in his throat. "You know that's not entirely true."

"Close enough."

He remained silent for several seconds, studying her as though she were a complicated puzzle that needed solving. She had to stiffen her muscles to keep from fidgeting under his intense scrutiny. With each breath she took, Elizabeth could feel her confidence slipping.

Hester had advised her to be bold. Luke, it would seem, was telling her to remain cautious. Which of them was right?

"For argument's sake, what sort of rules do you plan to break?"

The question took her off guard. She'd expected another warning. "I haven't thought that far ahead."

"You have already defied your mother's dictates regarding your clothing." He looked pointedly at her gown. "What else would you do?"

Glancing to the ceiling, she thought carefully about her answer. Possibilities tugged at her, tangling into a big, heaping ball of want.

She lowered her gaze. "I don't have the specifics sorted out, not yet. But I would do as much as I could without getting caught or jeopardizing my reputation."

Luke's sharp intake of air had Elizabeth's stomach twisting with tension. She refused to be dissuaded. Now that she'd voiced what was in her heart, she couldn't stop her mind from racing over all the possibilities spread out before her. There was so much she wanted to do.

She would make a list.

She was good at making lists, even better at following them. She could map out a specific plan and systematically mark off each item once she'd accomplished the task.

The force of her excitement felt strange, almost painful, as if a part of her that had been asleep was finally awakening.

"Careful, Little Bit, I see your thoughts clearly in your eyes. I fear you are heading into dangerous territory."

"Isn't it exciting?"

"It's terrifying." For a moment, there was something haunted in his eyes, but then it was gone and Elizabeth wondered if it had been there at all.

Her mind returned to her list. The first thing she would do was kiss a man, beneath the moon and stars, or perhaps . . .

Somewhere else, say, somewhere like a formal drawing room in a New York mansion. It would be so simple, so wonderful.

Be bold. Take a chance.

One small step. One tiny rebellion. If she lifted to the tips of her toes . . .

If Luke lowered his head just a bit . . .

What an exciting, frightening, marvelous thought.

Anticipation had her beginning her ascent, her eyelids fluttering shut of their own accord.

The sound of Luke's indrawn breath was muffled by the strike of determined footsteps approaching from the hallway.

Elizabeth jumped back a full two feet.

"That will be Aldrich," she said in a rush. The butler's purposeful gait was unmistakable.

"Consider yourself fortunate." Luke's lips tilted at a sardonic angle. "You have been spared a rather stern lecture, Little Bit."

She wrinkled her nose at the nickname. If Elizabeth didn't know better, she would think Luke had used it intentionally to distance himself from her.

Aldrich materialized in the doorway.

With his shoulders thrown back and his back ramrod straight, the butler shifted his very proper gaze from Luke to Elizabeth, Elizabeth to Luke. His eyebrows pulled together.

"Miss St. James, a package has arrived for you by special courier. The young man insists he was given instructions to deliver it only to you."

How odd. "I'll be down in a moment."

"Very good, Miss." Aldrich turned his frown onto Luke. "Mr. St. James is waiting for you in his study."

"Inform him I'm on my way."

"As you wish." The butler left the room, his back as pliant as a steel rod.

When it was just the two of them once again, Elizabeth could feel Luke's eyes on her. An overwhelming sense of embarrassment crashed in on her from all sides. She'd nearly kissed the man. He'd guessed her intent and hadn't been pleased.

Humiliating from start to finish.

She let the silence stretch for several seconds. When she glanced at him again, he looked wary, as if he wasn't sure what she might do next. For the first time in her life, Elizabeth felt a certain power that came with being born a female.

"Luke, I—"

"Not now, Elizabeth." He pierced her with a stern look. "We will continue this conversation later. When we do, we'll also discuss your plans concerning England."

"You have something to say about that?"

"I do." He did not look happy. That was . . . unexpected. Promising, as if he wanted her to stay in America.

A little jolt of pleasure passed through her.

"We will speak on the matter again," he said, exiting the room a second later.

Elizabeth hurried to the doorway and peered around the corner. Luke strode down the corridor with solid, deliberate strides. She admired the way he moved, all loose limbed and confident, like a panther.

Lucian Griffin was a man comfortable in his own skin. He was also a man who'd once embraced life to the fullest.

Elizabeth could learn a lot from him.

Chapter Seven

Elizabeth found the courier waiting for her in the foyer. He was young, probably fifteen, maybe fourteen. Thin and wiry, he was shabbily dressed, had ordinary features and slightly bemused gray eyes that watched her approach with obvious apprehension.

"I understand you have a package for me." She kept her voice soft, her smile bright.

The boy's Adam's apple bobbed up and down. "You are Elizabeth St. James?"

"I am."

"Then, yes." He cleared his throat, glanced around, swallowed again. "I was told to give this to you and only you."

He held out a package wrapped in brown parchment paper secured by a thin piece of beige twine. The size and shape gave away nothing of its contents.

Elizabeth reached out and took the package. "Thank you."

When she attempted to pay the boy for his trouble, he threw his hands in the air, palms facing forward. "I was already tipped by the lady who sent me here."

A *lady* had sent him. Elizabeth washed away a sudden bout of unease with several deep breaths.

"Nevertheless." She pressed several coins into his hand. "You came all this way."

Giving him no time in which to return the money, she thanked him again and escorted him out of the house.

Alone in the foyer, back flat against the black lacquered door, she studied the package. The plain wrapping gave no clue as to the sender's identity. There was no writing anywhere on the paper or discernable markings whatsoever.

Yet Elizabeth immediately knew who had sent the package. She knew what was inside. She closed her eyes and expelled a slight shuddering sigh. Why would Hester give away her beloved shawl?

Perhaps she hadn't.

Elizabeth had seen how much her friend valued the garment. She'd handled the silk so carefully, with a reverent touch.

A terrible, awful thought occurred. Remembering how ill Hester had looked, Elizabeth went still for a single heartbeat.

Please, no, Lord. Let me be wrong.

Fear had her tucking the package against her heart.

After a long hesitation, she hurried to the winding staircase. She conquered the stairs quickly, her slippered feet making soft swishing sounds on the slick, cold marble. At the second-floor landing, she could stand the suspense no longer and veered into the drawing room, where she and Luke had discussed breaking rules, the consequences of rebellion, and regrets.

It seemed the appropriate setting.

Bottom lip clasped between her teeth, Elizabeth sat on her favorite brocade settee and placed the package on her lap. She tugged on one end of the string. Nothing happened. She tugged again. At last, the knot released.

Ignoring the tiny flutter in her stomach, she peeled away the brown paper. With her heart in her throat, Elizabeth stared at Hester's keepsake box. A grim chill danced along the base of her spine.

She flattened her hand on the faded floral design. The wood was smooth beneath her palm, surprisingly warm. Eyes half closed, she removed the lid with much the same care as Hester had used. A thin layer of tissue covered the contents of the box.

Impatient now, Elizabeth dipped her hand beneath the paper and wrapped her fingers around soft, silky fabric. The remaining shreds of doubt disappeared.

With a flick of her wrist, she shoved the paper aside.

"Oh, Hester, whatever possessed you?"

Elizabeth lost her breath at the enormity of the gift.

She dragged her fingertips along the fringed edges. A second later, she gave in to temptation and draped the garment around her shoulders and moved to the mirror overlooking the room. She hardly recognized herself.

The woman staring back at her was a stranger. She was still Elizabeth St. James, but also . . . somehow . . . *more.*

Sighing in pleasure, she stroked the silk. The exquisite color added a rosy glow to her pale skin. She'd never worn anything so eye-catching. According to her mother, a lady of fine breeding was not to draw attention to herself. To do so was considered vulgar.

At the moment, Elizabeth didn't feel vulgar. She didn't feel scandalous, either. She felt empowered. What would her father and grandfather say if she wore the shawl tonight?

She would never know.

Tonight's gathering was a celebration for Caroline and Jackson. Elizabeth would do nothing to take away from the guests of honor.

Enjoying the feel of the shawl in her hands, she carefully refolded the delicate silk. As she placed the shawl in its nest of tissue, a piece of feminine stationary caught her eye.

Elizabeth retrieved the note, set the box on a nearby table, and sat down to read.

Hester's looping handwriting was still as pretty as Elizabeth remembered. For a moment, it was all she could do not to give in to the sense of terrible foreboding that sped through her.

Lowering her gaze, she read the opening lines.

> *My dear, sweet Elizabeth,*
> *I so enjoyed our recent visit. Our time together reminded me of all the good things in my life, you the greatest among them. The Lord has showered me with so much favor and goodness. I fear I let my melancholy overwhelm my faith and I forgot to count my blessings. Forgive me if I caused you unnecessary anxiety. That was never my intention. It pains me to say I am about to cause you more worry. Since last we met, my health has taken a turn for the worse. I am penning this letter from my hospital bed.*

Elizabeth's hand flew to her throat, alarm driving her to her feet. She looked frantically around, paced to the edge of the drawing room, then paused. Before she went to Hester, she must know all the facts. With Herculean effort, she willed herself to read the rest of the letter.

> *I imagine this news has you orchestrating a way to alleviate my suffering, at the very least sit at my bedside. Do not come. You will be turned away, for I have been denied visitors. Know that I am reconciled with my confinement and have complete confidence my Lord and Savior will heal me if it is His will. Or He will call me home. I welcome either outcome.*

Elizabeth had the presence of mind to sit before her legs collapsed beneath her. "Oh, Hester, why did you not tell me you were so ill?"

She forced herself to read the remaining few lines.

> *I have so little to show for my life. I find comfort knowing I played a small role in yours. You are my greatest achievement. I give you this shawl with the hope that you will live the life I never did.*
>
> *Do not be like me, Elizabeth. Live with boldness and joy and, most of all, passion.*
>
> *I pray your regrets are few and your adventures abundant.*
>
> *Yours, most humbly,*
> *Hester*

Tears sprang to Elizabeth's eyes. She dashed them away with an impatient swipe and read the letter again. Her vision blurred halfway through, and the tears returned. This time, she let them come. They trailed down her cheeks.

She must find a way to get to Hester.

You will be turned away.

She must try.

Placing the letter atop the tissue paper, Elizabeth picked up the box and hugged the treasured shawl tightly to her. She hurried forward, then came to an abrupt stop.

"Luke." The breath roared out of her in a furious rush. "You are finished with your meeting?"

"Yes." Two strong hands wrapped around her shoulders. "Something has upset you."

Willing her panic under control, she shook her head in denial. Her agony was too raw to put into words.

"Elizabeth." He pulled her closer, searching her face with those intense, all-seeing eyes. "Tell me what's happened."

As much as she wanted to soak up his strength, there was no time to explain, not if she wished to get to Hester. "It is nothing."

"It's something. You're shaking and"—he pulled her an inch closer, his gaze locked with hers—"you're crying."

She recognized the futility of denying his claim when the signs of her grief were still trailing down her cheeks. "I have had some distressing news."

Everything in him softened, his face, his mouth, even his stance. "Is it your mother?"

The question was so far off the mark and yet so very close to the truth. Hester had always been a sort of mother to Elizabeth. A sob slipped out of her.

Luke's arms instantly went around her.

Elizabeth desperately wanted to cling to him, but if she gave in and let him comfort her, she feared she would never stop crying. With enormous strength of will, she stepped out of his embrace.

He placed a finger under her chin and applied gentle pressure until their eyes met. "Talk to me."

This was the Luke that appeared in her dreams, tall and commanding, a portrait of masculine strength. A woman could count on a man like this.

Sighing, Elizabeth lowered her head, clutching the package in her arms as if it were a physical shield between her and this vibrant man. "It is not my mother. It is my former governess. She has taken ill."

"We'll go to her now."

Yes, take me to her.

She nearly said the words aloud. But what good could Elizabeth do for her friend?

"She has been refused visitors." She heard the tremor in her voice, the defeat. "I can't even sit by her bedside and hold her hand."

"I'm sorry."

His sincerity served to upset her further. The breath in her lungs grew cold as ice. Her heart was breaking, and she didn't know what to do to stop the pain. She adjusted the package in her grip, lifted her eyes to meet Luke's.

The quiet comfort staring back at her was nearly her undoing. The sting of fresh tears threatened.

Hester needed her, and Elizabeth could not go to her. She'd never felt more helpless, or more useless. She had family, money, and every luxury at her fingertips. What did Hester have?

Regrets. And a beautiful shawl she'd never worn.

It was all so tragic.

Voices drifted up from the foyer. Elizabeth recoiled, one hand flying to her wet cheek. She couldn't be seen in this state. People would ask questions, questions she wasn't feeling strong enough to answer.

Luke instantly took charge. "I'll see to your guests."

"No, Luke." She instinctively balked at the suggestion. "I cannot abandon you to a task that is my responsibility."

"Go, Elizabeth. Take a few moments to compose yourself."

Without waiting for her to respond, he took her shoulders once again and gently guided her toward the hallway.

"But the guests—"

"Will survive under my care." He leaned over her right ear. "I'll entertain them with my renowned charm and outrageous stories."

She nearly smiled.

Luke's relaxed manner made her feel less alone.

Before she realized what she was doing, she was in the hallway, facing the direction of her room and promising Luke, "I'll only be a moment."

"Take all the time you need."

At the sound of his deep, soothing tone, the agony Elizabeth felt became a tad more bearable. She hadn't expected to receive so much comfort from a man's voice. Then again, the voice didn't belong to just any man.

* * *

Luke watched Elizabeth cross to the other side of the corridor, the success of his brief meeting with Richard St. James all but forgotten. Her steps were slow and carefully measured. She looked small and alone. He was sorely tempted to call her back and offer her further comfort. He didn't, of course.

She needed a moment to gather herself.

He needed one as well.

Her tears had nearly brought him to his knees. Though Luke had faced down more than his share of female wretchedness, he'd never gotten used to the powerlessness that came with the experience. He'd wanted to erase Elizabeth's sadness.

He'd sent her away instead. It had been the right thing to do.

Luke had never seen her that openly upset before. Elizabeth was not a woman ruled by emotion. She was serene, calm, perfectly well behaved.

But as Luke silently reviewed each of his recent encounters with Elizabeth, he realized there had been something else in her manner, something he'd ignored, something not so serene or controlled as she spoke of her desire to rebel. And that desire was growing stronger in her. Luke dreaded what she might do next.

A memory flashed.

Elizabeth standing before him, in this very room, less than an hour ago . . . her rising up on her toes, him leaning closer.

He resisted the image, as he had all other inappropriate thoughts pertaining to the charming young woman.

Elizabeth was steady and predictable, her manners impeccable. She was not bold or impulsive. She was *not* a magnet pulling at his own rebellious nature. She was also . . .

Upset. And that slew him.

Perhaps he should see if she was all right.

He started down the hallway.

"Luke, I see you have arrived ahead of us."

Welcoming the interruption, Luke shifted his stance, and his attention, to his friend. "Jackson."

As they shook hands, Luke caught a movement on his left.

"Caroline." He released Jackson's hand and cupped hers. "You are even more beautiful than I remember."

"What a lovely thing to say." The smile she gave him was reminiscent of her cousin. Though Caroline had dark hair and startling green eyes, there were many similarities she shared with Elizabeth—the exotic tilt of their eyes; the creamy, flawless skin; the petite frame.

The cousins had met only a handful of months ago, as they'd been separated by an ocean and tragic events out of their control. The two could have easily become enemies. Instead, they'd become friends, closer than most sisters.

If anyone could help Elizabeth through her grief, this woman could.

"You are the exact woman I need."

"How very intriguing." The cultured British accent was the perfect accompaniment to Caroline's sculpted, elegant beauty. "Do explain."

"Yes, Griffin. Explain." Luke recognized the low growl in Jackson's request as a warning. It would seem the man was a protective husband.

He ignored his friend and pressed on. "I require your help with a rather delicate matter."

Two perfectly arched eyebrows lifted.

"It's to do with your cousin."

Alarm filled Caroline's gaze. "Is Elizabeth ill? Hurt?"

The worry in her tone was real, as real as the concern tearing through Luke.

"She isn't hurt." Not in the strictest sense of the word. She was, however, in pain.

He gave a brief overview of what he knew about Elizabeth's former governess, expanding on her recent illness and the hospital directive that prevented Elizabeth from going to her. "I believe your cousin could use another woman's—"

He was talking to Caroline's back.

Jackson moved in beside him. "I say, my good man, your way with women never ceases to amaze me."

The dry comment had Luke thrusting one hand through his hair. "I'm worried about Elizabeth. She's had a difficult time of it these past few months."

Jackson's entire demeanor sobered. "Has something else happened I don't know about?"

An ache started deep in Luke's chest, moved to his throat. "Nothing specific that I'm aware of. She puts on a brave face, but the business with her mother has left her reeling. On top of that shock, to be confronted with her governess's illness . . ."

For several seconds, Jackson stared down the empty corridor. "You mentioned her mother. Did Katherine attempt to contact Elizabeth while Caroline and I were away?"

"No, I don't believe so." She would have told him. Luke was sure of it.

"That's something, I suppose."

He wasn't nearly as certain as his friend. "Although I believe sending Elizabeth's mother to Florida was for the best"—banishment was a fitting punishment for a woman who valued her position among New York's social elite—"for all intents and purposes, Elizabeth lost an influential woman in her life. I fear she's about to lose another."

On top of that, the men in her life wanted to ship her off to England. While their wish might be to protect her and give her the fresh start she claimed she wanted, Luke thought Elizabeth had endured enough change in the past three months. She didn't need more. Not so soon.

"Relax, my friend." Jackson clasped his shoulder in a gesture of support. "Elizabeth is in good hands with my wife."

Luke took a stabilizing breath. Though he would like to go to Elizabeth, he settled for cooling his heels in the drawing room with Jackson.

Chapter Eight

By the time Elizabeth reached her room, she was almost composed. As she crossed to her writing desk with the keepsake box firmly in her grip, she experienced a moment of profound grief. The sensation was powerful enough that she had to pause momentarily or risk stumbling.

Some instinct warned her she would never see Hester again. She feared that her recent trip to the brownstone on Riverside Drive had been her last.

Oh, Hester, I cannot lose you.

Elizabeth's heart felt as if it were ripping in two. Helplessness and sorrow warred within her. She set the box on the spot where her lists had been earlier and looked down at her hands. They were shaking.

Lips pressed in a determined line, she formed two white-knuckled fists, then relaxed her fingers. She repeated the process twice over before she felt calm enough to trace her finger along the top edge of the box.

Hot tears pricked at the backs of her eyes. Elizabeth refused to let them form. She'd done enough crying for one evening.

Later, when the party was over and her guests were gone, she would indulge in her grief. But for the next four hours, she would pretend all was well in her world, dry-eyed and poised. It would not be easy, but she would set aside her sadness for Jackson and Caroline's sake.

Without thinking too hard about what she was doing, Elizabeth opened the box and gathered up the shawl. She pressed the garment to her face. The scent of jasmine and mint clung to the fabric. The familiar aroma reminded her of Hester.

Exhaling slowly, Elizabeth draped the garment over her shoulders and moved to the full-length mirror. Her stomach executed a long, slow roll.

"What a beautiful shawl."

Embarrassed to be caught admiring herself, every muscle in her body tensed. Just as quickly, peace invaded her heart, followed by a rush of pleasure.

"*Caro.*" Elizabeth spun around. She dashed to her cousin, practically flinging herself into the other woman's arms. "It's so good to see you."

They hugged for several long seconds.

"Oh, how I've missed you, dear Elizabeth."

The delight in Caroline's voice brought a fresh bout of tears. At least these were full of joy. "I've missed you, too."

Elizabeth hadn't realized how much until this very moment. Although she'd known her cousin only a short while, Caroline had become one of her most treasured friends.

As she gazed into the joy-filled face, Elizabeth found her own smile. Caroline had always been beautiful, but now . . . she glowed. "Jackson has made you a happy woman."

"He has. Oh, indeed he has. I am blissfully happy. But you, sweet girl"—her smile dropped—"are sad."

Elizabeth tried not to look as gloomy as she felt. "I've had some upsetting news."

Sympathy softened Caroline's features. "I'm so sorry about your governess. As I recall, she's a relatively young woman. Her illness must come as quite a shock."

"You know about Hester's decline?"

"Luke told us just now, when Jackson and I first arrived." Caroline rested her hand on Elizabeth's arm. "He's worried about you. We all are."

Telling herself she should be grateful she had so many people in her life who cared, Elizabeth let out an unsteady sigh. The move sent the shawl slipping off her shoulders. She caught the garment. Tenderly refolding the delicate silk, she placed it back in the keepsake box.

"I wish you wouldn't put that away." Caroline joined her at the writing desk. "That color suits you."

"But it's so . . . red."

"It's lovely." Caroline touched the thin fabric with her fingertips. "The rich tone enhances your complexion. You should wear red more often."

Elizabeth wished she had the courage to wear such a bold color in public. Rearranging the shawl in its nest of tissue paper, she let her hand linger over the cool silk. "Such a shame."

"Do you want to talk about your governess?"

Elizabeth snatched a quick breath.

Though she didn't have the time for an in-depth conversation— obligations awaited her in the drawing room—she found herself telling Caroline about her last visit with Hester. Elizabeth ended the story with "Her final words of advice were 'Be bold and never settle for a life half lived.'"

"Sounds as if your governess is a very wise woman."

There was no judgment in Caroline's voice, only vast amounts of compassion. Elizabeth thought of her cousin's childhood, of the things she'd been forced to do to survive.

Never once had Caroline complained about those difficult years, at least not in relation to herself. She did, however, lament over the life stolen from her mother. Rightfully so. "I'm sorry, Caro, for what my mother did to yours. I—"

"Stop right there." Caroline pressed a fingertip to Elizabeth's lips, her expression full of tender affection. "As I told you before, you are not to blame. I will not let you apologize for your mother's actions."

"Surely, when you look at me, you must see her."

"You are not your mother." With one seamless move, she pulled Elizabeth into another fast, fierce hug. When she stepped back, her expression was still warm. "I won't have you feeling guilty for something you had no more control over than I did."

"You are a good person, Caroline Montgomery."

"What a sweet thing to say, but we both know I'm not always good. In fact, I'm quite the challenge. Just ask my husband."

The twinkle in her eyes spoke of great affection and love for the man she'd married.

"I adore hearing you call Jackson your husband."

"Not as much as I love calling him that. Now." Her smile widened. "About this gorgeous shawl . . ."

She reached inside the keepsake box and, with a flourish more suitable for the theater, arranged the red silk over Elizabeth's shoulders. "Beautiful."

Unable to stop herself, Elizabeth returned to the mirror. Caroline moved in behind her and set her chin atop Elizabeth's shoulder.

"What a pair we make," she said on a sigh. "My dark hair to your light, my green eyes to your blue. We're practically polar opposites. Yet I see the family resemblance."

All Elizabeth saw was Caroline's vibrant beauty next to her predictable prettiness. The icy numbness of uncertainty that had plagued her for days returned with renewed force.

Caroline had been raised in poverty, scraping for every morsel of food on the streets of London. Such a childhood should have made her coarse and hard. Instead, she was a woman with natural grace, full of substance, goodness, and integrity.

In contrast, Elizabeth had been raised in luxury, with every advantage. She had a *reputation* for being good and kind.

Obedience did not make a person good or kind.

Who am I beneath the pretty outer shell?

A pale version of her cousin, at best.

Even their mutual grandfather recognized their differences. From nearly their first meeting, Richard St. James had seen Caroline as more than a beautiful face. He respected her brain and was already teaching her the family business from the ground up.

Whereas he was sending Elizabeth to England to find a husband.

"I believe"—Caroline lifted her chin off Elizabeth's shoulder—"that you are the most beautiful woman in New York, nay, all of America. Some man will be very fortunate to win your heart. I only pray he lives in New York."

"I . . . wait. What?" Elizabeth pressed a hand to her heart and spun to face her cousin head-on. "You know about my plans to go to England?"

"Luke told Jackson and"—she gave Elizabeth an apologetic tilt of her head—"Jackson told me."

Luke, Caroline, and Jackson. The three of them had been discussing her situation without her knowledge. Elizabeth didn't like knowing that, not one bit. Some of her annoyance sounded in her voice. "You don't approve."

Caroline didn't deny the accusation.

"For selfish reasons, I want you to stay in America. However"—she lifted a hand to prevent Elizabeth from interrupting—"it's your choice. The future is yours for the taking, and yours to control."

Having a choice wasn't the same as having control. Elizabeth was coming to understand that in ways she never had before. "My decision isn't final."

"I'm glad to hear it. Now brace yourself, because I'm about to add my advice to all the rest."

Irritation rose, the emotion clogging in her throat. Elizabeth was growing weary of all the people in her life offering her advice, no matter how well meant. There was too much noise in her head.

"Do what makes you happy." Gaze growing earnest, Caroline leaned slightly forward. "*You*, Elizabeth. Not the family, not Luke, not even me."

What a generous piece of advice. How she would miss her cousin if she journeyed to England. *If.* Elizabeth was no longer certain she would go. She wasn't certain she would stay, either.

She had family here in America, a handful of close friends, but what else? Her future held few options. She would eventually have to marry. Becoming a wife and running a large household was what she'd been trained to do. Even the banishment of her mother hadn't been solely to punish the woman but also to enhance Elizabeth's chances at making a suitable match. If her reputation was put into question, her prospects would diminish.

Would that be so awful? She was momentarily lost for an answer.

"Is it so terrible to lose the approval of your peers?" Elizabeth spoke without thinking. The moment the words left her mouth, she realized how they must sound to her cousin. Caroline had been judged wanting by the good people of New York, while Elizabeth continued to enjoy their favor. "I can't bear the idea of you and Jackson being shunned from society."

"My dear, sweet cousin." Caroline took her hands and squeezed gently. "Do not grieve for us. Jackson and I are quite happy with the way things turned out."

"You have no regrets?"

"Not one." The truth shimmered in her eyes, in the secret smile that slid across her lips. Caroline's reaction to life's disappointments was an inspiration, something to emulate.

"Oh, Caro, I'm so glad to have you home. You truly are the sister of my heart."

"And you are mine."

Still holding hands, they stood smiling at each other.

"I'm going to do a bit of meddling," Caroline warned as she straightened the shawl on Elizabeth's shoulders. "You've been too unselfish for far too long. From this moment on, you will take your governess's advice. You will be bold and seize the full, rich life you deserve."

Elizabeth gave herself a moment to let her cousin's words sink in. She couldn't deny the excitement that came upon her. Her breathing quickened in her lungs. One small step.

One tiny rebellion.

"I will take your suggestion under consideration." Elizabeth couldn't keep the smile from her lips, then sobered as she remembered her duty.

"Caro, would you do me a favor?"

"Of course. Anything."

"Will you return to the drawing room and inform the other guests I'll be there shortly?"

"It would be my pleasure." Caroline pressed a kiss to Elizabeth's cheek. And then she was gone.

Alone once again, Elizabeth turned back to the mirror. Eyes lit with conviction, she gave her reflection a knowing smile. "Here we go."

* * *

Impatient for Elizabeth's return, Luke stood apart from the growing crowd and took in the occupants of the drawing room.

Nearly all the guests had arrived. A fire in the large marble hearth had been lit to offset the evening chill. For his sister's sake, he should be mingling. This was Penelope and Simon's first event as an official couple since their engagement ball.

Luke couldn't drum up the enthusiasm. This was a friendly setting, and by all appearances his sister seemed to be having a splendid time. Simon stood by her side, smiling broadly. He looked relaxed, comfortable even.

The man's easy demeanor surprised Luke, and it wasn't the only surprise. He'd accepted an invitation to a party for a couple unwelcome in most New York homes. Had he done so because Penelope had asked it of him?

Of course, few declined an event held in Richard St. James's home. That didn't fully explain why Simon was here tonight. Luke narrowed his eyes. His future brother-in-law seemed exceptionally pleased with himself, as if he knew something the rest of them didn't. What game was he playing?

He presented the picture of a man besotted with his fiancée. Therein lay the problem. The picture was too flawless. Luke found it far too easy to distrust the man, for all his smooth-faced perfection.

"You're brooding, son."

Luke turned his head and confronted his father's icy disapproval. "I'm not brooding. I'm thinking."

"That's what you call it?"

His father was baiting him, but to what end? There was no cause for it, not at a private dinner party for a close family friend.

Lips pressed in a grim line, Luke shifted his attention to his mother. She sat perched on the edge of a small sofa, sharing the space with Jackson's mother, Lucille Montgomery. The long-suffering wife commiserating with the bitter, betrayed one.

That, Luke decided, was what happened when one partner in a marriage cared more deeply than the other. Both women had married knowing their feelings for their husbands were not returned. And they weren't alone in their lopsided display of sentiment. Marriages among New York's social set rarely brought happiness. Most produced misery and pain.

Luke frowned. When had he become so scornful of marriage?

How could he not be?

The examples of disastrous unions abounded everywhere. He didn't want his sister entering into the same trap as their mother.

There was still the possibility that Simon's affection for Penny was true. She could be entering the kind of marriage Jackson had with Caroline—the only example of a true love match Luke could call to mind.

Were his friends an exception?

Possibly. Probably.

"People are watching you." His father muttered the words under his breath. "At least try to look pleased when you glance at your sister and her fiancé."

Luke had nearly forgotten his father was still standing beside him.

"You know I have reservations about the match." He kept his voice low, his words cryptic, in the event people were doing more than merely watching him.

"You're being overprotective when there is no cause for it." His father kept his voice equally low. "Simon is a good man. He comes from one of the oldest and finest families in New York."

"Social standing does not guarantee a good marriage."

"Your sister is happy with the match."

Penny did look happy. At the moment, she and Simon were conversing with Jackson's grandmother, one of Luke's favorite people. A smile tugged at his lips.

Hattie Montgomery was eccentric, and had a big, booming voice to match her personality. She insisted everyone call her Granny. No one watching her animated conversation with the newly engaged couple would guess she'd recently celebrated her eighty-eighth birthday.

Granny's fondness for speaking her mind and her affection for Penny had endeared her to Luke years ago. She was one of the most powerful matriarchs of New York and an excellent judge of character.

Luke watched her interacting with Simon and Penny, taking in the scene as objectively as possible. Granny didn't seem as enamored with Penny's fiancé as she was with Penny. Something to ponder.

"I don't trust him."

If Simon proved unreliable or a danger to Penny, Luke would do what was necessary to put an end to their engagement.

"I know you've been asking around about your future brother-in-law. I'm warning you. Stop it now, before word gets back to Simon."

The gaze his father settled on him was that of a man used to issuing orders and having them followed. His eyes were harder than usual. Luke had seen that inflexible look once before, when he'd confronted his father about the paternity of Esmeralda's daughter.

They'd nearly come to blows. Luke had never brought up the subject again. The night of Penny's engagement ball had been the first time he and his father had spoken of the matter since that initial argument.

"You will do nothing to jeopardize the engagement. I want your word."

If anyone was going to jeopardize Penny's future happiness, it would be Warren. Only a select few knew his secret. Once Esmeralda and her daughter returned to America, the risk of exposure would increase dramatically.

What was his father thinking? Inviting his former paramour to perform in his private opera house was courting disaster. Did he think he was above the rules?

Obviously unaware of the direction of Luke's thoughts, his father proceeded to extol Simon's endless virtues and explain why he was the best possible match for Penny. Tuning out the litany, Luke continued watching his sister and her fiancé. He nearly relaxed, until he heard his father say, "He has a passion for the opera. In that we are alike."

Luke snapped his gaze to the other man. "How else are you two . . . alike?"

His father let out a hard, low hiss. "Watch yourself, boy. You are not without faults. You have no right to judge me."

"I won't deny I have an unsavory past." Luke's mind went to another place, another time, the memory of his actions a haunting reminder that his youthful indiscretions had come at a cost. "The question is, does Simon?"

"What does it matter?"

"I don't want Penny entering into a marriage that will cause her undue pain."

"The only pain she'll suffer is if Simon finds out about—" Warren pulled up short. Glancing around, probably to determine if anyone was listening, he stood tall. "I will not discuss this matter here."

Clearly finished having his say, his father walked off without uttering another word.

Luke returned his attention to his sister. Her smile seemed genuine. To be fair, Simon's solicitous consideration of her appeared equally sincere.

Perhaps, as his father suggested, Luke was being overprotective. There'd been a time when he'd had to be. Penny's childhood had been riddled with difficulty, her once stammering speech a source of much condemnation from her peers.

Luke was spared further contemplation when Caroline entered the drawing room. Alone.

Where was Elizabeth?

Annoyance with his father gave way to concern for his friend. He met Caroline in the center of the room. "Tell me she's all right."

"She is . . . melancholy. She will join us shortly."

The remark did nothing to erase Luke's unease. There was one sure way to settle his mind. "If you'll excuse me."

Caroline stepped in his path. "You are not thinking of going to her."

He lifted a questioning brow. "You believe such a move unwise?"

"I believe it's not necessary. She is only a few moments behind me." She glanced to her left, smiled. "Ah, there she is now."

Luke followed the direction of her gaze. His mind emptied of all thought.

Elizabeth stood poised in the doorway, her eyes scanning the crowd from one end of the room to the other. She was clearly looking for someone in particular. Him?

His chest contracted, squeezing the air out of his lungs.

He moved into her line of vision. After a moment, her gaze settled on him. She relaxed into a smile.

The impact was like a punch to his gut.

Compelled by some invisible tug, Luke took a step forward. A slash of red dragged his attention to her tiny waist, where she'd tied a thick silk ribbon. She hadn't been wearing that accessory earlier. The bold color matched the thin line of trim on her dress. Luke didn't know much about women's fashion, but she looked very pretty. The belt added a certain something.

At the same moment he entertained the thought, he overheard Mrs. Constance Newbury sniff in a very unladylike fashion.

"What is that girl thinking?" She directed the question at the stately older woman beside her. Luke couldn't remember her name. "Red is entirely inappropriate for an innocent young woman to wear, even if it is only a splash of color around her waist."

"Shocking," replied her compatriot. "Her mother would be horrified if she were here."

Luke's stomach rolled, as he understood all too well why Elizabeth had added the red sash. She'd taken another step away from her mother's oppressive influence, bolder than her previous ones, but nothing too scandalous and still relegated to her clothing. Unfortunately, this time a pair of nosy women had noticed.

Was this a precursor to continued defiance on Elizabeth's part, or a final show before she returned to her former, obedient self? Luke wasn't sure which was worse.

She was treading into territory fraught with unpredictable outcomes. And yet, there was something about this bolder Elizabeth that called to him. She was special, had always been so, but now he felt a tug of affection for her, one he absolutely did not want to feel.

He looked away, looked back again. Barely a handful of seconds had passed since she'd arrived in the doorway. Each one had felt like a lifetime.

There was something new in her eyes, a look that didn't belong to a young, naïve woman of twenty. Instinct warned him to put distance between himself and the enticing Elizabeth St. James.

Still smiling, she began moving in his direction, a disaster in the making.

Luke predicted a long, torturous evening ahead.

Chapter Nine

Elizabeth advanced on Luke, the red sash making her feel stronger, willing to take a chance. He watched her approach from beneath hooded eyes, his expression impossible to read. She was only partially aware of the other occupants in the room. The air pulsed with the din of a dozen different conversations.

Or was the drumming in her ears the sound of her own heartbeat?

She forced herself to look around, though her mind remained on Luke. She barely noticed the array of fashions worn by the other women, the fitted bodices and sleeves, the high lace collars. She hardly smelled the way feminine perfumes mingled with the scent of masculine colognes.

Luke had her full concentration.

A quick glance to her right told her that her grandfather stood on the opposite end of the room, conversing with his cousin Matilda. Aunt Tilly, as she insisted Elizabeth call her, had been one of the first American heiresses to journey to England.

Within a few months, the older woman had married the second son of a duke and by all accounts had gone on to enjoy a satisfying marriage.

Now a respectable widow, she loved sponsoring young American women in the hope that they would follow in her footsteps.

The two looked caught up in a serious conversation. Were they discussing Elizabeth? Surely not. Surely they wouldn't make plans without her.

But of course they would. They already had.

Concealing her annoyance behind a bright smile, Elizabeth put them out of her mind and continued in Luke's direction. The way he was looking at her, it was . . .

Oh, my.

What was it she saw in his eyes? Interest, perhaps masculine appreciation? Or was that a silent warning?

Her steps slowed to a crawl, then stopped altogether when he broke eye contact and melted into a group that included Jackson and Caroline. Undeterred, Elizabeth began moving again.

A friend of her mother's stepped in her way.

"Elizabeth." The woman dropped a glance to the red sash encircling her waist. Disapproval flared in her eyes, just a flicker but very real, before she hid it behind a bland smile. "Don't you look lovely this evening?"

"Thank you, Mrs. Newbury. I was thinking the same of you." Though conservative in cut and style, the light-green satin and cream lace were made of the finest fabrics.

A long pause ensued, which included a thorough head-to-toe once-over. Well aware of her role in this particular drama, Elizabeth held perfectly still under the rude assessment.

Finally, the woman lifted her gaze. "That color is simply divine with your skin tone."

Elizabeth didn't ask whether she meant the color of her dress or the twisted sash she'd fashioned out of Hester's shawl. "Thank you for saying so."

Another pause, followed by another, quicker appraisal. "It must have been difficult planning a dinner party without your mother's guidance."

Not so difficult, no. Wonderful, actually.

She nearly said the words aloud but caught herself.

"It was indeed a challenge." She spoke without inflection.

"I know you must miss her dreadfully."

Not even a little.

No, that wasn't entirely true. Elizabeth missed the loving, caring woman Katherine St. James had pretended to be. She missed the mother she'd once admired, the one she'd relied on to guide her through life. How naïve and trusting she'd been, how blindly loyal.

"I console myself knowing that Mother is having a grand time redecorating the family home in Florida." This time the words were harder to push past her lips and brought an odd sort of pang.

Elizabeth caught her bottom lip between her teeth before it trembled. If she continued embellishing the truth, she would hardly know what was real and what was false.

Guilt seared in her heart. Familiar resentment clogged in her throat.

The fabrications drawn up by her family were supposed to be for Elizabeth's protection. Her mother benefited most. Katherine's friends had no idea what she'd done. They didn't realize how self-serving she could be. No one in the family had known, either, until Caroline had shown up and exposed her shocking deeds.

Prior to that, everyone had believed Libby St. James had run off with a lowly stable boy for the sake of love. For years, Elizabeth's father and grandfather had mourned her abandonment of the family, never understanding why she hadn't contacted them.

Except . . . Libby had made many attempts to reach them. She'd sent letters home, nearly three dozen over a span of fifteen years, begging her father to let her return to the family fold. Richard St. James had never received those letters, because Elizabeth's mother had intercepted them.

The very worst part of the story was that Libby had died destitute in a run-down shack on the East End of London and Katherine's reputation had remained intact.

"I trust you correspond with her regularly."

Oh, the irony.

Elizabeth gave a slight incline of her head, this time unwilling to openly lie.

"In your next letter, do be sure to tell your mother that I asked about her."

"I will most definitely include your request in my next letter." Elizabeth managed to hold her smile. "If you'll excuse me, my aunt is motioning for me."

She didn't wait for Mrs. Newbury to respond before hurrying in Aunt Tilly's direction. The older woman was alone now. The light from the fire cast her features in partial shadow, emphasizing the soft angles of her face and the prominent beak nose that somehow worked with her eyes and mouth.

"Ah, Elizabeth." Aunt Tilly met her at the edge of the hearth rug. "Your grandfather and I were just speaking about our upcoming trip to London. I have grand plans for you, my dear."

Attempting to keep her tone light, her face serene, Elizabeth said, "I would love to hear them."

Her aunt launched into a detailed exposition.

Only half listening, Elizabeth cast a quick glance around, searching for Luke. He'd moved to another group that included his sister and her fiancé. His manner was deceptively easy, but Elizabeth noticed the tension in his shoulders, especially when he spoke directly to Simon.

"We will begin building your wardrobe immediately." Aunt Tilly glanced briefly at Elizabeth's dress. "Tulle and taffeta must give way to satin and other superior fabrics."

Elizabeth stifled a sigh. Here was yet another woman attempting to dress her.

"The conservative décolletage of your current gowns will have to be replaced with a more generous display of neck and arms."

"Truly?"

"You must stand out. But not too much, of course. I know exactly how far to go. When I am through with you, you will be the talk of London."

"I hope in a good way."

"Of course, of course." Aunt Tilly waved a dismissive hand. "Once we arrive in London, I will introduce you to a few friends at a small, informal tea. We will proceed from there to a private dinner party. The theater will be next. And then a ball. We will calculate each step carefully."

Caught up in her plans, Aunt Tilly continued mapping out her strategy for acquiring Elizabeth the perfect husband. The woman had missed her calling. The US Army could use her tactical mind.

"I believe I can secure us an invitation to the Duchess of Marlborough's annual garden party. Once you are accepted there, you will be accepted everywhere."

"Sounds wonderful." Elizabeth wondered what was wrong with her when even the prospect of meeting a duchess didn't spark anything more than mild curiosity. Certainly nothing close to the excitement she heard in Aunt Tilly's voice, her eagerness almost—*almost*—contagious.

Elizabeth attempted to tap into the older woman's enthusiasm. A trapped sensation stole over her instead. The sudden churning in her stomach made her head spin. The room grew unnaturally hot, so hot she feared she would faint. But her hands were like ice. She clasped them together, willing her stuttering heart to calm.

"It's important we pick the right clothing," the woman said, returning to her original topic of discussion. "As I always say, we are what we wear."

Elizabeth wanted to believe she was more than her clothing. A sense of urgency took hold. She must uncover what lurked beneath the hand-made gowns and perfectly coiffed hair before she sailed for London. *If* she sailed for London.

No matter what path she chose, action was required. A few rules needed to be broken, an adventure or two must be experienced. How else would she know what she was truly made of if she didn't push the boundaries and live a little?

While Aunt Tilly regaled her with all that lay ahead in England, Elizabeth's mind raced over the things she would do, the daring steps she would take, if she found the nerve. Some would require a partner.

Well, then, she would find a partner, a *willing* partner.

She knew she could, and probably should, enlist Sally's help. But that wouldn't be fair to the maid. As Elizabeth's paid employee, the young woman would have to go along with her schemes.

Elizabeth could go to Caroline. But her cousin was a newlywed, and she would soon begin working with their grandfather in the family business.

That left one option.

Elizabeth glanced surreptitiously across the room. Luke was engaged in a lively conversation with his sister. He leaned in and said something low. Penny laughed, and so did Luke. Elizabeth willed him to look at her. One more time. Just one more.

As if hearing her silent call, he turned his head and held her gaze. Her pulse roared into action as though the look were a physical touch.

Him.

Luke was the one Elizabeth would approach with her plan. Once she had a plan.

She would be careful, and not take too many chances with her reputation. No matter what, she would do nothing to prevent herself from fulfilling her duty to the family. No, not a duty. It was more than that. It was an honor, a privilege.

Nonetheless, she desperately wanted to go to Luke and demand he help her, as only a man with his past would know how to do.

Eyes fastened with his, she smiled.

He did not smile back.

She upped the brilliancy of her smile.

As if he'd turned off a switch, his expression shuttered. His attention turned back to his sister.

The connection was lost. But Elizabeth would not allow herself to be discouraged.

She was glad she'd switched his seat at the dining table. She would drop a few hints, see where that led. The evening stretched before her with endless possibilities.

As if on cue, one of the staff slipped into the room, gave Elizabeth a nod, then slipped out again. The first course was ready to be served.

Excellent timing.

* * *

Several hours later, Elizabeth stood alone in her room, shaking with frustration. The guests were gone. The party was over. Dinner had been a success.

Save for one minor disappointment—Luke.

Oh, he'd done nothing untoward or rude. If anything, he'd been an acceptable dinner companion, perfectly polite, a gentleman in both speech and manner. But he'd hardly spoken to her. When he did, he stuck to superficial topics. He'd commented on the weather seven times. She'd counted.

It was as if he'd erected an invisible wall around himself. But why? What had changed that he felt the need to pull away? He'd been so kind and supportive when she'd told him the news of Hester's illness.

Elizabeth moved to the fire already lit by her maid. Sally had been another disappointment. She'd failed to show up at the party.

In truth, Elizabeth hadn't been surprised. When she'd confronted the young woman, Sally had lifted her chin at a haughty angle and repeated her earlier argument about the inappropriateness of a servant mingling with guests.

Elizabeth didn't believe that was the reason for Sally's absence from the table, but she'd been insistent.

The fire cracked and popped, the flames spitting tiny sparks in every direction. Mesmerized by the golden light, Elizabeth moved a fraction closer. Desperate for the fire's warmth, she spread her fingers wide. The chill remained, navigating a path through her bones.

With a reluctant sigh, Elizabeth turned her back on the fire to pace the perimeter of the room. On her second pass, she caught a glimpse of herself in the full-length mirror. The red corded sash made her feel marginally better. But when she lifted her gaze and stared at her reflection, the color instantly drained from her cheeks.

Elizabeth saw her mother in her pale-blonde hair and doll-like features, in the small waist and perfect posture. Would she turn out like Katherine St. James in other ways?

For a moment, she stood rigid and unmoving, sending up a silent prayer that she would be able to step out from beneath her mother's shadow.

Hester had intimated that it wasn't too late to change. The question was, did Elizabeth have the courage to do more than wear last season's gown or fashion a belt from a shawl?

Luke had asked what rules she would break, if given a chance.

What *would* Elizabeth do? If she threw open the cage door and ignored the restrictions of her world, would she falter? Or would she soar?

The time had come to get serious about her next step. She would start by making her list.

Removing the shawl from her waist, she shook out the fabric and wrapped it around her shoulders. The silk felt cool on the exposed skin of her arms. Fortified with a rekindled resolve, she moved to her writing desk, sank into the velvet-padded chair, and pulled out a fresh sheet of paper.

Pressing her hand flat on the blank page, she let her mind drift. What would she do, if the rules didn't apply to her? What wonderful, glorious deed could she accomplish if she had the courage?

How far would she go?

Her heart behaved strangely in her chest, an animated pulse awakening in her ears, her throat, even in the spot behind her knees. Elizabeth drew in a slow, careful breath. While she certainly wished to start with a big, bold step, she knew herself well enough to know she needed to begin small.

She reached for a pen, then opened the silver inkpot that sat atop the desk. After dipping the nib in the ink, she wrote the number one. Beside the number, she added four simple words.

Wear last season's dress.

She'd already done that, twice now. No one had noticed.

Why would they? People saw what they wanted to see. When they looked at Elizabeth, they saw a passive girl, no longer a child but not yet fully a woman, either.

Setting the pen down, she stared at her looping, feminine handwriting. Each letter was perfectly executed, each word evenly spaced. Even the start of her list spoke of her careful nature.

She made her next entry a little off-center.

Walk in the rain.

There. Better. But not quite right. She angled her head and thought a moment. Item number two didn't seem bold enough.

Why not? The answer came to her a heartbeat later. She added another word.

Walk in the rain, barefoot.

Yes, that was it. Oh, how marvelous that would feel. She added four more activities in rapid succession.

Splash my bare feet in a public fountain.
Attend a vaudeville show.
Play a game of chance.
Ask a man to dance.

Feeling quite scandalous with that last entry, she knew she was ready to take the leap. With a fresh dip of pen to ink, she wrote number seven.

Kiss a man.

No.

Kiss a man under the moon and stars.

Yes. *Yes.*

Seeing the words penned in her own handwriting thrilled her to the marrow. Elizabeth didn't need to list the name of the man. She knew exactly whom she wanted to kiss her. Or perhaps she would kiss him. *That* would certainly shock Mr. Polite and Mannerly.

She smiled, having no difficulty imagining those intense tiger eyes widening in surprise, then narrowing with something far more personal. A look not dissimilar to the way he'd stared at her when she'd first arrived at the party tonight wearing Hester's shawl around her waist.

Head bent, she continued. Now confident she was on the right track, the rest of the list came quicker. She didn't worry about prioritizing yet. That could come later.

With fast pen strokes, Elizabeth added items as they came to her. Some were silly and not necessarily something she *needed* to do, such as swing on a trapeze or drive a motorcar.

Others were serious pursuits that, hopefully, would help her become a better person. She needed to stop relying on other people's advice. This wasn't about winning approval but about breaking free.

Thinking bigger now, beyond her own wants and needs, she wrote down item number twelve.

Live the life of a servant or factory worker for a day.

Walking in someone else's shoes would open her to the needs of people living without the advantages she enjoyed.

Mind reeling with all the adventures awaiting her, Elizabeth's hand flew across the page. Whether she chose to sail to London or stayed home, by accomplishing the items on this list, she would become a woman of substance and prove to herself she was destined to live life on her own terms. She would know how far to go and when to pull back only if she pushed to the very edge of propriety.

She reached the end of the page.

There was room for one more item. This time, her hand shook as she wrote.

Confront my mother.

The list was complete.

Elizabeth set down the pen and stared at the piece of paper. As she read through each item, she became aware of a feeling she'd had earlier in the night, a sort of tingling in her limbs that urged her to be cautious going forward.

The sensation intensified. It took several deep pulls of air to modulate her breathing. Of course she was experiencing a rush of trepidation. Everything on her list would require daring and no small amount of pluck.

She read through the items again.

The order was a bit chaotic, with no real attention to priorities. No problem—she would revise as needed.

Satisfied at last, she placed the lid back on the inkpot and returned the pen to its holder. Once she'd restored order to her desk, she picked up her list and folded the paper once, twice, three times, then hid it in the pages of her Bible.

Straightening, she secured the shawl around her shoulders. Elizabeth St. James had spent enough of her life being passive.

With her list as her guide, she would do more than she'd ever dared. She would know more than she'd ever known.

Most of all, she would *be* more than she'd ever been.

Chapter Ten

Shrouded in the gray light of dawn, Elizabeth pulled the hood of her cloak down over her face and dashed up the steps leading to the four-story house. Made from brown bricks and sand-colored limestone, the building had a masculine elegance similar to its owner.

The early-morning mist swirled around her, nipping at her cheeks. She huddled deeper inside her cloak and watched her breath plume out in front of her. Regardless of the cold temperature, this was her favorite time of day, when night surrendered to dawn and everything began anew, when unrealized possibilities hovered within reach.

From somewhere in the distance, the muffled creak of a wagon wheel contrasted with the boom-spit-boom of a motorcar coughing to life. The world was awakening, and so was Elizabeth.

She felt vibrant, alive, ready to conquer the next phase in her plan to become a woman of substance.

Her first adventure was but one knock away.

Slipping a hand beneath the edges of her cloak, Elizabeth touched the red shawl she'd tucked inside. The silky garment's presence reminded her why she'd alighted from her bed at such an early hour. Seven days had passed since she'd agreed to go to England, and nothing had changed in her life. She had seven weeks left to discover what lay beneath her carefully constructed veneer.

From the safety of her hooded cloak, she contemplated the pair of mahogany double doors. Hand rising, she paused mid-reach and stabbed a glance to her right, then to her left, then back to her right. The street was sufficiently deserted.

Satisfied she wouldn't be seen entering the house of an unmarried man, she lifted the brass knocker. Let it fall with a hard bang.

Nerves reared. She battled them into submission and made another slow, comprehensive study of her surroundings. Alone still.

She knocked again.

No answer.

Had she arrived too early? It wasn't yet seven o'clock, but undoubtedly someone in the household was awake. She lifted her hand to knock again. And met empty air.

"Oh." She stumbled forward—straight into a pair of strong, muscular arms. "Luke."

He smelled of soap, coffee, and some sort of intriguing spice.

"I . . ." She shoved to a standing position, pleased at how quickly she found her balance. "I wasn't expecting you."

"Who, exactly, were you expecting, Little Bit?" A muscle shifted in his jaw, the only sign of his agitation. "This is, after all, my home."

"Well, yes. I am aware of that." She made a grand show of straightening the hood of her cloak, tugging it lower over her face. "I thought your butler would answer the door."

"I don't employ a butler."

"Oh. Well." She hadn't expected that. "Oh."

He glanced over her shoulder. "Where is your maid?"

"At home."

A moment passed, just a tiny one, when everything seemed to slow down and wait. From the glint in Luke's eyes, it was clear he was not happy to see her. The man was a study in masculine impatience. Refusing to break the silence first, Elizabeth lifted her chin.

Several tense seconds passed. Her hands began to shake. She clasped them in front of her and counted off the next few seconds in her mind. One. Two.

Three.

"You are alone?"

Elizabeth wasn't sure how he'd managed it, but the man actually hissed out the words.

"I am, yes."

Releasing a heavy sigh, he shook his head in exasperation. "I will probably regret asking this, but how did you get here?"

"I walked."

"Of course you did." His snort of displeasure did not bode well for the rest of this visit. "It's twenty blocks from here to St. James House."

She lifted a shoulder, letting the gesture speak for her.

"You should not have come"—he reached for her, took hold of her arm in a gentle but firm grip—"but now that you are here . . ."

With a quick yank, he pulled her inside the house and shut the door with a resounding bang.

Elizabeth winced at the sound. She winced again when Luke fixed his gaze on her. His eyes were filled with apprehension, an uneasy mosaic of gold and amber framed by long, dark lashes beneath a bold slash of sandy-colored eyebrows.

Needing something to do with her hands, she shoved the hood off her head, then reached for the top button of her cloak.

"Don't bother removing your cloak. You aren't staying."

Oh, but she was. At least long enough to present her plan. Apparently, she would do so while wearing her cloak. So be it.

Elizabeth would never know where she found the courage, but she smiled up at him, a big toothy grin that was full of confidence she didn't particularly feel.

He rewarded the gesture with a grimace.

This was the reception she'd feared.

In the heavy silence that hung between them, she took in his casual appearance with a quick head-to-toe glance. The last time she'd seen him, a mere seven hours ago, Luke had been dressed in formal evening attire.

This morning he wore dark pin-striped trousers and a plain linen shirt. He hadn't attached the collar yet, nor had he put on a tie, a vest, or a suit coat. A small towel adorned his left shoulder. His square jaw was dusted with fine stubble, and a lock of golden hair tumbled over his left eye.

Elizabeth's heart switched places with her stomach. She'd caught him preparing to shave. The intimacy of the situation stole her breath. A part of her wanted to stand here in the foyer and simply stare at Luke in all his casual glory. This was the man his wife would meet every morning upon waking. They would share a kiss to start off the day. The moment would be light and tender and—

Her stomach took a fast, hard tumble.

Bad place for her mind to travel.

Luke had a rough edge in the dull morning light that called to a very female portion of her nature. She shifted, briefly wondering if she should have approached him at his place of business instead of his private residence.

Well, as he himself said, now that she was here . . .

"Do you want to know why I've come?"

"No."

It was the exact wrong thing to say. Something inside her broke, fracturing the part of her character that cared what others thought. Elizabeth had had just about enough of well-meaning friends and family treating her like a child, guiding and advising her as if she didn't have a brain inside her *pretty little head*. "I have come to offer you a proposition."

He gave her an impassive stare. "You walked twenty blocks in the cold dawn air to present me with a . . . proposition?"

"You don't have to make it sound so sordid."

His lips did not move from their flat, straight line.

There was a long moment of silence, during which he glared at her. And she glared right back.

"Might we have this conversation in a more comfortable setting?" she asked.

For several seconds, he didn't respond.

Unmoving, hardly breathing, she continued holding his stare. She could do this all day, one of the few benefits of her mother's rigorous training. *A young woman of fine breeding never fidgets.*

As she predicted, Luke was the first to break.

"Follow me." He took off down a wood-paneled corridor.

Elizabeth had to take two steps to match each one of his long, ground-eating strides. The way he moved, all sinewy strength and fast, fluid movement, reminded her of a male lion that ruled his domain.

They rounded a corner and, if she wasn't mistaken, Luke picked up the pace. Now he was just being ornery. With her breath coming quickly now and her feet moving far too fast, there was only time for impressions. They passed several rooms en route to wherever he was taking her.

The first was sparsely decorated in muted grays and deep blues. There was a formal dining area of sorts, with a table, three high-back, claw-footed chairs—why only three?—and a sideboard. The lack of charm in the décor could be forgiven. Luke had been back in America only a few months, not nearly enough time to furnish a home properly.

Oh, what Elizabeth could do with this house. The feminine touches she could add to the large, airy rooms.

At the end of the second hallway, Luke entered a library, much smaller than the one in her grandfather's house and all the more welcoming because of it. This room had received more care than the others.

The rich, dark wood and deep earth tones reflected Luke's personality to perfection. The floor was covered with a large woven carpet hailing from the Far East, its intricate pattern the same muted colors as the furniture and draperies.

Spinning in a slow circle, Elizabeth let out a happy sigh.

Bookshelves lined three walls, every shelf overstuffed with books. Her fingers itched to run across the leather spines as she investigated the titles. Were they organized by subject or author? The fourth wall boasted a marble fireplace with an unlit pile of wood.

She could spend hours in this room, enjoying a book and a cup of tea beside a fire, cozied up in one of the two wingback chairs covered in burgundy leather. Luke would be in the matching one, bouncing a fair-haired toddler on his lap and—

Not the point of your visit.

Elizabeth cleared her throat. "Do you wish to hear my proposition now?"

"Not especially."

The man was bone stubborn when he wanted to be. Why had Elizabeth not noticed that about him prior to this morning? "I find that odd since you invited me inside your home and brought me to your favorite room—"

"How do you know this is my favorite room?"

She offered him a bright smile. "The newspapers and open books gave you away." To punctuate her point, she waved a hand in the direction of an overstuffed ottoman covered with both. "As I was saying, you brought me to your favorite room. I can thus assume you want to hear my proposal."

Hitching a hip on the edge of the room's lone desk, he gave her a very long, very thorough appraisal. "Let's get this over with, shall we?"

Impossible, insufferable man.

Elizabeth would not be intimidated. She would, however, need a moment to gather her courage. With smooth, easy steps, she made her way to the window, staring outside without really seeing the street and buildings beyond.

She was suddenly afraid.

Not of Luke, never of him, but of herself. Of what she might do if he turned her down. There was no other man or woman she trusted to help her. He *must* agree to her proposal.

She pivoted to face him, only to discover he'd taken several paces toward her. He'd moved quickly, without a sound. There was a fresh intensity in his bearing. *This* was the man who'd spurned society without concern for what others thought of him.

Elizabeth liked this Luke, rather a lot, perhaps a bit too much. If he agreed to her request, one of them could end up hurt. Probably her.

"Perhaps I should come back another time." A temporary retreat, that was all. She wasn't giving up completely.

She made for the door.

"Oh, no, you don't." He moved with lightning speed, barring her exit with his big body. Feet splayed, arms crossed over his chest, he said, "You have come this far, at great risk to your reputation. I insist you see this through, Little Bit."

"I need your help."

He inclined his head ever so slightly. "With what?"

Of course he wouldn't make this easy. His demeanor was anything but welcoming, and he was standing too close on purpose. She couldn't think properly. A stab of pain extended from a spot behind her right eye all the way to her left temple.

At least Luke appeared equally on edge. He was outwardly calm and self-possessed, but Elizabeth noted the tension in his neck and shoulders, in the lines stretching out from his eyes and mouth.

"You are different this morning, Little Bit." He reached out a hand toward her, then dropped it back to his side without making contact. "You are more . . ." The long, quiet stare he gave her accomplished more than a string of sentences could. Whatever he thought of the change in her, it wasn't flattering.

"I am more . . . ?"

"Reckless." There was admonishment in his tone, but also something else. Respect, perhaps?

A rather inconvenient surge of pleasure surfaced.

"You've stalled long enough. Let's have it." He wound his wrist in the air. "Tell me why you came to my home, in the dead of night—"

"It's early morning."

"You came to my home," he repeated, "at an inappropriate hour, risking your reputation, and I want to know why."

In that moment, the monumental consequences of her behavior struck her full force. Not the consequences to herself—she'd weighed and measured those several times over—but to Luke. She'd put him at risk. Penelope, too. If Luke's behavior was thrown into question, the gossip could then spread to his sister, for no other reason than their close association.

"Luke, I'm sorry. I made a mistake coming here."

To her utter shock, his entire manner softened, and he gave her arm a reassuring pat. "It's done now."

Oh, right, perfect, now he acted all kind and considerate, which only served to make her more aware of how little she'd thought through this portion of her plan. What if someone saw her leaving his home and he was forced to marry her for propriety's sake? He would grow to resent her, and that would break her heart. Elizabeth didn't want either of them trapped in a marriage for all the wrong reasons.

A shiver raced through her at the thought.

"You're cold."

"Only a very little." She burrowed deeper inside her cloak. "It's chilly out this morning."

"Come." He took her hand and tugged her toward the center of the room. "Have a seat by the fire."

A reluctant laugh slipped out of her. "It isn't lit."

"Easily remedied." He rolled up his sleeves, stopping at the elbows, crouched down, and removed the grate. The muscles of his shoulders bunched and released with his efforts.

Elizabeth couldn't take her eyes off him rearranging the wood, looking very capable and male. In a futile attempt to find a comfortable position, she shifted, stretched out her legs, pulled them back in.

While he coaxed the fire to life, they spoke of nothing but inconsequential matters. Talk turned to the dinner party the previous evening, both in full agreement it was nice to have Jackson and Caroline home.

During this moment of relaxed conversation, Elizabeth found she enjoyed Luke's company. She had for some time, and decided to be glad she'd chosen him to be her accomplice. The man was maneuvering his way into her heart. She'd like to think he cared for her, too. But if he wanted more than friendship, he would have made his intentions known by now. Maybe, if she was smart and wily, she could make him see her as more than a child, more than his sister's friend, more than his Little Bit.

Time to state her business.

She waited until he stood calmly before her, rolling his sleeves back in place. The scent of burning wood and sulfur wafted on the air.

From her perch on the edge of the chair, Elizabeth was once again struck by the casual, easy way Luke moved and how his tall, lean frame was enhanced by the expert fit of his trousers and shirt. He appeared relaxed. But weeks of watching him at parties had given Elizabeth a keen sense of his various moods. The man was coiled tight with tension.

Standing, she squared her shoulders and dug deep for the courage to say, "I have come to ask for your assistance. I wish to break a few rules."

The only sign of his surprise was a slight narrowing of his eyes, barely perceptible unless one was watching him closely.

Elizabeth was watching him very closely.

"What sort of rules?"

"I'm not talking about anything too terrible or scandalous."

He lifted a golden eyebrow.

"Mostly insignificant, meaningless little acts."

The eyebrow lowered. "Perhaps you should let me be the judge of that."

The very opening Elizabeth hoped he would present.

"I have made a list." She reached inside the cloth purse hanging from her wrist. "If you would take a look, you will see that—"

"Stop right there."

She blinked up at him, surprised by the abrupt tone. Lips clamped firmly together, she thrust the list in the space between them instead. Had she waved a poisonous snake in front of his face, she couldn't imagine a more horrified expression contorting his handsome features.

"Don't you want to see my list?"

"No."

Stubborn, *stubborn* man. "Once you know the things I wish to do, you will see there is no cause for concern."

"Still no."

Her breath grew hot in her lungs. "You're being very narrow minded."

"I am being cautious on your behalf."

"How do you figure that?"

"I'm fairly certain whatever is on your list, if accomplished, will lead to your ruin."

Wasn't he full of judgment and condemnation? "I don't care."

He sucked in a sharp breath. "I find that hard to believe."

Maybe she did care, a little, but she cared more about the future. She would not stay locked in her gilded cage.

Arguing with the man was clearly the wrong approach. She switched tactics.

"Please, Luke. You must help me." She softened her voice to a breathy whisper. "You are the only man I trust to embark on this adventure with me."

* * *

Luke closed his eyes against a wave of exasperation. Who was this woman in his home? This bolder Elizabeth was a complete mystery, one he had no chance of solving with her standing so close.

Scrubbing the back of his hand across his mouth, he ordered his mind to focus on the matter at hand. When he was finally calm enough to look at Elizabeth again, he was confronted with a pretty blush spread high on her cheeks.

Not so bold anymore.

Good. Balance was somewhat restored in their relationship. Luke had no business thinking of Elizabeth St. James as anything but his Little Bit, his sister's dearest friend since childhood, the woman who'd nearly married his closest friend.

"Why come to me?"

Her silk-encased shoulders rose and fell. "I should think it obvious. You are, after all, a worldly man with considerable experience behind you. Your guidance will come with a vast array of knowledge I simply don't have."

She had him there, which was why he was the very last man she should approach. No, she shouldn't be approaching *any* man. A wave of possessiveness swept through him, but he refused to acknowledge the emotion.

This madness had to stop. He took her arm in a gentle grip and attempted to steer her toward the door.

Revealing a stubborn streak he hadn't known existed, she pulled free of his hold. "Luke, you know why I have to do this. If I don't, I fear I will disappear into a black void of nothingness."

Granted, she was being unnecessarily dramatic, but he did have a good idea what she was feeling. He even understood her reasoning, on an intellectual level. That didn't mean he would be a party to corrupting her innocence, no matter how *insignificant* or *meaningless* her list of adventures turned out to be.

"At the risk of sounding redundant, and I do hate to sound redundant," she said, "I have nothing to show for my life other than my impeccable reputation."

"What's wrong with having an impeccable reputation?" He'd worked hard cleaning up his own.

"Actually, I would relish society's high esteem if I knew, without a doubt, I was more than the product of my upbringing."

"You are more."

Her breath expelled on a deep, weary sigh. "How can you know that?"

"I know you."

"You can't possibly. I don't even know who I am." She lifted serious eyes and shoved the list into the space between them. "Will you help me find out?"

Maintaining a calm pose became a lesson in torture. The woman had no idea what she asked. The danger she was putting herself in by coming to a man like him.

"You cannot risk your standing in society, Little Bit." He pushed the hand holding the list away from him. "The cost is too high, the risk too great."

Could he sound any more pompous, any more arrogant, any more like his father? Warren Griffin had uttered those very same words to Luke, regarding both his personal life and his business pursuits.

The situations were not the same. The matter of a young woman's good name was at stake. Luke's thoughts shifted to Penelope. If he found out she'd gone to a gentleman's residence without the benefit of a chaperon, no matter the time of day, he would lock her away until her wedding night.

Jaw firm, eyes not quite meeting his, Elizabeth carefully tucked the list inside the cloth purse hanging from her wrist. "If you refuse to help me, then I will approach someone who is more agreeable to a bit of adventure."

Not while he still had breath in his lungs.

Given their history, Luke could be a gentleman about this. He could take pity on Elizabeth and provide her an exit that would allow her to maintain a portion of her dignity.

No time for that. The woman was on a mission. Her mind was set. He would have to rely on shocking some sense into her.

A plan formed in his head. It was a little underhanded, but reason hadn't worked.

"Very well, Little Bit. You have won me over."

"I have?"

"What can I say?" He added a bit of charm to his smile. "You are a fierce negotiator."

"I am?" she replied in a careful voice, clearly suspicious of him now. Wise woman.

He shot out his hand. "Let's have a look."

When she simply stared at his open palm, he wiggled his fingers in a silent *hurry-up* gesture.

"Oh. Yes. Right. You want to see my list."

Head down, she dug around in her purse. The way she fumbled with the strings, and nearly dropped the tiny bag on two separate occasions, told Luke he'd adopted the perfect strategy in their battle of wills.

With a triumphant grin, she placed the list in his hand.

Closing his fist over the piece of paper, he let his fingers linger over her hand a shade past polite. Her sharp inhale was its own reward.

The infamous list now in his possession, he held her gaze, taking his time unfolding the paper.

She swallowed.

Excellent. He was making her nervous. Her impatience all but vibrated out of her.

Holding back a smile, he lowered his head and studied the page. Elizabeth had pretty, neat handwriting. Very feminine, very much as he would expect.

He read the first item aloud. "Wear last season's dress."

She'd already accomplished that one and survived completely unscathed.

Perhaps he was overreacting. Perhaps she didn't plan to push the boundaries too far.

He continued reading.

Walk in the rain, barefoot . . . Attend a vaudeville show . . . Play a game of chance.

All the adventures were, as she'd claimed, relatively innocuous. Though they seemed to escalate in risk.

"Well?"

"I'm still reading."

"Would you mind hurrying up?"

Hearing something in her voice, he cast a surreptitious glance in her direction. She stood there, waiting, her gaze unwavering and direct, not an ounce of embarrassment.

Luke was actually feeling better, until he read the sixth item on her list: *Ask a man to dance.*

His stomach dropped. That one could prove problematic, depending on the man. With the proper supervision, however, the task was manageable.

Number seven.

Kiss a man under the moon and stars.

His heart stuttered in his chest. He felt a muscle twitch, then tighten in his jaw. He'd read enough. He need not continue to know

Elizabeth's thirst for adventure was stronger than he'd anticipated. She had no idea what she was getting herself into.

Luke knew.

Mouth grim, he thrust the list back into her hand, closed her fingers over the paper.

"So?" Her ridiculously long eyelashes fluttered. "Will you help me?"

Reckless. The word kept showing up in his mind.

Luke put the rest of his plan in motion. He began with a frank question. "Let's talk about number seven. Why under the moon and stars?"

Her cheeks turned a becoming pink. Not quite meeting his eyes, she gave a self-conscious shrug. "For the romance, of course."

"The romance," he repeated, not sure why her answer rankled.

She lifted her chin at a haughty angle. "Without a bit of romance, what's the point of breaking the rules?"

Luke's patience snapped. The woman definitely needed to learn a lesson. And he was just the man to do the teaching. Better him than someone who might exploit her innocence.

"You believe it would be romantic to kiss under the moon and stars, as opposed to, say . . . on a rooftop . . . or"—he moved to within inches of her—"in a man's favorite room?"

The shock that jumped into her eyes was exactly the reaction he'd intended. A promising start.

Gaze locked with hers, he reached out, slowly, deliberately, fully aware of the predatory nature of the move.

She looked at him with wide eyes, so trusting, so captivating in the glow of the fire. She was made to be admired by firelight, pale and delicate, her skin radiating good health.

A burst of tenderness flooded his senses, his heart, his soul.

Drawn to her in ways he'd never been drawn to a woman, he ran a finger along the curve of her cheek, tucked a wayward wisp gently behind her ear. "So pretty."

"Luke."

His name was like a caress, encouraging him to continue. He leaned in closer, moving with considerable care, as if she were a skittish colt poised to bolt at any moment.

He brushed his mouth across hers.

Enjoying the sensation more than he should, he loitered a moment, his lips barely touching hers. She began to shake. No, that was him. What was he doing?

The lesson had gone awry.

With considerable effort, he shifted back a step.

Her hand flew to her lips. Blinking rapidly, eyes a bit dreamy, her breath came in fast, erratic spurts. Luke had done that to her, with nothing more than a sweep of his lips along hers. What would her reaction be if he put some effort into it?

He wanted to know. God forgive him, he wanted to discover what lay beneath that prim façade and serene smile.

Dangerous territory.

Elizabeth dropped her hand and gave him a secretive little half smile. "That was rather quite nice."

Nice?

"Thank you, Luke." That female smile moved into her eyes, turning the clear blue to a smoky gray. "Although you didn't kiss me under the moon and stars, I believe I'm moving in the right direction. I can now mark number seven off my list."

He'd taken a strategic misstep.

The woman was supposed to have learned a lesson, not be encouraged to continue her outrageous quest in earnest.

"That was not a kiss." It was a matter of principle he make that clear.

A look of confusion stretched across her features. "No?"

"Not a proper one." He leaned over her and whispered close to her ear, "When I kiss you properly, Elizabeth, you will know."

Chapter Eleven

Slightly dizzy from the mysterious heat spreading through her limbs, Elizabeth digested Luke's words. Had he just promised to kiss her again?

When I kiss you properly, Elizabeth, you will know.

"Perhaps you could show me what you mean?"

"Absolutely not." Expression closed, he crossed his arms over his chest. "Nor will you embark on a quest to tick off any more items from your list. Better yet, give it to me."

"Why?"

Impatience surfaced, glowing in his eyes as hot as the flames burning behind him. "So I can put an end to this nonsense."

"No."

After a brief flick of his gaze toward the fire, he advanced on her, his intent obvious. "Give it to me."

"No."

He sprang for her.

Anticipating the move, she was already spinning around and bolting for the hallway.

"Get back here, Little Bit."

Oh, no. The man could not kiss her one moment and then call her by the childish nickname the next.

She whipped back around. "I don't want your help after all. I'll approach someone more agreeable. Forget I was ever here."

He stalked into the hallway after her. "Who do you have in mind?"

She hadn't worked that out yet. "Someone."

"You will not approach another man with your proposition." He strode toward her with long, unhurried strides. The look on his face was frustration itself. She was clearly trying his patience.

Well, he was trying hers.

"You cannot stop me."

He raked a hand through his hair, not one wasted move. Even in his irritation, Luke was in complete control of himself. Elizabeth would have stopped and admired that impressive trait if she wasn't equally annoyed with him.

"This scheme of yours is a spectacularly bad idea."

She vehemently disagreed. "My future has been preordained from the crib, every step mapped out, every decision already made. As a result, I am almost perfectly useless for any task but marriage."

"That's not true. You are gifted in countless areas."

She'd just bared her soul to the man, yet he refused to acknowledge the truth of her situation. "You are missing the point entirely."

"Elizabeth. Look at me."

"I would really rather not."

His hands moved to frame her face, and he waited until her eyes met his before speaking again. "I understand why you wish to spread your wings. But your route is far too dangerous."

"This is the path I choose. It is my life, my decision."

Still cupping her face, he pressed a gentle kiss to her forehead—of course—and smiled at her with such tenderness, a thread of hope bloomed in her heart.

"There are other ways to taste adventure without jeopardizing your reputation." He lowered his hands. "Let me help you find another way. We'll formulate a new plan, together."

Translation: *You can't be trusted with this task on your own.*

Elizabeth supposed she should look on the bright side. At least he was amenable to helping her reach her goals, if not in the way she chose to do so.

"I don't know if I can agree, Luke." She lowered her head so he wouldn't see the flash of hurt moving inside her. "I'll have to think about your offer."

"That's all I ask."

No, he was asking so much more.

"We'll discuss moving forward at a more appropriate hour," he told her. "In a less scintillating environment."

He was back in his role of protector. The man was nothing if not consistent.

"In the meantime . . ." He pulled the cloak's hood over her head and directed her to the back of the house. "I'll drive you home in my motorcar."

"I prefer to walk."

He started to argue.

She cut him off. "We cannot be seen leaving your house together."

"I don't like the idea of you out on the streets alone at this hour."

"I made it here without incident. I'm perfectly capable of finding my way home in the same manner."

On this point, she would not bend.

"Good-bye, Luke." Refusing to hear another word of protest, she slipped out the door to the sound of his muttering.

* * *

Elizabeth hastened down the sidewalk with fast, purposeful steps. A cold sweep of air slipped beneath her cloak, sending a chill down her spine. She tugged the hood lower over her eyes.

The calendar claimed springtime had arrived, but the season was stubbornly refusing to show its face. Cold mist hung on the air like a filmy curtain.

She was glad for the warmth of her cloak.

She was *not* glad for the results of her trip to Seventy-Seventh Street.

Lucian Griffin was the most stubborn, hardheaded, arrogant male of her acquaintance. Did he truly believe she couldn't walk twenty blocks on her own? Apparently so, proof positive he would forever see her as a wayward child in need of a man's protection.

Elizabeth thought of her cousin. In the name of survival, Caroline had done things Elizabeth could hardly comprehend. She'd picked pockets, played games of chance, traveled to a foreign country entirely on her own. Caroline was clever and resourceful. Elizabeth was also clever and resourceful. She merely had to tap into the part of her that shared the same blood as her cousin.

She glanced to the heavens, thought about praying, but the words wouldn't come. There was no harm in wishing for a taste of adventure in the way she chose, and on the terms she set. Luke was wrong to dissuade her from her quest.

Elizabeth would change his mind. Or find a more willing partner. Oh, but Luke was her first choice. The *only* choice that made sense.

When I kiss you properly, Elizabeth, you will know.

The memory of his mouth on hers had her hand lifting to her lips. Buildings on either side of the street cast long, dark shadows at her feet, broken only by the weak sunlight that peeked through a seam in the grubby gray clouds overhead. The sidewalks were virtually empty, much as they'd been when she'd left St. James House an hour ago.

One hour, that's all it had taken for Luke to quash her plans.

A minor setback, nothing more. If Luke thought he could talk her into a tamer approach to breaking the rules, he was very much mistaken. Her determination carried her the remaining nineteen blocks.

The moment Elizabeth entered St. James House, warmth curled around her from every direction. She was in the process of removing her gloves when the butler appeared in the foyer.

"Good morning, Aldrich."

"Miss Elizabeth." The butler's face held a blank stare that must have taken years of practice to master. "You are up early."

Though she didn't owe him an explanation, Elizabeth didn't want him telling her father or grandfather about her impromptu outing. There would be questions, questions she had no intention of answering.

Glancing at the stately clock nestled in an alcove by the staircase, she read the time. Seven o'clock, hours before she normally alighted from her room. No wonder Aldrich's eyes held a slightly inquisitive glint.

"I couldn't sleep, so I decided to go for a brisk morning walk. The cool air was quite refreshing."

Two bushy eyebrows lifted toward the receding hairline. "No doubt it was."

The man was certainly well trained. Despite the questions swirling in his black-eyed gaze, he voiced none of them.

Elizabeth shed her cloak and handed it to the butler. He turned to go. She nearly called him back when she realized the shawl was still stuffed inside the lining. She would have to retrieve it later.

At the top of the stairs, she started down the hallway toward her room, then changed direction when she noted the light coming from her father's study.

For months, she'd been furious with him for banishing her mother to Florida. Katherine St. James should have received a harsher punishment.

Elizabeth knew she wasn't being fair to her father. He'd done what he felt was right and what would ultimately benefit her. She'd been too upset to acknowledge that he'd suffered his share of pain. How distressing it must have been to discover he'd married a woman who'd deceived him their entire marriage.

The pang in Elizabeth's heart was sorrow. She'd played her part in their strained relationship and owed her father an apology.

Redirecting her steps, she knocked tentatively on the door. It swung open from the gentle force, and Elizabeth entered the room. Her father stood by the hearth, which boasted the remains of smoking embers from a dying fire. His shoulders were slumped, his head lowered.

He looked thoughtful.

No, he looked defeated. "Father?"

His red-rimmed, miserable gaze connected with hers.

"Elizabeth." He attempted a smile, but couldn't hide the strain shadowing his eyes and leeching his face of healthy color. "I didn't hear you come in."

"You left the door half-open."

"Ah." The word hung between them.

Elizabeth searched for something to say to break the tension. Her father had once been free with his affection, ready to laugh. He'd given of himself, asking for nothing in return.

Much had changed in the months since her mother's treachery had been uncovered. This morning, however, her father seemed even more dejected than usual. What had happened, Elizabeth wondered, since last evening?

Lowering her gaze, she noticed he held a letter in his hand. Alarm filled her, and she moved a step closer. Angling her head, she caught a glimpse of the handwriting.

Months-old hostility replaced her concern.

Elizabeth recognized the bold slash of ink across paper and yet found herself asking, "Is that from Mother?"

He nodded. "We have been corresponding on a regular basis."

Blood crashed through her veins. "You . . . *what*? Why? What does she want from you?"

With a surprisingly steady hand, her father folded the crisp pages and stuffed them in his coat pocket. "Forgiveness."

A familiar, white-hot anger flared to life. How dare her mother ask such a thing? "She can't have it."

"Elizabeth, I understand you're angry. I certainly see—"

"Why aren't *you* angry?" The cold fury stirring inside her had once felt foreign but was familiar now, growing stronger, morphing Elizabeth into someone she hardly recognized. "She betrayed the family. She betrayed you. She kept your sister from coming home, your *own* sister. Libby died destitute and impoverished because of Mother's actions, or did you forget that part?"

"I won't deny what your mother did was reprehensible." He released a heavy sigh. "She claims she is sorry."

"I very much doubt that."

He winced as though she'd kicked him in the shin. "I believe she is sincere."

A hot ball of dread pooled in Elizabeth's stomach. Her desire to mend matters with her father was lost in the sensation. How could he entertain forgiveness?

"Mother isn't sorry for what she did. The only reason she admitted to anything was because her deceit was exposed."

Had Caroline not come to America to seek justice, had she not confronted Katherine with her suspicions, the family would still be ignorant of her selfish character.

"You are being too hard on your mother."

"And you are not being hard enough." He'd adored his sister. Even when he'd thought Libby had abandoned the family, he'd insisted on naming Elizabeth after her. Elizabeth was proud to carry her aunt's name.

"How many letters have you and Mother exchanged?"

"Several."

A fresh spurt of panic trickled down her throat. "You've read several of her letters *and* responded."

"Your mother deserves a chance to explain herself."

Elizabeth's head throbbed. She pressed her fingertips into her temples, but the pain failed to subside.

Her mother had intercepted nearly three dozen letters from Libby. In an effort to ensure Libby understood she wasn't welcome, Katherine had returned all of them unopened. Libby had died thinking her family didn't want anything to do with her. Now, Katherine sent letters—*letters!*—to her husband begging for his forgiveness.

"You shouldn't have opened them. You should have treated Mother with the same coldhearted silence she gave Libby."

"You don't mean that."

"Yes, I do."

Both breathing hard, they stared at one another in stiff silence.

"Your mother requests another chance to state her case, and I'm inclined to give it."

"What does Grandfather have to say about this?"

"He's in agreement with you."

Good. That was good. "You must realize Mother only wants to come home because she misses her life as a prominent member of New York society."

Disapproval moved in her father's eyes. "When did you become so cynical?"

Elizabeth could pinpoint the exact moment. When her mother had shown her true nature. The words she'd flung at Caroline, with the bulk of New York society watching, had been unconscionable. She'd called Caroline a fraud, a liar, and a cheat.

For out of the abundance of the heart the mouth speaketh.

"Katherine St. James is not a good person." There, she'd said the words that had been on her tongue for weeks. Instead of feeling better, Elizabeth felt worse. She felt shameful, as if passing judgment made her no better than the woman she criticized.

"There is good in all of us, Elizabeth, even in your mother."

Once upon a time, she would have agreed. "That remains to be seen."

Shaking his head, her father gave her a look of profound sadness. He was clearly disappointed in her.

Well, she was disappointed in him.

Marcus St. James had always been able to see the good in others. When faced with an offense, he was slow to anger, quick to forgive. His greatest strength had become his greatest weakness.

"Why show mercy to a woman who withheld it from your sister?"

"Your mother deserves grace, as does every child of God."

"What of Libby?" The tears that burned in her throat sounded in her voice. "How can you claim Mother deserves grace when she withheld it from *your sister*?"

Elizabeth could not emphasize the connection enough.

"You are missing the very point of grace." Her father took her hand and linked their fingers as he'd done when she was a child. "It is unearned and freely given. The Bible is clear on this."

There was no argument in the face of such truth. "I'm sorry, Father." There weren't enough words in the English language to express her remorse. "I cannot find it in my heart to forgive her, not after what she's done."

Sighing heavily, he released her hand. "We are called to look past a person's behavior and to see them as God sees them."

Elizabeth had looked into her mother's heart. She'd seen ugly intent. "I don't believe she's changed."

"Maybe she hasn't." He executed a small, nearly imperceptible nod of agreement. "She has been my wife for twenty-five years. I won't turn my back on her completely."

The more her father argued in her mother's favor, the more stubborn Elizabeth became on the matter. "She can't come home."

He acknowledged her words with a slight bow of his head. "No, she cannot. Not yet."

"Never. As a point of honor, she can never come home." Even if Elizabeth sailed to England and made a life for herself among the British, her mother did not belong in this home anymore.

"She has been secluded from her family and friends for months, Elizabeth, long enough to contemplate the error of her ways."

"You can't be thinking of letting her come here to state her case."

"No, I will go to her."

"Oh, Father. You are too good, too trusting." He was setting himself up to be hurt again.

"I leave at the end of the week," he said. "When I return, we'll discuss your trip to England."

"I thought the plans were complete."

"I am thinking of going with you."

"I think that's . . . a lovely idea." Her father could use the change of scenery. It would do him good to get away from New York, St. James House, and the memories that plagued him.

For the first time in a week, the thought of sailing to England didn't carry so much weight. Elizabeth's mood lightened considerably. But then she looked at her father again.

His eyes were full of pain, and Elizabeth ached for him. He'd done nothing wrong, except fall in love with a woman he never really knew, a woman who could very well fool him again.

"There is nothing I can say to dissuade you from going to Mother?"

"She is my wife."

He said this as though it were explanation enough. Perhaps it was. Elizabeth thought of the wedding vows Jackson and Caroline had recited barely a month ago. They'd promised to love one another in sickness and health, in good times and bad. *In betrayal?*

Her father took her hands, squeezing gently. "Try to understand why I am making this trip. I will listen to your mother's pleas. After twenty-five years of marriage, I owe her that much."

It was more than the woman deserved.

Elizabeth was suddenly exhausted. She'd given her opinion. There was nothing more to say. "I wish you Godspeed."

Once she was back in her room and alone with her thoughts, she prowled around like a caged animal. Her mind was still in the study with her father. He'd asked her to show her mother grace.

It was an impossible request, one that revealed the true condition of Elizabeth's own heart.

Was she like her mother after all?

Was she cold and heartless? The question terrified her because she feared perhaps, maybe, she was both.

She knew she was supposed to forgive her mother. But a moment ago, when her father had given her insight into the pain he carried, Elizabeth had seen another casualty of her mother's deceit.

How was she supposed to forgive that?

Retrieving her Bible from the nightstand, she flipped to the conversation between Jesus and Peter about forgiving others. The book fell open to the exact page she wanted, the binding giving way because Elizabeth read the passage nearly every night.

She ran her fingertip over the text, paused at the passage she wanted. Peter had just asked Jesus how many times he was supposed to forgive someone who sinned against him.

Till seven times?

Jesus's reply still confounded Elizabeth: *I say not unto thee, Until seven times: but Until seventy times seven.*

Mulling over the words, she shut her eyes. She'd heard several sermons on the passage. Jesus had been speaking in hyperbole, his point being that forgiveness was required of all His children.

"Lord," she whispered. "I can't forgive my mother." *I can't.*

Despair washed through her.

Everyone told Elizabeth she was good. They said she was sweet, kind, and caring. She wasn't good. She wasn't sweet or kind or caring. She was angry and bitter.

She was her mother's daughter.

"I am not my mother."

She wasn't like her father, either.

Frustrated with herself, she set aside the Bible and sank into her favorite chair.

If she was honest with herself, she would admit that her change in mood wasn't solely because of her conversation with her father. The shift had begun after Luke kissed her. She'd been shocked, and a little thrilled, and then he'd ruined the moment with his typical overprotective, brotherly behavior.

Jumping to her feet, she took another pass around the room. All but marching now, her arms swinging so hard the purse still wrapped around her wrist slapped against her thigh.

Frowning, she loosened the strings and tugged off the offending bag. The crackle of paper prevented her from flinging the purse across the room. She retrieved her list, pausing over entry number seven: *Kiss a man under the moon and stars.*

She went to her writing desk, dipped her quill in the inkpot, and struck through the words. Drawing her bottom lip between her teeth, she rewrote the entry: *Kiss a man properly under the moon and stars.*

Other entries needed revising, as well. She continued making her way down her list, adding specifics where she'd failed to do so earlier.

With or without Luke's help, Elizabeth's rebellion was about to begin in earnest.

Chapter Twelve

Unwilling to let the headstrong woman walk home alone, Luke had followed Elizabeth back to St. James House. He'd maintained a respectable distance so she wouldn't see him and thereby misinterpret his motives.

If she'd caught sight of him, no doubt she would have had a few things to say to him, none of them flattering. She could label his behavior any way she wished—overprotective, rude, high-handed, masculine conceit—Luke didn't much care. It was not in his nature to allow a woman of his acquaintance to walk alone on the streets of New York, regardless of the hour.

The moment she disappeared inside the mansion, he'd turned around and retraced his steps to his own home. As he entered through the back door, he had only one desire: forget he'd ever kissed the confounding woman who'd shown up on his doorstep unexpectedly.

Reckless, improper, risky . . . those were a few of the *unflattering* terms that came to mind concerning Elizabeth St. James.

He banished the woman from his thoughts and went in search of a moment of peace. He found himself standing in his library once again, Elizabeth still in his head.

Battling unwanted sensations, Luke sank into the chair behind his desk and shut his eyes against the memory of the very sweet, deceptively innocent woman.

The images came, anyway.

Kissing Elizabeth had been a mistake. And yet, pressing his mouth to hers had felt as natural as taking a breath, as if he'd finally come home. For those brief moments, with his lips skimming hers, Luke had let his heart lead the way.

Even now, the lingering scent of jasmine and sandalwood teased his senses, making him yearn to drag Elizabeth back into his arms, to kiss her properly this time, and to . . .

Petrol-powered engines.

Mass production lines.

Manufacturing standards.

Luke forced his mind to concentrate on his automobile company, rather than picturing the way Elizabeth had looked the moment he'd lifted his head from hers. She'd appeared both shocked and wildly pleased, which had brought him great satisfaction and . . .

Capital gains.

Sales projections.

Competitive pricing.

Those were the things that must occupy his thoughts, nothing else. Nothing. Else.

Rolling his shoulders, Luke shoved Elizabeth to a quiet corner in his mind, pulled open a desk drawer, and retrieved the contract Richard St. James had sent over by messenger two days ago.

Focus eluded him yet again. This time, it wasn't the kiss that overwhelmed his thoughts. It was Elizabeth's dreaded list. Or, more accurately, the first seven items on her list. He shuddered to think what else she'd included beyond those.

Perhaps he should have read the dratted thing to the end. At least then he would know just how far she meant to go. She'd already taken a serious step in the wrong direction, with no small help from him.

Luke would be lying to himself if he said that Elizabeth's proposition didn't intrigue him. Helping her experience adventure was precisely the sort of endeavor his former, rowdier self would have relished. Pity, really, but Luke had to think of his sister's future, not his own wants. Until Penny was happily settled, he would not think, do, or say anything to bring disgrace upon the Griffin name.

Course set, he put the disturbing Elizabeth St. James out of his mind and set about making his automobile company a reality.

He studied the legal agreement that would set wheels—literally—in motion. He absorbed one word, one sentence, one page at a time, pulling his focus in tight and filtering out everything around him. He savored the idea of owning his own company and looked forward to controlling his destiny. The day was nearly here when his legacy would no longer be tied to his father's.

Focus, he ordered his wandering mind.

He absorbed the legal language as if it were as fundamental to his existence as air. It was tiring, meticulous work, and he let the task consume him. This was why he'd come home, to take his life in a new direction, to create a company that fit his sensibilities and penchant for taking risks.

Or so he told himself.

Running the London offices had suited his skills and personality just as well. With an ocean between them, he'd been free of his father's grip as surely as he would be when he started up his own company.

Luke had come home for other, more personal reasons. He'd missed his life in America. He'd also missed his sister and mother, his friends, even a certain woman with blue eyes and pale-blonde hair and . . .

Focus.

Satisfied the terms of the contract met his parameters, he gathered up the pages and stuffed the entire document inside a leather satchel.

Pulling out his pocket watch, he flipped open the lid and calculated that he had just enough time to finish shaving, don the rest of his business suit, and drive across town for his morning meeting with Richard St. James.

An hour later, Luke arrived at the building on Forty-Second Street and pushed through a pair of heavy gold-plated doors. Although Richard owned the entire thirteen-story building, St. James Industries took up the top four floors. The rest were leased to other businesses.

Richard's office was on the thirteenth floor and required Luke to take an elevator. As he stepped inside the metal cage and gave the attendant his destination, he thought of Elizabeth. She'd claimed she felt trapped in her current life and accused him of not understanding why. Problem was, he did understand. He was even sympathetic to her plight.

Enough to help her spread her wings, as if she were a bird set free from her invisible cage?

No, not if it meant ticking off items from her ridiculous list. There had to be another way to help her experience adventure without putting her future in jeopardy.

If he didn't come up with a counterplan soon, Luke feared she would seek out someone else, a man, perhaps, one who didn't appreciate the risks. The possibility of anyone but Luke kissing Elizabeth under the moon and stars unraveled all sorts of unwanted emotions inside him.

The elevator came to a grinding halt.

"Here we are, sir, the thirteenth floor." The attendant released latches and then slid aside a series of wrought-iron doors.

Luke exited the contraption and proceeded down the hallway. He'd nearly made it to Richard's office when he came face-to-face with Marcus St. James heading in his direction.

After they greeted one another with a handshake, the older man stepped aside so Luke could pass. Luke hesitated. "You won't be joining us for the meeting?"

"My presence isn't necessary."

This was true. The deal was practically done. All they had left to do was sign the contract.

Nevertheless, Luke would like to hear Marcus's thoughts on several details regarding the start-up of the company. He respected the way the other man's mind worked. Much like a brilliant chess player, Marcus St. James was able to calculate risks and see potential pitfalls five steps ahead.

When Luke said as much, the older man smiled. It was the first genuine smile Luke had seen on his face in months.

"Make no mistake, my boy, I have several opinions to share. Unfortunately, an unexpected matter has come up that requires my immediate attention." Even though his voice was perfectly cordial, the strain in the man was hard to miss.

Luke looked closer, seeing the lines around his eyes and the additional streaks of gray in his hair. Clearly, the recent months had been as hard on Marcus St. James as they had been on his daughter.

"I'll schedule another meeting at a more convenient time," Luke said.

"I'll be out of town through the end of next week, perhaps a shade longer." Mr. St. James paused. "I'll contact you as soon as I return, and we'll set something up then."

Luke nodded. "Very good."

Since both had places to be, they went their separate ways.

After giving his name to Richard's secretary, an older woman with kind eyes, graying hair, and a stern demeanor, Luke was told to go in straightaway. "No need to knock," she added. "Mr. St. James is expecting you."

Upon entering the cavernous room, the sound of a pen scratching across parchment paper mingled with the tick-tick-ticking of a clock.

The dark wood paneling on the walls, the leather furniture worn to a fine patina, and the intricately designed rugs all spoke of a commitment to quality. The high ceilings gave the room a feeling of grandeur and permanence, much like the man at the helm of St. James Industries.

Luke stopped in front of the large mahogany desk bracketed by a wall of windows on the left and a row of bookshelves on the right. He cleared his throat.

Richard St. James set down his pen. A lifetime of experience showed in the startling green eyes that met Luke's. "You're on time."

"It never occurred to me to be anything but punctual."

"Admirable."

"Efficient," Luke corrected, not wishing to start their business association with misconceptions, no matter how small.

A half smile tilted the older man's mouth. "Did you have any concerns or questions regarding the contract?"

Appreciating the straightforward approach, Luke answered with equal frankness. "Your attorney sufficiently addressed my issues and made the requested changes." He dug inside the satchel and, with a firm grip, produced three copies of the contract. "I am prepared to sign the document at your earliest convenience."

He placed the stack of papers on the desk.

"Well, then, have a seat and let's get down to business."

Luke did as requested, choosing the wingback chair on his left.

"Though I'm looking forward to our association, I have to wonder"— Richard's eyes showed no emotion as he leaned slightly forward—"why did you come to me with this venture instead of your father?"

Perplexed as to why the man was raising the question now, when there'd been ample opportunity during their previous meetings, Luke thought through his answer.

As he had thus far, he responded with complete honesty. "You are known for your forward thinking and have a reputation for taking calculated risks. My father is more"—he searched for the right term— "conservative in his business dealings."

"Ah, I see. Marcus likewise believes the financial risk isn't worth the investment."

"We both know otherwise." Luke had done extensive groundwork before approaching Richard St. James. He'd visited several British automobile manufacturers while still living in England. On the whole, they were far superior to their American counterparts, especially in terms of engineering and design.

"I have weighed the advantages of the various cylinder designs, and the disadvantages. I understand the difference between several types of engines, but I admit there are gaps in my knowledge." Luke paused. "As you already know, I plan to hire experts from England, engineers and mechanics with the necessary skills to make our venture a success. I wouldn't have approached you otherwise."

"Yes. Yes." Richard leaned back in his chair. "I'm curious, do you prefer three-speed or four-speed transmissions?"

"Four." He went on to explain why.

If Luke hadn't been studying the shadowed planes of Richard's face, he might have missed the respect in the other man's eyes.

After a short pause, Richard nodded. "You will be pleased to know my son and I have approached the owners of Leighton Industries. After ironing out a few sticking points on both sides of the deal, they have agreed to our terms and will sell the company to us."

"This is excellent news." Luke couldn't hold back a smile. Leighton Industries was the premiere maker of multicylinder engines. Buying the company would keep the entire manufacturing process within one house.

"Once we have a quality product," Luke told the other man, "I'll increase the company's profile by organizing a series of weeklong races similar to the ones held in Nice, France. We'll invite automobile clubs from around the country to enter their motorcars."

Proving his mind was still sharp beneath the shock of gray hair, Richard asked pertinent questions regarding what constituted a quality product and the timeline for getting the proposed races up and running.

Luke explained his plan, candidly admitting there were several details that needed addressing.

"I'd like my son to weigh in on those."

"Marcus has already agreed to meet with me."

"Outstanding." Richard asked a few more questions.

Prepared for each of them, Luke answered thoroughly yet succinctly.

At last, the older man rang for his secretary. The moment she appeared in the doorway, he said, "Please inform Mr. Montgomery we are ready to sign the contracts."

"At once, sir."

After she left the room, Richard addressed Luke once again. "While we wait for Jackson, I would like your thoughts on another, more personal matter."

Sensing what, or rather *who*, the older man wished to discuss, Luke tried with limited success to swallow back a wave of trepidation. "All right."

"I believe you are closely acquainted with my granddaughter."

A weight settled in Luke's stomach. If Richard knew just how closely acquainted Luke was with Elizabeth, the man would not sound so calm. "Elizabeth and I are friends."

Something came and went in the other man's eyes, a speculative gleam that warned Luke to be on his guard. "I understand she told you about her decision to go to England and why."

"She mentioned it, yes."

Richard watched Luke a long, tense moment, his expression giving nothing away. "I'm worried she is not as pleased with our plan for her future as she has led her family to believe."

Luke knew Elizabeth was struggling with her decision. He also knew she had deeper concerns about her future. But to say so would reveal just how close he and Elizabeth had become. No matter how much he disagreed with her desire to rebel, Luke would not betray her confidence. Not yet. He still held out hope he could steer her in a less risk-filled direction.

"What makes you think she is having doubts?"

"She is showing increasing signs of strain."

Frowning now, Luke turned Elizabeth's situation over in his mind, viewed it from several different angles. He concluded her grandfather was correct. She was becoming increasingly more agitated.

He knew why, of course, at least in part. "The situation with her mother has hit her hard, perhaps harder than any of us have come to realize. She wants a fresh start, away from the memories, and believes moving to England is the answer."

A pair of bushy white eyebrows traveled upward. "Elizabeth told you this?"

"Yes."

"What are your thoughts on the matter?"

Luke didn't hesitate to give his opinion. "It would be a mistake to send her to London at this time."

Or ever.

The other man looked prepared to press for more information, but Jackson entered the room and said, "I understand you need me to witness your signatures."

* * *

Later that afternoon, Elizabeth received a note from her cousin inviting her to dine at the newlyweds' house that same evening. Though short notice, she accepted Caroline's request with a combination of gratitude and relief. Elizabeth was still upset with her father and didn't think she could face him so soon after their difficult exchange earlier that morning.

She could think of no better way to spend the evening than with Caroline and Jackson, two of her favorite people. More importantly,

Elizabeth would not have to put on airs for their benefit. She might even take the opportunity to mark off another item from her list. Caroline was a master at cards. Her gift with numbers made her a fierce competitor, the perfect person to teach Elizabeth how to win. Because, really, what was the point in playing cards if not to win?

Feeling lighthearted, she alighted from the hired carriage at precisely seven o'clock. She could not help the wave of pleasure that coursed through her as the door swung open and she was greeted by a properly stone-faced butler. For all their claims of appreciating modernity, Jackson and Caroline were rather traditional in some ways.

Her point was further maintained when the butler accepted her cloak without actually looking at her, and then said in a cultured British accent, "Mr. and Mrs. Montgomery are in the green parlor."

"And this is where?"

"One story directly above where we are standing now."

"Thank you."

Heading toward the sound of muffled laughter, Elizabeth climbed the center staircase to the second floor. At the top of the landing, she heard a familiar voice rise above the others. Her heart lurched against her ribs.

She stopped walking.

For several seconds, she stared blindly ahead, realizing she wasn't the only dinner guest. Luke had been invited as well.

Elizabeth had not expected this. Her hand went to the locket she'd hung around her neck. Thumbing open the latch, she stared at the small piece of red silk nestled inside the oval casing.

Seeking a constant reminder for what she had to lose, and what she had to gain, Elizabeth had snipped off several pieces of fringe from Hester's shawl and placed them in an assortment of lockets. The one she wore tonight was a cameo given to her by Penelope on her last birthday.

Luke's laughter rang out, a very male sound that called to a very female part within Elizabeth.

Her feet began moving before her mind registered what she was doing. She snapped the locket shut and let it fall back to its place over the center portion of her bodice. The moment she entered the green parlor, her gaze tracked to Luke's.

Those changeable amber eyes locked with hers. He lifted an eyebrow. She lifted one as well. And so began an odd battle of wills.

Briefly touching the locket, Elizabeth adjusted her smile to one of poised serenity. Her stomach became a frantic flurry of activity. Matters were made infinitely worse when he returned her smile with one full of silent promises.

Something inside her stirred, unfolding like flower petals opening for the sun. She did not care for the sensation, because deep in a secret place of her heart, she enjoyed it entirely too much.

Caroline caught sight of her. "Ah, Elizabeth, you have arrived at last."

The words had her blinking at her cousin. "I hope I'm not late."

"You are right on time." Caroline greeted her with a kiss to her cheek. "Luke only just arrived himself."

Against her better judgment, Elizabeth glanced in his direction once again. All his fierce attention was still focused on her, which made it very hard to forget the last time he'd looked at her that way. Right after he'd kissed her.

The memory was too intimate, too personal, and so very wonderful. She swallowed a sigh and turned her attention to her cousin. "Are there more guests coming?"

"We are a small but intimate group of four. Now come." Caroline took her hand and dragged her deeper into the room. "Say hello to the others."

Jackson greeted her first, in the same manner as his wife had, with a kiss to her cheek. This was the man she'd nearly married. *What a mistake that would have been.*

Stepping in front of Jackson, Luke took her hand. "Good evening, Elizabeth."

"Luke."

Still holding her hand, he dropped his gaze momentarily over her dress. "New?"

"Yes." She heard the defensive note in her voice. After much debate, she'd given in and worn the blue silk from Paris, but only after promising herself she would wear it again before the season was over. When she told Luke he would see the dress again in the near future, he did not smile. He did not give her a single sign of encouragement.

He did not let go of her hand, either.

The meaning behind his reaction wasn't hard to discern. He still didn't approve of her plan. Well, so what if she broke a few rules? What was the harm?

There is no such thing as harmless rule-breaking.

Elizabeth could practically hear him saying the words. She also became aware of the stretching silence that had fallen between them. Her mouth opened, but nothing came out. It was so unfair. Luke's very presence robbed her of thought. At least he seemed equally afflicted. Wasn't that gratifying?

They were rescued from the awkward moment when Caroline suggested they go in to dinner since everyone had arrived.

Elizabeth took her place at the table opposite from Luke. She spent the first two courses ordering her heartbeat to calm. By the third course, her composure was nearly restored, and she was able to engage in polite conversation. Though the experience proved torturous from start to finish.

In such a small gathering, it was impossible to ignore the man seated across from her, though he seemed perfectly capable of ignoring her. He laughed as Caroline regaled him with a story about a street carnival she and Jackson had strolled into while in Venice. "The man juggled fire."

"Actual fire?" Luke asked, as though this were a real possibility. "That must have been quite a sight."

"It was, indeed," Jackson claimed without a hint of irony.

Eyes narrowed, Caroline pointed at her husband. "The flames were on a stick, as you well know."

"How would I know that?"

"You were there," she reminded him.

"True, but I was too busy watching my beautiful wife to notice something as mundane as fire on a stick."

"Good answer." Caroline beamed at her husband. Jackson matched her smile. Something very sweet, very personal passed between them.

Elizabeth looked away, uncomfortable witnessing the moment. A twinge of sadness nipped at her. She wanted that sort of closeness with a man she loved, who loved her in return. Her attention returned to Luke. For the first time all night, his gold eyes softened as they held hers.

In the flickering light of the wall sconces, his features took on a turbulent edge, a man with secrets that continually haunted him. Elizabeth longed to reach out and soothe away his pain. She curled her hands into fists. She supposed some women might find Luke's mysterious aura appealing. Not Elizabeth. Except that, of course she did. She found everything about him appealing.

The fourth course was set in front of her. Her appetite gone, she made a project of cutting the roast duck and pushing it around on her plate. Under normal circumstances, she would consider tonight's dining experience a pleasant respite from what would have been a tense evening with her father. These were not normal circumstances. Any event with Luke in attendance took on a different feel.

"Is the duck not to your liking?" His rich, velvety voice deprived her of logical thought.

"On the contrary." She speared a piece of meat with her fork and forced a smile. "It's quite wonderful."

"Such certainty, and yet"—he dropped an amused gaze to her plate—"you haven't taken a single bite."

She looked down. "I was speaking of the previous course."

His mouth quirked up at one corner. "Of course you were."

She took the bite, studied his handsome face as she chewed. Luke sampled his own duck, his gaze never moving from her face.

Only when Jackson said his name did he break eye contact and answer a question about the possibilities of a six-cylinder engine, whatever that meant. The discussion segued into a lengthy dissertation on automobile manufacturing. With nothing to add, Elizabeth listened in fascinated silence. The brief interlude gave her time to recover her equilibrium.

She cut a glance across the table, noticed her cousin wasn't engaged in the conversation, either. Instead, she was watching Elizabeth. Closely. Intently.

Elizabeth looked down at her plate, then just as quickly glanced back up. Caroline was still watching her, just as closely, just as intently. Then she looked pointedly at Luke, back to Elizabeth, back to Luke again.

With each pass, Caroline's expression turned more and more thoughtful. Speculation glimmered in her shrewd gaze.

Alarm filled Elizabeth. Her cousin knew. She *knew* Elizabeth had feelings for Luke. Her suspicions were confirmed when, at the end of the meal, Caroline suggested the two of them leave the men to their business.

"You don't wish to join us?" Jackson asked, looking perplexed. No wonder. Though it was tradition that the men and women separate for a time after a meal, the newlyweds were anything but traditional.

"We will join you, eventually. But first"—Caroline linked arms with Elizabeth—"I want a nice long chat with my cousin."

Chapter Thirteen

Caroline waited until Jackson and Luke left the dining room before she untangled her arm from Elizabeth's. Peering into the hallway, she let out a quick breath of air, then swung around to face Elizabeth directly.

She wasn't sure what she saw in her cousin's eyes, but Elizabeth had a feeling she knew what Caroline wanted to discuss. Not wanting to know, she spoke first.

"That was a lovely dinner," she said, innocence itself. "Your cook should be commended on her skill."

"I'll pass along the compliment." Caroline stepped closer. Close enough to reveal the speculative gleam in her eyes. "You like him."

Elizabeth nearly gasped at the blunt statement. Thanks to her mother's training, she was able to hide her reaction behind a flat, congenial smile.

"Jackson is really quite wonderful," she declared, rather pleased with her quick-wittedness. "I deem him the perfect match for my very most favorite cousin."

It was a deliberate misunderstanding, Elizabeth knew. Apparently, Caroline recognized the tactic as well. Hands planted firmly on her hips, she released a long-suffering sigh.

"I am your only cousin." An impressive eye roll accompanied this statement. "And we both know I was referring to Luke."

"Of course I like Luke." Elizabeth gave a little huff of laughter to cover the nervous note she heard in her voice. "I like all my friends."

Another deliberate misunderstanding, but if she admitted the truth out loud, even to Caroline, she would no longer be able to pretend she felt the same for Luke as she always had.

Unfortunately, her feelings were growing stronger, deeper, becoming the kind that lasted a lifetime. And now someone had noticed. Not just anyone, either, but her observant cousin.

"You consider Luke nothing more than a friend?" Caroline asked this with no small amount of skepticism.

"That's right."

Caroline leaned in closer, her green eyes unwavering. "So, you and Luke aren't—"

"There is no *me and Luke*."

One dark brow arched.

"If you don't believe me, ask him."

"Perhaps I will."

What a horrifying, terrible, awful thought. "Please don't."

"Elizabeth." All signs of teasing left Caroline's eyes. "What's going on with you? I'm worried. You aren't your usual carefree self."

She couldn't argue the point. "A lot has happened since you left for your honeymoon. A lot has changed in my life."

Everything has changed.

"I get the impression that Luke has something to do with your agitation. He's become important to you, perhaps more than you know what to do with."

How could her cousin know that? "We are friends, nothing more."

"Oh, it's more. In fact"—Caroline paused, as if needing a moment to gather her thoughts—"you look at him as I once looked at Jackson. And Luke looks at you the way Jackson once looked at me."

"How, precisely, do we *look* at one another?"

"With longing."

Elizabeth tried to laugh. The effort nearly choked her.

Swallowing, she waved a dismissive hand. It was either that or burst into tears. Her cousin was partially correct. But she had some of the particulars wrong. At least, in Luke's case. "He thinks of me as a little sister. In his mind, I still have one foot in childhood."

"You are quite mistaken. No man looks at a woman the way Luke looks at you and thinks of her as a child."

"He calls me *Little Bit*." She closed her eyes against the humiliation. "He's been using that ridiculous nickname since I wore pinafores and ribbons in my hair."

"Do not devalue your shared history. Because of it, you and Luke have a closeness that runs deep."

"Luke and I are friends, Caroline, nothing more."

"So you already said, several times, in fact." Caroline let out a soft chuckle. "And before you reiterate your point yet again, I'll remind you of the night you received the distressing news about your governess. Luke was consumed with worry for you. No man agonizes over a woman's well-being like that when he considers her a mere friend."

Elizabeth swallowed, took a hard pull of air, swallowed again. There was no excuse for feeling so thoroughly moved by her cousin's observation. The sensation slipping through her felt like . . . hope. "Luke is a good man, one of honor and integrity. He would have done the same for any number of people. You are reading too much into his behavior."

"Am I?"

"If he were interested in more than friendship, he has had months to declare himself."

That, Elizabeth realized, was a critical detail she must keep in mind when hope reared up again. She and Luke had been guests at the same balls, parties, and private dinners this season. For months, they'd been thrown into one another's paths over and over again.

Except for that first evening when he'd arrived home from England, he'd never once asked Elizabeth to dance. He'd never once sought out her company, never once made a point to speak with her unless they were seated next to each other at dinner.

No, whatever Caroline thought she'd seen in Luke's eyes, it had not been masculine interest. He'd probably been plotting ways to keep Elizabeth from continuing with her scheme.

Depressing thought.

"Elizabeth." Caroline took both of her hands. "Talk to me. Tell me what's so wrong with the possibility of you and Luke becoming more than—"

"Will you teach me how to cheat at cards?"

Caroline's eyes widened. "Pardon me? I don't believe I heard correctly. You want me to . . . what?"

Pleased her tactic to change the subject had worked so well, Elizabeth held back a smile. Gloating was unladylike. Besides, her cousin's shocked expression didn't fool her. "You absolutely heard what I said."

Caroline made a face. "I was hoping you would withdraw the request if I gave you the chance."

"I truly wish to learn."

"But why? I don't understand why you would wish to gain a skill that is unnecessary, underhanded, and, for want of a better word, dishonest."

The very real confusion in Caroline's voice gave Elizabeth pause. Had her cousin been judgmental or angry, she might have brushed off her request as a lark.

Instead, wishing for at least one ally in her quest for adventure, she found herself revealing the events of the past weeks. Starting with her father and grandfather's humiliating reaction when she'd told them she would go to England as they'd requested.

"I can see where that would upset you," Caroline said. "But I don't understand how that relates to cheating at cards."

"There's more."

Next came an exposition on the disastrous results of her first attempt at rebellion, then her visit with Hester. "The details of which you already know."

Caroline nodded, her eyes full of sympathy.

Encouraged by her cousin's lack of condemnation, Elizabeth shared her very real fear that she would never become a woman of substance. "And so," she concluded, "I made a list of all the things I would do if the rules of society didn't apply to me."

Now that she'd come to the end of her tale, she could finally manage to breathe calmly.

For several seconds, Caroline watched her closely, then said, "May I see the list?"

"I don't carry it with me." Luke's attempt to destroy the piece of paper had taught Elizabeth a valuable lesson. She'd spent the afternoon memorizing each of the twenty tasks. When she'd finished, she'd tucked the list away in a safe hiding place—between the pages of her Bible. "One of the tasks I wish to accomplish is to play a game of chance."

"That's not what you asked of me," Caroline pointed out, eyebrows raised.

With a wry twist of her lips, Elizabeth lifted a casual shoulder. "I knew if I asked you something outrageous, you would attempt to negotiate down to a lesser task."

To her astonishment, Caroline dissolved into a fit of laughter. "Elizabeth, my dear, sweet, clever cousin. You are already far wiser and full of far more substance than you realize."

"Then you'll play a game of chance with me?"

"No."

Elizabeth's heart dropped. Here was yet another person turning her down. Just how many disappointments must she endure?

"I'm going to do you one better." A mischievous twinkle lit in Caroline's eyes. "I'm going to teach you how to cheat at poker."

"Oh, Caro, truly?"

"Truly, as long as you promise only to play with me and never tell Grandfather I taught you."

"Done and done."

Minutes later, Elizabeth sat across from her cousin at a small table in a parlor with green wallpaper and countless paintings on every wall.

Caroline held a deck of cards in her hands, a secretive smile on her face. "There are three basic rules to cheating."

Feeling incredibly alive and more awake than she had in weeks, Elizabeth clasped her hands together in her lap and patiently waited for Caroline to reveal the first rule.

"Number one. Always maintain control of the game." She shuffled the deck as she spoke, shifting the placement of the cards with a fast, sure hand. That sort of natural confidence and skill must have taken years of practice.

"You maintain control in two ways." She squared the deck. "The first is rather obvious, but imperative. Always deal the cards yourself. The second requires feminine wiles."

Elizabeth couldn't fathom the need for those in a game of chance. "What sort of wiles?"

"That's a lesson for another time. Suffice it to say, you keep the other players' attention on you and not their cards." Caroline batted her eyelashes. "This is incredibly important when you're in the process of dealing."

With a flourish, she placed the deck of cards in her palm and, with fast, quick flicks, tossed them around the table one by one into five individual piles. Her hands moved at such speed, Elizabeth could hardly keep up.

"We won't be able to do this once you leave for London," Caroline said without looking at the table.

"Is that your subtle way of trying to talk me out of going?"

Caroline smiled. "Is it working?"

"Caro," Elizabeth said on a sigh. "You know I love you, and I would like nothing more than to—"

"Say no more." Head lowered, she reordered the deck of cards, switching the top half with the bottom half. "This must be your decision." She lifted her gaze. "My only wish is to see you happy."

That was her wish as well. There were countless reasons to go to England. But there were just as many keeping her here, the woman sitting across the table one of the most persuasive.

Elizabeth thought of the rest of her family. The cause of her argument with her father was something to consider. One day, he would forgive her mother. He would let Katherine return to New York, if not to St. James House, then to another home.

Then what?

Caroline interrupted her train of thought with another rule. "Number two. Avoid winning too often."

"Why?"

"You don't want to draw unnecessary attention to the game. Refer back to the first rule as to why. Successful cheating begins with control."

Caroline spent the next ten minutes explaining the rules of poker, using the hands she'd dealt as examples.

When they had gone through all five sets of cards, Elizabeth was slightly confused. "It seems luck plays a rather large role in winning."

"Which is why you must control the deck. Let me show you what I mean." She collected the cards from the table in a seemingly orderly fashion. While her hands were busy, she turned the conversation to her honeymoon, expanding on the various sites she and Jackson had seen.

Enthralled, Elizabeth found herself asking all sorts of questions about each of the cities they'd toured. Before she knew it, Caroline had dealt another five hands and was pushing back from the table, grinning broadly.

She'd done something during the deal, but Elizabeth couldn't figure out what. "What did I miss?"

"This." Caroline revealed the hand she'd dealt herself—a royal flush.

Elizabeth gasped. "You just cheated." She looked at the cards laid out on the table. "But I don't know how you did it."

"Let me show you."

Fascinated, Elizabeth watched her cousin choose another hand from the cards left on the table, plus two extra. She placed the seven cards on the bottom of the deck, careful to keep them there while she shuffled. Every time she dealt a card to herself, she pulled it off the bottom of the deck, while she gave the other players cards off the top.

The first time through this process, Caroline worked slowly so Elizabeth could see what she was doing. The second time, her hands moved with phenomenal speed.

"Do it again."

Caroline did as she requested. Even when Elizabeth watched the procedure closely, she failed to detect the con. "You are very good."

"I had to be." She left the rest unsaid. Cheating at cards had been a matter of survival for Caroline, something she would never have done had there been any other choice.

"Your turn." She handed the deck of cards to Elizabeth. "We'll start with shuffling."

While Elizabeth attempted to copy her cousin's earlier moves, Caroline revealed the third and final rule. "Never fleece a man of limited means."

"That seems only fair." Now that they were deep in the game, Elizabeth would have asked Caroline more about her childhood, specifically the kind of men she'd *fleeced*. But she heard the crisp strike of boot heels coming from the hallway.

"We're about to be found out," she whispered.

Caroline didn't seem concerned, which said much about her marriage. Clearly, Jackson knew about his wife's past and the things she'd done in order to feed herself. Yet he didn't hold her actions against her. Probably, like Elizabeth, he admired her for having overcome her impoverished upbringing.

The men appeared in the doorway.

Luke entered the room first, took in the scene, and, reading the situation accurately, bellowed, "What's going on here?"

* * *

Luke ignored the irritation in his tone, the thickness in his throat. What he could not ignore was his panic. Elizabeth had begun making her way down her list—on her own, without him—and she was already on number five. He'd read far enough down the page to know what came next.

Ask a man to dance.

There was a ball scheduled next week at the Waldorf-Astoria, thrown by family friends in honor of Penelope's engagement. Elizabeth would surely be there. Luke could hardly contain his dread. If she approached the wrong man . . .

The thought didn't require finishing to send his gut tossing.

Elizabeth was more stubborn than he'd imagined. She was also delusional if she thought he would allow her to continue ticking off items as if there were no consequences for her actions. There were *always* consequences.

"Explain yourself." The words sounded imperious even to his ears. He didn't care. He had to get through to her. Someway, somehow, he had to appeal to her sense of reason.

"Though I owe you no explanation, as you have surely ascertained, I am playing poker." She said this in an entirely rational tone.

A very irrational emotion slammed through him hard and fast. "What game did you say you were playing?"

"Poker."

He felt his eyes widen.

"No, that's not quite accurate." She lifted her chin, the blue world of her eyes full of defiance. "My cousin was teaching me how to *cheat* at poker."

Luke had forgotten the other woman in the room. At the reminder, he rounded on Caroline. "Why would you do such a thing?"

"She asked."

The soft chuckle coming from the man at his side had Luke glaring at his friend. He unclenched his jaw long enough to say, "You approve of this?"

"I don't disapprove." Jackson chuckled again. "It's not as if Elizabeth is planning to embark on a life of crime."

"That remains to be seen," he muttered under his breath. Having failed to read through the entirety of her list, Luke had no idea what the obstinate woman had planned. For all he knew, she could have included countless unlawful activities.

Probably, she hadn't; this was Elizabeth after all. But the possibility was there.

In that moment, his apprehension was overwhelmed with a primal need to wrap her in his arms and protect her from the world, from herself. From him, and men like him who would prey on such innocence.

He looked at her again and caught his breath at the eyes staring back at him. They were huge in her face, and slightly worried. *Good.* She should be worried.

"This madness has to stop." He did not give her a chance to reply. His next words rode along on a rush of irritation. "I want your promise, and I want it now."

Her eyes narrowed, her expression ripening with defiance. Under different circumstances, Luke might find her backbone admirable. She looked stunning in that moment, her righteous indignation coloring the delicate, sculpted bones of her cheeks.

Luke lost his train of thought. He knew he had a point to make. At the moment, he could do no more than stare at the long, spiked lashes encircling those enormous eyes. Elizabeth St. James was a beauty.

Not the point.

What was the point?

From somewhere off to his left, Jackson said his name.

"Luke," he repeated when Luke patently ignored him. "Don't you think you're turning a simple game of cards into a far bigger concern than the situation warrants?"

Perhaps he was. Perhaps he wasn't. If only he'd taken the opportunity to read Elizabeth's list in its entirety, he would know for sure. "I'll admit that teaching her how to play poker is a relatively tame endeavor. Teaching her how to *cheat* at poker is not."

"*Cheat*, such a harsh word," Caroline said, her lips pursed primly. "I was merely demonstrating a unique approach to a game of cards that will ensure my dear cousin wins every hand she plays in the future."

Luke gritted his teeth. There were too many people in the room, too many allies on Elizabeth's side.

"I'd like to speak with Elizabeth alone."

Silence fell as Jackson and Caroline considered his request. They looked to one another, no doubt preparing to argue with him.

Luke didn't give them the chance. "I'm not going to harm her, if that's your concern. I merely have things to say I don't want either of you hearing."

"You're not helping your case," Jackson argued as only a man with a law degree could.

"Nevertheless."

In the end, it was Elizabeth who settled the matter. "I will give you five minutes."

Oh, she would, would she? "I need ten."

"Five, no more."

"Fine, I'll talk fast. You"—he pointed at Jackson, then signaled to his wife—"leave us."

When the door closed behind them, Luke turned to Elizabeth. He was trying very hard not to think of the last time they'd been alone. He was trying even harder not to take her in his arms for an encore performance of the kiss that hadn't really been a kiss at all.

Splitting hairs.

Despite his growing agitation, Luke meant what he'd said. He had no intention of harming her. This meeting was about protecting her from herself. And, possibly, from him.

He clasped his hands together behind his back and adopted a reasonable tone. "I thought we agreed this morning that you and I were going to reformulate your plan."

Gaining her feet, she moved to a spot before him, while also keeping a polite distance. Now she showed caution? Now?

"That was your idea, not mine," she reminded him. "If you may recall, I did not agree to your suggestion."

And yet, he'd held out hope that she would. "I'm not trying to annoy you. I'm trying to protect your reputation."

"I . . . know." She wrapped her arms around herself, and, standing in that vulnerable pose, she looked small and fragile. She also looked . . . crushed, which only served to make him feel more protective. More frustrated.

If only I could make her understand.

When he spoke his voice was too rough, too full of the annoyance he couldn't completely tamp down. "I'm not opposed to helping you test the boundaries. I'm merely opposed to the route you've chosen. It's reckless."

"I am not"—she unwrapped her arms and poked him in the chest, hard—"reckless."

She went for another poke. This time, he caught her wrist before she made contact. "I didn't say you were. You're twisting my words. I said your plan is reckless."

"I spent a lot of time thinking it through."

Not enough.

Holding his silence, and her wrist, he cocked his head at a sardonic angle. Saying nothing seemed to be the wisest approach.

She tried to tug her wrist free.

He held on with a firm but gentle grip.

"Think about it, Luke." Tug. "I came to my cousin." Tug. "In the privacy of her home." Tug, tug. "And asked her to teach me how to play cards."

"You mean cheat at cards."

"Whatever." She waved her free hand in the air as if batting away a pesky fly rather than a valid argument. "My point is that my actions were far from *reckless*. In fact, I would argue the opposite. No one but the four of us need ever know what happened here tonight."

He found himself oddly comforted by her argument. This time, when she tugged on her wrist, he let her go. "How many items have you ticked off your list?"

"This was the first one."

That was . . . unexpected. "You are not going in order?"

"That would take away the spontaneity."

Of course it would.

"All in all, I had great fun this evening. Please don't spoil it for me." The smile she gave him nearly ripped his heart out of his chest.

Her course was set. He saw the familiar obstinacy in her eyes.

"There is nothing I can say to change your mind?"

"I am determined. And Luke"—her smile turned blinding—"your five minutes are up."

Chapter Fourteen

The trouble with keeping secrets was the weight put on a man's conscience. Even if the secrets weren't his own.

Perhaps *especially* if they weren't his own.

The morning after the dinner party with his friends, Luke dragged himself out of bed before dawn and made the short walk to his childhood home. The cycle of sins, lies, and deceit ended with him. Now that the contracts were signed, and his automobile company was more reality than concept, it was time to inform his father he was breaking out on his own.

The news shouldn't come as a shock. Luke had given Warren plenty of advance warning this day was coming.

Nevertheless, he predicted a difficult conversation ahead.

Having carefully planned his arrival to catch his father before he left for his place of business, Luke was mildly put out when the butler informed him Warren was not at home.

"What about the rest of the family?"

"I believe your sister is still abed. Your mother is in her greenhouse."

"Thank you, Winterbotham."

Dawn had barely broken when Luke trod through the sunken gardens toward his mother's favorite building on the property. Dew moistened the ground at his feet, muffling the sound of his footsteps. Birds chirped their happy greetings. A squirrel hurried up a tree.

Taking an easterly route, Luke passed the ornamental pond near the wrought-iron bench he'd shared with Elizabeth the night of Penelope's engagement party. The memory of that encounter brought a smile to his lips. Though there had been tense moments between them that evening, and since, the moments alone in this garden had been a turning point in their relationship.

Now, the pleasing scent of jasmine, lilacs, and roses would always remind Luke of Elizabeth. He couldn't bear the idea of her moving to England. The British wouldn't appreciate the complicated mix of sweetness and feistiness, of shyness and nerve. They wouldn't—

His feet ground to a halt.

Familiar notes from the first act of *Carmen* floated on the air. Luke knew the piece well. Sung by the mezzo-soprano lead, "L'amour est un oiseau rebelle" was the entrance aria for the main character.

The music wafting on the still air could mean only one thing: rehearsal for the upcoming performance had begun earlier than usual.

Luke changed direction.

Instinct warned him not to enter his father's private opera house. It was the same feeling Luke had experienced all those years ago when he'd come upon Warren and Esmeralda embracing. Even if he found nothing inappropriate this morning, he sensed he would come away angry.

Turn back.

He continued on.

Turn. Back.

He entered the building.

Besieged with an ominous sense of déjà vu, he paused just inside the threshold and took in the scene up on the stage. He counted a total of five people gathered. Four of them made sense: his father, a beautiful young woman, an older woman at the piano, and a famous voice coach—Marco, Marcella, Mercutio? Luke couldn't remember the man's name.

The fifth person sitting in the front row gave him pause. His sister was not still in bed, as Winterbotham had led Luke to believe. She was fully awake and dressed for the day, watching the rehearsal with rapt attention.

Did Penelope know about Warren's passion for turning his protégées into his paramours? Luke narrowed his eyes. His sister seemed lost in the music, oblivious to the undercurrents between her father and the young singer.

"Again, Juliette." The voice coach spoke in a thick Italian accent that Luke suspected wasn't wholly authentic. "And this time try to display more longing. We must know of your secret hopes from the very first note."

Under the coach's direction, the girl launched into the famous opening verse. *"L'amour est un oiseau rebelle"*—love is a rebellious bird— *"Que nul ne peut apprivoiser"*—that none can tame.

Gut roiling, unable to turn away, Luke propped his shoulder against the wall and watched the rehearsal, telling himself he would not leave until he told his father of his future plans.

His father's latest "project" glided to center stage, arms outstretched as she lifted her voice in song. She was young, of course—Warren's paramours were always young—probably only a few years older than Penelope. She was also very pretty.

Listening intently, Luke had to admit the girl had a respectable talent, not great, but good enough to launch a brief career on the stage. Then again, Luke had an aversion to opera that matched his father's love for it. Luke abhorred the music, or what he considered the equivalent of screeching. The melodrama was always over the top, and the tragic endings far too depressing. His opinion was, of course, skewed by events of the past.

With an angelic smile that lacked the longing the coach had requested of her, the girl launched into another verse.

"L'oiseau que tu croyais surprendre"—the bird you hoped to catch— *"Battit de l'aile et s'envola"*—beat its wings and flew away.

Although she wasn't as talented as some of the others before her, she had their same look. Smooth porcelain skin; liquid, doelike brown eyes; and the wild, dark curls that spoke of an exotic heritage.

Warren Griffin was nothing if not consistent. The girl was the very image of the singers who'd come before her, all of them mere copies of the original.

A memory flashed of Esmeralda on this stage. She'd been the first, the best. None of the women following in her footsteps had come close to her talent.

As if sensing his presence, Penelope turned her head and gave him a wiggle of her fingers. Nodding in return, Luke maintained his relaxed posture. Though he tried for her sake, he could not prevent a frown from forming on his lips as his sister joined him at the back of the room.

She kept her voice low to prevent interrupting the rehearsal. "You're up early this morning."

"I was going to say the same of you."

She glanced back to the stage, sighed wistfully. "I wanted to catch a portion of Juliette's rehearsal before I have to travel across town for my appointment."

"Dress shopping with friends?"

"The florist to finalize my selections for the wedding, then luncheon with Simon." Her smile brightened when she said her fiancé's name.

One would think Luke would be relieved to see his sister so happy. One would be wrong. Especially after what he'd learned last night when he and Jackson had left the women to their *long chat*.

Oblivious to what was really going on in the green parlor of Jackson's home, Luke had taken the opportunity to quiz his friend about Penelope's fiancé. After verbally dancing around the issue, Jackson had eventually agreed with Luke's estimation that the man might not be what he seemed. Then, he'd said, "I believe you were once acquainted with his cousin Albert."

Luke's guard had immediately gone up at the reminder. He'd taken great pains to forget the months he'd spent running in the same circles as Albert "Bertie" Phineas Fitzgerald III.

Apparently, he'd succeeded, and thus had missed the familial connection between Bertie and Simon.

"Do you not like the music?" Penelope asked.

Luke attempted a light tone. "I like it fine."

"You are a terrible liar." She pointed to a spot in the dead center of his forehead. "Your expression is every bit as soft as granite."

She was no doubt correct. Luke never could fake appreciation for the art form that had destroyed his parents' marriage. He glanced to the stage, drew in an unsteady breath. "I prefer the theater, primarily Shakespeare's tragedies. There is far less drama."

Penny laughed, as he hoped she would.

His father's latest protégée began the next verse. Jenny, Julie—no, Juliette—sang with a sensual voice, the tone slightly deeper than the sopranos his father usually preferred.

Luke attempted to separate his personal opinion of the opera from the music flowing from the stage, and by doing so realized the girl was better than he'd originally supposed. Penelope sighed beside him, her eyes shutting momentarily, her face a look of absolute joy. He loved seeing his sister happy. "You really do love opera, don't you?"

Opening her eyes, she beamed up at him, innocence shimmering in her gaze. "Very much." A delicate frown crossed her features. "I wish father would have let me continue my lessons. I should have enjoyed tackling complicated arias like this one."

It was only then that Luke remembered how Esmeralda had taught Penelope to sing. Though basic, and nothing compared to the training

Warren's paramours received, the lessons had played a large role in helping Penny conquer her stammer. No wonder she missed singing.

"When was the last time you had a lesson?"

"Not long after Esmeralda left for her initial European tour." The one that had launched her international renown.

Penelope braided her fingers together, her gaze reflective. "I miss her, you know, and Sophie even more. The time they were in our lives included some of the happiest days of my childhood."

Luke made a noncommittal sound deep in his throat. They had been some of his worst.

"Did you know Father used to take me up Fifth Avenue in his carriage, just the two of us?" Penelope asked.

"I didn't."

"He and I would visit Esmeralda and Sophie at their little house. The four of us would go ice-skating or stroll through the park at a leisurely pace, then Sophie and I would eat gooey cakes afterward."

An ironic smile tugged at Luke's lips. Though it was clear Penelope had fond memories of that time, it was also clear she had no idea about the true nature of Warren and Esmeralda's relationship. Luke would hate for Penny's recollection of those seemingly spontaneous visits to become tainted if she discovered the truth.

How could Warren have been so selfish? Taking Penelope with him to his paramour's home, the one he'd purchased for sinful reasons. While he spent time with Esmeralda, he'd encouraged his legitimate daughter to cultivate a friendship with his dark little secret.

What sort of man did that? So many innocent lives damaged for one man's desires. Luke wondered if Warren had any remorse, any regret, over his behavior.

Luke prayed Simon was a man of integrity. He wanted Penny happily settled, far, far away from Griffin Manor.

"What have you heard of Esmeralda in the years since they left for Europe?" he asked.

She shook her head. "Only what I read in the papers. Did you know she is returning to America?"

"I heard."

Penelope shifted her gaze to the stage. "I do so hope she'll follow through with her promise and perform for us here."

"I have no doubt she will." Warren would never let the world's most celebrated diva come to the city and beg off from singing at least one aria for him and his friends.

"Oh, oh." Penelope clapped her hands together. "Maestro Marcella is giving Juliette notes on her performance. I should like to hear what he has to say."

"By all means."

She gave Luke a hasty farewell and an even faster kiss on his cheek, then hurried to take a seat in the front row. Luke returned his attention to the stage. The voice coach commanded Juliette to begin the next song, the one where Carmen beguiles Don José with a seguidilla, singing of a night full of dancing and passion with her lover.

Nothing but misfortune and heartache awaited the character. Art imitating life.

Luke thought of the performance in a few weeks. Some of the most important men and women of New York, dressed in all their finery, would fill up every one of the plush velvet chairs. An invitation to one of Warren Griffin's operas was much sought after.

Of course, Luke's mother would be missing. As was her custom, she would take to her bed, claiming a headache. Luke took his gaze off the drama unfolding on the stage and glanced around. His father had redecorated the interior, sparing no expense. The expert woodwork, elaborate chandelier, and vibrant frescoes made for a luxurious décor seen in all the larger opera houses.

He closed his eyes for a moment—just one—and realized his mistake. The heart-wrenching melody washed over him. Luke whipped open his eyes and focused on his father. Warren had yet to look away from the stage. His fierce attention focused solely on Juliette; he was oblivious to all else, ignoring everyone, everything, but the woman on the stage.

She sang directly to him, watching him like a rabbit watched a hawk swooping in, with doomed fascination. The arrogant smirk and entitlement that poured off Warren Griffin had Luke's gut roiling again.

The music hit a crescendo, dragging his attention back to the stage. Juliette was yet another young woman making a very bad mistake. She had no idea the price she would soon pay for her career. Luke could try to warn her, as he had the others. Yet he doubted she would respond any differently than those before her. Among Warren's protégées, longing for success had always trumped the threat of lost innocence.

He'd seen enough.

As he headed for the door, Luke remembered why he'd come. He'd failed to reveal his future plans to his father.

Another time.

* * *

Luke exited the building.

Head down, he walked quickly, not really knowing where he'd end up, just that he had to get out of his childhood home.

His father was the worst sort of hypocrite, cultivating his next mistress less than a hundred yards from where his wife nurtured her hothouse flowers.

Unfair? Absolutely.

The world they lived in was unfair, and all the more reason Luke had to stop Elizabeth from ticking off items on her list, including number seven. *Especially number seven.*

He couldn't prevent Juliette from taking the wrong path. He *would* prevent Elizabeth.

Time passed.

He kept walking, conquering one block after another.

More time passed.

Someone called his name. Luke's steps faltered at the familiar voice. *What are the odds?*

He'd carefully avoided this meeting for months. He'd circumvented the places he'd once frequented in hopes of preventing a one-on-one conversation with this particular man.

Luke looked around, attempted to gather his bearings. Without realizing it, he'd covered nearly a dozen blocks and was now standing in front of the Harvard Club, at an hour he knew would cause this very sort of problem.

His past stared back at him from the face of a man he'd once considered a friend. No, Bertie had never been Luke's friend. They'd only run in the same crowd for six months. Five months and twenty-nine days too long.

"Well, well, if it isn't Lucian Griffin in the flesh. Good to see you, old boy." A hand clapped him on the back. "What has it been? Two years? Three?"

"Three." Luke kept his voice even, his expression devoid of emotion.

"How have we managed not seeing one another for that long?"

"I've been out of the country."

"Ah, yes, I recall hearing something about that. It appears the other rumors are true as well."

Luke stiffened. "What rumors?"

"You're a changed man." Bertie gave him a thorough once-over.

Luke treated the man with equal irreverence, taking in the changes. There weren't many. He was of an average height and build, his face was still classically handsome, his hair still dark and fashioned in the latest style. The red-rimmed eyes indicated a long night of carousing, and the evening attire was a sure sign Bertie had not been to bed yet.

Though Luke knew Bertie's true nature, many did not. The man was slick, living a double life that few outside his inner circle knew about. All that mattered to the New York upper crust was that Bertie came from a well-respected family with ties to the most influential men in the country.

As Jackson's wife often said, people saw what they wanted to see. When they looked at Bertie, they saw a man full of charm and wit who lived a blameless life. It was, of course, a well-honed lie. Once he left the more sedate functions, Bertie preferred running with men of loose morals. He skillfully kept his debauchery to areas of the city no proper gentleman dared frequent.

"You coming or going?" Bertie hitched his chin toward the club.

Luke hesitated. Bertie was trouble, but he was also Simon's cousin. Just how close were the two? One sure way to find out. "I'm heading in."

"Join me for a drink, my old friend."

The request was meant to goad him. Bertie knew Luke had quit drinking long before they'd parted ways. He'd made a host of bad decisions prior to that critical one, so becoming sober had been Luke's way of maintaining some semblance of control. A false sense of security, to be sure. He'd sinned in other ways that hadn't involved alcohol. In that respect, Luke was no better than his father.

Judge not, that ye be not judged.

They entered the club in silence. Luke gave Bertie a sidelong glance and caught the other man smirking at him in return. He wanted to wipe that look off his face. With his fist.

Think of your sister.

He forcibly unclenched his fingers, silently vowing to do whatever it took to secure Penny's future. If spending an hour in Bertie's company meant finding out whether or not Simon was cut from the same cloth as his cousin, then that was what he would do.

As they climbed the wide stairwell, Bertie regaled Luke with his doings since last they'd met. Taking in his surroundings, he listened with only half an ear. There were two types of members who patronized the Harvard Club at this early hour: men of industry starting their day with a hearty breakfast, and men of leisure finishing up their evening of play in the same manner.

A fire was lit in the great fireplace, flicking shadows across the intricate designs of the rugs and the portraits of prominent members framed on the walls.

Bertie's friends were already gathered haphazardly in chairs facing the marble hearth. The sound of their laughter told Luke they'd continued their evening revelry with more drinks.

Fortuitous. *In vino veritas.* In wine, truth. This was the exact chance Luke had been looking for to uncover information about Simon.

The group welcomed Bertie, all but cheering his arrival.

Luke sat in an empty chair and looked at the assembled gathering. He knew every man by name. They ranged in ages from twenty-four to thirty-five, two younger than Luke, the rest older. Though each came from a background similar to his own, and all had attended Harvard, he would call none of them friends.

"My good man, you're back."

Luke knew the reference wasn't to his return to the country but to this depraved circle. "Not permanently."

"Pity."

The speaker sat directly across from him. Silhouetted by firelight, Benjamin Carlton's face was all planes and hard lines. He was the oldest of the group. A banker of wealth and some renown, Ben was a genius with numbers and had a strong taste for Scotch. In lucid moments, the man lamented his inability to avoid overindulging. If the dark hollows beneath his eyes and his bloated cheeks were any indication, he'd lost the battle for sobriety. Luke felt sorry for Ben. The man was caught in a vicious cycle.

"We knew you couldn't stay away." This statement came from Kelvin Grimshaw, a man whose penchant for decadence was rivaled only by Bertie's.

Luke looked at the remaining three men, an unholy trinity of debauchery. Each had his own vice of choice, and each face held a decidedly more wicked smile than the last.

I spent six miserable months with these men.

He'd like to blame his lack of judgment on his father, but that wasn't true. Luke was accountable for his choices, including his time spent with this sort.

Awake to righteousness, and sin not.

He had much to answer for, including his worst sin—hurting a woman who'd been a temporary part of this group. Abigail, a freethinking artist and poet, had fallen for Luke. He hadn't realized how hard until it was too late.

In his defense, he'd done nothing to encourage her affection, except insist she be treated with kindness and respect. Something the others rarely did where women were concerned. Thinking this meant he shared her feelings, she'd declared herself. He'd let her down as best he could, but there had been witnesses, the men in this group among them.

Abby's devastation over being spurned in so public a manner threw her into a deep melancholy. Her downward spiral was the final push Luke had needed to change his ways. He'd been hovering at a crossroads, knowing if he didn't make a complete break he would become as cold and unfeeling as these men. He'd left the country, hoping his absence would not only help Abby recover, but also prevent his own heart from growing as callous as Bertie's.

Luke recently got word Abby was living in Paris with a colony of fellow artists. He prayed she was happy.

The waiter came with another round of drinks.

"Now that the gang's all here, it's time for our weekly review." Bertie pulled out a slim black leather-bound notebook.

The others followed suit.

Luke's shoulders bunched. He should have expected this. Why had he not expected this?

Bertie and his cronies kept a running tally of their conquests through the year. They assigned a point system to certain types of women. A woman with questionable morals was worth one point, and a virgin was worth twenty. Points were assigned at varying degrees to women between the two opposing spectrums. On New Year's Eve, the man with the highest total score won the sum of $500.

Luke stood, bile rising in his throat. He would find out about Simon from another source.

Slicing a sly glance in his direction, Bertie opened the book to a page near the center. "Don't you want to know which lovelies are on my list this year?"

"Have you no shame?" Luke leveled a crushing glance at the other man, then turned it on the others.

Red-faced, Ben and Kelvin looked away. The other three held his gaze, bold and unflinching, with just enough meanness in their eyes to warn Luke their hearts were even harder than he remembered. He'd been right to distance himself from this group. He regretted only not doing so before hurting Abby.

"Still squeamish, old boy?" Bertie released a low, wicked laugh. "Still touting the virtues of integrity and the fair treatment of women?"

"Every woman deserves respect, no matter her station in life."

Bertie sneered.

Luke wasn't through. "You treat women as if they're possessions that you can buy and sell and then discard when you grow bored."

"What can I say? I like their company, but especially the pure and untouched." He winked at his cohorts. "Corrupting an innocent is a powerful temptation I simply cannot resist, hence the reason I win this game every year."

Luke stiffened at the words. He didn't miss Bertie's sarcasm or the calculating glint in his eyes. The man was as bad as Warren Griffin.

No, he was worse.

At least Warren considered himself in love with his mistresses, fleeting as the feeling proved to be. Bertie didn't care about the women he ruined. He cared only about the points they represented on his list.

Luke thought of Elizabeth and her very different, far more innocent list. She was precisely the type of woman Bertie couldn't resist. Proper and perfectly bred, with her quiet smiles and impeccable manners, she was all that was good in their dark world. And she was looking for a man to help her taste adventure. If she approached Bertie . . .

Rattled by the thought, Luke snatched the book out of Bertie's hand, looking for her name. She was listed halfway down the back page with other untouched debutantes Bertie had been unable to conquer but still considered fair game. Penelope was on the list as well.

Violence moved through Luke. "You're done, Bertie."

"On the contrary, I'm only just getting started."

"If you continue with this despicable game"—Luke tossed the book at him—"I'll make sure the good people of New York know who and what you are."

"Go ahead and do your worst." Bertie waved off the threat with a contemptuous flick of his wrist. "It will be my word against yours."

A valid point. Luke hadn't been as proficient at covering his tracks as Bertie. Though few people knew the particulars of his wayward activities, it was no secret that he had a questionable past. Conversely, almost no one knew the depths of Bertie's depravity.

"One more thing." Bertie smirked. A viper poised to strike, he met Luke's gaze and said, "You attempt to reveal my game to anyone outside this circle, and I *will* go after your sister."

There was a collective gasp at the threat. To target a man's sister was the highest form of treachery, even for this bunch.

A flood of hot fury coursed through Luke. Controlling his temper, barely, he gave Bertie a small but deadly smile. "Touch Penelope, go within ten feet of her, and I will kill you."

He meant every word.

Bertie blanched, then recovered quickly, the viciousness in his eyes turning the irises black as hate. He cut a look to his friends. "I do love a challenge."

"She's engaged to your cousin," one of the others reminded him, looking as uncomfortable as a man with his lack of morals could.

"Simon is a prig and a prude. He won't be able to satisfy her, anyway."

Luke reached down, grabbed Bertie by the lapels, and yanked him to his feet. "You touch my sister or try to ruin her engagement," he growled in a voice only the two of them could hear, "and you will regret ever knowing me."

Bertie must have seen the truth in Luke's eyes, because he raised his hands, palms facing forward. "Hey. Hey, now. I was only jesting."

"Stay away from Penelope."

"I heard you the first time. Besides"—Bertie shrugged, no small feat considering his position—"she's too bland for my taste."

Luke dropped the man back in his chair.

Now that there was a safe distance between them, Bertie called him a vile name. Luke sneered in return.

"You know as well as I that my birth was legitimate."

A snicker came from one of the minions.

Making a show of straightening his coat sleeves, Luke turned on his heel and exited the building. He did not look back. Considering his foul mood, he thought this best. One look at Bertie's smirking face and he would punch the man, hard. A show of violence would only encourage him.

Out on the sidewalk, Luke glanced to the sky.

While he'd been in the club, the weather had taken a turn for the worse, as had his day. Gray, squalid clouds rolled in from the east. They moved at a slow, lazy pace, and were too pale to be holding significant amounts of water. There was plenty of time to get to his office before the rain let loose. Or . . .

With lists on the brain, Luke took a detour.

Chapter Fifteen

Late last night, flushed with success after crossing an item off her list, Elizabeth's thoughts had turned to her father. She spent several restless hours turning their quarrel over in her mind, trying desperately to see his side.

By the time dawn spread weak tendrils of light into her bedroom, she'd come to the conclusion that she owed him an apology for her angry words. She might not believe that Katherine St. James deserved a second chance, but her father did. Arguing with him had only served to make him more determined. *Like father, like daughter.*

Elizabeth loved him too much to let him leave New York thinking she didn't support him. She went in search of him early the next morning, desperate they reconcile their differences before he boarded the train to Florida.

It took searching the entire mansion, gardens, *and* carriage house before she finally found him. He was in his dressing room, packing for his trip. He must have moved up his departure. Elizabeth stood on the threshold, clutching the locket holding the piece of Hester's shawl for courage.

Now that she'd found her father, she struggled with what to say, how to tell him she understood why he'd agreed to meet with her mother.

Problem was, Elizabeth didn't understand, hence her sleepless night.

Holding the locket gave her added strength, enough to swallow back the tidal wave of powerlessness that crashed over her as she watched her father direct Aldrich and two of the other servants through the room. Marcus didn't snap out the orders, not precisely, but there was a decided lack of warmth in his voice.

The man who'd always been so patient, so levelheaded and self-possessed, was gone. She blamed her mother for the change, which made forgiving her practically impossible.

She is your mother. There is good in her.

Elizabeth wanted—needed—to believe her father's claims. She wanted the woman from her happy childhood back, the one who'd given her no reason to doubt she was treasured and loved.

Please, Lord, help me . . .

The rest of the prayer wouldn't form in her mind. Apparently, her stubborn streak ran deep.

Sighing, she focused on her father once again. The mid-morning light streaming through the window at his back showcased the changes in him.

He was still a striking man. But his once-dark hair now had thick strands of gray threaded through it. The laugh lines around his mouth held a hint of strain.

His perpetual grimace told its own story.

Marcus St. James was suffering. Not solely because of her mother, but because of Elizabeth's lack of understanding. Why couldn't Elizabeth find it in her heart to forgive like him? What hidden flaw in her character made her so pitiless?

Her father gave Aldrich a curt nod. The butler shut the trunk's lid and secured the latches, then directed the other two men as they lifted the large piece of luggage and proceeded to leave the room.

Elizabeth shifted out of their way.

Unaware of her presence, her father continued packing. In a small valise, he placed personal items from his dresser: a comb, a shaving kit, a handful of pressed handkerchiefs. Just how long was he planning to stay in Florida?

He probably didn't know. His mission could take a day or quite possibly weeks. Elizabeth felt an undertow of yearning. She wanted to let go of the anger she felt toward both her parents. If only she could be sure her mother truly felt sorry for what she'd done to their family. If only she could comprehend her father's need to take this trip. If only. If only.

"If only," she whispered.

"Come in, daughter." Her father didn't look up from his task as he made the request. "And close the door behind you."

Elizabeth didn't move from her spot on the threshold.

There was unmistakable weariness in her father's voice. Her dread for his well-being was palpable. A second time in two days, she'd come to make amends and found herself unable to say the words. "Please, Father, I beg you to reconsider this trip."

He turned to face her, a patient look on his face. "You know why I have to go."

"She'll hurt you again." *And me. She'll hurt us both if we let her back into our hearts.*

"I promise you, Elizabeth, I will not allow your mother to return unless I'm confident she's truly repented of her actions."

He was already halfway to forgiveness, all because of a handful of carefully penned letters. They'd had this argument too many times for Elizabeth to think she could make him see reason at this point.

Still, she tried. "There is nothing I can say to change your mind?"

The question was the same one Luke had asked of her just last night. Like she had then, her father held firm now.

"My course is set."

His eyes glittered midnight blue, nearly black. He was a husband determined to restore his marriage with the woman he'd pledged to love until death do them part. Evidently, he took his wedding vows seriously. There was tremendous honor in that kind of devotion, stubbornness as well.

"I will always love your mother. But that's not the only reason I am making this trip now. I must—" He glanced around the room, then drew in a sharp breath and started again. "Even if I discover your mother hasn't changed, even if she doesn't ask me for my forgiveness, I must find a way to forgive her."

It humbled Elizabeth that her father was right.

Why did he have to be so . . . *good*?

Why did she have to be so . . . *unforgiving*? This insight into her nature was painful.

"I have to find a way to forgive her, Elizabeth. Or I will never be able to live with myself."

Marcus St. James had always been the obedient son, the caring, faithful husband, always doing the right thing, for all the right reasons.

Look how that turned out.

Elizabeth reached for the locket with a trembling hand, forced her breathing to calm. Twenty-five years from now, this could be her arguing with one of her children, struggling for a way to forgive her husband's betrayal. It was the very worst outcome but also a very real possibility when two people married for the sake of money and status.

Her thinking wasn't entirely rational, she knew. After all, she could end up marrying a good man, one full of integrity, who genuinely loved her, or at the very least liked her.

Then again, she might end up with a cold, hard-hearted man who cared about nothing other than his reputation among his peers.

There was yet another scenario. She could enter the marriage from a point of strength. She could go in with some experience behind her, a woman of substance, less obedient than her father. *And more . . . jaded?*

She was already more jaded, compliments of Katherine St. James. *How does this end?*

Her head grew dizzy, and the room began to swim before her eyes. She had an ally in this house, at least, someone with considerable influence in this family. Knowing her strategy was spectacularly unfair to her father, she let go of the necklace and pressed on, anyway. "You would defy Grandfather's wishes and allow Mother to come home?"

Hands frozen over the contents of his valise, her father was silent for several long seconds.

Then, snapping the case closed with a hard flick, he shot Elizabeth a fierce glare. "My decision is made."

Very well, Father, Elizabeth thought, *if this is what you want . . .*

For the duration of five heartbeats, there was no sound in the room but the shuffle of her father's feet as he moved toward the door.

"The hour is growing late," he said, drawing within a foot of her. "I don't want to miss my train."

His voice was unemotional as he spoke, but the pain in his eyes had Elizabeth holding her tongue. A sense of helplessness worked through her.

At a loss for words, she stepped aside. "Good-bye, Father."

Reaching up, he cupped her cheek. "Good-bye, my dear."

He entered the hallway and headed for the great staircase leading to the foyer below. Elizabeth couldn't let him leave angry. *Let not the sun go down upon your wrath.*

"Father, wait." His long strides outdistanced her nervous little trots. When she caught up with him, she willed herself to smile. "I love you."

"I love you, too." Dropping the valise, he opened his arms wide.

She leapt into them without hesitation, clinging to his shoulders as if she'd never see him again.

"We'll get through this, my dear." He whispered the words near her ear, stroking her hair as he had when she was a girl.

Throat constricting, Elizabeth swallowed a sob. She would not cry another tear because of her mother. She would find the strength to put the past behind her. She would find the courage to forgive the unforgivable.

One small step.

Straightening her shoulders, she dug deep inside her angry heart and found a small, tiny spark of courage to say, "Give Mother my regards."

* * *

Thirty minutes after her father left the house, Elizabeth was back in her room, studying the list. Other than wearing last season's gown, she'd accomplished only one additional task.

Two down, eighteen to go.

Time was running out.

There had to be something she could do today, maybe even two or three somethings.

Several tasks appealed to her, some of which she could accomplish on her own. Two of them, *Swing on a trapeze* and *Drive a motorcar*, required a bit of cleverness on her part. The circus was scheduled to arrive in two days. There had to be a way for Elizabeth to sneak into the tent before one of the performances, or perhaps after. She would come up with a plan later this afternoon.

Drive a motorcar.

She could do that anytime she wished. Her father had taken a hired coach to the train station. His motorcar was still in the carriage house, just sitting there all alone waiting for her. Once she managed to get the engine started, where would she go?

As Elizabeth contemplated her options, Sally entered the room.

Hiding the list behind her back, Elizabeth smiled at the maid. "Good morning, Sally."

"You wished for me to remind you of your dress-shopping appointment with your Aunt Tilly."

"That's today?"

Sally nodded.

The idea of being poked and pinned and prodded from multiple angles, then forced to parade in front of full-length mirrors held little appeal. New gowns could wait.

Decision made, she penned a quick note of regret, included a request to reschedule another shopping trip at her aunt's convenience, then handed the letter to Sally. "Please deliver this to my aunt right away."

The young woman hesitated before saying, "You want *me* to go?"

Surprised at the question, Elizabeth raised a brow, met the maid's eyes, and said, "I want to ensure she receives my regrets long before we are due to meet."

"Of course." Sally sighed. "I will leave straightaway."

One look at the downcast gaze made Elizabeth wonder at the maid's reluctance. "You don't wish to deliver the note."

As if searching for an answer, Sally slid a glance around the room, her gaze latching onto the window overlooking the street beyond.

"On the contrary, I look forward to indulging in a bit of fresh air." Still looking out the window, she pressed her lips tightly together. "Though I had better hurry if I wish to make the journey before the rain lets loose."

Rolling thunder punctuated her words.

Before the maid exited through the adjoining door, Elizabeth called her back. "Once your errand is complete, take the rest of the day off."

Sally eyed her a long moment. "I just had my half day on Sunday."

"At least take an hour and practice your piano."

Something close to pleasure entered the young woman's eyes. Not for the first time since Sally had entered her life, Elizabeth wondered what the maid was hiding.

What was her story?

Her work was excellent, and her devotion to her position with Elizabeth was without question. Yet there was something not quite altogether true about the picture she made in her crisp uniform. The stunning young maid had a regal bearing more suited for the upper classes. And her skill at the piano spoke of extensive training, something Elizabeth had discovered quite by accident.

"You have a lovely talent," she added by way of encouragement. "It would be a shame not to sharpen your ability."

"If that is what you wish."

"It is, yes."

Smiling ever so slightly, Sally turned to go.

Several minutes later, the sound of a rumbling engine had Elizabeth rushing to the window overlooking the street below her bedroom.

At the same moment Sally wove her way through traffic with the hood of her cloak pulled low over her face, Luke climbed out of a fancy silver motorcar. He immediately went to work securing a black oilcloth to steel rods, eventually pulling the thick tarpaulin up and over the seats, thereby providing a sufficient covering from the incoming rain.

What was Luke doing at St. James House?

Maybe he was here for Elizabeth. What a promising thought. Hidden inside the drapery, she watched him look to the east and smile.

Following the direction of his gaze, Elizabeth noted the rain clouds rolling in, turning the sky a dismal gray. Her fingers curled around the paper in her hand. The list. Of course.

Of course.

Glancing at her entries, she read one of the items aloud. "Walk in the rain, barefoot."

Oh, Luke.

Without thinking too hard about her actions, Elizabeth dashed out of her room and sped down the hallway. Moving at a fast pace that was as close to a run as possible without actually being a run—*Girls of fine breeding do not run*—she descended the winding stairs and entered the foyer.

Aldrich opened the front door, and Elizabeth drew to an abrupt stop. The skirts of her pale-green day dress whirled around her legs.

Luke stepped inside, caught sight of her, and smiled.

Her heart lifted and sighed. "Good morning, Luke."

He peered around Aldrich's stiff shoulders. "Good morning, Elizabeth."

Dividing a glance between them, the butler looked about to say something, evidently thought better of it, then left them alone after executing a curt head bob.

And then there were two.

Elizabeth searched for something witty to say. "It's good to see you."

"And you as well, Little Bit."

She was so pleased he'd come for her that she didn't mind the nickname. In truth, the way the words curled off his tongue gave her a pleasant little jolt.

Lowering his voice to a sultry tone that sent shivers over her skin, he leaned in close to her ear. "It's a nice day for a walk, wouldn't you agree?"

Her breath caught in her throat. He *had* come for her. "I believe there's a threat of rain."

The smile he gave her curled her toes. "I hoped you would notice."

This time, her heart didn't just sigh, it screamed, *Hallelujah*. Luke had really, truly come to take her for a walk in the rain.

The moment lost its charm when the sound of purposeful footsteps drew to a stop behind her. Clearly, she and Luke were no longer alone.

"Luke, my boy." Her grandfather's booming voice ricocheted off the marble flooring. "You caught me just leaving for the office. But now that you are here, I have something I'd like to run by you."

"But, Grandfather, he has come to—"

A flash of warning showed in Luke's gaze before he focused his full attention on her grandfather. "Well, then it's fortuitous I'm here."

"Not anymore," Elizabeth muttered under her breath.

Obviously hearing her, Luke shot another quick warning glance in her direction.

Oh, really. What did he think she would do? Jump into his arms and demand they conquer the seventh item on her list, *properly*, in front of her grandfather? As much as she would like to surprise both of these men with a bit of outrageous behavior, she wouldn't dare do anything to upset her grandfather. She couldn't bear the idea of losing his respect.

That, she realized, was part of the problem.

Elizabeth was obedient to the bone. She cared what others thought of her, especially these two men. Luke was still sending her covert warning looks, even as he spoke with her grandfather in a carefully modulated tone.

A part of her wanted to ruffle that sedate exterior, as much to shock him as to prove to herself that she could make him notice her, in a way a man noticed a woman.

With barely a word of good-bye, the two men left her staring after their retreating backs. They crossed the foyer and headed down the hallway toward the library.

Neither looked in her direction.

She caught a portion of their conversation, terms like *chassis*, *horsepower*, and *petrol-powered engines*. The same words Luke and Jackson had tossed around last evening at dinner.

Elizabeth had no idea why Luke was discussing motorcars with both Jackson and her grandfather. Something to do with a business venture, no doubt, but she would never know for certain, because she would not be asked to join the conversation.

"Some things never change," she said on a sigh. And they never would change if she didn't take matters into her own hands.

If not now, when?

Craning her neck, she waited until the men disappeared around the corner. She continued waiting until she heard the creak of a door opening and then the click of it shutting closed again. Only then did she make a face.

Luke had all but ignored her once her grandfather had arrived in the foyer. Elizabeth was completely, totally, almost certain the man had sought her out to go walking in the rain.

Now that the idea of accomplishing the task with him was in her head, she couldn't imagine ticking off that particular item alone, or with anyone else. But the opportunity was lost, at least for this morning.

That didn't mean she had to stand here wringing her hands.

She hurried back to her room. Ever since her father had left for the train station, she'd been feeling out of sorts.

I will always love your mother.

The words echoed in her head. Around and around they swirled, mocking her, challenging her. What sort of love looked past the unforgivable?

She knew, of course. Only a love powered by the Holy Spirit could accomplish that level of selflessness.

Though she desperately wanted someone special in her life, Elizabeth feared she wasn't capable of that kind of unconditional devotion. She feared she had her mother's selfish heart. Only when she was tested would she know for certain.

The realization was a blow to her very core. Enough thinking. She'd spent far too much time in her head for far too long. Time to take action.

Throwing open her closet doors, she considered her clothing. Though she didn't know what task she planned to accomplish, she knew she would need to wear a dress that would not draw attention.

A dark color would work best, the kind usually reserved for mourning. Appropriate, she thought, as she donned a dark-purple, rather boring gown. With each task she completed, she would shed another piece of the old Elizabeth and make way for the new.

After lacing up her black ankle boots, she grabbed Hester's shawl. With the garment draped over her shoulders, she reviewed her list. Luke had indicated he'd come to take her walking in the rain. Well, not really, but she was going forward with that assumption.

Now that he was on board with her plan—surely, he was on board—she would attempt one of the tasks that didn't require a partner.

Unless she waited for him to finish speaking with her grandfather . . .

Her eyes latched onto *Kiss a man properly under the moon and stars.* Elizabeth was relatively confident a kiss would be just as romantic in the rain. All it would take was a little patience and some quick thinking. Or . . .

Why not steal Luke away for the entire day? They could take in a vaudeville show. Though Luke hated the opera—they had that in common—he enjoyed the theater. They had *that* in common, as well.

Oh, how she longed to discover what other likes and dislikes they shared. If she could convince him to spend the day with her . . .

No, she couldn't.

Could she?

Maybe. Possibly.

No.

Luke was a man of business. He had commitments, employees under his care. People counted on him. Once he left St. James House, he would head to his office and get to work.

Bottom lip caught between her teeth, Elizabeth studied the remaining items not yet crossed out, all eighteen of them. Eighteen! A staggering number.

Her eyes landed on number seven again.

When I kiss you properly, Elizabeth, you will know.

As the unveiled promise slid through her mind, her heart did a little jig. Stupid, stupid heart.

Frustrating, frustrating man.

How could Luke say something so provocative and then lecture her on the dangers of rule-breaking?

Elizabeth would very much like to show him . . .

Her eyes landed on the center of the page. *Drive a motorcar.* "How hard could it be?"

Ten minutes later, sitting in her father's two-seater Oldsmobile, Elizabeth had her answer. Driving a motorcar was impossible without the proper training, something which Elizabeth did not possess.

What a dismal beginning. She couldn't even start the engine. Frustrated but not defeated, she exited the car and, hands on hips, stared at the seemingly innocuous machine. Last night, Luke had told Jackson, *Motorcars are the future.*

Elizabeth stomped her foot in frustration. She knew the gesture was childish but found she couldn't help herself. She wanted to be a part of the future, not stuck in the past. Yet, here she was, held back by lack of knowledge. A machine would not get the best of her.

With a soft whoosh of air, she put her back to the offensive vehicle, wrapped her arms around herself, and looked up at the sky. The earthy scent on the air and the pale, swiftly moving clouds promised a pleasant spring shower.

Could she?

Dare she?

The sound of motorcars passing by on the street ridiculed Elizabeth, highlighting her failure to start the engine of her father's Oldsmobile. At this rate, she would be setting sail for England with less than half her list complete. Unacceptable.

She approached Luke's silver motorcar.

One small step.

One tiny rebellion.

Not nearly good enough.

Elizabeth was through being tentative. The time had come for one large, bold step.

Luke would certainly be surprised and would probably return her to St. James House once he discovered what she had planned.

But maybe, just maybe . . .

She approached the car, looked over her shoulder, and listened for the sound of footsteps. It was nearly impossible to hear anything over the raging of her pulse in her ears.

With as much grace as possible, which was to say very little, Elizabeth crawled into the backseat, clicking the door shut behind her. She wiggled onto the floor, knees pulled up and wrapped inside her arms. Not enough covering. She pulled Hester's shawl over her head and allowed the resulting darkness to embrace her.

The toe of her boot dug into something soft. A blanket. She threw that over her head as well, grateful for the additional covering.

Willing away her nerves, Elizabeth strained to hear something, anything. There was a drumming in her heart, an anticipation that had been building for weeks.

Not more than five minutes later, the sound of familiar male voices flowed over her.

"I'll say one thing. You know your engines, Luke, my boy. I'm impressed with your vast knowledge and expertise. I predict a lucrative venture for us both."

A low chuckle followed. "I look forward to working with you, Richard."

Elizabeth shifted, lifting the very edge of the blanket for a better look.

The sun chose that moment to peek out from the clouds, shining over both men. But it was Luke who captured Elizabeth's attention. The thin ray of light illuminated his hair, turning it a million shades of gold. He really was a handsome man. The straight, perfectly proportioned nose; the square jaw; and the cheekbones that could have been sculpted out of marble all spoke of his excellent breeding.

He would father beautiful children. She could see their blond curls, their beautiful tawny eyes. Elizabeth took a deep breath, tried to make herself as small as possible, and prayed she wouldn't be discovered until she and Luke were away.

Even though she was watching him closely, she felt rather than saw a subtle change in him. His shoulders shifted, flexed, and then went still again.

She'd been found out.

Elizabeth took a quick, steadying breath and prepared for the worst. Closing her eyes, she waited for the inevitable revelation, followed by the dreaded reprimand.

Nothing happened.

The men continued speaking as if neither had seen her.

Could she be so fortunate? She dropped the edge of the blanket and forced her breathing to slow down.

Their conversation had shifted sometime during Elizabeth's quiet moment of panic. They were now discussing the private performance early next month at the opera house connected to Luke's childhood home.

"Will I see you there?" Luke asked her grandfather.

"I'm afraid I have another engagement. I trust you'll be there."

Luke cleared his throat. "Of course."

He sounded . . . troubled, more than the situation warranted, even for a man who disliked opera. Though Elizabeth would prefer to skip the performance, she was glad she'd accepted the invitation. She sensed Luke would appreciate an ally.

The engine roared to life, pushing the thought out of her mind. Elizabeth's heartbeat caught the rhythm of the purring motor, and her fear of discovery disappeared as Luke put the car in gear.

From her vantage point on the floor, and with the stingy light of the darkening sky, Elizabeth could barely make out the back of Luke's head. They bounced along the road, hitting a few too many bumps for her liking.

For a brief moment, she considered revealing her presence. But they were still too close to St. James House. Luke could easily turn around and deposit her on the very spot where this adventure had begun.

She held silent.

They hit another bump, and then another, and then one more, each hard jolt jarring Elizabeth's body and rattling her teeth. She prayed the road would smooth out soon. Perhaps if she made herself smaller, the bumps wouldn't hurt quite so much.

Tucking her knees up under her chin, she shut her eyes and proceeded to do complicated math problems in her head.

Fifty-two times twelve equals six hundred and twenty-four.

Bump.

Elizabeth's chin slammed against her knees, sending the trail of numbers straight out of her head. If she didn't know better, she'd suspect Luke was intentionally driving over every pothole in Manhattan.

Bump.

Bump. Bump.

Grinding her teeth together, she continued concentrating on mathematics. *Seventy-eight divided by six equals—*

Bump, bump, bump.

Oh, for crying out loud. That last one had to be the size of a small canyon. They hit another, even larger bump. She had to cover her mouth with her hand to keep her yelp from spilling out.

"Had enough?" The calm, amused voice cut through the roar of the engine.

Tossing aside the blanket and Hester's shawl, Elizabeth smoothed a hand over her hair, stretched out her legs, then pulled herself up to the seat. "You, Lucian Griffin, are a very bad, mean, mean man."

Chapter Sixteen

Holding back a chuckle, Luke slowed the motorcar and, seeing that they were alone on the road, glanced at Elizabeth over his shoulder.

She glowered back.

Well, all right, then.

He rearranged his face in a look of mock horror, putting some real effort into the task. "I might be mean, but you, Little Bit, are a menace to any rational man's sanity."

Her glower deepened.

There was nothing compliant or obedient about her now. She was stunning in her indignation, her eyes a dove gray in the pale, weak light. No, blue gray. They seemed to change color even as he watched her, the irises darkening with emotion.

What passion. Staring at that beautiful, dramatic face, Luke felt the stirrings of male interest, a sort of yearning, the kind he'd never felt for a woman.

He whipped his attention back to the road. He had no right thinking of her as anything but his Little Bit.

After hitting every pothole in the street, he had anticipated some level of irritation on Elizabeth's part. What he had not expected was his reaction to her outrage. Her face was transformed, and he felt as though he was looking at Elizabeth yet someone else entirely.

The soft glow of her skin and the fullness of her lips belonged to a different woman, one who knew what she wanted out of life and was determined to get it, with or without his help.

Hard not to admire that level of commitment to a goal.

Luke had a moment of clarity. Elizabeth didn't need to go on any quest to become a woman of substance. She already *was* one. She simply didn't know it yet.

There was no joy in the knowledge, no triumph. Because if Luke recognized her unique appeal, so would other men.

After leaving Bertie and company, Luke had decided to approach Elizabeth again about her list. No, that was a lie. He'd come looking for her because he'd needed her purity, her goodness.

You, Lucian Griffin, are a very bad, mean, mean man.

Elizabeth had no idea how accurately she'd summed up his nature. Abruptly, he laughed.

"I'm glad one of us finds this situation amusing."

He didn't find any of this funny. When other men discovered what Luke already knew, there would be a mad dash for Elizabeth's attention. As if to put a fine point on the thought, the temperature dropped several degrees. The cold air swept over him like a menacing breath.

"Where are we going?" she asked, her voice a study in peevishness.

He could tell her he'd gone to St. James House to steal her away for the day. He could tell her his original plan had been to take her out to the country, where they could walk in the impending shower without being seen. He could also tell her that stowing away in his backseat had been unnecessary.

But it was a matter of principle he not make the next few minutes easy for her. "You'll have to wait and see."

A rustle of material accompanied her sniff of irritation. "Take me home."

"And waste all your efforts?" He swerved to the right, this time missing the crater in the pocked street. Out of the corner of his eye, he noticed how the sudden movement threw her off balance.

"You did that on purpose."

Taking satisfaction in her surly tone, he blessed her with a brief sidelong glance. "I'm thinking this little adventure of yours isn't going the way you planned."

A roll of distant thunder punctuated his remark.

"I didn't have a plan."

The sound he made was half laugh, half hiss. "Why doesn't that surprise me?"

"It was more a guideline."

His grip tightened on the wheel. "A . . . guideline."

"One I am regretting with each passing moment."

It was about time the reckless woman started thinking rationally.

"You can let me off at the next street corner. I'll make my way home on foot."

"I'm afraid I can't do that."

"Why not?"

"Gentlemen do not allow ladies of their acquaintance to make their way home alone, on foot or otherwise."

"Oh, honestly, you allowed me to do so the other morning."

He hadn't done any such thing. But with the dark mood she was currently nursing, Luke decided no good would come from correcting her misconception on that score.

"Luke, this is 1901. We are living in a brand-new century where possibilities abound." She set her elbows on the back of his seat and leaned forward, a piece of her hair tickling his cheek. "Women can do all sorts of things alone."

Another low chuckle reverberated from deep within his chest. "Including stowing away in an unattached man's motorcar?"

"Well, yes."

They rolled along in silence for several seconds. The Brooklyn Bridge loomed large and sturdy in the distance. Luke had half a mind to do as Elizabeth requested and return her to the safety of St. James House.

In for a penny, in for a pound. "I assume stowing away in my motorcar is one of the items on your loathsome list."

She sighed dramatically. "I should have known you would be rude and sanctimonious."

"Actually, I'm being patronizing. And you didn't answer my question."

"No, Luke, stowing away in your motorcar is not on my list." She sniffed indelicately. "Such ego."

He felt his lips twitch. The woman certainly had cheek. He'd give her that. He counted to five, then glanced at her over his shoulder. "You still haven't explained why you were hiding in my motorcar."

"My current presence in your motorcar is a means to an end, a way to forward my plan that wasn't really a plan, as you oh-so-helpfully pointed out." She paused to take a breath. "I had hoped to mark number ten off my list."

"What is number ten, precisely?"

She pasted a winning smile on her face. "Drive a motorcar."

"Your father and grandfather own motorcars."

"There you go again, being oh-so-helpful."

Ignoring the sassy remark, he veered the car to the far right side of the road, pulled to a stop, and turned a questioning look on the woman in his backseat.

Back ramrod straight, she took her time smoothing her skirts around her. "If you must know—"

"I must."

Her gaze narrowed.

He waited.

"If you must know," she began again, "I couldn't figure out how to start the stupid engine of my father's Oldsmobile. And, so"—she lifted her hands helplessly in the air—"here I am."

Luke had been right. Elizabeth St. James was a menace, a danger to herself and the rest of New York City.

Okay, the latter might be a slight exaggeration.

"Let me see if I understand the sequence of events. You decided to drive a motorcar, a simple enough task on your list, seeing as you have access to not one but two stellar machines. But, apparently, *simple* isn't in your vocabulary."

"You don't have to be snide."

He continued as if she hadn't spoken. "When you couldn't figure out how to start the engine, instead of asking your grandfather's chauffeur for advice, you stowed away in my motorcar."

The eyes that met his were a stormy blue. "While I'll admit you make a valid point—"

He lifted an eyebrow.

"*Several* valid points," she amended, sighing dramatically. "I'm on a deadline, Luke. Time is running out."

"You still plan to go to England and marry a Brit?" Emotion scraped the words raw.

"Yes."

If she'd slapped him in the face, he wouldn't have been more surprised. He scooped a hand through his hair, ignoring the big, gaping pit that now sat where his stomach used to be.

"I set sail for England in just over six weeks," she added for emphasis. "And I've only accomplished two items on my list."

"That's two more than last week."

She swallowed, glanced away, then boldly looked back at him. "Will you help me tackle the rest?"

The plea in her big, fathomless eyes cut him to the core. Needing a moment, he glanced up at the sky. The sun hid behind dull gray clouds, creating a gloomy feel to the air, a perfect match for his mood.

He adjusted his shoulders as if taking on a weight. Then, shifting slightly, he reached over the seat and took her hand, linking their fingers together. "If I agree to help you, you have to give me a say over the items on your list. I insist upon it."

The eyes that met his were narrowed to tiny slits, blue lightning to match the thunder outside. "Coming to you was a bad idea. I won't trouble you with this again." Yanking back her hand, she reached for the door handle.

"Elizabeth, wait."

Her hand dropped away from the latch, and she slowly, almost reluctantly turned back to face him.

"Don't look so tragic, and listen to me. No sighing, no interrupting, just let me have my say."

After a brief hesitation, she nodded.

His eyes slid past her, brushed over the hood of the motorcar, then slid back to her face. And then Luke said the three words that would change both their lives forever. "I'll do it."

"Do what? I need you to be more specific."

Give the woman an inch . . .

"I'll assist you with the tasks on your list."

"You . . ." She puffed out her cheeks, released the air. "Oh, Luke, you truly mean it?"

If it meant having this woman look at him like *that*, he would attempt to move the moon and stars with his bare hands. "I do."

"Thank you."

The pleasure in her gaze was his undoing. He suddenly, desperately, wanted to share one of his greatest passions with her, and so he said, "Want to learn how to drive a motorcar?"

"Yes. Oh, yes." Her face lit from within, and her smile was the same one she'd given him after their brief kiss. The one that had hardly been a kiss and yet had left him reeling.

His heart lurched in his chest.

This is a bad idea.

"One lesson. But not in Manhattan, somewhere out in the country."

"I'll take what I can get."

"Come sit in the front with me." He patted the empty seat beside him.

With ingrained dignity, she exited out on the street, secured her pretty red shawl around her shoulders, then reentered the motorcar a second later, settling on the exact spot he'd indicated.

The interior immediately shrank, the extra space crowded out by her very presence. Her scent hit him like a punch to the gut, and there it was again, the whirlpool of feelings and emotions sweeping away all common sense.

He examined every angle of her face, her smiling mouth, her beautiful eyes, then quickly looked away and focused on getting them out of Manhattan. After releasing the brake, he worked the foot pedals, moved the hand controls into the proper positions, and then pulled away from the curb.

"Here we go." Elizabeth's voice held nothing but excitement at the prospect of learning how to drive his motorcar.

Luke felt nothing but dread.

* * *

In her shadowed side of the front seat, Elizabeth battled a very real desire to gloat. At last. At last! Luke had agreed to join her on her quest. She hid a smile of triumph behind her hand.

Luke's stony silence disturbed her not one bit.

Clutching the shawl around her shoulders—*Oh, Hester, I wish you were here*—Elizabeth watched the scenery roll past. Large private homes soon gave way to multistory buildings that housed businesses.

Glancing from left to right, right to left, she was aware of every sight, sound, and smell with a clarity of sensation that had her breath coming in snatches.

She was especially conscious of the man beside her. The way he worked the controls, with such precision and skill, made her stomach pitch. Luke had a quiet, confident edge that made Elizabeth feel all twitchy inside.

They were halfway across the Brooklyn Bridge when she decided she'd left him to his silence long enough. "How much longer before I get to drive?"

"Soon."

She didn't especially like that answer.

"Is it difficult?"

"At first."

Wasn't he a plethora of information?

As if hearing her thoughts, he flicked a glance in her direction. "It gets easier with time and practice."

Glancing up to the sky, she noted that the clouds were darker now, fat and swollen, poised for their watery attack. A little hum worked its way past her lips. "I would think driving a motorcar is harder in the rain."

"You would be right."

The first droplets hit the windshield. More followed.

Well, drat. She closed her eyes momentarily, listening to the patter of raindrops on the tarpaulin overhead. She breathed in deep, drew in the scent of rain and petrol and Luke.

"We'll have to hold off on your lesson," he said, turning the motorcar onto a dirt road. He steered them under a large shade tree and cut the engine. "We'll wait out the rain here."

She nodded, forced a smile to hide her disappointment. This didn't have to be a bad thing. There were other items on her list. Outside the rain pattered on, and . . .

Her disappointment instantly vanished. She swiveled her head. Her gaze met Luke's. "I have a sudden passion to take off my shoes."

He laughed, a quick, pleasant sound that filled the interior of the motorcar. "Ah, my dear, sweet Elizabeth. There is no one quite like you."

"Is that a good thing?"

Eyes twinkling with humor, he leaned toward her, lowering his voice to a near whisper. "A very good thing."

Oh, my. She shook off a delicious shiver and stared into his mesmerizing eyes.

A blanket of silence enveloped them, fractured only by the sound of raindrops hitting the makeshift roof. Despite the chill in the air, a feeling of warmth stole over her.

"Let's get to it," he suggested, looking pointedly at her feet, then getting to work on his own shoes.

I'm really going to do this. It occurred to her that this was to be a real adventure. The first time she'd ever done anything just for herself. She couldn't think of anyone she'd rather share the moment with than Luke.

At his suggestion, she removed her gloves and shawl as well. "You'll want them dry when we're back in the car."

"I hadn't thought of that."

Finishing before she did, he spared her one last glance before exiting his side of the motorcar. Too impatient to wait for him to open the door for her, she scrambled onto the grass and met him five seconds later near the tree trunk.

He took her hand and, in silent agreement, they stepped out from beneath the leafy canopy, heading into an empty field. The rain was a slow, steady stream falling from the sky, cool on her skin but not unpleasant. Elizabeth had never felt more glorious, more aware of every sight and sound. A million wildflowers blanketed the field, a kaleido-scope of color against a carpet of green.

They walked in silence, hand in hand. Wet grass tickled between her toes. She laughed. Emotion was gathering inside her, something she recognized as happiness. The rain slowly let off, turning into a misty drizzle.

Luke stopped walking and shifted in front of her.

Through the gray haze of rain, their eyes met with a force that nearly flattened her. A thousand words passed between them without a sound.

Shivering slightly, Elizabeth dragged the dripping hair out of her face. Too many feelings tugged and tangled inside her. She felt jittery inside and alive, so alive it hurt. She closed her eyes, tipped her head back, and let the rain trickle down her face.

"Elizabeth." Luke's voice was low and gravelly and full of something she'd never heard in it before, something solely for her. "Look at me."

She did as he requested. He'd collected silver points of rain every-where, on his hair, his shoulders, his eyelashes.

His hand came up and cupped the back of her head, drawing her closer. Just a little bit closer.

"Are we about to cross a line?" she asked.

"Look behind you, Elizabeth. We already have."

He was going to kiss her.

His eyes locked with hers.

Her hands went to his shoulders.

For a moment, his mask fell and emotion showed through the misty droplets of rain, so clear, so real, something she understood on an elemental level. Gaze locked with his, she didn't have to search long to see her own tender feelings mirrored in Luke's expression.

This man, she wanted *this* man, not an English lord, not a man chosen by her father and grandfather, no one but Luke. And maybe, finally, he was beginning to see her as more than his Little Bit.

His head moved toward hers, obvious intent in his eyes, then paused. "I'm trying to do right, to be honorable."

Tomorrow he could have honor. Today, she wanted him to be hers, with no conditions or concerns for the future, just the here and now. Just one glorious moment that she could keep with her for eternity.

Feeling unusually bold, she pulled him closer to her, until her hands were clasped behind his neck. She could feel the shift in his breathing, the tension that would have been undetectable were she not so close.

His eyes darkened. Something not altogether tame flashed in their depths.

The world faded away, and there was nothing but the two of them, in the middle of a rain-drenched field, scandalously barefoot, Luke's golden gaze on her face, his masculine warmth chasing away the cold.

She whispered his name, so soft even she wasn't sure she'd spoken.

His lips came down on hers.

The kiss was unhurried at first, slow and tender. Then it changed, becoming a bit more desperate. Elizabeth's knees threatened to give way. She nestled deeper into Luke's embrace, as if she'd been waiting for this moment all her life, as if she'd been waiting for *him* all her life.

Not too far from the truth.

A sigh worked its way up from the bottom of her toes and stalled in her throat. It was a golden, perfect moment she never wanted to end.

But then his head raised, just enough that their lips were no longer touching and their eyes could meet. What she saw in his glittering gaze stole her breath.

She started to speak. His mouth closed back over hers.

Her breathing accelerated, feeling after feeling crashed over her; this was where she belonged, in Luke's arms.

A clap of thunder had him pulling abruptly away.

She opened her eyes and then wished she hadn't. Luke looked at her, horrified, a man who'd come to his senses.

Self-preservation forced her to turn her eyes from the sight of his obvious self-reproach. She stood blinking and trembling as reality erupted in her heart.

"Little Bit—"

"Don't call me that."

His jaw steeled. "I meant it affectionately. You'll always be my Little Bit."

"I know." Which only made the situation a thousand times worse.

"I'm sorry, Elizabeth." He swept the back of his hand across his forehead. "I should never have kissed you."

He sounded so remorseful, so sincere in his contrition, and that was the most humiliating part of all.

"Please, Luke, don't apologize." Anything but that. "It will only make this moment more uncomfortable for us both."

Glancing away, he took an unsteady breath, shook water out of his eyes. "I care about you, Elizabeth."

"I know."

"You're special to me. Never would I set out to hurt you."

And yet, he already had. *"I know."*

Oh, wonderful. She was beginning to sound like a talking bird.

A jumble of emotions battered her composure. She squeezed her eyes shut and forced her unsteady legs to hold her upright.

"I wish to go home now." She pressed her fingertips to her temples. "My head is beginning to pound."

Long seconds passed before he nodded. Taking her hand, he escorted her across the open field in complete silence. What a disaster.

Inside the motorcar, Luke handed her the blanket. "To keep you from getting cold."

"Thank you."

The ride back to the city was accomplished in silence. There was no more talk of driving a motorcar. The rain had stopped, leaving a cold, wet mist in its wake.

Huddled in the warmth of the blanket, Elizabeth glanced at her reflection in the glass windshield. The woman staring back at her looked small and tormented. The day had turned out so very differently than she'd planned. A bad time for doubt, but she couldn't help herself.

She sat in the murky light of the aftermath of her failure, wondering how something so wonderful had taken such a terrible turn. Her face burned. She wanted to disappear, to evaporate like the water on the windshield.

But the lure of freedom beckoned, and she thought, *No, a minor setback will not keep me from pursuing my quest for adventure.*

One sticking point with that: this particular setback didn't feel minor. It felt very, very major. And utterly confusing. Luke had been fully engaged in their kiss. The overall experience had been really quite wonderful, life altering.

Up until the moment he'd shoved away from her.

Head cocked, Elizabeth glanced over at the man.

Oh, Luke.

Guilt rolled off him in waves, and that gave her pause. Luke was overprotective by nature. How many times had she watched him rescue Penelope from all sorts of disasters, real and perceived? Elizabeth had no doubt he would die before he hurt a woman.

Oh, Luke.

What a man he was. Tall, honorable, with shoulders broad enough for a woman to set her cares upon, if only temporarily, and know he would move the earth, moon, and stars to rectify the problem, even if he was the cause.

Oh, Luke.

In that moment, Elizabeth fell a little in love with him.

She whispered his name, tentative at first, then bolder when he didn't respond. "I have a question for you."

Fisting his hands tightly on the steering wheel, he gave her one curt nod.

"Was that a proper kiss?"

He sucked in a hard breath. And then something miraculous happened. His lips curved in a tilted smile that would have dropped her to her knees had she not been sitting. "Yes, Elizabeth, that was a proper kiss."

"I knew it."

Chapter Seventeen

Sneaking into St. James House in the middle of broad daylight turned out to be far easier than Elizabeth had imagined. Even wet and bedraggled from her walk in the rain, she managed to slip through the halls and corridors without crossing paths with a single person.

Of course, at this time of day, the servants were hard at work.

Elizabeth made a promise to herself. She would thank each of them for playing a crucial role in the household. Not now but later, when she was in dry clothing and her hair was no longer a tangle of unruly wet curls.

Entering her room, she made another promise to herself as she padded across the ornamental rugs to her dressing chamber. Before the month was through, no matter what the future held, Elizabeth would complete her list. And she would do so without anybody's help.

She would fail or succeed on her own.

Every mistake and misstep would be hers, alone.

If she did something to throw her reputation into question, she would drag no one else into the ensuing scandal with her. Not her family, not her friends, and definitely not Luke. She loved him too much to—

Her hand flew to her mouth. Love?

She loved Luke?

Of course she loved him.

It had always been Luke, even when it hadn't, even when her mother had promised Elizabeth to another man.

Initially her feelings had been based on childish adoration, a young girl longing for an older boy to notice her. Her feelings had matured over time, and Elizabeth had grown to care for Luke with the desperate passion of a teen emerging out of childhood, caught in her first throes of infatuation.

Now, she loved him as a woman loved a man, with her whole heart and soul.

"I love him." Speaking the words out loud made them so much more real. Elizabeth would forever remember this moment. The moment when she decided to stay in America and win Luke's heart.

She felt weak and strong at once, fearful and daring.

The door swung open, and Sally entered the dressing chamber. There was a beat of silence as the maid took in Elizabeth's disheveled appearance.

"I got caught in the rain," she defended.

Sally's eyes skimmed past her face, brushed over her wet clothing, then slid up to her hair. The young woman repeated the process, this time pausing at Elizabeth's bare feet. "Where are your shoes?"

"I left them in—" *Luke's motorcar.* She stopped just short of incriminating herself. "I left them . . . behind."

She did not explain further.

The maid's expression turned troubled, betraying an emotion Elizabeth couldn't decipher. Something about that look sliced through the fabric of her composure. "You have something to say."

"Let's get you out of these wet clothes, before you catch your death."

Elizabeth felt the echo of a smile play across her lips. That hadn't been what Sally meant to say. She let it go because the soggy, wet brocade weighed three times more now than it ever did dry.

By the time she was sitting at her dressing table in a fresh dress, with Sally attacking the tangles in her hair with a brush, the clouds had scattered completely. Ribbons of sunlight coaxed their way through the beveled windowpanes, creating a medley of flickering shadows in the room.

"How did Aunt Tilly receive the news I was skipping out on our shopping excursion?"

"She seemed a bit miffed, but not overly so." Gently working on a particularly stubborn knot, Sally hitched her chin toward Elizabeth's writing desk. "I set her response with the other letters that came for you while you were out this morning."

Letters. How Elizabeth had grown to hate them. Dread settled heavy and cold in her belly. Had her mother written her?

Desperate for a distraction, she captured Sally's gaze in the mirror. The young woman looked quickly away.

"I can't help thinking you have something you wish to say to me, something about my outing."

Sally's eyes went wide and uncertain before a blank expression covered her features. "Nothing comes to mind."

"I believe that's the first time you've ever openly lied to me."

The maid's hand froze, the brush still tangled in Elizabeth's hair as her mouth dropped open.

Taking advantage of Sally's momentary shock, Elizabeth continued. "I don't understand your reticence. You've been free with your opinions in the past, and have offered very good advice on several occasions."

Color drained from the young woman's face. "I would never presume to tell you what to do."

"Of course you wouldn't." Elizabeth offered a smile she hoped would alleviate the maid's anxiety. "Please, Sally, I would very much like to hear what's on your mind."

A wisp of a sigh slipped out of the other woman.

"Please."

"I was in the music room when you arrived home." Sally showed grave interest in the hairbrush. "I saw you climb out of Mr. Griffin's motorcar."

A burning throb knotted in Elizabeth's throat. "Did anyone else see?"

"I don't believe so, no."

Something in her voice put Elizabeth on guard, that and the way the maid refused to meet her eyes. "You don't approve."

Sally's nervous gaze continued chasing around the room, landing everywhere but on Elizabeth. "It is not my place to approve or disapprove."

No, it wasn't. But Elizabeth considered the woman a friend, perhaps her closest in recent months now that Penelope was spending more time with her fiancé. Sally's reticence to give her opinion didn't make any sense. "Luke is a good man."

"They all are, at first." The air around the maid crackled with unveiled resentment.

"Did a man hurt you, Sally?"

The maid cast Elizabeth a grim, pained look. "When a woman falls in love, she goes quiet and small. She sacrifices everything, only to lose herself in the process."

No, that couldn't be true. Elizabeth refused to believe that. She could think of one example that proved Sally wrong. "Caroline hasn't lost herself, quite the opposite. Loving Jackson has enriched her life."

Sally acknowledged this with a half smile. "Caroline is the exception. For the rest of us, love is nothing but an invitation to pain."

"Oh, Sally." Elizabeth quickly gained her feet and took the maid's hands in hers. "Whoever he was, he didn't deserve you."

Tears pooled in the other woman's eyes. "Tread carefully, Elizabeth. When it comes to a man, decisions made quickly are regretted for a lifetime."

Here was more advice on regret. Everyone seemed to have an opinion on what she should and should not do. Was this to be the theme of her life? Was she to receive warnings at every turn?

"We can't always trust the heart to lead us in the most suitable directions." Sally's face took on a grim expression as she tugged her hands free. "The heart lies."

The maid bent to pick up the pile of wet clothes. Hester's shawl was as wet as all the other garments. Perhaps it was even ruined. Elizabeth would find a way to restore the silk to its former glory. Even if she couldn't, she would not regret taking the shawl with her today. It had been a really good day.

She made a soft, satisfied sound deep in her throat.

"I'll leave you to read your letters in peace," Sally said as she made her way to the door.

Elizabeth waited until the maid left the room to retrieve the list she'd tucked inside the pages of her Bible. Sally had warned her that the heart couldn't be trusted. She claimed the heart lied. Elizabeth didn't believe that.

Her feelings for Luke were real and true and based on something bigger than herself, something beyond what she'd ever experienced before.

She glanced down at the Bible, opened to Paul's letter to the Romans.

Let love be without dissimulation. Abhor that which is evil; cleave to that which is good.

As she let the words sink in, Elizabeth had an epiphany.

God was love. The Lord was her example. Everything she did must be based in love. At her writing desk, she shoved aside the stack of letters and dipped her pen in the inkpot.

Bottom lip caught between her teeth, she crossed out several items that simply weren't important anymore and added two new tasks that would change how she approached life forever.

Love without reservation.
Live every day to the fullest.

* * *

Luke drove away from St. James House almost immediately after seeing Elizabeth tucked safely inside the house. He was three blocks gone when he noticed she'd left her shoes sitting on the floorboard of his motorcar.

At the sight of the tiny, female footwear, he realized five fundamental truths at once. First . . .

He'd kissed Elizabeth—*properly*—in the cold, drizzling rain. Instead of returning her to her home—which, now that he had time to think about it, would have been the honorable thing to do—he'd taken the very pure, entirely too innocent girl out of the city to an open field in the country, never once caring about the consequences.

And that brought him to the second fundamental truth.

If he found himself in a similar situation sometime in the near or distant future, he would repeat the experience moment for moment. He would kiss Elizabeth again, without hesitation.

And that brought him to a third fundamental truth.

He had no regrets. None. Not one. Absolutely zero.

And that brought him to number four in the chain of fundamental truths.

Luke was, indeed, as Elizabeth maintained, a very bad, mean, mean man.

And *that* brought him to the fifth, most fundamental of the fundamental truths.

He would end up hurting her, eventually.

Elizabeth was everything he had never been—good and kind and full of hope. She made him want to be the man he saw in her eyes. But the six months he'd spent in Bertie's company was as much a part of

Luke as his education and family name. His past could never be erased. The pain he'd inflicted could never be taken back.

The best way to protect Elizabeth was to let her go. Even if that meant spending the rest of his life plagued with what might have been.

Arriving at his destination, Luke steered the motorcar to the curb. He kept his hands on the steering wheel and took in Griffin Manor from his vantage point. Even if rehearsal had gone long, his father would have left hours ago. Penny would be enjoying luncheon with her fiancé.

That left Luke's mother, the woman he'd come to see.

After yanking off his driving gloves, he rubbed both hands over his face. The calm he sought drifted just out of reach.

Another fundamental truth materialized.

Luke was better for knowing Elizabeth. At another time, as another man, he would have already begun courting her in earnest.

The image of her dreamy blue eyes flashed in his mind. No woman had ever looked at him that way, as if she believed he was goodness itself, as if he were a man worth believing in. For an instant, with her wrapped in his arms, Luke had allowed himself to imagine he could be that man.

A flood of remorse coursed through him, for what he'd done and his inability to change the past. Knowing it was for the best, Luke would openly encourage Elizabeth to travel to England with her aunt Tilly. He trusted the older woman without reservation and knew Elizabeth would be in good hands.

The thought brought no comfort, only sadness, a dismal mood in which to go in search of his mother. He found her in the greenhouse, her hands deep in dirt, surrounded by muggy hot air and colorful flowers of numerous varieties. As an expert painter might wield his brush, Violet Griffin brandished a gardening trowel, her creations true works of art.

Even in her gardening clothes, she held herself with dignity, the wife of a powerful business titan. Violet was tall and lithe, and her face showed the signs of continued exposure to the sun. Her once caramel-colored hair now held thin streaks of gray.

The love he felt for this woman was real and complicated, sullied by the secrets no child should know about his parents.

"Good afternoon, Mother."

She turned at the greeting, a smile on her lips. "Lucian." Her eyes swept over him. "You got caught in the rain."

He laughed, the sound ragged in the silence of the greenhouse. "I took my motorcar for a drive."

"You and your motorcar." Her brow furrowed just barely as she set down the trowel. Picking up a rag, she wiped the dirt off her palms. "Your father told me you have plans to start an automobile company."

"You spoke about me with Father?"

She tossed the rag atop the trowel without taking her eyes off Luke's face. "We discuss both you and your sister nearly every night at dinner."

"I didn't realize you still"—he paused, thought best how to continue—"dined together."

His words were greeted with blank bewilderment, followed by a look of dawning comprehension. "Of course we dine together, nearly every evening. We are married. It is what a husband and wife do."

It was Luke's turn to stare in bafflement. He had no reply to this, none whatsoever. He'd always assumed his parents were estranged—how could they not be?—and lived separate yet parallel lives.

His mother patted his arm. "I see I have shocked you."

"I am"—he cocked his head, attempting to process what he'd just heard—"puzzled."

"Ah." She stepped toward the door, paused when she drew alongside him. "Now that the rain has stopped, I would like to investigate my rose bushes. Won't you join me, son?"

Stepping onto the gravel path outside the glasshouse, Luke walked quietly beside his mother. Their progress down the walk was slow, due primarily to the fact that his mother stopped every three or four steps to examine one of her flower bushes. She favored cheerful, varied plants.

The sky was bright now that the clouds had vanished, and a family of bees was hard at work in the sweet-smelling blossoms lining the pathway.

"Is it safe to say you are put off by marriage because of the example you have been given in this home?"

Luke was surprised by the blunt question. "I am not averse to marriage." *In theory.* "But it would take finding the right girl to entice me to take the plunge."

You've already found her.

He resisted the thought. If he hurt Elizabeth, it would slay him.

"Oh, Lucian." Digging out a pair of clippers, his mother cut a group of enormous yellow blooms and then handed them off to him. "Matters are far worse than I feared."

His alarm must have showed, for his mother patted his arm again, this time a show of reassurance.

"You have avoided marriage because you believe mine is unhappy."

Again, he thought, how could it not be? "Isn't it? Father is—"

"A man with a great many passions."

"You know about his many . . . passions?"

"I said my wedding vows understanding exactly what sort of man I was marrying."

She looked off into the distance, her gaze circling past her garden, past the grand mansion, pausing on the smaller building where Warren's current paramour had spent the morning preparing for her debut. "Your father and I have found our rhythm. He may wander at times, but he always comes home."

Luke had heard his mother's rationale before. Hearing it again, spoken in such simple terms, was laughable in its understatement. The press of outrage on her behalf pushed him to ask, "How can you accept Father's *passions* and *wanderings*"—the terms stuck in his throat—"with such ease?"

"I didn't say it was easy." She put great effort into plucking a series of brown-edged leaves from a bush. "Our shared life is worth the occasional season of pain."

That was her reasoning? That was how she slept at night? He thought of Sophie. "What if his past shows up, hypothetically speaking, in a form you cannot dismiss?"

"That would never happen. Your father is too smart for that."

His mother didn't know about Sophie, Luke realized. Could Warren's deception be any more complete?

"That is not the sort of marriage I wish for Penny."

"Or, I dare say"—his mother's smile turned sad—"for yourself."

"I would rather never marry than enter into a union like yours and father's." Though he meant every word, he hadn't intended to sound so harsh. "I apologize. I did not mean to pass judgment on your choices."

"Yes, you did. But that's beside the point."

"What is the point?" He didn't know anymore.

She sighed, her face growing thoughtful, as if she needed a moment to choose her words.

"Mother?"

"I am trying to help you let go of your anger toward your father. Here, give me those." She reached for the flowers in his hand. "You're strangling them."

Luke looked down, frowned at his hand. He was gripping the stems so hard his knuckles had turned white. Carefully peeling his fingers away, his mother took the bunch of flowers.

"Forgive your father, Luke. I have."

His mother asked too much. Warren Griffin continually inflicted pain on her, some of which she didn't even know about, and she accepted it as if it were a normal part of marriage. If his father suffered even a small amount of remorse, perhaps Luke could find it in his heart to forgive. As matters stood, he could not.

In that moment, he understood Elizabeth's animosity toward her mother on a whole new level. She carried a great burden, and was clearly suffering, while all he'd done was think of her reputation. "I have to go."

"Where?"

"To help out a friend." And he would do so without Elizabeth ever knowing his involvement. Luke may not be able to overcome his past, he may not be able to release his fear of repeating the sins of his father, but he could do something to ease the burdens of a woman he adored, maybe even loved.

It required calling in several favors—and a considerable amount of money. But a week later, as Luke watched the carriage pull away from the hospital in the direction of the train station, he knew he'd done the right thing.

For one brief moment, his heart didn't feel so hard, and his burdens felt a little lighter.

Chapter Eighteen

Three hours after seeing the hired conveyance off to the train station, Luke hired another carriage, this one for him.

Dressed in formal evening attire, he alerted the driver of his destination. "The Waldorf-Astoria. You may drop me off at the corner of Fifth Avenue and Thirty-Third Street."

"Very good, sir."

Placing his hat and gloves on the empty spot beside him, Luke leaned his head against the cushions and closed his eyes. He could have driven his motorcar, but his thoughts were too muddled with the events of the past week to concentrate. Tonight would be the first time he'd see his parents stand together in public since Penelope's engagement party.

His mother's startling revelations had forced Luke to rethink everything he thought he knew about their marriage. Violet Griffin was evidently content with her life and didn't mind her husband's infidelity. Or at least turned a blind eye to his *wanderings*.

Then again, Violet didn't know the entirety of her husband's secrets. She didn't know about Sophie.

Would his mother be so quick to push Luke to forgive his father if she knew the truth?

For one black moment, he was tempted to tell her. To what end? The disclosure would release his burdens but would only cause his mother pain. The facts wouldn't change.

Luke clamped his jaw shut, grinding his teeth together until they throbbed.

Keeping Warren Griffin's secret was becoming nearly too hard to bear. The worst of it was that an innocent young woman had no idea who her father was or that she had a half brother and sister. Sophie deserved to know the truth. Perhaps she already did.

Blowing out a frustrated hiss, Luke lifted his head and glanced out the window. People rushed about, no doubt hurrying home or to some sort of special occasion.

The current event requiring Luke's presence was yet another ball celebrating Penny's engagement, given by Mavis and Leonard Newman, close friends of Simon's parents.

Luke didn't know the couple very well. They were among the more conservative of the old Knickerbocker families, rivaled only by Simon's family. Luke had nearly completed his investigation of Penny's fiancé. So far, the man appeared to be the solid, upstanding citizen everyone thought him to be. Luke still wasn't convinced.

The carriage came to an abrupt halt, jerking Luke's attention to the snarl of traffic on the streets. They were still three blocks from the hotel. Hoping to avoid this very thing, he'd left his home an entire hour after the official start of the party. Clearly, he should have waited two.

He disembarked from the carriage and, after paying the driver, conquered the remaining blocks on foot.

Luke crossed onto Fifth Avenue.

The lofty hotel loomed half a block ahead. All slanted slopes and hard angles, gables and turrets, tile roof–topped balconies, alcoves, and plant-filled terraces. Not yet a decade old, the hotel was already considered the social center of New York.

The interior was as lavish as any grand hotel in the world. Wood-paneled walls and rugs with swirling patterns of several shades of blue glittered under the silvery light of the chandelier. Having been here for a ball years ago, Luke knew he needed to take one of the elevators to the top floor.

The crush of people was unprecedented and required every ounce of his patience as he made his way through the wide hallway into the actual ballroom. At least a hundred voices clamored for supremacy, each trying to be heard above the loud din.

Although he thought he'd seen opulence in the grand homes in London, Luke was still struck by the beauty of the Waldorf ballroom. The elegant decorations, abundant with greenery and an assortment of white flowers, sparkled under the long row of crystal chandeliers hanging from the high ceiling.

The golden, silvery light provided an old-world feel to the party. An added touch of glamour came from the guests themselves. The ladies wore lavish, colorful ball gowns. Like Luke, the men were clad in formal black.

The ballroom didn't fall silent as he entered, but there was a definite lull in conversation among the guests closest to him. He smiled and greeted everyone he knew, then proceeded to find his sister.

Several feet later, he spotted Penelope standing with Simon. She didn't look as small and vulnerable as she had at the ball announcing their engagement, but she didn't appear fully comfortable, either.

Once again, Simon was doing all the talking.

A familiar protective instinct took hold as Luke watched Penelope with her future husband. She didn't like attending balls or parties, but Simon apparently thrived at them.

The poor girl needed a distraction. Perhaps a dance with her favorite brother was in order.

Luke navigated the crowd and had nearly made it to his sister when Simon escorted her out onto the floor himself. At least Penny was smiling now.

Releasing a relieved breath, Luke continued moving through the room, straight for the buffet tables lining one entire wall on the west side of the building. As he wended his way through the hordes of party guests, he paused at intervals to speak to friends and acquaintances, stopping to kiss the hands of several older ladies he knew were friends with his mother.

He'd nearly made it to his destination when a low, wicked laugh sent a chill up his spine. That laugh belonged to the man he'd nearly throttled a week ago in the Harvard Club.

Luke's pulse picked up speed. Blood rushed in his ears. Memories yanked at him, the ones he'd ruthlessly blocked the last time he'd encountered Bertie. They came at him harder this evening, emptying his mind of everything but a miserable sense of guilt and regret.

He hadn't expected Bertie's presence at Penelope's party, though he should have. The man was Simon's cousin after all, and a favorite among the upper classes of New York. Bertie relished his reputation as a pillar in the community, a man who was everything polite and proper—on the outside. Luke knew far too well the man was nothing but evil on the inside, a user of people, especially women.

Luke recalled the challenge Bertie had tossed at him in the Harvard Club, and his presence tonight made a sick sort of sense. Luke fought the urge to close his eyes. If he did, he'd be back to the time when he'd called Bertie friend, when he'd thought he could escape his father's influence.

He'd gotten involved with a man far worse than Warren Griffin.

Bertie had introduced Luke to a world of decadence, filled with glamorous women and men who relished the finer things in life. The women were sophisticated, world weary, and fast. Dazzled at first, Luke had enjoyed their company, both publically and in private. There'd been no promises made, no suggestion of a future. His relationship with Abby had seemed as casual as the rest, the rules the same. But then she'd revealed her love for him.

Luke had been completely taken off guard. Looking back, he realized he could have handled the situation with more delicacy. He hadn't meant to hurt her, but he had. Instead of escaping his father's sins, he'd followed in Warren's footsteps. And Bertie had been more than willing to pick up the pieces, hurting Abby in far worse ways.

But this wasn't about Abby, or Luke. *Not about you.* It was about the innocent woman Bertie had in his sights.

Not about you.

The words finally sank in, releasing Luke from the past, at least temporarily.

Mouth grim, he looked in Bertie's direction. Who was he charming?

The man's back was to Luke, preventing him from seeing Bertie's companion. A woman, he knew. Luke could see her gloved hand gesturing as she spoke. He could also make out the outline of her dress. It was not the usual pale-colored gown of an innocent. Rather, it was the definition of drama, the blue silk a rich sapphire that sparkled in the chandelier light.

Relief nearly buckled his knees. Evidently, Bertie was chatting up an older woman, or at least one with a bit of experience behind her. No innocent girl would wear a gown that bold and eye-catching. Luke was just turning away when Bertie shifted and the woman in question came into focus.

No. *No.*

Luke staggered back a step.

Bertie was speaking with . . .

No. Not her. Not Elizabeth.

His throat began to burn.

Elizabeth had no idea the danger she was in merely talking to a man like Bertie. The very real possibility of her ruination hit Luke like a solid punch to the gut. After his altercation with the odious man, Luke should have foreseen something like this. He should have been better prepared.

232

Luke was back on the move, all but shoving his way through the party guests. His ambition had one focus now: save his sister's friend—*his* friend—from Bertie's clutches.

After his own boorish behavior of late, Luke owed Elizabeth that much, and he was a man who always paid his debts.

Catching sight of him, Elizabeth's eyes widened, then softened with something that looked like pleasure. She was happy to see him. Luke found himself caught between yearning and frustration.

Their gazes fastened, stuck, held. He smiled.

She smiled back.

Bertie followed the direction of her gaze, frowned at Luke, and then said something to Elizabeth that had her breaking eye contact, and now she frowned as well.

Luke increased his pace, determined to separate Elizabeth from Bertie as fast as humanly possible. *Some have not the knowledge of God*—the Bible verse had never been truer than in the case of Albert Phineas Fitzgerald III.

Had Bertie decided upon his next conquest? *No.* Luke all but broke out in a run, coming to a stop at a less-than-polite distance from the innocent young woman he'd kissed not once but twice. A stark reminder that he was no more deserving of her smiles than Bertie was.

"Luke." He loved the way she said his name, with a mix of fondness and delight, as if she'd been waiting for his arrival.

"Elizabeth."

As was becoming a habit whenever they were close, he had to remind himself this was his Little Bit, that same skinny kid who'd played hide-and-go-seek with his younger sister.

Except, their relationship was morphing into something new, something charged with tension and awkward pauses and . . . kisses. *Can't forget about the kisses.* Ever since Penelope's engagement party something had changed between them.

Everything had changed.

Elizabeth had changed.

She'd done something remarkable with her hair. The mass of blonde curls had been captured in a loose knot, and she'd twined pearls and ribbons throughout, all of them red. She looked sophisticated, mature, no longer a girl but a woman in full bloom.

His heart yearned.

Panic reared.

He had to get her away from Bertie.

"Luke." She touched his arm, the connection as natural as her smile. "I believe you are acquainted with Mr. Fitzgerald."

"We know one another." Luke flexed his neck to relieve the knotted muscles there. "We attended Harvard at the same time."

"Luke and I were more than classmates." Bertie eyed him narrowly, then smiled benignly at Elizabeth. "We were once very good chums, but that was before he left for London."

"I hadn't realized you two were that intimately acquainted." Elizabeth said this directly to Luke, her confusion very real.

Bertie responded for both of them. "We were as close as brothers, practically inseparable for a time." He chuckled. "The stories I could tell."

Luke shot the man a silent warning. "It was a long time ago."

"Not that long." Bertie's smile turned sly as a snake's. "We must get together and reminisce about old times."

Elizabeth divided a look between them. Clearly reading the tension, she gave Luke's arm a reassuring squeeze before releasing her hold. "Mr. Fitzgerald was just expounding on the wonders of vaudeville."

"As I was saying, you must attend a show, Miss St. James, as soon as possible." The man's manner was all politeness. "You won't have lived until you do."

Inside his chest, Luke's lungs tightened. Attending a vaudeville show was on Elizabeth's list. Had she shared this with Bertie?

"Oh, my, Mr. Fitzgerald." Her lips curved in a half smile that didn't quite meet her eyes. "That's certainly an ardent endorsement."

Bertie's smile was full of slimy charm. But his eyes had a calculating glint, black, sharp, and predatory. "I am enthusiastic about many things, Miss St. James, vaudeville being only one of them."

"Oh. Yes. Well . . ." Elizabeth clearly had no idea how to respond to that. Luke had a few ideas, all involving his fists.

"I see I have made you uncomfortable." Bertie's voice turned conciliatory. "That was not my intention."

Elizabeth's smile slipped. "I'm sure it wasn't."

Bertie accepted her words with a brief nod, then turned his head and shot Luke a grim twist of his lips meant to annoy. "Been to the Harvard Club lately?"

If circumstances were different, and this wasn't a party in Penelope's honor, Luke would have no qualms about wiping that smirk off the man's face.

Luke focused on Elizabeth. Only her. "Dance with me."

"I . . ." Her head angled in confusion. "Now?"

"Now."

Elizabeth blinked up at him, then at Bertie, her gaze bouncing between them with fast, nervous flicks. "But I am in the middle of a conversation. I cannot simply—"

"Dance with me," he repeated, the command only a fraction less abrupt than the first time he'd uttered it.

"Luke." She laughed, the sound short and husky. "What's gotten into you? I've never known you to be so rude."

"I apologize. My *enthusiasm* got the best of me."

Bertie snorted.

Luke ignored him. He rifled through the items he'd read on Elizabeth's list, then said, "I wish to speak with you about a fountain I came across the other day."

"You wish to speak with me about a fountain?" She looked confused. Then, slowly, understanding dawned in her remarkable eyes. "Oh, a *fountain*."

He reached out, a silent invitation.

Bertie was not to be so easily thwarted. "Miss St. James, if you don't wish to dance with Luke, I will happily take a turn around the floor with you."

"I'm sorry, Mr. Fitzgerald, but I have already promised Luke this dance." She turned slightly, missing the hard look that came into Bertie's gaze.

Urgency riding him hard, Luke took Elizabeth's hand.

The inevitable kick in his gut came right on schedule, as it always did whenever he touched her. It wasn't an altogether awful feeling, reminding him of the sensation he felt in the middle of a thunderstorm. Or a light rain shower in a deserted country field.

Elizabeth felt it, too. Luke knew this by the way her breathing quickened. She had no idea the sort of man Bertie was behind the polished veneer, no idea how close she'd come to ruination.

At least she was safe now, or as safe as she could be in the company of a man with a questionable past like Luke's.

Determined to enjoy their dance and put all other thoughts aside, he guided her to the center of the parquet floor. With the first strains of a Viennese waltz drifting over them, he pulled her into his arms and gazed into eyes of a mesmerizing, dreamy blue. Home.

At last, Luke was home.

* * *

Matching her steps with his, Elizabeth happily settled into Luke's arms, loving the feel of his strong embrace. At last, she was right where she wanted to be, with the man she loved. She breathed in his warm scent, and her entire being calmed.

Ever since their walk in the rain, and the kiss that had changed her life forever, Luke had not been far from Elizabeth's mind. In truth, she'd been thinking of him earlier, back when Mr. Fitzgerald had first approached her. She'd wondered where Luke was and, not seeing him anywhere, had settled for the other man's company.

Then, Luke had appeared in the ballroom. Their gazes had connected across the room. His eyes had held such a look of determination that she'd felt an answering twist of emotion in her heart.

He'd behaved more protective than usual, as if he didn't trust Mr. Fitzgerald. Or perhaps it was Elizabeth he didn't trust. Surely, Luke didn't think she would approach the other man with her list. There was something *off* about him. Luke had nothing to worry about, not when it came to Mr. Fitzgerald, or any other man for that matter.

Pulling her a fraction closer, Luke guided her through a series of spins that left her pleasantly dizzy.

Elizabeth laughed. She was suddenly having a lovely time, and Luke was the source of her joy. She'd been waiting for his arrival for a full hour and couldn't help wondering why he'd arrived late.

She'd known the moment he'd seen her. His gaze had locked onto her over the sea of twirling bodies and party guests. She'd watched, with her heart in her throat, as he approached through the maddening crush. He'd been coming for her. And now he wanted to discuss another adventure on her list.

Only this moment mattered. Only this man.

Their eyes met. This time, a charge as strong as lightning flashed between them.

She laughed again. "You were quite forceful back there."

He said nothing.

"If I didn't know better, I'd say you didn't want me talking with Mr. Fitzgerald."

Still, nothing.

His silence told her she was right. The knowledge made her bolder. While he spun her through another series of turns, she said, "You don't like him."

He tugged her closer and took them through a series of complicated steps that spoke of his expertise on the dance floor. The man was full of hidden talents.

"Bertie is not a good man," he said through a tight jaw.

Elizabeth had sensed as much, though all accounts said otherwise. The man was considered quite a catch.

"Steer clear of him, Little Bit. He's dangerous."

Something in his gaze said he had information about Albert Fitzgerald that would shock her. "If you say to avoid him, then you must have a very good reason why."

"What?" His eyebrows lifted. "No argument?"

She shook her head.

Luke backpedaled, leading them into another turn. And then another. The intricate series of steps made her feel exhilarated and full of . . . something. Anticipation, perhaps?

Smiling into Luke's handsome face, which was still scrunched in a frown, she followed him smoothly through the steps of the waltz. One. Two. Three. One. Two. Three. Elizabeth studied him a moment in silence. His hair was slightly disheveled, as if he'd dragged both hands through the strands more than a few times.

He was worried. About her. He cared. About her. Her heart lifted and sighed.

Reaching up, she gently touched his cheek, then dropped her hand when she realized where they were. "Thank you, Luke."

"For . . . ?"

"For worrying about me."

He drew in a few unsteady breaths, his remarkable control returning with each exhale. "I don't want to see you hurt, Little Bit."

There was something in his voice, affection and maybe even fear, a tone that told her there was more between Luke and Albert Fitzgerald than he was letting on. Though curious, she didn't want to spend these precious moments talking about a man she hardly knew.

Luke was here. They were dancing. The evening was perfect. The other day she'd decided to attack her list on her own. But if Luke was still offering to help her, perhaps this was the perfect way to win his heart, one lovely adventure at a time.

"I also want to thank you, ahead of time, for helping me with the rest of my list and—"

"I'm not helping you with the list you showed me." He leaned in a fraction closer. "You cannot go on in the manner you've begun. There are too many problems that could arise, too much risk, too many wrong turns."

"That's the point. I *want* to take a few wrong turns."

"You wouldn't say that if you knew what lay around the corner."

And they were back where they'd begun.

Her throat squeezed shut. She pushed her next words out on a frustrated sigh. "Luke, please—"

"No."

How was she supposed to get through to him when he kept interrupting her? "Perhaps I'll dance with Mr. Fitzgerald after all."

Horror filled his expression. That was oddly, incredibly heartwarming.

"You will not approach Bertie." His hand flexed at her waist. "Promise me, Elizabeth."

"I . . . Why don't you trust Mr. Fitzgerald? What do you know that I don't?"

Luke stopped abruptly. "Let's go." He took her hand and guided her across the dance floor at a clipped pace. Elizabeth had no recourse but to follow.

There was time only for brief glimpses and nods as they moved from the dance floor, past the banquet tables, past friends and family, to a door leading out to the balcony. Peering around Luke's broad shoulders, Elizabeth took note of the clear sky beyond the wall of windows. The moon and stars sparkled in the black fabric of the sky, casting the area in silvery light. It was a romantic setting for another kiss, perhaps in a shadowed corner.

Her heart tripped over itself.

Every step she took grew lighter, and lighter still, until she was practically gliding above the floor. The smells of baked sea bass and lobster dripping in butter wafted on the air, along with a mixture of other savory scents, sweet honey, and freshly baked bread.

She hadn't eaten tonight, a situation that wouldn't be remedied anytime soon. She cared not one whit.

Luke continued to guide her through the labyrinth of party guests. Elizabeth could alleviate his concerns about Mr. Fitzgerald if the man would slow down long enough for her to do so. She loved Luke, but it was more than that. She trusted him. She'd always trusted him, and always would. If he said to stay away from his former friend, she would.

Elizabeth absently noted the smiling faces passing by in a blur. Luke was certainly in a hurry. Matriarchs shared conversation with younger women. The whispers were nothing new, especially the ones about her. "She's the perfect completion of her mother's hard work."

Another mentioned how very sad it was that Katherine had grown ill and couldn't be here to watch her lovely daughter bloom into a young woman sought after by every eligible bachelor at the party.

"It really is a pity," another commented. "Katherine is always a wonderful addition to any gathering."

True, Katherine St. James was very popular among her friends. How little they knew her.

"Such a good girl."

How little they knew Elizabeth. Plotting how best to get Luke in a dark corner wasn't the portrait of propriety they attached to her.

More smiles and nods were thrown their way. Did no one notice Luke was all but dragging her along behind him?

People see what they want to see. Caroline had said this to Elizabeth once. At the time, she hadn't understood what her cousin meant. Now, she did. In Caroline's case, people saw a street urchin unworthy of them. In Elizabeth's case, they saw the perfect debutante who never disobeyed or questioned her place in society.

Oh, how she wanted—*needed*—to prove she was more, so much more. Would completing the list be enough?

As Luke guided her through the open balcony doors, there was an electric feel in the air as his long strides slowed to match her pace. Elizabeth glanced at his profile. So handsome, so frustrating, so convinced she was some wayward child in need of a good scolding.

Enough.

Chapter Nineteen

Elizabeth stopped abruptly and pulled her hand free. "Luke, wait, slow down."

He swung around to face her. *Slam.* The intensity of his frustration—frustration with her—shoved her back a step. Elizabeth straightened, dragged in a lungful of air, and told herself she was imagining the blow.

But, of course, she wasn't. She couldn't remember having been so aware of a man and what his presence did to her heart rate.

The paper-thin moon cast the balcony in silvery light. Music drifted over them, a Viennese waltz by Johann Strauss II. The moment would have been perfect, the setting spectacular, but for two distinct points, both problematic in their own right: Luke was looking overly serious. And they weren't alone. People milled about them. Several smiled or nodded their way.

Seeking a bit of privacy, Elizabeth moved into the shadows. Luke nudged her back into the light. The man was proving entirely too proper.

Angling her head, she stared straight into his blazing eyes.

"Luke." She slipped once again into the shadows, stopping on the edge of an alcove and waiting until he reluctantly joined her. "You do realize that I am not a child, nor am I without sense. I can make my own—"

"Not another word, Elizabeth." His tone was immovable steel. But at least he didn't move away from her, or try to get her to return to the center of the balcony. "You will not continue down the course you've set for yourself."

And now she knew why he stood in the alcove with her. He wanted privacy so he could lecture her. Beastly, frustrating man.

"You are completely misreading the situation."

"I won't see you ruined."

Elizabeth felt her eyes widen. She'd never seen Luke this grave. "You weren't this concerned when we were strolling hand in hand in the rain. What's changed?"

He clenched his jaw so hard a muscle jumped. "Albert Fitzgerald is not the man he portrays to the world. There are ugly layers beneath that suave veneer, dark layers."

This pronouncement didn't surprise her. Most people weren't who they pretended to be—not her mother. Not her father. Not even Luke. He was supposed to be a man with a questionable reputation, a little wild, a little audacious. Yet he continually behaved above reproach and continually put others ahead of himself.

"You will not approach Bertie with your proposition. I won't allow it."

He wouldn't *allow* it?

Now he'd crossed a line. "It's really not up to you, and it's certainly none of your business."

"You made it my business when you came to me with your ridiculous list. At an inappropriate hour. In the privacy of my own home."

"What a stunning prude you've become."

The insult missed its mark.

"The worst of it, *the very worst of it*"—his voice lowered to an ominous level—"is that you don't even know how close to disaster you've come, Little Bit."

She flinched at the nickname, but he gave her no time to respond.

"You are a kitten attempting to run with jungle cats. You must steer clear of Bertie—of all men, for that matter."

"Including you?"

"Especially me."

He looked tired, heavily burdened. "Oh, Luke, you really are a good man. I'm starting to like you very much, even when you're being bone stubborn."

He looked around, scowled, then pulled Elizabeth fully into the alcove, away from prying eyes. With shadows covering his face, he spoke in a low, nearly imperceptible voice. "You cannot go around asking men to help you break the rules of society, no matter how silly or unfair those rules may seem."

"I have only approached you."

He raised a single dark eyebrow, nearly impossible to detect in the shadows, but Elizabeth was close enough. "Do you mean to say that you didn't have plans to ask Bertie to assist you—"

"No." She paused when conversation around them halted, lowered her voice to a whisper. "I did not. There's something about him that makes me think of slimy, slithering creatures."

An involuntary shudder passed through her.

"You're right to be afraid of him."

Drawing in a deep breath, she said, "Luke, I understand the dangers of my quest, truly, I do. But I can't continue as I have been." She absently touched the locket around her neck, found the courage to add, "You know why."

His gaze ran over her face, dropped down to her necklace, turned thoughtful. "That's a stunning piece of jewelry. Is it new?"

A sigh leaked out of her. This was her chance, perhaps even her last, to win Luke to her side. The locket was a good reminder of why Elizabeth must make this move, with or without his help.

Again, she lifted her hand to the necklace, released the latch, and showed Luke the piece of red fringe. Then, lifting her hand to her hair, she indicated the ribbons she'd made from the scarlet garment.

When she explained where the scraps had come from and why she wore them, Luke's expression softened. "I've been where you are, Little Bit. I understand the need to break free."

The change in him, the sudden sadness, had her touching his sleeve. "Will you tell me what led to your rebellion?"

"Perhaps I should." He guided her out of the dark alcove and into the light.

Still gripping her hand, he pulled her toward a bench, indicated she take a seat. He joined her a moment later.

It was all perfectly proper. Elizabeth sighed. There would be no kiss under the moon and stars tonight.

"You've indicated that I can't possibly understand what you're suffering, but you're wrong, Elizabeth." His eyes were brilliant with emotion. "I discovered something about my father that revealed a different side to his nature. It doesn't matter how, or even what, only that I will never look at him the same."

"I'm sorry."

He kept talking, barely acknowledging her words. "I went a little wild, began hanging out with a rowdy crowd."

"That's how you know Mr. Fitzgerald."

"Yes." He turned his head, commanded her gaze. "I did things I can never undo." He shifted in his seat, cast around a moment, presumably to make sure they weren't drawing unwanted attention. "I'm trying to preserve your honor. The very thing I have lost."

"Luke, you are the most honorable man I know." The very reason she'd approached him in the first place.

"You're wrong, Little Bit."

"If you have such concern for my reputation, may I suggest you follow through with your agreement to assist me? What better way to keep me safe than to stick by my side?"

"Your trust in me is misguided."

"I disagree." She gave him her most confident smile and stood. Looking down at him, she felt emboldened enough to reach out a hand to him.

Frowning, he stood a second later. But didn't take her hand. The man was as obstinate as any she knew. She rather liked that about him.

"I'm about to do something very inappropriate," she warned, stepping closer. "Lucian Griffin, may I have the next waltz?"

The echo of a smile curved his lips. "I'd be delighted to dance with you."

She shook off a delicious shiver, and, this time, when she reached out to him, he took her hand and tucked it in the crook of his arm. They entered the ballroom and were immediately accosted.

"Elizabeth St. James," said the scolding, matronly voice. "You have been a very naughty young lady."

She and Luke had been found out; that was her first thought. But that couldn't be right. They hadn't done anything wrong. *This time.*

"I'll need you to be more specific, Aunt Tilly. What, exactly, have I done to upset you so?"

"You know perfectly well what you did." The older woman wagged a finger at her. "You begged off from our shopping trip and have yet to reschedule."

"That is a grave offense, indeed." Luke couldn't hide the momentary flash of amusement in his eyes. "You should be ashamed of yourself."

Aunt Tilly bobbed her head in agreement. "Indeed, she should."

"I do apologize." Elizabeth pursed her lips into what she hoped was a contrite expression. "I'm sure I'll be available to go shopping sometime . . . soon."

"Oh, no, I'm onto your slippery tactics. You won't put me off again. My schedule is quite tight, but I'm free two weeks from Wednesday. You will meet me at Bergdorf Goodman, one o'clock sharp. I'll take no excuses."

Elizabeth couldn't think of a worse way to spend an afternoon. An army of seamstresses stuffing her into dresses while her ribs cracked and her organs were crushed.

Of course, even if she were to voice her misgivings, they would be of little concern to Aunt Tilly, and so Elizabeth took a deep breath and said, "I'll be there."

"Excellent." The older woman smiled triumphantly. "Oh, look, it's Isadora Covington. I haven't seen her in ages. Good-bye, dear."

"Good-bye."

Aunt Tilly bustled off, calling after her friend.

Elizabeth sighed. "You were right, Luke."

"Though I do love to hear those three little words, especially when uttered in front of my name, what was I right about?"

"Regrets." Elizabeth sighed dramatically. "I shall regret my upcoming shopping excursion with a grand passion."

His only response was a low chuckle.

* * *

"Do a little spin for me, dear, so I may see if the material flows in an attractive manner around your form." Aunt Tilly gave this directive from a silver brocade divan in the fitting room of Bergdorf Goodman.

Fixing a smile on her face, Elizabeth did as she was ordered, taking a slow, measured turn, then executed another one when the older woman twirled her finger in the air and said, "One more time, please."

Elizabeth finished her spin and waited.

"Lovely," Aunt Tilly declared as she reached out to grab a tea cake from the tray brought in by the store's floor manager. "I predict you will be the belle of a winter ball in that gown, once the alterations are complete."

"It is beautiful," Elizabeth agreed, smoothing her hand down the cool, shimmering silk.

She returned to the raised platform, and the team of seamstresses moved into place, manipulating and pinning the evergreen silk. The material was of the finest quality and complemented her skin tone, giving it a rosy glow. But Elizabeth had been through too many fittings in her life to find any excitement in the process today.

Had she truly thought shopping in a department store would be any less trying than in a Parisian couture house?

The experiences were nearly identical. For hours she was measured, poked, and pinned, while only being allowed to move when told to do so.

Knowing what was expected of her, she held perfectly still. Out of the corner of her eye, she watched one of the young seamstresses tuck and drape the material at her waist.

When the girl turned her attention to the hem, Elizabeth had an unencumbered view of the mirror. She inspected her new gown with a critical eye. It was indeed lovely, as lovely as any of her dresses made by French hands. Lifting her gaze, she studied the cameo hanging around her neck.

What lay inside the locket reminded Elizabeth of her list, of the too-few items she'd accomplished. The circus had come to town. Unfortunately, she hadn't flown on the trapeze. There'd been too many people milling about. At least she and Sally had gotten close enough to a camel to pet his bristly fur. The creature had rewarded their bravery by spitting on Elizabeth's foot. A pair of ruined ankle boots had been well worth the experience.

Smiling at the memory, she reached up and clutched the necklace, then immediately dropped her hand when the seamstress ordered her to be still.

From her spot on the divan, Aunt Tilly began a chattering litany about the type of ball gowns that were all the rage among British women. These *simply divine* creations were made in subdued colors, nothing too bold, and were cut from thin materials such as gauzes, laces, and softer silks. Seemingly unaware that she carried the one-sided conversation, Aunt Tilly prattled on. And on and on and on.

Elizabeth let her mind wander to the rain-drenched field where she'd kissed Luke.

For a fleeting moment he'd been all hers, and she'd been bold, and her life had been anything but boring or predictable. For that one gloriously fleeting moment, Elizabeth had been anything but passive. She'd been passionate and shared a connection with the man she loved, a wonderful, scandalous connection that she would very much like to repeat a hundred, nay, a thousand times over.

A ghost of a smile crossed her lips at the thought, then fell away just as quickly. There would be no repeat of that day's remarkable adventure. Luke had been too horrified and guilt-ridden over his behavior to initiate another kiss. Sadly, he hadn't made a single unsavory overture since.

I could kiss him.

Elizabeth's smile returned.

Already, her life was changing. She was reaching for more, doing more, becoming . . . more.

Live every day to the fullest. Love without reservation.

Her life was already fuller, richer, all because of the chances she was taking, because of knowing Luke, and because of her kinship with Caroline. When her cousin had first arrived in America, she'd been understandably distant. Even after the family connection was revealed and verified, she'd held a portion of herself apart from the family.

Elizabeth hadn't blamed her cousin. Caroline had every right to keep her distance.

There'd been a time when Elizabeth had been convinced that Caroline hated her. But Caroline had eventually accepted her. And while their relationship was still evolving, Elizabeth was learning what it meant to care for the woman as more than a cousin, as a sister. Loving without reservation was easy when it came to Caroline. It was easy with the rest of her family, save for one person.

Elizabeth thought of the two unopened letters on her writing desk, resting in the same spot where Sally had deposited them days before. Both were from her mother; Elizabeth had recognized the handwriting in a single glance. No doubt each page was filled with explanations, false apologies, and pleas for forgiveness. She had no wish to read those words. *Liar.*

She desperately wanted to read her mother's letters. She couldn't. She wouldn't. Something in them might cause her to have a change of heart. Forgiving her mother would be the ultimate betrayal to Caroline.

Or would it?

Perhaps one act didn't automatically lead to the other. Perhaps—

"You'll want to add extra trim to the dress. Embroidery wouldn't be out of the question, and perhaps some additional lace down the front of the bodice." Aunt Tilly scrambled to her feet and headed for a wall of accents. Studying the choices of ribbons, buttons, and lace, she said, "Something that will draw attention to your lovely long neck."

The older woman picked up two spools of cream lace, one slightly darker than the other, and, for the first time in her life, Elizabeth made her opinion known. "No lace."

Aunt Tilly glanced over at her. "What's that, dear?"

Elizabeth squared her shoulders and firmed her chin. "I don't want any additional lace on this dress. There is enough already."

There was a long pause, during which Aunt Tilly's eyes narrowed ever so slightly.

If the rushing in her ears had not been so loud, Elizabeth would have heard the sound of footsteps approaching.

"I agree completely," said a musical voice with an Italian accent. "More lace would only detract from the exquisite cut of the neckline and your beautiful face."

An unfamiliar young woman appeared in the mirror. Her arresting features and a mass of chestnut curls piled atop her head spoke of a foreign heritage. She was exotic, beautiful, with the kind of loveliness reminiscent of another time, another world. Her smiling eyes weren't brown, nothing so mundane, but the color of burnished old gold. Elizabeth knew those eyes.

She'd seen them in another face.

But that couldn't be right.

Something akin to shock clogged in her throat. She felt a nudge of foreboding, which she ruthlessly suppressed. "Do I know you?"

The young woman held her gaze a long moment, her mouth forming into a pretty pout. "You don't remember me."

"Should I?"

Smiling again, eyes twinkling with mischief, the girl sang the opening bar from *Carmen*, her voice as velvety rich as her mother's.

"Sophie! Sophie Cappelletti, is it really you?"

"*Sì, bella*, it is I."

Elizabeth needed no further confirmation. Uncaring she was crushing the silk of her new dress, she grabbed her old friend and hugged her tightly. The years fell away, and Elizabeth was back in the gardens of Griffin Manor, playing a rousing game of tag with her two favorite friends, Penelope and this young woman.

"The last time we met," Elizabeth said, "we were children."

"What fun we had, *amica*."

Elizabeth stepped back and studied the stunning face, finally seeing the girl she'd once called friend. But the first thing she'd noticed about her old friend hadn't been her delicate features, or her gorgeous hair, or even her lilting voice, which carried the sound of her Italian heritage.

No, the first thing Elizabeth had noticed about Sophie Cappelletti was her stunning eyes. The shape, the exotic tilt, and the unusual color were a flawless reproduction of Luke's. And Penelope's. And . . .

No, it couldn't be. But of course it could. Memories nagged at her. Luke's proclamation about discovering his father wasn't the man he pretended to be.

Elizabeth's thoughts were interrupted by Aunt Tilly's voice.

"Who is this lovely young woman? I don't believe we've met. Or have we?" Eyes locked on Sophie, confusion in her gaze, Aunt Tilly began the process of trying to place the face with a name.

Elizabeth made the introductions.

"Aunt Tilly, this is Sophie Cappelletti. Sophie, this is my aunt Tilly—I mean, Lady Matilda Effingham." She lifted a questioning glance at the older woman. "Is that the proper title?"

"Close enough." With a quick slash of her hand, she dismissed Elizabeth's question. And Elizabeth. "Cappelletti . . . I know that name. How do I know that name? Oh, yes, Esmeralda Cappelletti."

"She is my mother."

"But of course." Aunt Tilly shook her head, laughing as if surprised she hadn't made the connection sooner. "That explains why you look familiar."

Sophie's face went dead white, a clear indication that Elizabeth's suspicions of her parentage were warranted. For her part, Aunt Tilly didn't seem to notice. She was too busy gushing over the incomparable Esmeralda Cappelletti.

"I had the pleasure of attending one of your mother's performances in London. Exquisite voice, captivating stage presence, really quite delightful."

Recovering from her initial reaction, Sophie pasted a pleasant smile on her face. "I'll pass along your words of praise."

"Please do. Oh, to think, I have come this close"—Aunt Tilly lifted her hand, closing her forefinger within an inch of her thumb—"to meeting the most celebrated diva of our generation."

As Aunt Tilly expounded on Esmeralda's wonderful, charming, not-to-be-forgotten talent, Sophie's expression didn't change. She continued smiling stiffly, unmoving, hardly even blinking.

At last, Aunt Tilly took a breath. Elizabeth seized the opportunity to send the woman in search of another new dress for her to try on. It would mean an additional hour of being pinned and poked, but she wanted a brief moment alone with her friend and had been unable to think of another solution.

She had so much to ask Sophie, so much she wanted to know. But they were strangers now.

Needing privacy for their conversation, she sent the seamstresses away as well. Once she and Sophie were alone, she placed a hand on the other woman's arm. "I'm so glad you're home."

"Home," Sophie repeated. "Yes, I am home."

She shifted her gaze to where Elizabeth was touching her, staring at her hand for a long moment before placing her palm atop Elizabeth's. When she lifted her head, her expression was full of anguish.

"Do you remember the games we played?" Sophie asked, changing the subject with an alacrity that would have impressed Elizabeth if she hadn't been concerned for the repercussions of the girl's presence in New York, months before Penelope's wedding. "Hide-and-go-seek was always my favorite."

Elizabeth agreed with a smile and a nod. She couldn't seem to push words past her throat as time shifted and bent in her mind. Memories once again bombarded her in a shocking assault to her senses.

Sophie's mother in the private opera house . . .

Day after day, the children sent outside to play in the gardens . . .

The endless rehearsals they weren't allowed to attend, the ones they were . . .

Warren Griffin always there, offering his opinions, his direction . . .

The absence of Violet Griffin at the formal performances . . .

"Oh, Sophie, you look so much . . ." *Like Luke and Penelope* was what she wanted to say. Instead, she tempered her speech. "So worldly, far more than when we were children."

Sophie laughed, a pretty, melodic sound. "I suppose that's because I have traveled the world."

At last, Elizabeth found her smile. "I can only imagine how exciting that must have been. I suspect you have seen great wonders."

"*Allora*, yes. But America is my home."

Home. The way she said the word, with reverence and conviction and furious intent. That sense of foreboding returned. "Are you here for a long visit?"

"I am here to stay."

"How . . . wonderful."

They shared a tense smile.

"Have you seen Penelope yet?"

"Not yet." A flash of guilt crossed Sophie's face. "Soon."

"She will be so happy to see you."

"Will she?" Something unpleasant came and went in the other girl's face, full of intent. "I wonder."

A gasp worked its way up Elizabeth's throat. She swallowed it back. Unfortunately, her fear remained. Fear for her friend and the repercussions to her and her family, particularly if what she suspected had brought Sophie to America was true.

If Elizabeth noticed the family resemblance, others would as well.

She knew it wasn't her place to interfere. Griffin family matters weren't her concern. But Elizabeth couldn't help worrying, not only for Penelope, but for Luke, and Sophie, too. If she was Warren's daughter, she deserved to take her place in the family.

At what price?

"Penelope is engaged to be married."

Two perfectly winged eyebrows lifted. "Is she?"

"His name is Simon Burrows. He's from a proper Knickerbocker family. His reputation is impeccable."

Sophie's gaze hardened. "You are telling me this to warn me."

"No. Well, yes. Penelope is my closest friend. And so are you, Sophie," she added hastily when the young woman's gaze darkened even further. "I would not wish for you to be harmed, any more than I would want Penelope hurt."

Sophie stared at her, seeming to consider her words, weighing and measuring.

There was a chill in the air now, seeped with emotion.

Sophie's breathing hitched, making her tremble. Only then did Elizabeth realize she was still clutching the other woman's arm. She released her grip and looked into the hauntingly familiar eyes. There was so much need and defiance staring back at her, so much loneliness and disillusion, and a wild, desperate hope. Elizabeth hurt for this woman, her friend.

Was it any wonder she'd always loved Sophie? She was related to two of her favorite people. Not simply related, she was their half sibling. The revelation would cause a great scandal. Luke had warned Elizabeth that disobedience came at a cost. She'd been too headstrong, too naïve and selfish to understand. Her pitiful little list of rebellions seemed trite now. Except for one of the most recent entries.

Love without reservation.

Suddenly, she knew exactly what to say to ease this woman's mind.

"I will stand by you." She would do the same for Penelope, and for Luke. "No matter what happens in the next few days, Sophie, I will not forget our friendship or what we once meant to each other."

Abruptly, Sophie's tattered control broke. Great, raw sobs poured from her as she stood rigidly, her hands clutched tightly together at her waist. With tears streaming down her cheeks, Sophie's eyes were locked with Elizabeth's as if the past connecting them was her only hope.

Grasping the enormity of her friend's torment, Elizabeth wrapped her arms around the girl as tightly as she could. In the midst of the emotional chaos, her mind went to Luke.

Luke. She must warn him before the scandal broke.

Chapter Twenty

Luke was deep at work reviewing an article on the benefits of a four-speed transmission versus a three-speed when a knock came at his office door. Concentration sufficiently shattered, he looked up. "Enter."

His assistant, Franklin Southerland, a thin young man with regular features and a tentative smile, stuck his head in the room. "Excuse me, Mr. Griffin, I know you requested not to be disturbed, but a young lady is here to see you."

"Did she give her name?"

The clerk's Adam's apple was bobbing, and his gaze danced around the room, landing nowhere in particular. "Miss Elizabeth St. James, sir."

Luke scrubbed the back of his hand across his mouth and glanced at the clock on his desk. Four o'clock, three hours after the shopping excursion Elizabeth had scheduled with her aunt.

His first instinct was to send the troublesome woman away. He did not have time for another argument concerning her bothersome list. He certainly didn't have time for her quiet smiles and unforgettable adventures in the rain and the way she made him yearn for things lost to him years ago.

There was no room in his life for Elizabeth. His burdens were already too heavy.

She isn't a burden. She's the one person who soothes away your cares and eases the load you bear. Just being in her presence makes you calm, and a happy future seems possible.

That was exactly the kind of thinking that would lead to her ruin. Luke would only fail Elizabeth, eventually, as he'd failed all the others he loved. Maintaining his distance was crucial. Detachment was the best way to establish the parameters of their relationship.

Who was he fooling? Elizabeth would trample over any boundaries he tried to set. She was as stubborn as he was. The thought made him unreasonably cheerful.

"Mr. Griffin?" His assistant's usually calm countenance appeared a bit ragged at the edges. "Shall I send her away?"

"No. Bring her in. But give me five minutes before you do." He needed to fortify himself, assemble some armor before facing Elizabeth.

"Very good, sir."

The clerk left the room, pulling the door shut behind him.

Running his hands through his hair, Luke made his way around his desk, the wide surface filled with automobile periodicals and engineering books.

At the window, he took a long pull of air, released it slowly, deliberately. Luke considered himself a man of control, except when it came to Elizabeth. She always managed to slip past his defenses. He was already halfway to giving in to whatever she asked of him, and she hadn't even entered the room yet.

Exactly five minutes after Mr. Southerland left the room, he reentered, Elizabeth one step behind.

Luke schooled his features into a blank expression. "Elizabeth, please, come in."

"Thank you."

His well-honed composure evaporated the moment he caught sight of her face. Barely concealed panic played across her features. Forcing his alarm to subside, he adopted a casual pose and sat on the edge of his desk and asked, "To what do I owe this honor?"

"I've come with some distressing news."

His heart pounded against his ribs, and his breath hitched in his lungs. *She's in trouble.*

That list. That blasted list of hers. He should have destroyed it when he'd had the chance.

Now it was too late. He swallowed the lump in his throat. "Tell me what's happened."

Hesitating, she glanced at Franklin. The gesture reminded Luke they had an audience. He seemed to do that a lot in her company, his focus so much on her that he forgot there were other people around.

He dismissed his clerk. "Close the door on your way out."

"As you wish."

While the other man left the room, Luke kept his gaze on Elizabeth. Her shoulders were unnaturally stiff. She looked vulnerable, distraught. Luke wanted to go to her, to soothe away her anxiety. He wanted to tease a laugh out of her like he had when they were children. Yet he sensed it wouldn't help and possibly would only make matters worse.

"Elizabeth," he said softly, tenderly. "Look at me."

Slowly, she lifted her head and started walking again, crossing the expanse of hardwood flooring between them with short, anxious steps. When she was within two feet of him, she stopped. Her floral scent hit him like a rough blow to the heart.

Luke tried to think brotherly thoughts. But Elizabeth's pleasing smell, along with the memory of their kisses, made his efforts fruitless.

He looked into her face. His heart lurched, and a sense of urgency surged. Elizabeth was upset, though she hid her reaction behind a benign smile.

Affecting a bland expression of his own, he went to her, knuckled an errant curl out of her eyes. "Tell me what's brought you to me."

She drew in a shaky breath, blinked several times. For a shocking moment, Luke thought she was going to cry. He took her hands in his. "You can tell me anything, Elizabeth. I won't judge you. Whatever it is you've done, I'll find a way to fix the damage."

He would go to whatever lengths necessary to erase that terrible look of pain in her eyes. But what if he couldn't? What if she'd gone too far?

"That's oddly sweet, and yet a bit insulting." She let out an unlady-like snort. "Have no fear, Luke, my reputation is firmly intact."

"Then why are you so upset?" As soon as the words left his mouth, he knew. "Your mother. She's come home."

"No, it's nothing to do with me."

"Then why—"

"I ran into an old friend of yours this afternoon." Misery fell across her face. "A woman you haven't seen in many years."

Luke recognized the curling in his gut as dread. He quelled the sensation and forced himself to ask, "Does this woman have a name?"

Elizabeth nodded. "Sophie Cappelletti."

Though not the name he was expecting—he'd thought Elizabeth had met Abby—the dread he'd felt earlier remained. "You spoke with her?"

"We had a long visit."

He released her hands, shoved his own in his pockets. "She is . . . well?"

"Very well. She has become a beautiful woman." Elizabeth walked slowly to the window, looked out. Twisting the handle of her cloth purse in agitation, she pivoted back around. "She has the most amazing eyes."

He knew where this was going, considered stopping her, and yet let her continue, anyway.

"They're an unusual color, not quite brown, but a lovely golden shade." She drew alongside him. "I've only seen eyes that color on three other people."

"Me, Penelope, and our father."

"Yes."

Legs shakier than he'd like, Luke turned away, tugged at his lapels. One thought dominated the twisting in his chest. Elizabeth knew. She knew Sophie was his half sister.

"Does Sophie know the truth?" he asked.

"That's why I'm here. To warn you."

Guilt spiraled in him for not trying harder to reach out to his half sister. What Sophie must be suffering, the fear, the confusion, the need for answers. Luke had grappled with all three himself, not well, and certainly not with dignity, and he wasn't even the most affected party.

Elizabeth came around to him, touched his arm. "How long have you known she is your sister?"

"I've suspected for years but have never received actual confirmation. Until now."

"Oh."

Seconds ticked by before Elizabeth removed her hand from his arm. She regarded him with patient, solemn eyes, the look giving Luke the impression her next words would be far worse than all the others before. "I believe Sophie has come to confront your father."

This was Luke's greatest fear. Yet he couldn't fault Sophie's desire to stand before Warren Griffin and demand answers. She deserved to know the truth, no matter how ugly. She deserved to be acknowledged.

"What are you going to do?"

"I don't know," he admitted, a dozen thoughts colliding into one another in his head. Hands still in his pockets, he rocked back on his heels, rolled forward again.

"Will you try to stop her?"

"She is my sister." Which didn't answer the question. "I won't deny her, or turn my back on her, if that's what you mean. She is family. She deserves to take her place among us. But if she confronts my father in a public manner . . ."

"Your family will be ruined."

Lips twisted at a wry angle, he nodded. "I don't care about the repercussions to me. Or to my father." Warren Griffin had brought this on himself. "But I do care what this will do to my mother. And to Penelope. I fear she will suffer the most."

"Oh, Luke." Eyes full of agony rolled up to his. "You don't think Mr. Burrows will break off the engagement if the truth comes out before the wedding, do you?"

Luke laughed harshly, the sound ragged in the silence that had fallen over the room. "That's exactly what I suspect the venerable, uptight Simon Burrows will do."

"He could surprise us."

"He could." Luke didn't hold out much hope for that. He'd done his research, turned over every rock. Simon was a man of honor, without a blemish in his past. "But I doubt it."

"We must warn Penelope."

"Yes." And his mother—Luke must alert his mother. He must also distance himself from Elizabeth, immediately. Any dishonor that touched him could not be allowed to rub off on her.

He'd been waiting for this day for years, preparing for the disgrace that would come when Warren's secret came to light. He had expected to feel any number of emotions, when in truth, he felt nothing, nothing but an empty inner calm that shouldn't exist.

The wait was over.

"Luke?" Elizabeth moved to within inches of him. Her eyes were troubled and should have been full of judgment but held only affection, devotion, and something stronger, something he dared not hope for.

"You know I will stand by you."

He smiled. He could not help it. How remarkable she was, a woman full of substance and character and goodness. Glorious at times, when she wasn't frustrating him. Luke would do anything—sacrifice everything—to make her happy, even if that meant cutting her out of his life. He adored her. He might even be in love with her.

He was in love with Elizabeth?

Possibly.

Probably.

He crushed her to him and set his forehead to hers.

"Elizabeth." Her name came out as a ragged sigh. Pressure built in his throat, burned behind his eyes.

"Luke. Oh, Luke." Trembling in his arms, she feathered her long, slim fingers through his hair. She had a soothing touch, a healing touch, and he wanted to bask in the joy of her. "It's going to be all right."

No, it wasn't. Soon, very soon, nothing would be right again. But for this moment, with the world locked on the other side of the office, Luke would allow himself to be selfish. He would think of Elizabeth as his. Only his.

"Elizabeth." He buried his face in her hair, breathed in her scent of lilacs and jasmine.

This was where she belonged, in his arms, in his life.

He could hear the voice of reason telling him to release her. The longer he held on to her, the harder it would be to let her go. He kissed the top of her head, stroked a hand over her hair, prayed for some semblance of control.

When she pulled back to look at him, he lowered his mouth to hers. The kiss started gentle, but it quickly got out of hand. He immediately set her away from him.

They stared at one another, breathing hard, both caught in a storm of emotion. And then she was back in his arms. Luke would never know which of them moved first—him, her, both perhaps.

Wrapping her tightly to him, he allowed himself one more moment, one final indulgence, then stepped away from her again and turned his back on her. "I have to go."

"Go? Go where?"

"I'll see you home first."

"I'm not going home."

He didn't look at her. "You are."

Moving around him, eyes shining with sympathy, she took one of his hands and placed a kiss to his palm. The gesture was so unexpected, so gentle, his heart tripped over itself. To keep from pulling her close, he folded his arms across his chest.

"I want to be with you when you speak with Penelope."

"This is a family matter." Unwilling to drag her into this drama, he hardened his heart. "You are not family."

Eyes bleak, she said, "Please don't shut me out."

"That's not what I'm doing."

"Even if you don't want my support, I know some of what Penelope will be experiencing when she discovers the truth about her father. I can be a comfort to her."

She made a valid argument. Luke nearly relented. But, as she herself said, Elizabeth had endured her own pain in recent months. He wanted to shield her from suffering any more.

"Go home, Little Bit."

"Why are you pushing me way?"

"You must disassociate yourself from my family or risk suffering guilt by association."

"Right, now I get it." She smiled, though her smile was anything but pleasant. "This is yet another of your misguided attempts to protect me."

"Misguided? Hardly."

"I thought you knew me."

"I do know you." He reached for her.

She shrank from his touch. "You think I would desert Penelope and Sophie, for the sake of my own reputation?"

"That's not what I said."

Her cheeks colored to a deep, angry red. "You think I would desert *you*?"

Luke swallowed around the knot in his throat. "I know you wouldn't."

Therein lay the problem. Elizabeth would fight for those she loved, at great risk to herself. She was the very definition of Christian integrity. He could send her home, but he knew that wouldn't keep her from standing with him and his family.

"I have another idea," he found himself saying. "I'll go to my father and let him know of Sophie's plans to confront him."

Elizabeth's eyes widened. "What do you think he'll do?"

"He will make matters right with my mother and Penelope and, of course, Sophie."

"And if he doesn't?"

"Then I will."

* * *

The sound of piano music greeted Elizabeth when she entered St. James House. She didn't recognize the piece, but she recognized the quality of the playing.

Happy for the distraction after the emotionally draining time in Luke's office, and during the tense car ride to St. James House, she divested herself of her cloak. Then, she made her way to the music room.

Pausing at the top of the stairs leading into the sunken space, Elizabeth shut her eyes and let the music flow over her.

The haunting melody matched her mood. Her mind instantly went to Luke and the way one corner of his mouth had lifted in a sad smile during their difficult conversation. Elizabeth worried for him. He was so strong, so in charge, so willing to take care of the people in his life. But she knew he was suffering unspeakable guilt over what his father had done to the women he loved. Luke shouldered their burdens and did what he could to protect them from harm.

Elizabeth adored the competent way he entered a situation and took charge. But who took care of him?

Who protected him? Who stood for him?

No one. He was alone, so alone.

He needs me.

He refused to accept her support.

Elizabeth wanted to weep in frustration. She could be his helpmate, the one person who would stand by him, always, who had the honor of sharing his joys and sorrows.

Sighing, she dropped her head, studied the toe of her boot.

She would never be that woman, not as things stood, not unless Luke stopped seeing her as yet another person requiring his protection. She ached to convince him she was his perfect match. There had to be a way to make him see her as a woman he could count on. A woman he could take rest in and turn to when he found himself overburdened with life's cares.

That was the biblical model of marriage and the life she wanted with Luke.

The playing stopped abruptly. "Is someone there?"

"Just me, Sally."

Elizabeth entered the music room. The heels of her ankle boots clicked across the wood-slatted floors, bouncing off the walls and high-vaulted ceilings designed specifically for acoustics.

Stopping near the piano, she smiled at her maid. The young woman sat at the bench, her lace cap sitting beside her. She'd let down her hair, and now it hung in thick caramel waves past her shoulders. There was something in her eyes, a vulnerability that was foreign to the Sally Smith whom Elizabeth knew.

The maid looked as haunted as the music she'd been playing.

"Please don't stop on my account," Elizabeth told her, meeting the maid's eyes. "I never tire of listening to you play."

Sally reached for her cap, twisted the edges between her fingers, before returning it to her head. "I've been at it for nearly two hours. I could use a break."

Knowing her maid didn't like answering personal questions, Elizabeth considered leaving it at that. But something about the woman's posture told her to press on, if for no other reason than to let her know someone cared about her. She started with a simple statement. "I'm glad you feel comfortable enough to take me up on my offer to play whenever you have a free moment or two."

Sally smiled, the sadness still in her eyes.

"Someone once said music expresses that which cannot be put into words and that which cannot remain silent."

"The quote is attributed to Victor Hugo."

Elizabeth started. The maid knew the saying was from the famous playwright and poet? Where could she have learned something like that?

Sighing, Sally stared wistfully at the piano, ran her fingers over the black lacquered wood above the ivory keys.

"It's such a beautiful instrument." She played a few bars of a Bach concerto before drawing her hands away and setting them carefully on her lap. "The tone is excellent."

Elizabeth could tell by the reverence in Sally's words that the young woman had a great affection for playing the piano. *Love without reservation.* Elizabeth was too late to help Hester. But she could do something tangible and lasting for Sally. Even if it was as simple as encouraging her to pursue her passion for music. "Where did you learn to play so exquisitely?"

Sally flinched. The reflexive gesture gave Elizabeth the impression she'd pushed the maid too far and now Sally wouldn't answer her question. But after dragging air into her lungs, she said, "My mother taught me."

Relieved the young woman had responded, Elizabeth pressed for more. "Is she still alive?"

Her hands flexed in her lap. "No."

"Do you have any other family?"

Sally shook her head, refusing to meet Elizabeth's gaze. She didn't doubt Sally was alone in the world, yet her reluctant answers only raised more questions and made her more determined to help her friend. What kind of sad, lonely world did the maid inhabit, where she had no family to lean on and no one but Elizabeth to share confidences with? "I'm so sorry."

Sally acknowledged her words with a head bob. She looked about to say more but then took another breath and turned away from the piano, sufficiently ending that portion of their conversation. "Another letter came for you this afternoon"—the maid's eyes went dark and turbulent—"from the same Florida address as the others."

Her mother had written her again. That made three letters.

"I set it with the previous two, along with several invitations and a letter with an Arizona postmark."

How odd. Elizabeth didn't know anyone living in Arizona.

"Thank you, Sally." Eager to solve the mystery, she started for the door. "I'll head upstairs straightaway."

"Would you like me to come with you?"

She was not so fragile that she needed company opening a letter from an unknown address. "Stay, play awhile longer."

Sally looked longingly at the piano, back at Elizabeth. "You are certain?"

"Beyond certain."

Minutes later, she sat at her writing desk, Hester's shawl wrapped around her shoulders. The rain had done its damage, and the silk was ruined, but Elizabeth didn't care about the garment's appearance. Only what it represented.

The first thing she noticed was how Sally had organized the pieces of correspondence in three neat piles.

Elizabeth tackled the largest stack first. An invitation to a ball, three requests for her attendance at various dinner parties, one to a soiree for ladies only, and a hastily scribbled note from Penelope reminding Elizabeth about the performance of *Carmen* in her father's opera house the following evening.

Apprehension took hold of Elizabeth. She remembered Sophie's vulnerable expression in the department store. There'd been resentment and purpose in her gaze as well. If the girl wished to confront her father, and wanted to do so with the most impact, the performance would be the perfect place.

One question would be all it would take: *Are you my father?*

Quick, clean, and tidy, with unimaginable repercussions to the guilty and innocent alike. The damage would be great and impossible to undo.

A burst of panic had her writing a quick response to Penelope. Not only would Elizabeth attend the performance, she would make sure she sat beside her friend. And Luke. She would be there for him as well, whether he liked it or not.

Heart in her throat, Elizabeth penned another quick note, alerting Luke she would be at the opera and expected to see him there. He would understand the hidden meaning in her words.

That deed done, she set aside both notes, knowing she would have Sally deliver them later, and studied the next two stacks. One included her mother's three letters. The other held a single letter from Tucson, Arizona.

A rush of emotion clawed in her throat. The handwriting was familiar and dear. The letter was from Hester. Tears pricked but remained unshed.

Elizabeth forced herself to remain calm, to think logically. If Hester had written her—from an Arizona address, no less—that meant her former governess was doing better. More importantly, she was alive.

After securing the shawl tighter around her shoulders, she ripped open the envelope.

> *My dear, sweet Elizabeth,*
> *I pray this letter finds you well and that the shawl I sent*
> *you is showing a bit of wear.*

Smiling, Elizabeth glanced at the garment in question. The ends were frayed where she'd snipped off the fringe to put in the cameo and other lockets. There was also a sizable section missing where she'd cut into the shawl to make hair ribbons. Most telling of all, the silk was faded to a drab red from its time in the rain. "Hester," she whispered, "I think you would approve."

Elizabeth lowered her head and continued reading.

> *I am writing from my new home, St. Mary's*
> *Sanatorium in Tucson, Arizona.*

Elizabeth's hand flew to her throat. Hester was living in a sanatorium? That could mean only one thing.

> *Have no fear, my dear. I do not have tuberculosis.*
> *My lungs are merely weak. I have been in residence less*
> *than a week, but I already feel at home. I am enjoying*
> *fresh air, sunshine, and friendship. I felt especially strong*
> *yesterday and accompanied two of the sisters on what they*
> *call a "begging tour" to raise money for the Indian schools*
> *they built in San Xavier and Komatke. We also sought*
> *funds for their orphanage.*

I am pleased to report that the Sisters of St. Joseph and I are of a like mind. I have found my calling, Elizabeth. The Lord has been very gracious at a time I thought my life was over. This is the adventure I have always sought, in a most unexpected yet fulfilling way.

Elizabeth sighed, the happy sound filling the room. "I am so pleased for you, my friend."

In closing, please thank your young man for me, not only for his generous donation to our cause but also for making the arrangements to send me here. Had Mr. Griffin not found this sanatorium, I would have been forever stuck in that horrible hospital bed, full of regrets.

I will write again soon. If you find a moment, I would love to hear where my shawl has been.

Yours, most humbly,

Hester

Elizabeth reread the letter, quicker this time, then refolded the paper and placed it in the drawer with the others Hester had sent.

Oh, Luke, you dear, wonderful man. His actions had probably saved Hester's life.

Struggling to absorb the extravagance of his gift, she took a long breath. He loved her, the dear, wonderful, stubborn, stubborn man; nothing else explained the lengths he'd gone to in order to give Hester a comfortable new life.

There was a drumming in Elizabeth's heart, an anticipation that had been building in her ever since he'd taken her walking in the rain. This was the confirmation she'd been seeking, the realization that she could have more, *be* more, if she was willing to take a chance.

Love without reservation.

Retrieving her Bible, she pulled out her list, studied the entries. Hester had been her inspiration to start the journey. Now, she was the reason Elizabeth assessed the direction she'd initially taken.

She'd been raised in the church, taught to serve people in need but only from a distance.

What she'd really done was live for herself, selfishly resisting the blessings she'd been given, wanting more than duty. More than blind obedience. More than marriage to a stranger for the sake of the family.

How shortsighted she'd been.

No wonder her life had seemed so empty. She'd been chasing the wrong adventures, searching for validation in the wrong places, from the wrong people.

Oh, Elizabeth still wanted more. But now she wanted more of a chance to impact others. Urging Sally to play the piano whenever she wished was a start, but it was not nearly enough. Perhaps she could nurture the maid's talent in a way that would lead her to a better situation. Elizabeth wouldn't stop there. She would help others in need and expand her influence beyond her small, privileged world. The world Katherine St. James found so appealing.

The unopened letters from her mother caught her attention.

She sat staring at them, the familiar handwriting blurring before her eyes, riveting her attention until her chin dropped. A swarm of unpleasant memories swirled in her mind, taking her back to the day she'd discovered her mother's true nature. The reflex to throw the letters across the room came fast and hard. No. She would not give in to emotion. She'd been a coward for too long.

Chin firmed, shoulders square, Elizabeth opened the first of the three letters and read her mother's words.

Chapter Twenty-One

The twelfth annual performance of *Carmen* had yet to begin. A problem had broken out backstage, delaying the opening act by ten full minutes. No, make that—Luke flipped open his pocket watch—fifteen minutes. And counting.

Fidgeting uncomfortably in their chairs, the gentlemen of the orchestra gave one another helpless shrugs. Their instruments were tuned, their sheet music neatly organized in front of them, but they hadn't played a single bar of the famous opera. Not even the prelude.

From his spot at the back of the theater, Luke inwardly cringed. He, along with the roomful of 150 invited guests, could hear a pair of raised female voices arguing in Italian.

Eager for a glimpse of the drama unfolding behind the velvet curtain, the audience leaned forward in their seats, tongues wagging. Luke shuddered to think what conclusions they'd already drawn. This particular performance would be the talk of wealthy New Yorkers for months to come.

"Mio Dio, non posso sopportare altri insulti!" shouted one of the voices.

"É lei che mi insulta!" came the reply.

The room gave a collective gasp. Then . . .

The whispers began again in earnest.

Luke had no idea what either woman screamed at the other, but he recognized the voices. One was from Warren's past, the other from his present.

A sense of inevitability took hold. And Luke realized he'd failed the women in his family. This evening was not going to end well. Whether he interfered or kept out of the fray, Warren Griffin's past had caught up with him. The ensuing scandal was but moments away. All Luke could do now was manage the aftereffects.

He let out a slow, careful, silent push of air. The gesture reduced the tension between his shoulders not one bit. Given a choice, he'd prefer to leave the theater this very minute. He didn't dare. He needed to be present in case the worst happened.

When the worst happened.

"*Io canterò per essere al comando!*"

"*Dovrai passare sul mio cadavere! Non siete in grado di cantare le arie di* Carmen*!*"

Luke knew he should probably head backstage and see if he could calm the raging female tempest. But his father had threatened him with bodily harm if he got involved. Luke didn't fear Warren's fist. No, what kept him rooted to the spot was a very real sense that if he put himself in the middle of the women's argument, he would only complicate matters.

This was his father's battle. Not his.

Still. Dread filled him. He shifted his stance, ran his gaze over the assembled crowd. There wasn't an empty seat in the tiny theater. Some of the most powerful men in New York sat beside their equally influential wives, the latter hungry for a juicy scandal. They would get their wish soon enough.

Penelope and Simon had taken their seats in the front row. They seemed oblivious to everything around them, their heads bent in quiet conversation. Simon's hand rested on Penelope's arm in a protective gesture. This wasn't the first time Luke had watched the two closely, but it was the first time he saw what he'd been unable to discern because of his own prejudice.

Simon was, indeed, devoted to Penny, and she to him.

That devotion will be tested before the night is through.

For months, Luke had worked hard to prevent this very thing, a futile attempt on his part to control the people around him, his father in particular.

Warren Griffin was an arrogant man, full of entitlement, and unwilling to change.

Luke didn't often pray. He did so now, lifting up a fervent request that the Lord protect the innocent in the room tonight.

Please, Lord, this is all I ask.

Opening his eyes once again, he focused on the woman sitting on Penelope's left. Elizabeth had arrived later than many of the other guests, but her presence next to Penelope gave Luke a moment of peace.

Unfortunately, the way she flinched every time a string of angry Italian burst through a seam in the curtains indicated she, like Luke, feared what was to come.

She shot a nervous glance over her shoulder, as if looking for someone in particular. Not someone, him. From his vantage point in the shadows, Luke watched her a moment in frozen silence. His breath caught in his throat. She was so lovely.

The shock of her beauty never ceased to call forth a strong visceral response in him. He gave the sensation free rein tonight, let his breathing quicken and his heart pound wildly in his chest.

The green-and-gold gown she wore shimmered in the soft glow of the theater lighting, taking on the same hue as the heavy velvet curtains covering the stage. She looked delicate, beguiling, and yet also dynamic. The unexpected flares of fiery mischief lurking beneath the doll-like beauty captivated Luke. Enthralled him.

Called to him.

As if she sensed his presence, her gaze sought and found his.

She smiled.

Despite the apprehension pooling in his gut, he smiled back. He'd evaded his feelings for so long, this poignant moment extorted the last scraps of calm he possessed.

Leaving her seat, Elizabeth joined him at the back of the theater, setting her back against the wall. "I looked for you earlier."

"I only just arrived."

She worried her bottom lip. "Did you speak with your father?"

He nodded. "The conversation did not go well."

An understatement. His father had been full of denial and fury. There hadn't been an ounce of remorse in Warren's bearing. Luke had looked. His appeal to Warren's character had fallen flat. A man couldn't change unless he wanted to do so. Warren did not want to change.

"I was afraid of that." Elizabeth said something more, but her words were lost under a river of furious Italian expletives. He knew *exactly* what those meant.

Feeling her flinch beside him, Luke turned to Elizabeth and caught her staring up at him. In her evening slippers, she stood to the height of his chin. Mesmerized, he held her gaze. The look in her eyes was tenderness itself, a look full of affection and . . . love.

She loved him.

The revelation caused him an instant of absolute peace. He loved her in return, with everything he was. Suddenly, he wanted to tell her everything in his heart.

Now was not the time. This was not the place.

The precious moment lasted three, perhaps four heartbeats. Luke tried to collect every second and commit it to memory so that in the future when he closed his eyes, Elizabeth would be there, smiling at him as if he were the most special man in the world.

"While I have your attention . . ." She paused. "I would like to say thank you, Luke. What you did for my friend." Another pause. "It was . . . I can't begin to tell you . . ." She gave an anxious little laugh. "There are no words to express my gratitude."

Having a hard time keeping up with her erratic speech, he asked, "What exactly do you think I did?"

"You made arrangements for Hester's move to St. Mary's Sanatorium. It could not have been easy or, dare I say, without great cost to you."

Luke went still for a heartbeat. Elizabeth wasn't supposed to know what he'd done for her former governess. Hester had promised to keep his involvement only between them. He thought back to their conversation. He'd asked her to keep quiet. Had she actually agreed? The older woman had patted his hand, smiled, then thanked him profusely, but no, she hadn't given her word.

"Don't look so grim, Luke. Hester is greatly appreciative."

"I didn't do it for her. I did it for you."

"Luke." In a sweet tone most effective for its softness, she said, "I . . . Oh, Luke, I . . . *Thank you.*"

The love was there, in her eyes, in her tone, taking over, filling his heart, and releasing the years of built-up anger, tearing down the wall he'd erected between them. He felt defenseless against the sensation, against her.

You could have a life with her. Not without bringing harm to her. "Go back to your seat."

"I want to stand by you." Her words held a double meaning.

"I don't want to ruin you by association."

"Of course you don't. You can't; it's not in your nature."

"You don't understand." He took a stabilizing breath. "There are things I've done in my past that cannot be undone. You could be harmed merely by standing beside me tonight."

"You don't mean to insult me. I know that." She cut him a quick, irritated look. "So I'm going to change the subject."

Before he could say a word, she hurled into a lengthy dissertation on the weather. Luke felt his lips curve upward, especially when she expounded on the virtue of spring rain showers.

How could he not love this woman?

How could he let her go to England?

In the middle of her ridiculous speech, the shouting stopped suddenly, the silence more jolting than the screeching Italian.

A hush fell over the theater.

Luke's father appeared from behind the center slit in the curtains, then took up a spot near center stage. His features were set and stern, matched only by the severity of his black coat and crisp white shirt. He looked put-upon, a man pushed to his limits. No wonder—mediating an argument between two divas required fortitude.

"There will be a change in the cast this evening." Warren paused, looked over his shoulder, grimaced, and continued. "It is my great honor to announce the lead mezzo-soprano role will be sung by the incomparable . . . Esmeralda Cappelletti."

A murmuring went up from the crowd.

The performance of a lifetime was upon them.

At the same moment Warren nodded to the orchestra, the door on Luke's right swung opened with a bang. All heads turned, including Luke's. Elizabeth's hand went to his arm.

In stepped a stunning young woman a few years older than Penelope. She hovered at the entrance of the theater, poised and unmoving. She scanned the crowd, found who she was looking for an instant later.

Warren's face went completely ashen.

Luke exchanged a bleak look with Elizabeth.

"That's Sophie." Her voice came at him as if from a great distance. He nodded. He didn't need confirmation. Those amber eyes didn't lie.

Luke reached for a calm that didn't exist. Sophie had a beautiful, dramatic face, the perfect mix of exotic and innocent. She had her mother's dark hair and regal bearing. She had her father's eyes. And she was Luke's sister.

His sister.

Gaze fixed on Warren, Sophie began walking toward the front of the theater.

Luke went on the move as well. Elizabeth was one step ahead of him, calling after the girl.

Sophie ignored her.

Luke pulled Elizabeth to a stop near the front row. This wasn't her battle. It wasn't his, either.

Eyes on the drama developing steps ahead of them, she reached out, laid a hand on his in a natural show of comfort he knew was innate to her.

All this time, Luke had been worried Elizabeth would do something reckless and ruin her reputation. Deep down, he'd known she was too smart for that. He was the real danger to her good name, though not in the way he'd feared.

He glanced at Penelope. Her mouth had fallen open, and she started to rise. Simon held her in place.

A cold, deadening sensation filled Luke's lungs as he twined his fingers through Elizabeth's.

Her gaze was locked on the stage. A gasp slipped out of her. Luke didn't need to look to know who'd joined Warren on the stage. He felt Esmeralda's presence in his gut, in the kick of antagonism that hit him square in the heart.

Luke knew how this ended. His grip on Elizabeth's hand tightened. He was probably squeezing a bit too hard. He couldn't help himself. She was his only lifeline in a sea of uncertain emotion.

Let her go, he told himself. *Let. Her. Go.*

He couldn't make his fingers cooperate, couldn't seem to distance himself from her.

Let her go.

Elizabeth was the one who pulled away from him. The absence of her touch was staggering, the pain sharp and unexpected.

But instead of leaving him, she moved closer and linked her arm through his. Her eyes filled with understanding and something even more disturbing. Sympathy.

He didn't want her sympathy. He wanted her free of scandal. It was the one gift he could give her.

He began to step away from her, to distance himself from what he saw in her eyes. She tightened her grip and smiled sweetly. Luke became aware of whispers rising from the audience and turned back to the stage.

"Who is she?" He didn't know who asked the question. He was too focused on Sophie's face, on the fear and bitterness and inflexibility there.

"Do you know who I am?" Sophie demanded of Warren.

Esmeralda tried to speak. "Now, Sophie, this is not the time for dramatics."

Actually, Luke thought perversely, this was the perfect time for dramatics. Sophie could not have timed her arrival better.

"Do you know who I am?" she repeated, ignoring her mother, ignoring the crowd, ignoring everyone but Warren.

"I know who you are."

"Will you acknowledge me?"

Warren winced. "It appears I do not have a choice."

"Sophie? Sophie Cappelletti?" Penelope shrugged off Simon, a tentative, hopeful smile on her lips. "Is it really you?"

The question broke Sophie's concentration for a split second. She glanced at Penelope, smiled sadly, turned to Luke, gave him a similar look, then turned back to Warren.

"I see I have interrupted something of a family gathering, a performance of sorts. I suppose I should have waited until morning, but I simply could not bear another night without knowing my fa—"

"*Silenzio!*" Esmeralda stepped in front of Warren, glaring at her daughter. "Sophie, you will not do this tonight."

"But, Mamma, I already have."

There was an enormous pause, silence falling over the room right before the gossip exploded in loud, easy-to-discern phrases of condemnation.

Yes, Luke thought grimly, Sophie had done enough simply by standing before Warren. She need not say another word. The audience did the talking for her.

"She is the very image of him."

"The eyes. There can be no mistake."

"I wonder if there are others like her."

Everyone's attention was riveted on Warren and Sophie. No one noticed him and Elizabeth in the shadows.

It was the incentive he needed to untangle their arms and step away from her. "Go home," he told her. "Before it's too late."

Luke had to find his mother and warn her. He also had to go to Penelope, except . . .

He *didn't* have to go to her. Simon had his arm around her shoulders, drawing her against him, the move one of protection. The man was standing by his fiancée.

"I won't leave you." At the same moment Simon said the words to Penelope, Elizabeth said them to Luke.

He turned his head and saw the truth in her eyes. She would jeopardize her future for him. She would throw away her standing in society and suffer scandal for him.

He loved her too much to let her make such a sacrifice. The look she gave him was nearly his undoing.

"Go away," he said, his voice harsh with desperation. "I don't want you here."

"Luke," she whispered, tears filling her eyes.

He repeated the words.

"Please don't push me away." She grabbed his arm, her grip surprisingly strong. "I love you. You big, handsome, stupid fool, did you hear me? I love you."

She loved him. Joy filled him, bringing him hope.

He wanted to say the words back to her. But if he did, she would be linked to him forever. Her future would no longer be hers, her choices no longer her own. "Sometimes," he said, "love is not enough."

* * *

"You don't mean that." Elizabeth stepped toward Luke, lifting her hand and touching his jaw. "Love can conquer anything."

For a fleeting moment, she thought he would tell her he needed her and wanted her to stay by his side. But he didn't. He pulled away from her touch and stepped back, refusing to meet her eyes.

She considered his beautiful, stony face, knowing this was her last chance to convince him they belonged together. That no scandal was too big to keep them apart.

"You once accused me of being reckless and not considering the consequences of my actions. But I know exactly what I'm doing." Closing the distance between them, she lifted on her tiptoes, prepared to kiss him in front of anyone who cared to watch.

He evaded the move with a small side step. The message was clear. He didn't want her with him now, or ever. At least that's what his actions said. His eyes told a different story.

Scowling, she opened her mouth to speak, only to have him interrupt her.

"I won't bring scandal on you, Little Bit." He said the nickname with admiration, affection, and love. So much love. "I want you to go to England as planned, and live happily ever after with your British lord."

Elizabeth heard what he didn't say. He wanted her away from New York. Away from him. "I can only be happy with you, Luke."

"I won't be happy with you."

Having said those horrible, awful, untrue words—*Lies, lies, lies*—Luke pulled away from her, literally and figuratively, as Elizabeth watched helplessly. He shifted his stance so she had a view of his hard, inflexible profile.

His pain was tangible, and her heart broke for him. Bone-deep grief knocked the breath out of her. Refusing to let him shut her out, she stepped around him and forced him to look at her.

"Move aside, Elizabeth. I need to find my mother and . . . prepare her."

Giving her no chance to respond, he pushed past.

She stopped him with a hand on his arm. "This isn't over. *We* aren't over."

"Yes, Elizabeth, we are."

He exited the theater without a backward glance. In her heart, she knew he needed to find his mother and tell her of the scandal coming her way. But Luke didn't have to do that alone. How dare he leave her behind?

She wanted to go after him, but she knew he wouldn't appreciate her persistence. Another time, perhaps, but not tonight.

Seeing that Penelope was in good hands with her fiancé—how reassuring—there was nothing left for Elizabeth to do but go home. She found her grandfather's chauffeur waiting for her by the motorcar. "Please, Jefferies, take me home."

"Yes, ma'am."

Elizabeth sighed, leaning her head back against the upholstery. She let the motion of the vehicle calm her, enough to make plans. She would approach Luke again in the morning. She would present the reasons they belonged together in calm, succinct terms.

They arrived at St. James House all too soon.

Hurt and confused by Luke's refusal to rely on her, Elizabeth trudged inside the giant entryway, defeated but not beaten. There must be a way to prove she was sincere, but how? She'd secretly wanted a love like Jackson and Caroline shared, one of sacrificial devotion. She'd found that with Luke. She hadn't wanted scandal, but she wouldn't run away from it, either. She and Luke would weather the gossip together.

He would send her away if she didn't have a solid plan in place when she faced him. How was she supposed to make him see that she didn't care about her reputation if preserving it meant losing him?

Her father met her in the foyer, an apology in his eyes.

Elizabeth moved in his direction and kissed his cheek. "Welcome home, Father."

"Elizabeth, if you would be so good as to join me in the parlor." He made a sweeping gesture with his hand. "I have something I wish to discuss."

One look at his face told her what she needed to know. He'd forgiven his wife and was prepared to tell her why. Elizabeth thought of the letters she'd read yesterday afternoon. There were phrases penned in her mother's elegant script that had suggested sincerity, pleas for forgiveness that gave Elizabeth cause to believe she was truly contrite. Yet there were other sentences that had revealed a strong desire on Katherine's part to place the blame everywhere but where it belonged—on herself.

On the whole, the letters had softened Elizabeth's heart a bit, at least enough to hear her father's arguments with an open mind. But she wasn't in the mood to do so tonight. Not with Luke and his family's trouble filling her head. "I'm tired, Father. Can this please wait until tomorrow?"

"I'm afraid it can't." Her father hesitated, and she turned to face him, gauging his mood and seeing the apology again. "You have a visitor, Elizabeth."

Relief nearly buckled her knees. Luke had come for her. Somehow he'd beaten her home. But that couldn't be right. He would never abandon his family at such a time as this. That wasn't the man she loved.

Elizabeth met her father's gaze. It was filled with guilt and regret, and she knew who was waiting in the parlor before he said, "It is your mother."

So. The ghastly evening was not yet over.

"She cannot be here." The wariness in her voice was a perfect match for the turmoil swirling in her heart. "Grandfather would never allow it."

"Richard has graciously given me thirty minutes to make my case." Her mother moved into the foyer, hand extended to Elizabeth. "Won't you hear me out?"

She considered ignoring her mother's request, but she thought of the three letters she'd read, each more passionate than the last. Somewhere, deep inside, Elizabeth was still a little girl working to earn her mother's approval. Even knowing the risks of letting down her guard, she wanted to believe that every word and sentiment expressed in those letters was real. She wanted to believe her mother was good and kind.

Hating her own weakness, she followed her parents into the parlor. The three of them sat in silence, until Elizabeth couldn't stand the quiet a moment longer. "Where is Grandfather?"

Her mother dipped her head, sighed tragically. "Richard does not want to hear anything I have to say."

Elizabeth couldn't blame him. She suddenly wanted to run from the room and never look back. But she was here now, and cowardice had no place in this conversation.

Ask for my forgiveness, Mother. Say the words. Apologize. Then I can go to my room and formulate a plan to win Luke's trust.

"I understand your cousin has returned from her honeymoon."

"Do not mention Caroline in this house. You do not have the right."

"No, I suppose I don't." Her mother's pale-blue gaze, so like her own, showed signs of repentance. Was the emotion real? Or a calculated pretense to play on Elizabeth's sympathies?

"I merely wished to point out that your cousin has found happiness." Katherine said this without a hint of irony. "All is as it should be."

That was her mother's flimsy defense? "No thanks to you."

"Elizabeth," her father scolded, "there is no cause to be rude."

Perhaps not, but the resentment she'd held at bay for months threatened to burst out of her mouth in a string of accusations. None of which would change the events of the past. "Say what you came to say, Mother."

"I am sorry."

Struck by the sincerity in the words, Elizabeth leaned forward and studied her mother's face. She looked the same. Her beauty, the one gift she'd transferred to her daughter, was undeniable. There were a few new lines on her face and neck, and her light-blonde hair was streaked golden from time spent in the Florida sun.

"You are sorry for what?" Elizabeth pressed.

There was something in her mother's eyes, a hint of humility that gave Elizabeth hope she'd truly changed. But then, she spoke. "I am sorry for what I've done."

I am sorry for what I've done. Not *I'm sorry for hurting Caroline.* Not *I'm sorry for betraying my family.* It was as Elizabeth feared. Katherine St. James was sorry for being sent away, for losing the life she valued above all else, not for destroying innocent lives. She hadn't truly changed.

"What do you want from me?" She heard the tremor in her voice, hated the weak sound.

"I want your permission to come home."

Elizabeth shrugged one shoulder. "That decision is not up to me. Grandfather is the one you should be asking."

Her mother eyed her closely, and one side of her mouth turned down. "You have changed."

Praise God. "I suppose I have."

"You have become alarmingly strong-willed."

"I certainly hope so."

Katherine's mouth thinned. "Is this your cousin's doing? This lack of respect for your own mother?"

"If you mean to suggest that I have become more like Caroline, then I will take that as a compliment."

Her mother stared at her in muted shock.

Needing to think, to digest the past ten minutes, Elizabeth exited the room without uttering a single word of farewell. She walked with slow, steady strides, head high, chin parallel with the floor. She waited for the pain to hit her, the sadness that Katherine St. James would never fully regret her actions. Elizabeth felt nothing but a vast, gaping hollowness deep in her soul. And she knew why.

Tonight had been her opportunity to let go of the past. She'd failed to say the words necessary to gain her freedom. Moreover, she'd refused to grant her mother mercy simply because the woman hadn't displayed enough remorse.

Elizabeth's footsteps faltered, then stopped altogether.

She was withholding forgiveness for the wrong reason, waiting for her mother to *earn* her compassion. Elizabeth reached for the locket around her neck.

A month ago, she'd embarked on a journey for independence. She'd begun like a fluffy white cloud, blown around by every wind. The list had been a prelude, a shallow attempt to find a purpose for her life.

Elizabeth had been fooling herself, thinking a few adventures would make a difference. She could accomplish every task on her list, and she would still not be free. If she was to become a woman of substance, a woman who could look herself in the mirror every morning without wondering if there was *more*, she had to release her anger. Only then would she find her purpose and become the woman she was meant to be.

She returned to the parlor.

Other than a slight widening of her eyes, her mother had not moved, a striking, composed woman who appeared younger than her age, groomed and polished in her Parisian gown. Marcus had joined his wife on the settee. He looked as stricken as Elizabeth felt.

The two sat holding hands, unmoving, blinking at one another in strained silence as if unsure what to do next.

When Elizabeth went to stand before her mother, she swallowed back a wave of consternation. Why was it, she mused, that she perpetually felt inadequate around the woman who had given birth to her?

For several seconds, she just stood there, her heart hammering, trying to gather the words that would set her free.

"You have hurt many people, Mother. I am the least of them." Elizabeth drew in a quick breath, proud of the steadiness in her voice. "It is still Grandfather's decision, but if you wish to come home, I will do nothing to prevent your return."

Her mother rose, her face showing genuine signs of stress.

Standing eye to eye with the woman who had caused so many of her loved ones pain, Elizabeth dug deep and found the courage to release the last of her hostility. "I forgive you."

Chapter Twenty-Two

In the calm after the emotional storm that had raged all through the night, Luke stood in the library of Griffin Manor, eyes gritty, head pounding. He'd left his mother resting quietly in her room, her trusted maid by her side. Though she hadn't known the truth about Sophie, Violet Griffin hadn't been particularly surprised her husband had fathered a child out of wedlock.

And yet, coming to grips with Warren's betrayal would take time, including perhaps a month-long trip abroad.

The scandal would be tremendous, on the same scale as when Jackson's father had run off with his own wife's sister. By now, with the sun rising, the story of Warren's illegitimate daughter was being discussed, dissected, and judged in every home across Manhattan.

Luke clenched his fists. He knew his mother was hurting. He just didn't know how to ease her pain. And that made him feel helpless.

He hated feeling helpless.

The hard work of staring down the gossip would begin in a handful of hours. For now, Luke studied the other occupants in the room.

His sister and Sophie were huddled together in an overstuffed chair by the fire. Simon stood beside the mantel, looking down at the women with the same powerlessness Luke felt.

"I'm sorry, Penny." Sophie's voice shook with obvious shame and remorse. "It never occurred to me what my actions would do to you or the rest of your family. I've been so angry for so long, I only thought of myself. It was very badly done on my part."

Proving she was the best of all the Griffins, Penelope pulled the other girl into her arms and stroked a soothing hand down her hair. "You are the injured party, my dear, sweet friend. Not me, not my family, and definitely not my father."

She said the last two words through gritted teeth. Luke found Penelope's control impressive. She had every right to be angry with Warren, yet she set aside her own pain to help another woman through hers. His sister was one for the ages.

Elizabeth was the same sort of woman, with a similar depth of character.

And you sent her away.

His blood ran cold at the memory of her devastated expression.

"If I had only suffered a few sly glances, I might have kept the secret forever." She sniffled, wiped at her eyes, then sighed. "But my mother has always enjoyed drama, on and off the stage. She changes the story about my father depending on her audience, and that has proven a problem. All my life, I've had to listen to the speculation, the hushed whispers, but it was the open criticism that hurt most. The names I have been called . . ."

The feeling of helplessness came at Luke again, harder and with more force. He'd never put much stock in what other people thought about him, but he'd never had to endure the kind of censure Sophie described. "Has it been bad, Sophie?"

"You have no idea." Red-rimmed eyes turned his way. "I'm not like my mother, Luke. Despite my actions tonight, I abhor drama of any kind.

I just . . . I'm just so tired of the lies. They had to stop. I tried to approach Warren here at this house, and again at his office. He turned me away both times. I could think of no other way to make him acknowledge me."

"You did what you had to do," Penelope assured her, no judgment, no condemnation in her voice.

A sob slipped out of Sophie. "I would understand if you wished to refute my claim publicly. I would not hold it against you."

"We will not deny you," Luke vowed. "You are our sister."

"There is nothing more important than family." Penelope hugged the girl again. "We stick together and stand by each other. It is our way."

Sophie gave them both a shaky smile. Penelope murmured something Luke couldn't quite make out. Sophie responded in an equally low voice.

As the women huddled together, their voices barely audible, Luke looked at Simon over their heads. With a hitch of his chin, he motioned for the other man to follow him out into the hallway.

Seconds later, Simon stood before him, composed, coolheaded, the ultimate man of integrity. Tonight, he'd proven solid in his devotion to Penelope. Still, Luke wouldn't breathe easy until he knew, without a doubt, that his future brother-in-law understood what he was in for in the coming weeks, months, perhaps even years.

"You surprised me tonight."

The other man sniffed, his eyes radiating disdain and the judgment lacking in Penelope's behavior toward Sophie. "It was shabby of you to doubt my love for your sister."

Perhaps it was, but Luke had no remorse. "Penelope's future happiness matters to me."

Simon's entire bearing went stiff. "Her future happiness matters to me, as well, far more than my own."

A pall of silence enveloped them, broken only by the sound of the soft female voices coming from the library. "Your good name will suffer once the scandal spreads," Luke pointed out. "Are you prepared?"

"There is nothing to prepare for." Simon sent him a long, pitying look. "My good name will see us through this debacle."

"And if it doesn't?" Luke pressed. "Will you have a sudden change of heart and abandon my sister?"

Simon's fist went up, quick and furious.

Luke shifted smoothly to his left, catching the bulk of the blow on his right shoulder. Had he not been expecting the move, he would have been sporting a black eye later that afternoon.

Rubbing his shoulder—the man clearly didn't pull his punches—Luke gave Simon a wry look. "I deserved that."

One side of Simon's mouth kicked up. "Yes, you did." Shaking out his hand, he scowled. "Your concern for your sister is commendable, though wildly misdirected. Penny is worth ten times the man I will ever be, but she has agreed to marry me, and I am smart enough to know the blessing I have been given."

"That was some speech."

Simon continued as if Luke hadn't spoken. "If, as you suggest, Penny and I are shunned from society, then so be it. I would rather spend the rest of my life with your sister as my wife than enter another ballroom without her by my side."

There was sincerity in the man's voice that could not be faked, especially by someone like Simon, who lacked a sense of humor. "I was wrong about you," Luke admitted.

"You are wrong about a great many things."

Luke lifted an eyebrow. "Such as . . . ?"

A flash of pity moved in the other man's eyes, which he converted into a superior smile that set Luke's teeth on edge. "You should not have sent Miss St. James away. She is stronger than you give her credit for and would have brought you comfort during this time of uncertainty."

His shock couldn't have been greater had Simon challenged him to a duel. "You know about . . . Elizabeth and me?"

"You're not the only man investigating his future brother-in-law."

Well, well. He'd underestimated Simon Burrows. The realization brought him a moment of peace. Penelope was marrying a good man.

"You should apologize to Miss St. James."

Some of Luke's surprise edged into irritation. "You're giving me advice on women now?"

The superior smile widened. "Which one of us is happily engaged, and which one of us is pining for a woman he doesn't deserve?"

Luke rolled his throbbing shoulder at the rhetorical question. He *was* pining for a woman he didn't deserve. He thought of Elizabeth's steadfastness, her promise to stand by him. He'd all but thrown her out of his life. Worse, he'd told her to go to England and marry her British lord.

An ache started in his gut and ripped through his chest. What had he been thinking? He couldn't let her marry another man. She was his, the woman of his heart.

Whenever he mentally reviewed the past few months, Elizabeth was in every moment worth remembering. Since the first ball after his arrival back from England, Luke had fought to keep this woman at arm's length, to remember she didn't belong to him. Even when she was no longer off limits, old habits had prevailed. Luke had maintained his distance, or had attempted to do so, never asking her to dance, keeping their conversations brief. But at every gathering, she'd been the one he'd sought out first.

And then he'd kissed her. Twice. The first time had been about discovery, a lesson for her that had turned into a revelation for him. The second time Luke pulled Elizabeth into his arms had been . . . perfect. The homecoming he'd been waiting for since his return to America.

How long had he been in love with Elizabeth?

As long as he could remember. Not always as a man loved a woman, but she'd always held a special place in his heart. When she was near, nothing else mattered.

He needed to make things right between them. Then, he would spend the rest of his life placing her well-being above his own. When he imagined their future together, he saw grand adventures, laughter, and children, a houseful of towheaded boys and girls with their mother's goodness and strength.

Luke would ask her to marry him today, *after* he apologized. He wouldn't relinquish the good fight until she knew the contents of his heart. "I have to go."

"Yes, you do."

Luke paused mid-step.

"You know, Simon. One of these days, you and I may become friends." He gave the man a hard pat on the back. "Today is not that day."

Luke left Griffin Manor with Simon's low chuckle resonating in his ears. Perhaps the man had a sense of humor after all.

* * *

Luke went straight to St. James House. Not wanting to waste a single moment, he didn't bother changing out of his evening attire. Though the hour was still early, the sun had already made its appearance, tinting the sky a golden, rosy glow that would forever remind Luke of Elizabeth.

She was everything good and beautiful in his life, a beacon of light in his otherwise dark world, and Luke had been a colossal fool of the first order.

Had he actually thought he could live without Elizabeth?

Had he truly believed staying away from her would keep her safe?

No one knew better than Luke did that life was messy. People surprised and disappointed, often in the same moment. Safeguarding loved ones from pain was an admirable pursuit but not always an easy feat.

In an effort to protect Elizabeth, Luke had hurt her terribly. He would make it up to her, somehow. Even if it took him fifty years, a hundred, he would show her how much he loved her, wanted her.

Needed her.

He bound up the front steps leading to St. James House. Pausing at the enormous front door, Luke battled back a rush of unease.

What if he couldn't convince Elizabeth that he loved her? He'd treated her dismally. The damage could be irreparable.

His heart started beating madly in his chest, like a small animal's fighting to free itself from a net. No. He refused to admit defeat, not yet. Not ever.

Jaw set, he stabbed the doorbell and kept his finger in place long past necessary. He would not be ignored or turned away this morning.

A bleary-eyed, somewhat annoyed-looking Aldrich let him into the entryway. The butler's weary posture suggested there'd been difficulty at St. James House the previous evening. It seemed a night of drama was enjoyed by all.

"Mr. Griffin." The butler angled his head in confusion. "I wasn't aware you had an appointment with Mr. St. James this morning."

"I've come to speak with Miss St. James."

Two bushy eyebrows slid up the other man's forehead. "That presents a problem, sir. She's not at home. She left the house nearly an hour ago."

Luke's heart took a hard plunge. He'd prepared for every possible contingency, except Elizabeth's absence.

Battling a thread of panic, he made himself speak slowly, deliberately. "Did she happen to mention where she was going?"

The butler lifted his chin at a proud angle. "Miss St. James is not required to reveal her comings and goings to me."

Apparently, Luke had hit a sore spot. "Thank you, Aldrich. I'll see myself out."

He exited the house and conquered the steps two at a time. His sole intent was to find Elizabeth as quickly as possible.

Raking a hand through his hair, he forced himself to stop and think logically. Where would she go at this hour?

Who would she turn to, if not him? He could think of only one person—her cousin.

Twenty minutes later, the door to Jackson's house swung open. The man himself stood on the other side of the threshold, his gaze clouded with something that might be called amusement. "You look dreadful."

Luke let out a humorous laugh. "It's been a long night, and proving to be an equally trying morning."

"No doubt." Jackson ushered him inside.

Only once he'd crossed the threshold did Luke notice the squirming orange ball of fluff tucked under his friend's arm. "Is that one of your grandmother's pomegranates?"

"Otis is a Pomeranian," Jackson corrected. "And yes, he belongs to Granny."

"How did he end up with you?"

"Caroline mentioned our desire to start a family. Granny was so over the moon hearing this news that she suggested Caroline practice her mothering skills on Otis."

"Ah." It was no secret that Hattie Montgomery was fond of her miniature dogs. Last Luke counted, she had seven of the little terrors in her possession. She treated them like her beloved children, outrageously spoiling them. To give one of her "babies" to Caroline spoke of the older woman's desire for a great-grandchild.

"I take it you want to see Elizabeth."

Relief nearly buckled his knees. "She's here, then."

"Possibly."

Which meant *yes*.

The fact that Jackson just stood there, unmoving, eyes slightly narrowed, pushed Luke's control to the breaking point. "You want to let her know I'm here?"

"I will. Eventually."

The remaining scraps of his control unraveled. "Get her now."

"Not yet." Jackson's voice was as flat as the thin line of his lips. "You need to calm down first."

"I am calm," he said through a tight jaw.

"And yet, I remain unmoved." Jackson shifted the dog to his other arm. "If it's any consolation, Elizabeth arrived dry-eyed and far calmer than you."

This didn't surprise Luke. "She has hidden depths and strength of character that goes far beyond mere kindness."

"You know her well."

Luke rubbed at the ache behind his temple. "Elizabeth is the best woman I know."

"Yes. She would have been a great help to you and your family last night if you would have let her stay."

Luke saw something in his friend's serious eyes: sympathy—commiseration, even. "Elizabeth told you about last night."

Jackson nodded. A multitude of questions swam in his gaze. He voiced none of them, no doubt out of deference for their friendship. Or he simply hadn't come to grips with the truth that Warren Griffin, a man he'd always admired, wasn't who he presented to the world.

"Then you are aware of Sophie Cappelletti's connection to my family."

"I know she's your sister." Jackson made a sympathetic sound that spoke volumes. "I also know Elizabeth tried to stand by you when the scandal broke, but you sent her away."

A familiar rush of guilt spread through him. "I did it for her own good."

"You're an idiot."

"I don't disagree."

"When a woman like Elizabeth pledges her devotion, you don't throw her out of your life. You take the gift God has given you and treasure her the rest of your days on this earth."

Luke didn't need his friend telling him what he already knew. "I didn't come for a lecture."

"You're going to get one. But not here. Out in the garden. Otis is overdue for his morning constitutional."

Luke considered shoving past man and beast and then searching the house for Elizabeth. He thought better of it when he saw the look in Jackson's eyes. Luke wasn't getting past him until he'd had his say.

Patience, he told himself, feeling anything but. *Patience.* "Lead the way."

They exited the house through the terrace doors and fell into step, old friends used to one another's pace. Neither spoke as they worked their way down the marble stairs leading into the gardens below.

The crisp morning air smelled like spring, sweet and fresh. A symphony of blooms colored the entire area, and Luke was reminded of the time he'd come upon Elizabeth in the gardens of Griffin Manor. That night had changed everything between them. That had been the first time Luke had allowed himself to think of her as anything but his sister's friend.

After setting the dog on the ground, Jackson straightened and turned to Luke, his gaze full of bafflement. "The news of your father's infidelity came as quite a shock. I had no idea about the true nature of Warren's character."

"Not many did. My father has kept his secret . . . passions well hidden."

Jackson studied him a silent moment. "How long have you known?"

Shame coursed through Luke, his skin burning hot. "A decade, maybe longer. Esmeralda was only the first of many, but I don't believe I have any other half siblings besides Sophie."

Sympathy returned to Jackson's eyes. "You have carried this burden with you all that time?"

Luke nodded.

"You could have told me."

He could have, on any number of occasions, but . . .

"To what end?" Luke shoved his hands in his pockets and glanced over the manicured lawn, raking his gaze across the flower bushes and shrub trees without really seeing them. "You've always admired Warren."

"I considered him a second father."

"He liked playing that role in your life." Luke remembered the countless times Warren had compared him to Jackson. *Why can't you be more like your friend?*

"I never understood why Warren gave my father money to leave the country with his lover. It makes sense now." Jackson's voice was bleak, his gaze troubled. "It's going to be rough going for your family in the coming weeks."

If anyone would know, it would be Jackson. He'd faced his share of gossip because of his father's scandalous behavior. He'd worked tirelessly restoring his family's good name, and had nearly succeeded, only to toss every bit of progress away to marry Caroline.

He claimed he had no regrets for his choice.

Luke believed him, especially now that he'd discovered his own love for Elizabeth. If she were the one facing family disgrace, Luke would stand by her without a moment's hesitation.

"The Griffin name will suffer some pretty heavy blows," Jackson said.

"We'll get through it."

"You won't do so alone. Caroline and I will stand by you."

Simon would stand with his family, as well. There would be others. Not many, but some.

"I have one question for you, Luke." Jackson glanced briefly over Luke's shoulder. "And I want an honest answer."

Knowing what was about to come, he prepared to answer from his heart. "All right."

"Do you love Elizabeth?"

"With every fiber of my being."

"Then why did you reject her support last night?"

Luke ran a hand over his face, the scratch of day-old stubble rough against his palm. "I can't tolerate the thought of her facing down a scandal that isn't hers to bear."

"Admittedly, neither can I." Jackson looked over his shoulder again. "We both know she doesn't understand what it means to be refused entry into homes where she'd once been a favorite guest."

Throat tight, Luke watched Otis chase a butterfly, yapping every time he made a leap in the air. "I don't want Elizabeth to suffer humiliation and exclusion because of her association with me."

"Nor do I, but, as she told me mere minutes before you arrived, it's her decision."

Despite the yawning pit in his gut, Luke felt a smile tug at his lips. That sounded exactly like the Elizabeth he'd come to know and love. He could imagine her scolding Jackson, hands on her hips, her eyes huge and sparkling with outrage on Luke's behalf. How he loved her.

"The best solution, the only solution, is to let her go to England. But"—Luke drew in a sharp breath—"I can't bear the idea of her marrying another man. I love her, Jackson. I can't live without her."

"Then fight for her."

Fight for her; the answer was really that simple. And yet, nothing about this situation felt simple. Luke refused to be daunted. He would humble himself before Elizabeth. He would bear his heart. Use whatever argument necessary. A bit of groveling couldn't hurt, either.

The idea of leaving this house without Elizabeth was incomprehensible. "I can't—"

"Then you're a coward."

"I can't," Luke repeated, more forcibly this time, "fight for her if you won't let me speak with her."

"Ah, well, then. Problem solved." Jackson clapped him on the shoulder. "She's right behind you."

Chapter Twenty-Three

Elizabeth spent three full seconds unable to take a single breath. Then, suddenly, air whooshed out of her lungs, and her breathing came in fast, lung-burning snatches. As if caught in a waking dream, she watched Luke turn to face her.

Something caught deep inside her, a feeling that her life had just begun, this moment, with this man. He loved her. He'd said the words. Not to her, not yet. But he would. She saw the determination in him, in every tense muscle of his big body.

"Elizabeth." Not quite smiling, Luke walked toward her with that swagger of his, his gaze on her face. No one had ever looked at her like that, as if she were the only woman in the world. A bud of happiness opened in her heart, blossoming with warmth and certainty.

It felt absolutely right that they pledge their love in a spring garden, with the scent of flowers wrapping them in a secret world all their own. They'd shared a similar moment when she'd come upon him the night of Penelope's engagement party.

"I'll leave you two alone." Jackson brushed past her, touched her arm with a sweep of his fingertips, then was gone.

Luke stood before her. He appeared rather worse for wear. He was still dressed in evening attire, minus the coat and tie. His clothes were rumpled beyond repair, and his shirtsleeves were rolled up to the elbows. Purple shadows had taken up residence beneath his eyes, and his face was etched with lines of exhaustion. He looked terrible.

He looked magnificent. And he was hers, all hers.

She wanted to reach up and touch his unshaven jaw, the sensation so intense her hands itched. But she resisted. *Not yet,* she told herself. *Talk first, touch later.*

Holding his beautiful gaze—the color of amber jewels—Elizabeth waited for him to say the three words that would begin the rest of their lives together.

"I'm a fool."

Not those three.

Elizabeth took a deep breath, a hitch catching in her throat.

"I have treated you dreadfully." His face radiated pain. "I turned you away when I needed you most."

"I understand why you did it."

"No, don't make this easy for me." He let out a long, tortured sigh. "I hurt you, Elizabeth. I hate hurting you. I vow I will spend the rest of my life making it up to you, if you'll let me."

Sounds of happiness climbed in her throat.

"I love you, Elizabeth. I love your goodness, your kindness, and your beauty. I love your heart and your ability to put others ahead of yourself. I also love your boldness and your desire to take risks. You're my perfect match."

Tears clogged in her throat, burned behind her eyes. Luke saw the woman she was beneath the perfectly groomed veneer, and he wanted her, anyway.

"I love you, Luke, with all that I am."

He took her hand in his. "I want your version of adventure, Elizabeth. I want to teach you how to drive a motorcar and walk in the rain until our clothes are ruined. I don't care if you wear last season's gown or a shawl made of scandalous red silk, as long as you let me be a part of your life."

"You really mean that, Luke? No more squawking about my reputation?"

"Reputation is nothing when compared to love."

"Oh. Oh, Luke." Could the man be any more romantic, any more wonderful?

"You taught me the true meaning of love, Elizabeth. You are my Little Bit, and so much more. You are my very heart." He kissed each of her hands and whispered again, "I love you."

Her breath caught as he lowered himself to one knee and cupped her hand in his. "Will you let me spend the rest of my life proving I'm worthy of you? Will you be my wife?"

She was crying now, the tears running down her cheeks in rivers of joy.

"I've made you cry." He was instantly on his feet, dragging her into his embrace. "Please don't cry."

She cried harder, holding on to him with all she had in her. The force of her feelings threatened to overwhelm her. When their children and grandchildren asked about this day, Elizabeth would tell them that Luke's declaration of love had been the most precious moment of her life.

"Elizabeth, I don't know what to do. I don't know how to convince you I am sincere."

"I believe you, Luke." She pulled away and saw the beginnings of despair in his eyes. He didn't understand why she was crying.

Lifting her hand to his jaw, reveling in the feel of the rough stubble beneath her palm, she said, "Yes."

"Yes?"

"Yes, Luke. *Yes.* I will marry you."

She was back in his arms before she finished saying the words. Luke crushed his mouth to hers.

They stayed there, holding one another tight, kissing, then pulling away, kissing again, whispering words of love, making promises, saying the equivalent of wedding vows.

In the circle of Luke's arms, Elizabeth felt warm and cared for and safe. Eventually, he set her away from him.

She frowned. "I wasn't finished kissing you."

"Don't tempt me, Little Bit." He gave her a mock scowl, and she realized how much she cherished the nickname. "I think there's been enough scandal for one day."

"Perhaps, but maybe there's room for a little harmless rebellion?"

He laughed, the sound washing over her, drying her tears.

Eyes full of love, he reached for her again.

This time, when he took her in his arms, he held her gently, tenderly. Elizabeth caught her breath and let it out in a sigh. For a moment, a lifetime of a moment, she simply held on to him and let the rest of her doubts slip away.

"I'm sorry, Elizabeth, I shouldn't have sent you away last night."

"I know, Luke, but now that I've had time to ponder the situation, I believe it was for the best."

"It was a mistake, one I won't ever repeat."

Head resting on his shoulder, she told him about her mother's return to New York. "She was waiting for me at St. James House when I arrived home last night."

"That had to have been a difficult conversation." He set her away from him again and stared into her eyes. "I should have been there with you."

"You were rather preoccupied." Cupping his cheek, she told him the rest. "I found it in my heart to forgive my mother."

"I'm glad. I would like to say, maybe, one day, I'll find it in mine to forgive my father."

He was suffering, and Elizabeth knew exactly what to say to him, the same words he'd given her in a garden much like this one. "The wound is fresh, Luke. Give it time."

"I don't deserve you." How gently he gathered her into his arms. Elizabeth thought she might cry again. "But I'm not letting you go. I want a lifetime of adventure with you. We'll start by working our way down your list."

"Actually, I have a new list."

"You've made another?" Chuckling, he pressed his lips to her hair. "Dare I ask?"

Holding back a laugh of her own, she stepped out of his arms, reached inside her sleeve, and drew out the list she'd tucked beneath the pleated cuff. "I believe you'll like this one."

She handed him the single sheet of paper. "Go ahead," she urged. "Take a look."

He lowered his head, snapped it back up again. "There are only three items here."

"I'm aware." She gave him what she hoped was her most encouraging smile. "Why don't you read them aloud?"

"Number one, live a life without regret. That seems rather"—he lifted his head—"ambiguous."

"Not to me. Several people have given me sound advice." All with her best interest in mind, she knew, and she adored them for that. "My father and grandfather suggested I start over in a new country. Hester inspired me to be bold and take risks. Sally warned me to guard my heart, while *you* helped me to consider the consequences of my actions."

"You are loved by many."

"This is true." Her blessings were so much richer and more enduring than the house she lived in or the clothes she wore. "You were all right and yet also wrong. Mistakes are inevitable. It's what we do with our failures that matters most. Do we let them define us and live with regret the rest of our lives? Or do we atone for our past, forgive ourselves, and move on a bit wiser?"

Luke's eyes softened with love, so much love. "You are a very smart woman."

Adoring the feel of his eyes on her, she pointed to the paper in his hand. "Read the second item on my list."

"Love without reservation."

"I believe that one's self-explanatory, as is the third and final item."

"Grow old with the man I love." He lifted his head, grinning.

"In case you have any doubts, Lucian Griffin"—she smiled broadly—"the man in question is you."

His expression held a hint of wonder. "I am completely, utterly unworthy of you, but I'm too greedy to let you go. I'll strive every day to make you happy. All I ask is a normal amount of patience when I disappoint you."

"I'll ask the same in return."

"We're going to have a good life together, Elizabeth St. James, one exciting, slightly scandalous adventure after another." He pulled her close. "There will be trials along the way, and the road won't always be smooth, but I'll catch you when you fall and love you until my dying day."

"We'll be together, Luke. And that's enough for me."

* * *

They agreed to a simple wedding ceremony in the gardens of St. James House. The bride's parents, having left for Florida two weeks prior, were not in attendance. The groom was better represented, at least by the females of his family and one future brother-in-law; his father chose to remain at home.

The only other guests were Caroline and Jackson Montgomery, Aunt Tilly, the entire Burrows family, the incomparable Hattie Montgomery, and, of course, Luke's new business partner, Richard St. James.

Too excited to sleep, Elizabeth rose early and dressed with care the morning of her wedding.

Determined to impress her groom, she wore a deceptively simple white gown of tiered lace trimmed with a million pearls, a thin scarlet ribbon along the neckline, and petite bows at the sleeves. The same white pearls and bold red ribbons were woven into her hair.

Confident she looked her best, Elizabeth reached up and anchored a final pin in her upswept curls and stepped back to study her reflection.

A smiling Sally joined her in the mirror. "You're nearly ready."

"I thought I *was* ready."

"Not yet." The maid bustled around her, pulling at invisible threads and brushing away nonexistent wrinkles. She worked furiously, much like a bee attacked a particularly large, fragrant flower.

At last, Sally stepped back and gave one solid nod. "Now," she declared, "you're ready."

Elizabeth stifled a grin. She would miss the young woman but knew Sophie Cappelletti could use the additional support and guidance as she navigated New York society.

To everyone's shock—Sophie's most of all—the mavens had rallied around the girl. Elizabeth suspected this was in large part due to Genevieve Burrows's influence. Simon's mother had proven as good as her son and was wielding her significant power among her friends to gain acceptance for Sophie in the most respectable homes across the city.

"Will you let Grandfather know it's time to begin the ceremony?"

"Of course." Before she left, Sally took Elizabeth's hands and squeezed. "I wish you the best of luck with Mr. Griffin."

"Thank you, my friend. And I wish you the same in your new position. I will miss you."

When she was alone once again, Elizabeth strolled to the window that overlooked the gardens below. The cool morning air seeped past the window casing and whispered across her face. Taking a moment to settle her nerves, she dragged in a slow breath and took in God's splendor.

The sun shone in a bright, cloudless sky. Not a single puff of white or dingy gray marred the pristine blue. Pity, Elizabeth thought; she would have enjoyed a light rain.

Nevertheless, she squeezed her eyes shut and prayed for her future with Luke. *Lord, may we not only be good to each other but good for each other. May we be better together than apart, and may You always be in the center of our marriage, guiding our every step.*

She turned and glanced around her room. She'd grown from child to woman within these walls. She'd made her list at the writing desk, wishing for more, grasping for more, eventually discovering the woman of substance that had always been inside her.

Hester's shawl caught her eye. Elizabeth hesitated, then, with unsteady fingers, picked up the remaining piece of ruined silk, nothing more than a tiny frayed scrap now. Tucking the fragment in the keepsake box, Elizabeth promised herself she would honor Hester's influence with wise choices, not only amid the adventures she and Luke shared but also in serving people in need.

The door to the adjoining room swung open and hit the wall with a soft thud. Elizabeth jumped away from the desk and, heart in her throat, spun around. Her momentary shock turned to pleasure as she caught sight of her cousin entering the room.

"Oh, Elizabeth." Caroline's words came out in a rush of pleasure. "It's quite possible you are the most beautiful bride I have ever seen. I predict Luke will fall in a dead faint the moment he lays eyes on you."

Elizabeth laughed at that ridiculous image. A single breath later, she was pulled into her cousin's arms.

Careful not to crush her dress, Caroline kept the embrace loose. "I don't know if I've said this before, but I'm so pleased you're marrying Luke. You are going to be very happy together."

"You're just relieved I'm not moving to England."

"There is that." Caroline released her hold, her expression serious. "But I would have endured a lifetime of separation if it had been what you truly wanted."

"I'm exactly where I want to be, with family and friends of my choosing." For what must have been the twentieth time since she'd risen from bed, her eyes filled. "I'm afraid I'm desperately emotional today. I keep having to brush away tears."

"Of course you're emotional." Caroline handed her a pretty embroidered handkerchief. "You're marrying the man you love."

Dabbing at her eyes, Elizabeth borrowed her cousin's words. "There is that."

They shared a laugh.

"I've come to tell you the minister has arrived. The guests are all assembled in the garden. We just need"—Caroline stretched out her hand—"the bride."

They made their way down the marble staircase. At the terrace doors, Caroline unlinked their hands. "This is where I leave you."

Swallowing, Elizabeth nodded.

With a quick smile and a backward glance over her shoulder, Caroline made her way into the garden. Stomach twisting into a dozen knots, Elizabeth peeked around the corner after her.

Penelope winked at her. Elizabeth winked back, and, just like that, her nervousness melted away. She was among friends and family. People who loved her. People she loved in return.

Feeling confident, Elizabeth moved into the center of the doorway and met her grandfather's gaze. His tenderness and quiet acceptance silenced her remaining apprehension. "You are making the right decision, my dear."

He need say nothing more. But, being the patriarch of the family and taking his role seriously, he did. "Luke is one of the finest young men I know. He will make you a good, solid husband, Elizabeth." Her grandfather's startling green eyes swam with watery emotion. "I could not have parted with you for any other man, not even one with a title."

"I'm so glad you approve, Grandfather."

He kissed her cheek. "Ready to get married?"

"Yes. Oh, yes." She settled her hand in the crook of his arm.

Without another word, he guided her down into the garden. The buzz of bees hard at work mingled with the musical notes of birdsong and leaves rustling in the breeze. Those sounds, as well as the scent of jasmine and roses, would forever remind Elizabeth of her wedding day.

She remained perfectly dry-eyed until she turned her attention to her groom.

Their gazes locked, and all other distractions vanished. In the span of a single heartbeat, a thousand words passed between them.

Luke. Her Luke.

Her husband.

So handsome, so upright. With him by her side, and her by his, their life together would be full of love and laughter, an example to their children of what marriage could be.

In pure Luke fashion, he sent her a spontaneous, captivating smile. The breath backed up in her throat.

Oh, my.

With his charming brand of arrogance firmly in place, he stretched out his hand and summoned her to him.

Her heart took a quick, solid tumble.

And then . . .

She simply . . .

Sighed.

No matter what hardships arose, no matter what challenges God brought their way, they would face each and every one of them together. Two cords linked as one.

When the traditional vows were complete, and Elizabeth wore Luke's ring on her finger, he continued holding her hand and said, "I'm yours, Elizabeth St. James Griffin. Heart and soul, forever."

She had to gulp several times in order to regain her voice.

"I'm yours, Lucian Griffin," she pledged. "No matter the place, the circumstance, or the season, I will always stand by you."

"My love." He lowered his forehead to hers. For a long moment, they simply stood there, unmoving, neither speaking, both breathing deeply. Elizabeth heard a shuffling of feet as everyone moved a step forward in anticipation of what the bride and groom would do next.

Elizabeth wondered that herself.

"I love you, Elizabeth. I will never leave your side."

"I love you, Luke," she said in return. "I'll always love you, through good times and bad, to the end of our days."

They parted, stared into one another's gazes. The moment of quiet solidarity was the most precious one they'd shared so far. And then, with their family and friends looking on . . .

Luke sealed their union with a kiss.

Epilogue

There was no traditional reception, because the bride and groom had to board a steamship. Elizabeth was traveling to England after all. Not to seek a husband, as originally planned, but as a bride. As Luke's bride.

A collection of wedding guests had gathered on the dock to send them off in style. Aunt Tilly would follow them to England a week later. She would not be traveling alone. Luke's mother had decided to join her new friend. They would stay in London a fortnight, then continue on to the Continent for a grand month-long tour.

With her new husband's arm wrapped around her waist, Elizabeth surveyed the assembled group.

Most smiled at them, while others—namely Elizabeth's grandfather and cousin—attempted to hide their teary-eyed emotion behind booming words of wisdom, in Richard's case, and a handkerchief, in Caroline's.

Elizabeth would not cry. She would not cry.

Oh, what did it matter? She let out a sob.

Misinterpreting the sound, Luke pulled her close. "We don't have to leave today. We can always wait a week or two—"

She kissed the rest of his words away.

"We're going on this adventure," she whispered against his mouth, then drew back and smiled into his beautiful amber eyes. She prayed every child she bore her handsome husband would inherit that stunning characteristic.

Later that afternoon, with New York fading in the distance and the sun fast approaching the horizon, Luke and Elizabeth were finally alone in their stateroom.

The sky was no longer an unblemished blanket of blue. Rain clouds had begun moving in from the east. With the balcony doors thrown open and a light breeze drawing the rain closer, Luke presented his wedding gift to his new bride.

"It is my greatest joy and honor to call you my wife. I look forward to each and every adventure we—"

"Share," Elizabeth finished for him, kissing him once, twice, three times.

A distant roll of thunder rent the air, pulling them apart.

"Open your gift, Little Bit."

The backs of her eyes stung at the way he spoke the nickname, as if he were promising delicious things to come.

Delighted at all they had to discover together, Elizabeth smiled up at her husband. The wind had tousled his hair, giving him a roguish appeal that called to the rebellious part of her. He was so handsome, so strong, so . . . *hers*.

She took the box wrapped in pretty white paper and a big red bow.

Bottom lip clasped between her teeth, she sat on the edge of a brocade-covered chair and placed the package on her lap.

"I hope you like it."

"I know I will. It's from you."

He chuckled. The sound sent a chill of expectation through her. Reminiscent of another time, and another package, Elizabeth tugged on one end of the ribbon. The knot instantly released.

Ignoring the tiny flutter in her stomach, she peeled away the paper and stared at a brand-new keepsake box with bold, bright flowers scrolled across the edges.

"It's lovely."

"There's more inside."

Flattening her hand over the pretty floral design, she removed the lid. A thin layer of tissue covered the contents of the box.

Excited now, Elizabeth dipped her hand beneath the paper and wrapped her fingers around soft, silky fabric. With a flick of her wrist, she shoved the paper aside.

"Oh, Luke. It's . . . oh!"

She retrieved the shawl. The floral pattern matched the one painted on the box, spring flowers of every shape and variety, much like the ones in the gardens of Griffin Manor.

Elizabeth lost her breath at the meaning behind the precious gift. Luke understood her in ways no one ever had. How could she not love him?

She dragged her fingertips along the fringed edges. A second later, she gave in to temptation and draped the garment around her shoulders and moved to the mirror.

Her breath caught. With the light stronger in this section of the room, she was able to see the crowning glory of her new shawl.

Red thread had been expertly woven throughout the design, all the way to the very edges of the fringe. The thin cord was barely visible, merely a touch of scarlet, and all the more powerful for the subtlety.

Sighing with pleasure, Elizabeth spun around and leapt into her husband's arms and pressed her lips to his.

It was a kiss, only a kiss, simply another wonderful moment among all the other wonderful moments of the day. What a glorious life they had ahead of them.

They pulled apart at the same time and smiled knowingly into one another's gazes.

The rain began then. Nothing more than a light drizzle, a refreshing spring shower that landed on the balcony floor in a soft, delicate patter.

"It's raining," she said.

Luke gave her the kind of grin that proved a portion of his rebellious nature still existed. "I have a sudden passion to take a walk around the ship's upper deck."

"I share that same passion."

"How fortuitous."

As they exited the room arm in arm, laughing, Elizabeth couldn't think of a better way to start their life together as husband and wife.

Discussion Questions

1. Why does Elizabeth seek out her grandfather in the opening of the book? What happens during the interview that upsets her? What does she decide to do about it?

2. How is Elizabeth viewed by others in society? Does this cause her concern? Why or why not? Have you ever tried to break free from what others thought of you? Explain.

3. Who does Elizabeth encounter in the gardens during her friend's engagement party? What about this encounter encourages her to continue on her quest to become more than the "finished product" of her mother's grooming?

4. Describe Luke's relationship with his father. Why do you think it has become so tense between them? Why does Luke want to start his own motorcar company? What does Warren reveal during their conversation at Penelope's engagement party? How does this create a problem for Luke?

5. Who does Elizabeth visit the day after the party? What happens during the visit that changes Elizabeth's view of herself and her future?

6. When Elizabeth tells Luke she wants to try a bit of harmless rebellion, he tells her there's no such thing as harmless rebellion. Do you agree with him? Why or why not?

7. What gift does Elizabeth receive from her former governess? How does this item play into her quest for adventure?

8. Why does Elizabeth seek out Luke at his home? What is his response to her proposition?

9. What does Elizabeth discover about her father and mother when she returns home from Luke's? Why does this upset her? Have you ever tried to forgive someone but couldn't find it in your heart to do so? Explain.

10. After witnessing the rehearsal in his father's private opera house, who does Luke encounter at the Harvard Club? Why is this troubling for him?

11. What happens when Luke discovers Elizabeth in his motorcar? How is this afternoon a turning point in their relationship?

12. When Luke arrives at the Waldorf-Astoria, who is Elizabeth talking with? How does he react?

13. Who does Elizabeth encounter when she goes dress shopping? What happens when she recognizes the young woman? What does she do immediately after leaving the department store?

14. What two women show up at the production of *Carmen*? Why does this set off a scandal? Why does Luke refuse Elizabeth's support? Have you ever tried to protect someone but only ended up hurting them instead? Explain.

15. How does Luke fix his mistake? What is Elizabeth's response to his declaration? What does Luke give Elizabeth as a wedding gift? Why is this special?

About the Author

Photo © 2012 Caroline Akins / One Six Photography

Renee Ryan is the author of twenty inspirational, faith-based romance novels. She received the Daphne du Maurier Award for Excellence in Mystery/Suspense in the Inspirational category for her novels *Dangerous Allies* and *Courting the Enemy*. She is an active member on the board of the Romance Writers of America. Ryan currently lives in Lincoln, Nebraska, with her husband. For more information on the author and her work, visit www.reneeryan.com.